Axioms

'Please . . .' he weeps. And what woman can fail to be moved by a man's tears? 'Please don't throw me out . . . I'll do anything you want.'

'I don't want anything,' Claudia hears herself say.

'Please, Claudie, please forgive me!'

Dorian is kneeling beside his wife. He puts one hand on her upper arm, the other on her thigh. This is his mistake. Words and tears might have melted her, but at his touch, his treacherous touch, she stiffens as if she is afraid of him, and yet equally afraid to move. There is something disgusting in his behaviour. Why can't he be more of a man? Even as the question utters itself inwardly, she knows with painful certainty that her husband has never been and will never be the sort of husband she can respect: honest, open, equal. And the question, wrung and fraught as it was, is followed by a resolution agreed upon in an instant among all the particles in her body: I will not be destroyed.

'I'd rather die,' she says.

SHEILA MacLEOD

Axioms

Methuen

A Methuen Paperback
AXIOMS

First published in Great Britain 1984
by Quartet Books
This edition published 1985
by Methuen London Limited
11 New Fetter Lane, London EC4P 4EE

Reproduced, printed and bound in Great Britain by
Hazell Watson & Viney Limited,
Member of the BPCC Group,
Aylesbury, Bucks

British Library Cataloguing in Publication Data

MacLeod, Sheila
Axioms
I. Title
823′.914[F] PR6063.A253

ISBN 0-413-57040-1

That girls are raped, that two boys knife a third
Were axioms to him who'd never heard
Of any world where promises were kept
Or one could weep because another wept.

W.H. Auden, 'The Shield of Achilles'

Axioms

I

When Dad left home all I thought was, what a fucking cliché; can't they see it's only the boring old male menopause? I was too disgusted with the pair of them to take any of it seriously. Parents and their sodding middle-aged problems! You see, it never occurred to me that he wasn't going to come back – to me. After all, he'd said, that memorable afternoon when he took me and Josh to the Ritz, that it was only a temporary separation.

The Ritz of all places! What a wank. We'd just been to see *Superman* at that cinema in Piccadilly Circus and he said it was handy, but I guessed it was because he still thought he was a famous star and such places were his natural (and deserved) habitat. And I felt tender towards my Dad, who was once a teenage idol and a household name, because he was getting old and a has-been, and that shouldn't happen to a dog. I held his hand and skipped along Piccadilly beside him, saying, oh supah, supah, Daddeh, in my posh voice. To humour him. To make him smile. You can imagine how sick I felt when I realized that my pity had been wasted and that all he'd been doing was sugaring the pill.

The waiter was polite, indifferent, and I could see that he didn't recognize my Dad. But then he was foreign – Spanish or something. I suppose he thought the two older women in the corner were staring at us because of our hair and the way we were dressed. At least I looked halfway normal, which was the way I liked to look in those days. I was even wearing a skirt. It was straight and black leather and came to four inches above my knees. With it I wore a huge pink fluffy sweater, ribbed tights to match and gold pumps. Only bits of my chopped-off hair were bleached, and it was too floppy to stick out all over my head the way I wanted it to.

Josh looked his usual cretinous self, with his stupid Mohican bright-red and the rest of his hair black and unevenly shaved with the traces of dye-stains still trickling on his neck because he never washed properly. Jesus H. Christ, you should have heard the moaning and yelling and throwing things round the bathroom every morning when he couldn't get the bugger to stand up, not even when it was stiff with soap! No need to go into the Freudian implications of *that*. He'd been told not to come back to school until he'd had it cut off. Of course Mum and Dad knew nothing about this. The innocence of middle age. They actually thought he was going off meekly to Fleet Valley every morning to study for his O-levels, looking like an anaemic refugee from a reservation.

The very sight of Josh made poor old Venables want to puke. And much as I wished the bastard would choke to death on his own vomit, I can't say I blamed him. It wasn't just the hair. It wasn't just the zits which were angry and red enough to be visible through layers of aeons of accumulated filth. No, the real turn-off for Venables, even in the pre-Mohican days, was Josh's clothes. Now, I don't know if you've noticed this, but what gets middle-aged people more worked up than anything else, is hair. Don't ask me why. And don't tell me either. I don't think I want to know what goes on in the murky recesses of their minds. Next to hair, it's clothes. You can be a right little cunt like Simon Peasemore, who's always going on about his Dad's souped-up bangers and how much they cost, or a pampered slag like Cheryl Berners, who's always flashing her real gold jewellery around, and the middle-aged will smile on you. But look like Josh (who has his moments, even I can't deny) or his mates, and those ageing lips will curl in supercilious disgust, so that there's no opportunity for them to engage in intelligent conversation of the sort they'd never get from Slime or Cheryl.

Anyway, on this occasion Josh wore his black bondage trousers with the zips up the side and the holes at the knees well frayed, but sporting a safety pin or two. His T-shirt, once white but now the same indeterminate grey as his cretinous features, was emblazoned with the blatantly untruthful slogan, I'm A Fucking Genius. (If there's a genius in our family, it's me, as I shall shortly prove.) His black leather jacket, studded and bezipped, was covered with badges of all denominations from swastikas to CND – not that he subscribed to either (or, indeed, any) organization. A length of bog-chain round his neck was fastened together in front with a mangy-looking dummy he'd nicked from a baby who'd dropped it from its pram in Tesco's. A broad leather band adorned each of his puny wrists, the studs glinting back and forth beneath the pastel-shaded lights as he rolled his own weedy tube of Old Holborn in a licorice skin.

Dad didn't give a screw about the way we looked. Mum did, but she pretended not to. Her clothes (but not her mind, which was rather eccentric) were always more conventional than Dad's. He dressed much younger than his age, which was something of an embarrassment to her. As it was to me. Josh, as far as I know, had no opinion on the subject. No doubt to him, Dad's loose, slubby jacket, faded blue jeans, pale-blue Kickers, cream silk shirt with a loosely knotted bootlace tie, all looked as far beyond the pale as your average businessman's quiet grey suit. But I thought that his new short haircut with the funny little quiff in front made my Dad look rather dashing. He looked more like an elder brother – a step-brother, perhaps – than a father. Though I'd have killed anybody who actually said so.

He ordered cream cakes for us, like we were still little kids dying to gorge ourselves on everything in sight. And chocolate eclairs. He must have forgotten about Josh's allergy. But I tucked in, just to please him, just to indulge him in his boyish pleasure. He didn't eat much himself, but chain-smoked. This should have alerted me, but I was too busy being Daddy's good little girl to give anything more than passing attention to the fact that he was behaving more like Mum than his usual non-neurotic self. I should have been alarmed rather than flattered by the careful way he seemed to be looking after us. He didn't even scold me for putting the wrong spoon (the one I'd been stirring my tea with) back into the sugar basin. Instead, he seemed fascinated by Josh's irritated attempts to scrape every vestige of chocolate from his eclair. Although his expression was kind of brooding, I felt a twinge of jealousy for this unwonted attention.

'Matilda,' he said suddenly, 'Josh.' We both stared politely at him. He was smiling with one side of his mouth only, a put-on smile, an actor's smile. I recognized it from his television appearances: self-deprecating, would-be appeasing. It said, love me, and his eyes were moist. I knew then he was going to say something vaguely unpleasant, but I assumed it was just another of his feeble attempts to play the part of the heavy father. This, whatever he was going to say, was something Mum had asked him to say. We would hear him in silence, agree with him shamefacedly, give our hypocritical promises and, that smile giving way to a more natural grin, everything would return to normal. And sure enough, on he went as expected: your mother and I have decided . . . This phrase (so often mocked in secret by me and Josh) was usually the prelude to a criticism of our lifestyle, especially our industry, tidiness, politeness, punctuality – or rather, our lack of these sterling virtues.

But what came next wasn't what I had expected at all. What he said was: Your mother and I have decided that it would be better for us to live apart for a short while. I was so relieved not to have to sit through another of his half-hearted lectures that I didn't take in properly what he was saying. So I asked him at once quite cheerfully, how long is a short while? He seemed surprised, perhaps a little annoyed with me. At last he said that it would perhaps be six months or so. Then, dimly, I began to suspect that my own life might be affected by this parental decision. I asked him what was going to happen to us, Josh and me. Oh, said he, you'll stay with your mother, of course.

Of course. Well, that was something definite, anyway. Dad would go away, as he was always doing. And we would stay with Mum, as we always did. Only this time it would be for six months instead of six weeks or so. Otherwise, nothing much would change. In short, big deal. I finished my millefeuille and took a chocolate eclair. It was at this point I realized Josh hadn't said anything. He was sitting there in that stolid way of his, like some dumb sheep, not moving a muscle. The tears were rolling down his face, leaving clean, pink tracks. I was shocked. Then I became uneasy. Even when Dad leaned across to give him a fatherly pat on the knee, Josh didn't move. He looked at Dad's hand but not his face. And I couldn't stop staring at him. Then he blurted out one word like it had been choking him: why?

It was Dad who became uneasy at this. He winced. He leaned back in his chair, away from Josh. He sighed. He lit another cigarette, drawing it slowly from his mouth in a gesture that turned into part of a shrug. Then, speaking very carefully, like Josh was some kind of foreigner, he said that at the moment he and Mum were finding it impossible to live under the same roof. And Josh, still not looking at him, blurted out again: why? Dad's eyes had a misty, faraway look. These things happen, he said. Then, almost as an afterthought, he added, there was another woman.

Another woman! It sounded so dramatic, like something out of a television play. I tried to conjure up a picture of this other woman, but all that happened was a blur of hair and mascara. Who was she? Dad said I didn't know her. When I asked him what sort of woman, he said it didn't matter, it was all over now. Well, I didn't see how that made sense. If it was all over, why was he leaving? But I couldn't very well accuse him of lying, now, could I? All he would say was, your mother insists. It was beyond me. Then I opened my mouth and put my foot in it. Another triumph for the International Year of the Child, I said lightly, and it's only February. I don't know what made me say it. Honestly, I don't. Sometimes these things, these words, emerge from my mouth before I've even thought them. Dad flinched. His composure was shattered. And I was frightened, frightened of my own power. He was supposed to protect me from myself. He wasn't supposed to show me that perhaps he needed protection from me. What the hell else are parents for?

It was Josh who spoke. It's not Mum's fault, he said. Of course not, Dad said, recovering somewhat. He was sorry but there it was. And there we were. None of us said anything for a bit. Dad kept taking breaths, like he was going to speak. Josh and me waited till he could get it together, whatever it was. If it's any comfort to you, he said at last, the whole business has been extremely painful for me. Well, there wasn't any way we could comment on that, was there? He didn't expect us to understand now, but perhaps we would when we were a little older. Painful. For him. He was right: I didn't understand. And I wondered if I ever would.

But on the silent journey home in our little yellow Citroën I began to remember things, things which had seemed vaguely wrong at the time, but not particularly important. There was that screaming in the night, which Josh pretended not to have heard. There was the way Mum and Dad would stop talking whenever I came into the room (and I thought they'd been discussing my misdeeds). The unusually bad meals. And Mum always being shut up in her study yattering on and on to some friend or other on the phone.

The phone. That was another thing. There was that phone call on New Year's Day when we'd come back from the Freeburgs' lunchtime party and Dad had gone off to the theatre for the evening performance of the panto, and Mum and Josh and me were sitting round the table playing tablanette. I answered the phone because I was nearest. A woman asked to speak to Mum. It was a short conversation, and afterwards I thought Mum was going to be sick or faint or something. She asked me who the woman had asked for. Her, of course. But she insisted, what name? Claudia Hughes. Was I sure she had asked for Claudia Hughes and not Claudia Grey or Mrs Grey?

I should explain that my Dad's stage name is Grey. His real name is Dorian Hughes (he's half-Welsh) but he called himself Grey after a character in some book by Oscar Wilde. Everyone said it suited him, but I didn't see the point of it, and refused to be known as Matilda Grey. Luckily, my Dad having become a has-been some years before I reached the relevant one of fourteen, it didn't happen all that often. But it happened to Mum all the time, because of course Dad wasn't a has-been at all to her generation. Some of them had even been known to ask for his autograph.

Anyway, I thought Mum's questioning odd and her behaviour even odder. But I had other things on my mind. When she said she didn't feel like going on with the game, I didn't object. Josh did because he was winning, as usual – he always cheats and then denies it. But even he must have seen that there was no point in arguing. It was then Mum made some remark about it being the first day of the International Year of the Child. So I suppose that when I mentioned it to Dad I must have made some sort of subconscious connection between the phone call and what he was telling us. Ah yes, the complexities of the human psyche – even that of a burgeoning little punkette like myself.

I described the journey home as silent, but that isn't strictly true. Dad kept trying to make conversation. Who was appearing at the Rainbow, who had won the *Melody Maker* poll, the banning of the Sex Pistols' latest album, and so on. I wanted to tell him that I was interested in other things besides fucking pop music. But somehow it didn't seem tactful in the circumstances. As it was, I just answered yes or no, and Josh didn't answer him at all.

That's what worried me. Now, I know that Josh gives the appearance of being as thick as nine short planks, but in his own way the stupid wanker is really quite intelligent. Lurking somewhere in the back of my mind was this horrible suspicion that he knew something I didn't. What's more, I didn't want to know it. It might harm me. Eventually, I knew, it would harm me. But whatever it was, I wanted to evade it for as long as possible.

II

Everything means something. Nothing is without significance and the nature of reality is essentially metaphorical. We ourselves are metaphors. Our bodies are metaphors transfigured by meaning. We are knit and unravelled by language, by discourse upon discourse, by silence upon silence. By discourse upon silence (plain, purl). And by silence upon discourse (purl, plain). And language, this language of the self-consuming, other-consuming self, never stops. Say or be said. Do or be done to. Eat or be eaten. Or so it seems. Say and be said. Do and be done to. Eat and be eaten. And so it seems.

The heavy enamel casserole gets placed on the hotplate with a little sunflower oil. Streaky bacon, onions and garlic get chopped and are fried; water is put on to boil; pasta is weighed, minced beef mashed. These actions have all been performed before. It was Claudia who performed them with love in her heart. It is still Claudia who performs them, but now there is a different quality to that love. It is no longer strong and nurturative, like the food itself, but is dissolving into pain and guilt, at odds with what it is doing. The beef gets turned over and over with the same skilled hands and the smell is as savoury as before. But in dreams there is no sense of smell or taste: the throat is closed. Claudia cannot respond to the stimulus. The food is not disgusting, but somehow neutral material like cloth or clay, absolved from all connotations of comfort or appeasement.

What has she done? She is suddenly and painfully a Judas. Her children, her children: they are going to be hurt because she has said that they must be. Is this what she has done? Her family: it is going to be broken apart, and the pieces kicked aside as if they were inanimate, unimportant. Has she done this? Has her pride transformed her into such a monster, the very antithesis of caring motherhood? She must call them back, her family, her own, her dear ones. She must spare them the agony of knowledge, an agony which she cannot confront herself.

Josh was six months old the first time it happened, and Claudia had just found out that she was pregnant again. As if that weren't bad enough, they told her at the ante-natal clinic that she had 'contracted a venereal infection'. She couldn't believe it. The doctor asked her if she had 'strayed'. At first she didn't even understand what he meant. He told her in gentle, professionally worded phrases, adding that she must question her husband. In answer to her apologetic questioning, Dorian denied that he had been infected. But he had to admit it eventually. That he had deceived her, that he seemed determined to go on deceiving her, was far worse than the act of infidelity itself. He couldn't understand that. What upset him was that she had found out in such an indirect way. He was angry with the doctor for having shocked and hurt her: he himself would never have done such a thing.

Dr Jaffa said, 'Why don't you divorce him? He won't change.' Dorian would have been so hurt to learn that Dr Jaffa thought so little of him. That was Claudia's first response. She was hurt too. But at the same time she was secretly pleased to have an ally. Years later, Dr Jaffa said, as if by way of reparation, 'Your husband is a very nice man.' But Claudia resisted this description too. What she needed to know then was that she, rather than Dorian, was somehow acceptable; that besides being a lucky woman, she was married to a lucky man. How, after that, could she tell Dr Jaffa about Gloria Crabbe? He diagnosed depression and sent her away with a prescription for protryptiline hydrochloride.

One day, coming home after some hours of filming which had started at eight in the morning, Dorian put his arms round Claudia and, crushing her against him, said desperately, 'I love her.' Claudia heard him start to say, 'I love you,' as he had said over and over the week before when they had all gone down to Brighton to shoot the crowd scenes on the beach. But on the word 'her', she staggered away from him, as if he had just stabbed her in the back. And indeed he had. Crabbe in several passionate love scenes was no mean rival. Hadn't her face been on the cover of every glossy magazine? Didn't her image invade men's dreams?

Claudia knew that actors tend to believe whatever they have to act, and in Brighton (almost a second honeymoon) she had been gratified to have her most optimistic view of Dorian confirmed: he was much too strong and sensible to be carried away by some piece of showbiz make-believe. All the more shattering to find that he was as much a prey to cliché as the next narcissist. The fact that Crabbe treated him like a pet dog did nothing to improve the situation, or Claudia's perception of it. Crabbe finally sent him packing home to his wife, who received him with open arms. Ah, what a scene of reconciliation followed! Tears and penitence on his side, tears and forgiveness on hers, and promises, such promises on both. Pabst himself couldn't have done it better.

She was thirty-two then, Dorian twenty-nine. And now she is nearly forty. Stirring the beef, she adds a splash of wine and pours another glass for herself. And she laughs abruptly, out loud, remembering her mother's favourite literal: 'Heavens, I'm thirty – give me a drink.' Her mother was always making jokes about age, most of which weren't funny at all. And not only jokes. All sorts of comments. 'I'm forty, Claudie. Can you believe it? Me forty?' 'Which of you is going to look after me in my old age?' Claudia's laughter turns as abruptly into hot, angry tears. Her mother never had an old age. She died of breast cancer at the age of fifty-seven.

The phone rings and Claudia stops crying, instantly alerted. Ever since New Year's Day there have been silent phone calls, especially at weekends. She doesn't know which is worse: the silence at the other end of the line or the mean little voice, triumphant in its meanness, which was to start her year with the words: 'Your bloke's having it off with some little tart.' And then rang off. And hasn't been heard since.

'Can you talk?' Juno asks.

'It's OK. He's taken them to a movie.'

'Are you all right? You sound kind of stoned.'

'Oh, yes, yes, I'm all right. I just don't like answering the phone.'

Claudia knows that this semi-truthful answer is on a level Juno can accept. No point in telling Juno that she was weeping for her mother and hence for herself; for the loss of her mother and hence for the loss of Dorian; for all impermanence and hence, vainest of all, for entropy. Like all sensible people, Juno accepts loss, impermanence, entropy. Juno has never married and is childless. These omissions make her, like Catholic priests or nuns, an expert on marital and parental problems.

'What's he going to do?' she asks Claudia.

'He's going to the Freeburgs' – well, for tonight, anyway.'

'The Freeburgs!' Claudia hears the tinkle of ice cubes and then the clunk of a glass on the marble table in Juno's telephone alcove. 'Oh Claudia, I can't bear it. Once he gets into their clutches, you may as well say goodbye to him for ever. They'll be delighted. They're like a couple of man-eating spiders. Why on earth is he going there?'

It was Claudia's idea, but now she can't remember why. 'It's near.'

'Greta will take him to her bed to console him. That is, if Vida the Vamp doesn't get hold of him first. But they'll probably share him, just like they share Leo.'

'We'll see,' says Claudia, but her nerve is shaken when she visualizes Dorian with Vida the Vamp and the Freeburgs – a foursome in Greta's waterbed – all laughing over silly little Claudie's uncool reaction to an everyday event. She realizes that she has wanted Dorian to become part of the unothodox Freeburg household in order to have things put in some sort of proportion. She wants the Freeburgs to reassure her that any worthwhile marriage is capable of withstanding repeated adulteries as long as both partners behave honourably towards each other. She is relying on them to demonstrate the superiority of openness to secrecy and deceit. She wants them – and this realization shakes her further – to save her marriage. 'They are my friends too, you know.'

'You mean Leo is,' says Juno. 'He'll be round your place in a flash. Or Clive will. You know he's got his eye on you, and he's just dying to slap Greta in the face by showing her he's got a mind of his own – which he hasn't, of course.'

'You make it all sound so sordid.'

'My dear, it is sordid. They're sordid people. They're the most corrupt people I've ever met.'

'Why are they corrupt? Surely they're two people who've managed to work everything out. Their marriage hangs together because they're both so tolerant – and honest.'

'Don't you believe it. There is nothing going on there. It's empty. Leo and Greta are in cut-throat competition with each other. That's why they stay together – so that they can keep scoring each other off. The one who screws most, wins.'

'Oh nonsense, Juno.'

'It's not nonsense, Claudia. I could tell you things about them to make your neat little haircut stand on end like your son's.'

'I've heard them all already, and I don't believe them.'

'I despair of you, Claudia. If they think your marriage has broken up, they'll rush in to pick up the pieces for themselves. Then they'll each swallow what they've got, just so the other can't get hold of it.'

'Oh Juno, you're absurd.'

'Absurd I may be. Naive I'm not. I think you should talk to Sonia. She's been through the whole thing twice.'

'I hardly know her.'

'So? You soon will. I'll arrange it.'

'All right, Juno.' No point in demurring.

'How about lunch one day next week? I know she's more or less free.'

'Well, I'm not.'

'Now, now, Claudia. You've only got two classes a week. How about Thursday?'

'I teach on Thursdays.'

'I know. At three o'clock. We'll have lunch first. The Indonesian in Meard Street.'

'Oh, all right, Juno.'

'Good.' Juno sounds cheerful. And yet it was Juno who said, when Claudia talked of separation, Baby, it's cold outside. 'See you at one on Thursday. Bye!'

Claudia will never get used to Juno's abrupt endings. She stands, vacantly holding the receiver for a moment before rushing back to the stove. It is time to add tomato paste. And to top up her glass. If only she could get drunk. Blind, crawling, screaming drunk. But the children need her to be sober, to be in control. Whatever happens, whoever screams, crawls, gets horribly drunk, Claudia must stay in control. That's what responsible forty-year-old women do. That's what mothers are for. She picks up her glass and throws it with a violence which surprises her against the tiles above the sink. Her body has spoken her mind.

Because the body cannot lie. Like Cassandra it is all truth and mainly unheeded truth. Even Dorian, professional performer, professional liar, has not been able to persuade his body out of truth. Her glittering moment of satisfaction over, Claudia pulls on a rubber glove and begins to pick the fragments of glass from the stainless-steel draining board, dropping them into the dustpan one by one. She is remembering the last time she and Dorian made love. It was last October on Josh's birthday in a hotel in Stirling during a tour of *The Italian Straw Hat*. It was half-term, time for a break and to take the children to Scotland for a week. Dorian forgot Josh's birthday. He and Claudia quarrelled. Had they not, they wouldn't have made love. After all, the affair with the little tart had been going on for the duration of the tour. Dorian had been claiming for three months that he was impotent.

It had happened before, once for nearly a year. Each time Claudia had suggested, with all due deference to male pride, that perhaps he should talk to Dr Jaffa. And each time Dorian had assured her that his failure, as he himself termed it, was the result of overwork and fatigue. It was temporary. He asked her to be patient with him. Thus, impotence became less a slur on his manhood than a test of her womanhood. Male inadequacy was to be redeemed by female forbearance, male frailty by female nursing. What else are wives for?

Claudia was left with the feeling that somehow it was all her fault, the more so precisely because Dorian insisted repeatedly that it was not. She was getting older, fatter, less attractive. He was bored with her, tired of her. But her virtue, her tolerance, would bind him to her for ever in sheer gratitude. Hadn't it always done so before? And didn't all marriages have their weak spots, their difficult times? Of course they did: ones which must be strengthened and worked through. It was only the immature and the feckless who ran away from adversity; the adult met it face to face fully aware that out of conflict comes strength and out of strength, growth. But try convincing Dorian of that. He just assumed that everything would turn out all right in the end, as it had always done before.

Bullshit! Claudia dumps the contents of the dustpan into the bin beneath the sink and slams the cupboard shut, giving it a good kick. There doesn't seem to be much wine left in the bottle. She can't have drunk it all. Wine bottles must be getting smaller. Yes, dear, in the same way as policemen are getting younger. And the peccadilloes of husbands less endearing.

Pasta gets drained in a colander, basil from a pot on the window-sill gets added to the meat mixture. The two are folded together, sprinkled with Parmesan and put in the oven. Claudia drinks the remaining wine from the bottle, which she then throws into the bin. The clash of glass on broken glass is musical. Lettuce gets washed; oil mixed with lemon juice. Once Dorian has left, she needn't bother to cook proper meals. Matty and Josh can help themselves to fish fingers and beans on toast, which they probably prefer anyway. And she herself can eat or not eat as she pleases. Dorian can feast on Greta's aduki pie and lentil salad, and purge himself of all the accumulated poisons of a diet too rich in yin. He can praise her cooking and she can listen to his troubles. They can have a wonderful relationship.

The Freeburgs will be warm and kind to Dorian and yet (she hopes) not unsympathetic to Claudia. They will devote a great deal of attention to the problem. They enjoy helping people to sort out their lives. The Freeburgs have an instinct for such things. And they are never wrong. It is only the wilful blindness or the pathetic hang-ups of other people that militate against their rightness. The Freeburgs inhabit the bleached-out landscape of the psychoanalysed, where the sun burns every grain of sand alike and even the smallest lizard, loosed from the swampy id, fails to find adequate shade. These lizards are their favourite pets. Claudia has brought them nets full of them and they have accepted them all gladly. They will always accept, never censure, never complain of surfeit. They know that all human intercourse is a matter of barter, that the home-baked wholewheat bread which they cast upon the waters of their friends' tears will be returned to them an hundredfold.

The Freeburgs always forgive. They forgive Claudia for her less than charitable attitude towards their fluctuating assortment of house guests: aggression is only to be expected from carnivores. They forgive her silk blouses and her leather boots: she cannot be blamed for having a sensitivity less refined than theirs. They even forgive Juno, who is American and understands them. 'They're Canadian,' she explains, as if this fact constituted one of life's major handicaps. Way back in Toronto and the mists of time, Leo deserted the nice Jewish wife he had known since childhood to run off with Greta, fifteen years his junior, French and a Catholic. Toronto couldn't contain them but London, in its vastness and indifference, has provided security and at least the appearance of forgiveness. Steadfast at the centre of their own painfully constructed universe, they cannot afford to recognize indifference. Because they are not condemned, they must have been forgiven.

To the forgiven, all things are forgiveable. Shriven, their stomachs pumped clean of the indigestible apple which flooded the system with knowledge of good and evil, they stand pristine in the ruined garden, naked and unashamed. How enviable they are. Can Claudia join their ranks? Can Dorian? Who can forgive the self more easily – the betrayer or the betrayed? And which can ever forgive the other?

A key turns in the front door. Claudia's body tenses, closes in on itself. She can't hear any voices. Footsteps scurry upstairs and are heard overhead. Bedroom doors open and shut quietly. Silence. Claudia experiences a moment of panic, pure and instinctive. The children, her children, have fled to their separate sanctuaries. She has made the wrong decision: she has betrayed them. And Dorian is walking through the hall towards her. Anticipating his undiluted physical presence, she feels suddenly sick. Since New Year's Day she hasn't been able to share a bed with him; now it seems she can't even share a room. She has made the right decision. Why then does she feel so frightened?

Dorian is not smiling. His expression is resentful and somehow furtive. Claudia's is resentful too, but questioning. Neither of them can speak. Her hands shaking, she lights a cigarette. He lights up another, sitting down opposite her, the length of the table between them. There is no ashtray. Claudia hasn't noticed its absence, doesn't notice the ash lengthen on her cigarette, allows it to fall in her lap, on the floor. Dorian looks irritated, fetches an ashtray and puts it in the middle of the table where neither of them can reach it properly.

'I've done as you asked,' he says. 'I hope you're satisfied.'

'What happened?'

'What do you think happened?'

The ashtray is smoked glass, one of a series that Dorian has nicked from Holiday Inns around the country. The wedding ring on the third finger of Claudia's left hand, now stretched towards it, cost two pounds, ten shillings second-hand from a jeweller's in Camden Town in 1963. The puzzle ring, red and white gold, on the third finger of her right hand, was a birthday present from Dorian in 1970, bought at a jeweller's in New York, the price now forgotten. Her cords were bought by Dorian's American Express card from the North London Jean Centre in Upper Street, Islington. The Cacherel shirt, which she rarely wears, dates from the sixties and was bought at cost price in Paris in 1967 through the good offices of an admirer of Dorian's. Her gold and jade earrings were chosen by Dorian in preference to the hoops she had picked out for herself from a stall at Camden Lock. What's mine is yours.

'I'm sorry,' she says. 'I'm sorry it was necessary for me to ask you.'

A.—2

'Necessary?'

'What else do you expect?'

'Oh, I expect whatever is necessary. What else can I expect?'

Put at a distance by this sarcasm, Claudia says, 'I don't see what it is you want of me.'

Dorian makes some vague gesture with both hands. 'I want you to believe in me.'

'How can I believe in you when I can't trust you?'

'But you must trust me. It's my only hope. Our only hope.'

'You're asking too much of me.'

'And you're asking too much of me.'

'Is being honest with me too much to ask of you?'

'If you loved me, you would trust me.'

'If you loved me, I could trust you.'

'When have you ever loved me?' Dorian asks hoarsely.

Claudia doesn't waver at this appeal to her womanly self. 'Why did you ever marry me?'

'Why did you marry me?'

'Why indeed?'

'I'll tell you why,' says Dorian. 'We got married because we were in love.'

'And now?'

'And now . . .'

The past tense, the present tense. Just a flick of the wrist, just one different key pressed on the typewriter: he/she loves; he/she loved. Is that all it takes? Dorian's jeans have been patched and darned by Claudia again and again; her neatly improvised stitches are evident at his knees, his pocket and the seam along his crotch. She has often washed his silk shirt by hand and ironed while it was still damp. The toast he ate for breakfast consisted of bread baked in her own special proportions of wheat to rye. The marmalade on it was made from Seville oranges cut up a year ago by her dutiful hands. His stomach is filled with the fruits of her labour. What's yours is mine.

'I wonder,' says Dorian, 'did you just want me to show myself up in front of my children?'

'If you didn't want your children to think that their father is a shit, then you shouldn't have behaved like one.'

'That's what you want them to think. That their father is a shit.'

'I thought it was best to put an end to all the mystification.'

'I hadn't noticed any mystification.'

'They had.'

'They're not old enough.'

'They are!' Claudia speaks passionately. 'And they're old

enough to appreciate that truth is always better than lies.'

'Always? Even when it hurts?'

'Why do people always say the truth hurts? It does, of course, but lies hurt more.'

'Only if they're known to be lies.'

'You mean, only if the liar gets found out.'

'You always have to have the last word, don't you?'

'No!' Claudia's voice almost breaks over the word. 'Can't you see? I've been begging you to tell me that I've got everything wrong. I want to be wrong. I want to feel that I can trust you. I want to believe that you're capable of telling the truth, but how can I when you actually tell me you're not? When you actually say that you can't undertake to be truthful with me? Well, I can't face living with lies for the rest of my life. I just can't.'

The room is full of cigarette smoke. Embattled, embittered, husband and wife stare bleakly through it at each other. Dorian and Claudia bought the mahogany table five years ago from Junk City at World's End. The chairs, their stuffing now protruding from the leather upholstery, were bought from the same place at the same time. The art nouveau posters were bought in a ragged state from a shop in Chalk Farm and framed by an old man near the Angel just after Matilda was born. Claudia found the firescreen on a skip a year or so after moving into the house. The honeycomb dish on the mantelpiece, the knob of its lid in the shape of a bee, was a wedding present from Dorian's best man, Ron. What's mine is yours, what's yours is mine.

'All right,' says Dorian. 'What do you want to know, Claudia?'

'What do you mean?'

'Seek and ye shall find. The truth.'

Claudia considers, but accepts the challenge. 'How many of these little scrubbers have there been?'

'Which little scrubbers?'

'The ones you love to screw.'

'Oh, those.' Dorian can take a challenge too. 'I haven't exactly kept a tally, but I'll do my best to remember. There was Marianne in Stockholm and Louanne in Sidney and Gracie in Chicago and Sharon in Hull. Those are the ones that, as it were, stand out.'

Claudia's incipient laughter freezes: Dorian is not joking. 'Oh my God,' she says. 'I don't want to know.'

'Then why ask?'

'I want to know why.'

'I don't know why. No reason.'

'There must be a reason.'

'You tell me.'

'Is it so important to you to be a star? To be eternally young?'

'It's not that. You make it sound so paltry.'

'That's what it is.'

'Thank you.' Dorian fetches another bottle of wine; Claudia takes the corkscrew from a drawer at her end of the table and pushes it across to him. 'It's only my whole career that you have just dismissed in your usual lofty fashion. The career which has kept the wolf from your door for the last sixteen years.'

'Is that all you are, that part of your career?'

'That's what I'm good at, Claudia, being an entertainer.'

'Don't bullshit me, Dorian. You're not content with being a mere entertainer. You want the whole showbiz glitter, glitter, big-time star, Oh how wondrous bright you are.'

'What's wrong with that?'

'I thought you were more than that.'

'Suppose I'm not more than that?'

But this is a possibility Claudia cannot take seriously. As far as she is concerned, Dorian is deliberately refusing to face up to the demands of his unconscious, where angels lurk alongside demons. She cannot understand that he is now telling her the truth she asked for to the best of his ability. 'You have to be,' she says. 'Anyone is.'

Dorian cannot understand that she cannot understand. As far as he is concerned, she is deliberately refusing to recognize certain basic differences between the two of them. 'Anyone who lived up to your puritanically high standards,' he tells her, 'would have to be a saint.' And he takes some wine to her in a clean glass before delivering the punch-line: 'Believe me, it's no fun screwing a saint.'

Claudia stares at him with dawning comprehension. 'What do you mean by that?' she asks shakily.

'What I say. You must admit that our sex-life was a disaster area.'

'A disaster area? It's been practically non-existent for the last five years.'

'And that's my fault?'

'It's not mine. I did what you wanted. I waited.'

'And masturbated.'

'Sometimes, yes.'

'I wasn't good enough for you.'

'*I* wasn't good enough for *you*.'

'You were too good.'

'Oh my God.' She hides her face in her hands, hides the threatening tears. 'I thought I was your wife. But all along I've been your mother. Can't you tell the difference?'

But Dorian doesn't know what she is talking about. Smarting at the injustice with which he is being treated, he remembers rejection where she has remembered forbearance. Any other woman would have told him, showed him, how much she desired him, instead of switching off as if such matters were of no importance. Any other woman would have recognized how lonely he became when he was away from home, how he needed the closeness and comfort of another warm body. Any other woman would have seen the naturalness of such needs instead of regarding them as major crimes against herself. But not Claudia. She can't admit to herself that men have needs, needs which women are lucky enough never to experience. She cannot tolerate weakness. She expects him to be the perfect husband. How grossly unfair she is.

Claudia cannot evade his unspoken accusation. When was it she began to die inside? Why don't you divorce him? He's not going to change. No, it wasn't then. She refused to believe Dr Jaffa. Your husband is a very nice man. It was then, wasn't it? It was after Crabbe that something happened, something died. Somewhere at the quick, something folded in upon itself, fearful, violated, and yet determined to remain unravished. Wounds don't heal; they just close over. Scabs are protective, and scar tissue shrinks, ashamed of its own ugliness, from being touched. It is the wound that must remain unravished, unmoved to pleasure and to pain alike. The body remembers and the body has its own tale to tell.

Oh but her forgiveness is so sweet! She has always bestowed it so freely before. Dorian cannot believe that she means to withhold it from him even now. She is shutting him out deliberately, to punish him, because she knows it is the one thing he can't bear. It's some kind of cruel game she's playing. There is only one strategy left to him.

'Please . . . ' he weeps. And what woman can fail to be moved by a man's tears? 'Please don't throw me out.'

His tears do indeed move Claudia, pulling her in opposite directions. She should weep with him, as she has done before; then all could be forgiven and forgotten. But her eyes are dry. The pitiable sight of him chills her into silence.

'I'll do anything you want,' he weeps.

'I don't want anything,' Claudia hears herself say.

'Please, Claudie, please forgive me!'

Dorian is kneeling beside his wife. He puts one hand on her upper arm, the other on her thigh. This is his mistake. Words and tears might have melted her, but at his touch, his treacherous touch, she stiffens as if she is afraid of him, and yet equally afraid to move. There is something disgusting in his behaviour. Why can't he be more of a man? Even as the question utters itself inwardly, she knows with painful certainty that her husband has never been and will never be the only sort of husband she can respect: honest, open, equal. And the question, wrung and fraught as it was, is followed by a resolution agreed upon in an instant among all the particles in her body: I will not be destroyed.

'I'd rather die,' she says.

III

Trust Josh to go and make a balls-up of everything by trying to go one better than anyone else. Nat and me had the whole thing worked out. No detail was overlooked, as they say. For starters, we both made sure we signed the register, morning and afternoon, before bunking off. But not Josh. Oh no. He couldn't be bothered, thought he'd get away with it for ever, thought old Venables wouldn't even notice. It doesn't do to underestimate the intelligence (and I mean intelligence – like MI5) of the opposition. All very well muttering, don't let the bastards grind you down. But it doesn't half make things easier if you're careful not to present them with the opportunity.

Nat said Josh must have wanted to get nicked. When the store detective tapped him on the shoulder, he had cassettes stuffed everywhere – inside his T-shirt, his jeans, up his sleeves. Enough to make him look like a Michelin man. So mind-bogglingly moronic. I mean, why the sod should he want to get found out? Unless of course he thought it would make him the big hero. The notorious Joshua Hughes, the despair of the psychiatric social services. That sort of crap. He should have known, anyone could have told him, that once that sort of thing starts, They never leave you alone. Never. You've only got to look at Nat himself to know that. Crazy like a fox is what he is. He's developed it. But my poor naive little ponce of a brother has the cunning and subtlety of a juggernaut.

We'd go to Rama Records, Nat and me, doing our teenage lovers act, arms round each other, oblivious to the rest of mortality, poor sods that they were. One time I heard some wanker of a public-school type saying to his horse-fancying little miss goody-two-shoes, do you think they actually look attractive to each other? People stared all right. How could they help it, seeing as how Nat was six foot tall and changed his hair colour every week? They stared at him while I got discreetly to work, slipping a few cassettes – never more than half a dozen at any one time – down the baggy sleeves of my knee-length sweater. We must have ripped off hours and hours of sounds that way.

Until Josh put paid to it all. None of the better part of valour for him. He only went and ripped off forty-seven – no less. Of course you've got to hand it to him for drama. And in a funny sort of way for courage. It wasn't, like Nat said, that he wanted to get nicked. It was that he didn't give a fuck whether he got nicked or not. I could sense that much, even though he never talked to me. He never did talk to me. Rumour had it that he talked to Nat in lucid intervals, but it didn't seem to have done him much good. I mean, Nat could have *told* him about the tolerant nature of our legal system and that our police are truly wonderful.

Nat was Josh's friend first. Josh was a loner till Nat arrived. I never understood how that happened, because at St Bartholomew's Lodge they all thought the sun shone out of his arse, just because he was on 'Top of the Form' and answered all his questions correctly, even though our team lost. I was just the pathetic little kid sister, always getting blamed for whatever went wrong and even sent to Child Guidance when I shrieked at the repulsive old Head for calling me a liar. (*They* thought I was OK, which was more than they thought of Josh, when he had to go a year later. They thought he was a nut case.) There weren't hardly any Arsenal supporters at Fleet Valley. Perhaps that was it. Josh never had anyone to go to Highbury with, because they were all buggering off to White Hart Lane. The week after Spurs massacred the Gunners *at Highbury* Josh didn't dare show his face at school. I think that's when he started bunking off.

Nat didn't have any unhealthy interests like football and heavy metal. He was into punk before anyone else and turned up in the maths class wearing a Sex and Drugs and Rock 'n' Roll badge, which Hazlitt confiscated at once and went twittering off to Venables. Nat was notorious. He ended up at Fleet Valley because no other school in the area would have him. But we had this wonderfully liberal Headmistress for our sins. She was always appearing on telly trying to look glamorous and talking about 'kids' and 'ethnic minorities' and all that crap. Joan Fairfax, whose name has become a byword in educational circles. That's what they always said. And then, likely as not, they would add the bit about how she refused to recognize a hopeless case. Nat must have strained her ostrich-like propensities somewhat: he could be spotted a mile off. In the metalwork class he made himself a new badge: Nicking and Fucking and Glue. But he wore that on a chain round his neck and only flashed it at the favoured few. Fairfax could hardly be said to be of their number.

It's odd, as I've said before, the things grown-ups get worked up about. Nat had nicked a few things, true. But what really got them going was the way he made these little cuts all over his arms and chest. Self-mutilation they called it, and sent him to see a psychiatrist. But when Nat called it body adornment and said it was part of a tribally based adolescent subculture, the psychiatrist laughed and sent him away again, saying he was glad to have met him. Of course he wasn't right either, as events have since proved, but he cheered Nat up terrifically.

I think the general idea was that Nat was a victim of circumstances, poor bastard. What They really meant was that he was a victim of divorce. Honestly, the way They went on about divorce, you'd think everyone in the country was living in a nuclear family with Mum, Dad, three point two children, point five of a dog and point seven-five of a cat. They must have known that by the time you get to be sixteen, you can't expect to live with both your parents any longer. Though of course the irony of it all is that that's exactly what Nat did. His Dad and his Dad's girlfriend lived in the basement flat. Nat, his sister, his Mum and his Mum's boyfriend (known to Nat as Motherfucker) all lived in the rest of the house. Enough parenting to satisfy even the most avid of social workers, I'd have thought. But not on your nelly. As far as They're concerned, Two-Parents is good and Four-Parents is just as bad as One-Parent. Talk about social control!

Now I can see why Josh became friends with Nat. Here was someone even further beyond the pale than him, someone who translated his ideas into more obvious forms of action than just bunking off. It's more difficult to see what Nat thought the attraction was. (Unless of course he fancied him – which I won't dwell on, as they say in Jane Austen. At least, not yet.) When I asked him, he said Josh was the first person he'd met who was brighter than him. Rather peeved (my own intellectual qualities were not cited), I said I was surprised to hear he should have such a problem, seeing as how he wasn't a Trappist monk. He didn't even get it at first. Typical. Boys are so absorbed in measuring themselves against each other (yes, I do mean that, too) that they don't even notice that one girl can have more brains than the rest of them put together.

I only got friendly with Nat when Josh brought him home. We

never talked to each other at school. For a kick-off, he never even noticed my existence. That's the trouble with being skinny and a late developer. Boys only notice the girls with tits. And then their tits is all they do notice. Who needs it? It annoyed me the way Nat ignored me. And when Josh was with him, *he* ignored me too. What was I supposed to do? Grow tits so as my own brother and his mates would talk to me? Well, I didn't, as it happens. And it was beneath my dignity to draw attention to myself in any other way. I ignored the two of them, didn't even say hullo. It was then (it seems) Nat started complaining to Josh, your sister doesn't like me. But of course I did.

So did Mum. Even Nat, with his inferiority complex, could see that. One miraculous Saturday we all had lunch together. Even Dad was there. Mum had done jacket potatoes and all sorts of salady things with different dressings, and Nat kept saying things like, ah, tarragon! And, how much garlic do you use in your aoili, Claudia? Partly to smarm up to her, partly to show that he came from a good middle-class home, and she should rest assured that he was a suitable companion for her darling son. She bought it, of course. She loved it. At last – a friend for Joshua. Nat's ginger hair was shoulder-length, his glasses (soon to be discarded in favour of contact lenses) thick and heavy-rimmed, his arms and legs too long for his clothes. But he was clean, said please and thank you in the right places, and didn't (or managed not to) swear. And I suppose that was enough for her.

Dad rabbited on in his usual fashion, telling amusing little anecdotes about himself and other showbiz folk. Mum sat at the other end of the table, pretending to listen in her usual bleak fashion and chain-smoking throughout the meal. Josh and I laughed at Dad's stories. Mum and Nat didn't. What's more, I was sure I saw them exchange some sort of conspiratorial glance. I'd always thought Mum a mean shit for not allowing Dad his little moments of applause. All the more so because she did it in such an underhand way, never interrupting but silently offering you another slice of bread or a second helping of apple crumble at the strategic moment. But when I saw Nat reacting in the same sort of way, I began to have misgivings. Neither of them said a word, but their *faces* were having a conversation about the quality of Mum's cooking, the state of Nat's stomach. And, underneath, about what a shit Dad was. Or so it seemed to me. My loyalties were torn. Either: Dad was a shit. Or: Nat was a shit. But seeing as how they weren't, I was back to square one: Mum was a shit. And yet I knew, deep down, that she was less of a shit than either of them.

After that, Nat could do no wrong in her eyes (well, for the time being, anyway). Nat was the exception to every rule. Emma, Cheryl, Bart, Slime and Spike were all turfed out of the house dead on ten-thirty, as if she was operating her own licensing laws. But not Nat. Poor Nat, she'd sigh, life must be so difficult for him at home. Nat was allowed to stay the night (in her study), share her cigarettes, call her Claudia, offer her advice about her wayward children. It was quite sickening. He loved it. She loved it. I was quite put off him.

But then it got to the point where he needed me. Well, not *me* exactly, but a partner, and I would do as well as anyone else. And better than most. On his own he was too conspicuous. If you're middle-aged, you'll simply have no idea of the way shopkeepers, usherettes, ticket-collectors, etc. freeze up at the sight of teenage boys and (metaphorically speaking) reach for their guns. Girls don't qet quite the same reaction, especially if they're little with middle-class accents and can look all sweetie-sweetie when they want to, like me. Together, we got away with daylight robbery. Literally. So you see I had my uses.

Of course everyone thought we were going out together. Much to my surprise, Mum didn't seem to mind a bit. (But then she didn't know about the nicking, did she?) It was Dad who minded, even more to my surprise. He said I was much too young. Too young for what, for Chrissake? What did he think we were doing? Well, whatever he thought, we weren't doing very much. At least, not at first. All the usual preliminaries, I suppose. Only once did we go the whole way, and then neither of us knew what we were doing, so we decided to leave it out for a bit and have a hassle-free business relationship. Which didn't prevent Nat from behaving as if he owned me.

I suppose Josh was the one who felt left out after that. We didn't take him on our expeditions, I've never quite known why. And when Nat said he should find himself a girl, Josh threw a mug of coffee at him and slammed out of the house. I thought that was the end of a beautiful friendship, but no, the next day they were carrying on as if nothing had happened. And I was the one who felt left out once again. Since Nat had appeared on the scene I'd more or less lost track of my girlfriends, who resented being second-best. Nat and Josh were all I had. And if Josh came between Nat and me, then certainly Nat came between me and Josh. Nat needed us both but he needed us separately. In fact I often felt he was taking some trouble to keep us apart. I couldn't understand why, but it made me slightly wary of him and I was glad we'd agreed not to be in love or any of that crap. You see, I think that even if you are young and foolish you can scent danger.

You're attracted by it, but if you've got any sense, you leap out of the way when it turns into a stink and threatens to overwhelm you.

But not, as in so many cases, Josh. Mum was horrified. The police called her just as she was about to go out to lunch with her bossy friend Juno and her feminist friend, Sonia. She had to go to the police station instead and listen to a sermon about her son's behaviour. So then she was late for lunch and went off to her class rolling drunk and shocked the shit out of her boss. So she came home all foul-tempered and refused to cook any supper. She kept calling Dad but he wasn't there and the people he was staying with didn't know where he was. It turned out he had a gig with Ron, but anyone would have thought he'd emigrated to Australia without a word, the way she was carrying on. So Josh didn't feel the full force of the paternal wrath (*sic*) until the next day.

By the time Dad arrived – an hour and a half late – Mum was practically beside herself. I could hear her pacing up and down the kitchen waiting for the kettle to boil, and once she yelled, I'll kill him, I'll kill him! I was scared. I admit it. I was scared rigid. I went downstairs and offered to make the tea – just in case she'd actually freaked out and was about to murder Dad. She sat at the table, her head in her hands, until I put the mug down in front of her. Then she said, oh, thank you, Matty love, as if she really meant it. I nearly cried. She looked so old and small all of a sudden, so frail, that I felt guilty about all the bad thoughts I'd ever had about her. So I said, airy-like, it's all right, Mum, and sat down with her. She kind of patted my hand and said, yes, it's all right, Matty, it's going to be all right. Then I knew I *was* going to cry.

But – saved by the bell – that was when Dad arrived. He apologized in his usual charming manner for being late, smiling, appealing, asking for some response. Mum was cooler than cool, and for one horrifying moment I saw him through her eyes, and I couldn't respond to him either. Apart from his exaggerated expressions of regret, he had no reason at all for being late. And he wasn't sorry, either. In fact, I had the feeling he was positively glad. But I couldn't understand why. Later he was to tell me that this was the moment when he realized that Mum was turning me against him. But she didn't. If there was any turning, I did it myself – and with his own help. That's what he always refused to recognize.

When Dad had taken Josh off for his man-to-man talk, or whatever it was supposed to be, I thought me and Mum might have our woman-to-woman talk. But as soon as she'd finished her tea, she said she had work to do and shut herself in her study. I was furious with her. I wanted to hammer on her door and yell, I'll kill you, I'll kill you if you don't talk to me! I don't know what came over me. I even stomped across the hall to the study, my fists at the ready. But when I reached the door I could hear her sobbing. My hands unclenching slowly, I leaned against the jamb for a moment, then went back up to my room and tried to concentrate on the causes of World War I.

Josh was gone only an hour. Dad brought him back in the car, but didn't come in. From where I was on the landing I heard him say, I think he's learned his lesson. I couldn't hear what Mum said – if anything – because Josh was clomping up the stairs. He slouched past me without a word or a look and shut himself in his room. I heard Dad laugh. Be reasonable, Claudia, he said, he's been let off with a caution, it won't happen again. Oh, says Mum, so that's what you think, is it? And then Dad saying yes, and Mum saying why, and Dad saying, why not? I thought they were going to have another row and when the door slammed shut I didn't know at first if Dad had come in or not. But then Mum called me.

She was leaning against the door, her hands held out towards me. When I took them, they were cold. My God, she said, I don't think I knew till today just what it was I was up against. And suddenly she hugged me. And I hugged her. And I didn't really want to cry because I felt strong. Then, holding me at arm's length because it was her that was near to tears, she said why didn't we have fish pie for supper. It's Josh's favourite, she said, do you mind? I didn't mind if it was his favourite or not, so I shook my head and led her into the kitchen.

IV

'Of course it's stealing affection,' says Juno. 'What's to worry about there? Nobody ever gets enough affection.'

'Which only means,' says Claudia with a sigh, 'that no one ever gives enough.'

'Of course.' Juno sounds jaunty. 'No point in feeling guilty about it. All our failures are ultimately failures in love, as whoever it was said.'

'I asked Dorian to raise his pocket money.'

'Money is hardly a substitute.'

'But I *do* love Josh.'

'Of course you do,' says Juno.

'Of course *you* do,' says Sonia.

But their reassuring smiles only serve to unnerve Claudia. She stares at the remains of the Indonesian dishes in front of them, the chilli-pink sauces separating into orange oil and greyish curds. She hasn't eaten much because the valium makes her hands shake. Sometimes – about an hour after she has taken one – she can manage. But now she is due to take another and her hands can only convey the food to her mouth in a hit or miss fashion, which she has been at such pains to conceal that she has waited for the rare moments when Juno and Sonia have been looking at each other in order to feed herself. But it simply wasn't worth the effort, so she gave up, telling Juno that she wasn't hungry. Sonia hasn't eaten much either, but then Sonia (says Juno) doesn't. So it has all been left to Juno, an avid eater at the best of times and always a careless one. Claudia and Sonia both watch her pick at the cold food, trailing grease across the paper tablecloth. The stains spread, as if determined to take over the whole area of white. Claudia is horrified. She wonders if she ought to go to the ladies' room and take the next valium in private.

But Sonia has anticipated her. She walks towards the red and white strips of plastic which constitute a curtain, small, slim, straight-backed, carrying an enormous leather bag under one arm. The waiters step aside. They watch her swish through the curtain and exchange a glance whose meaning Claudia can't read. Perhaps it is an orientally understated expression of lust. Hardly. Sonia provokes respect rather than lust. Lucky Sonia. People are always accosting Claudia, sometimes harmlessly enough, as on trains, for want of anything better to do than bore the nearest likely victim with chatter rather than yourself with silence; and sometimes more intrusively, more sinisterly. But who would dare accost Sonia? Tiny and unafraid, she goes apparently unarmed where and when she pleases. Her armour is her bearing and the brazen way she looks you in the eye, as if there she could read your intentions writ pathetically and all too articulately large. Sonia walks through life as if immune, like some alien in a comic-strip surrounded by its own impenetrable force field whose attempted broach brings annihilation in an instant.

Not so Claudia whose rounded, rather childish face invites approach or, she has sometimes been told, violation. It is not that she wants to be approached or, indeed, violated; just that she has never learned to experience an approach as a violation. Once on a tube a man approached her and offered her a great deal of money if she would go back to his flat with him. He was ugly and nervous and she felt sorry for him. She almost accepted. But common sense whispered of strangulation by tights and the possibility of torture. She was twenty. At primary school they used to sing a song called 'All the Little Pansy Faces', and once one of the nuns, in an access of misplaced zeal, applied the description to Claudia and her sisters. When they got home they stamped on all the pansies in the front garden. At Claudia's instigation. Their parents couldn't understand why such good little girls should behave so destructively.

Claudia fumbles impatiently in her bag. Why on earth is she recalling these stupid little incidents now? Why have so many memories of youth and childhood been surfacing lately? She tugs futilely at the lid of the plastic container before remembering that it is supposed to be child-proof and she must line up the arrows. The lid won't turn. It's like wearing thick gloves. And yet she doesn't want to ask Juno, as she has so often asked Matilda, for help. Tears of frustration beginning to cloud her vision, she takes the frail thing in both hands and manages to wrench the lid off with her teeth. There is something animal, more so than Juno's absorbed greed, in the body needing any substance so much. And now there is the problem of extracting one pill without upsetting the lot. Would it be better to hook one out or to spill one gradually on to the palm?

'It's going to be two years of sheer hell,' Juno says between mouthfuls, 'and then things will start to straighten out.'

Juno's voluminous sweater is stained from past meals among her chunky jewellery. Her skin is perfect, glowing, flushed. Her pale-blue eyes bulge slightly, perhaps because of the way she ties her hair back, and their gaze, following Claudia's attempt to swallow the pill, is deceptively bland. It is Juno's mouth which is her most expressive feature: it is always ajar. Even when she is not talking she breathes through it meaningfully, as if about to utter something of great moment.

'I can't keep up with you, Juno,' says Claudia. 'Two weeks ago you were urging me to keep my marriage together. Baby, it's cold outside, you said. And now you can't wait to see me divorced.'

'Divorce is hell,' says Sonia, sitting down in her place again, her make-up retouched. 'It takes three years to get over it.'

'Juno just said two years.'

'Two years? Three years?' Juno says brightly. 'What's that out of three score and ten? Life is hell, anyway. It's just a matter of making the most of it.'

'I don't see why it should be hell,' says Claudia.

'Life?' asks Juno. 'Or divorce?'

'I think, Juno,' says Sonia, 'that Claudia is still at the wide-eyed stage. She thinks that everything can be settled amicably, and that she and Dorian will never do anything as sordid as fight over money – or children.'

'Yes,' says Claudia. 'That is what I think. After all, we're adult –'

'Civilized human beings,' Sonia finishes for her. 'Yes, I've heard that one often before. Believe me, there's no such thing. Sex is supposed to bring out the beast in men, but in my experience it's the severance of sexual relations that does it. Hell knows no fury like a man scorned.'

'But I haven't actually scorned him.'

'You've thrown him out of his home. Do you think he's going to forgive you for that?'

'It's only temporary,' Claudia says doubtfully.

Sonia and Juno look at each other as though this too they have heard before. It would seem that Claudia has committed the arch crime: that of injuring male pride. She hadn't realized. If only someone would tell her what to do! And yet of course there is no one who can. You can't possibly throw away the best man you've ever had for one little hiccup. That was another thing Juno said two weeks ago before her apparent change of heart. But it wasn't like that. It wasn't a matter of a hiccup but of one big retch of dishonesty threatening to engulf her. Why don't you divorce him? It isn't like that either. Divorce is like giving up, running away. It isn't an ending that is necessary, but a change.

'My life began,' says Sonia, 'when my marriage ended.'

'Which marriage?' asks Juno.

'The first one doesn't count,' says Sonia.

'Sonia married beneath her,' says Juno. 'She was eighteen. A GI bride.'

'Of course I married beneath me,' says Sonia. 'Women always do. Marriage was made by men for men. It's about property. Once you know that, you know all you need to know.'

'But what else *is* there?' Claudia asks.

'Ask Juno.'

Juno flushes; Sonia should know better. 'Come on, Sonia,' she says, her voice pitched high and light as it always is when she is wounded. 'You know very well I'd marry Rupert tomorrow, if he asked me.'

'Why don't you ask him?'

'I did.'

'And he refused?'

'He said he'd think about it.'

Juno leans back in her chair with a triumphant smile and waves her hand at the waiter. There is a large hole under her arm. Claudia remembers meeting Rupert very briefly at one of Juno's parties. She had been well prepared: Rupert was an Old Etonian, very well connected, so interesting, so talented, so good-looking, and so very, very English. Just like all the men with whom Juno fell so hopelessly in love and with such painful regularity. They were also almost invariably homosexual – a fact which didn't deter Juno in the least. Claudia has often wondered if Juno's choice of men is, like her refusal to lose weight, an excuse for opting out of the sexual rat-race. It occurs to her now that maybe Juno, for all her obsessive interest in who is doing what with whom and how, is not really interested in sex at all – at least not as a participator. Maybe she sees it as a spectator sport, but has to profess for appearances' sake that she too is game. Well, she is quite safe, as far as Rupert is concerned, from being dragged into the fray. Claudia is sure of that.

'And here was I,' says Sonia in voice nice with ambiguity, 'thinking that you had the strength of mind to shun the whole business.'

Juno is studying the bill. 'I'll get this,' she says, producing her American Express card. 'You two had better save your pennies for the proverbial rainy day.'

'Thanks, Juno,' says Sonia. 'I'll reciprocate in July when I should get my next royalty cheque.'

'How do you survive?' Claudia asks worriedly, glimpsing life beyond divorce.

'Oh, a bit of this and a bit of that,' says Sonia. 'Certainly not by writing books. I'd earn more as an au pair.'

'The same way I survive,' says Juno. 'And the same way you're going to have to survive, Claudia, if you don't want to be dependent on Dorian for the rest of your life.' She hands the bill and credit card to the waiter with a flourish.

'Not only are women the losers in marriage,' says Sonia, 'but they also lose out in divorce.' She wriggles into her fur coat. It looks expensive, but old. 'Discarded wives. No matter what the reality is, that's how the legal system sees us. After all, it consists of men, doesn't it, and they've probably got discarded wives themselves. Women are expendable.'

'You mean,' says Claudia, 'we should have the decency to recognize when we've outlived our usefulness?'

'Unless we're recyclable,' Sonia says, pulling on her gloves. 'When I first went to see my lawyer he said to me, you've got clear eyes and good bones – all you've got to do is to make yourself marketable.'

'How outrageous!'

'Isn't it?' Sonia stands up, pulling her coat more closely around her, 'And now I'll leave you. I have the statutory fifteen hundred words to complete before I can watch that programme on the reallocation of the television franchises.'

'Well, mind you keep in touch with Claudia.'

'Oh, I'll keep in touch with Claudia,' Sonia says with a wink.

Juno orders some coffee, persuading Claudia to join her because there is plenty of time before her class. Claudia reckons she will have to leave in ten minutes. Sonia's departure has eased what she has scarcely perceived as tension. She finds it odd that Sonia and Juno should be friends: Juno often loquacious to the point of being unable to distinguish thought from speech and Sonia so measured in her utterances, giving nothing away; Juno so infatuated with the English class system, Sonia the inexorable meritocrat; Juno so large and blonde, Sonia so small and dark.

'Sonia's life seems very well ordered,' she remarks as the coffee arrives.

'Don't you believe it,' says Juno.

'Shouldn't I?'

'There's one thing you must accept,' says Juno, ignoring the question, 'and that is, everything is going to get worse before it gets better. Sonia's marriage was childless. And besides she's got her work. Josh is going to rebel in other ways against what's happened. So will Matilda. This is only the beginning.'

'Well, thanks for your optimism. What ordeals do you foresee?'

'Now, don't be like that, Claudia. You can't expect them to go along as if nothing had happened to their lives.'

'I know, I know. And what the hell do you think has happened to mine?'

'You at least have the choice.' Juno pours the slopped coffee from her saucer back into the cup with admirable dexterity. 'They're completely helpless in the face of your decision to get rid of their father.'

'Just a moment,' Claudia interrupts. 'That's not what happened. Are you trying to say I should have covered up and pretended everything was fine, in order to spare the children?'

'I'm not saying you should or you shouldn't. I'm telling you what you've done.'

'So I'm the wicked parent. I'm not the one who's been lying and cheating and ignoring my children's needs, but I'm the wicked parent. I'm just the one who wants to live openly and without hypocrisy. But I'm the one who's going to get the blame.'

'Of course you are.' There is a cheerful lilt to Juno's voice.

'You're going to be the only one around to blame, aren't you?'

Claudia groans. 'But it's so unfair.'

'Of course it's unfair,' says Juno. 'Life is unfair. You're an idealist, Claudia, and you're going to have to pay the price.'

'What price?'

'You're going to have to live with the fact that nothing and no one is ever going to live up to your expectations.'

Claudia groans again. 'You make it sound like a penance. And now I'm going to be late for my class.'

'No, you won't,' says Juno. 'We'll take a cab. I'll come with you as far as Knightsbridge.'

The grimy snow banked along the kerbs and gutters has been thawing for three days now, and the cold is bitter enough to sneak through the holes of the most ingenious thermal underwear. Passing cars can hardly avoid spraying pedestrians with slush. Pedestrians themselves are forced to make their narrow way between such sporadic onslaughts and the continuing obstacle of black plastic rubbish bags, which have not been collected for weeks. Marauding animals – dogs, cats, rats? – have contrived to rip several apart, allowing the contents to spill on to the pavements of Wardour Street and there defrost into a second putrefaction. This morning, outside the police station in Savile Row, Japanese tourists were taking pictures of each other among the debris. They will show them to their relatives at home as proof of Britain's crumbling economy. They even snapped the bobbies, two by two, to show that order was still being maintained with typically British insouciance.

Juno begins to talk about her fibroids, a subject that has been in abeyance since she has learned about Claudia's troubles. Sleet from a pitilessly leaden sky joins the steady droppings from the eaves and scaffolding as if to emphasize that there is no hope to be gained from looking upwards. My life began when my marriage ended. But Sonia was younger then. And talented. And determined. She turned herself from Mrs James Ravelston, the radical journalist's wife, into the famous novelist Sonia Ravel; as if she had merely been waiting for half a chance. What hope is there for Claudia? Looking downwards and watching the tan of her thin leather boots assume the same deep monochrome as the pavements and the wintry afternoon light, she hears Juno say that she is suffering from Nun's Disease. And she laughs involuntarily at the quaintness of it.

'It's true,' Juno insists. 'It's something that happens to women who haven't had children. So be thankful for your brats, my dear.'

'Oh, I am,' says Claudia, a certain grimness to her sincerity.

Juno ignores the grimness. 'I can have surgery now or leave it for a year and see what happens. If it's OK, it's OK. But if it isn't, then the longer I leave it, the nastier the operation will be. And the more expensive.'

'All right,' says Claudia. 'So it's a gamble. But we do have a National Health Service in this country, you know.'

'And look at the state of it! Anyway, Claudia, you know what we Americans are like. We don't trust anything we don't have to pay for.'

'Well, perhaps you should get it over and done with.'

'And mess up my chances with Rupert?' Juno demands, wounded that her friend should consider condemning her to such a circumstance.

Claudia hesitates. They have reached Oxford Street and she is distracted by the need to find a taxi. 'How,' she asks carefully, 'would having an operation mess up your chances with Rupert?'

'Because,' Juno wails, 'it means I probably wouldn't be able to have a child!'

A 73 bus pulls up at the traffic lights and Claudia considers taking this rare opportunity and jumping on. But of course she is not going home. And Juno has found a cab. She is waving and yelling taxi, taxi, like someone in an Ealing Studios film and unlike anyone else Claudia has ever actually known. The taxi-driver looks resigned. What is left of daylight begins to fade more rapidly as the traffic slows down towards Marble Arch.

'His parents are waiting for him to produce a son and heir,' Juno explains. 'Good God, Claudia, it's his duty. I think we should be able to come to some sort of arrangement.'

Claudia has heard this line of argument before, and she knows that Juno is being perfectly serious. Once, half in fun, Juno drew up a list of the men she would choose to father her child; but then the idea took told of her, and she decided to write to them all, whether or not she had met them, to proposition them. Claudia and others had to dissuade her. But Claudia wonders now if there were not some element of honesty transcending social convention in Juno's plan of action. What sort of transaction, after all, is marriage itself? And shouldn't you choose the father of your children with all due care? If marriage is a property deal, then it should be conducted as cannily as any other investment. Neither sexual attraction nor romantic love, nor even a combination of the two, are ones which are likely to yield an increasing rate of interest.

'Is that really what you'd like?' Claudia asks. 'I'm sure that in many ways it's ever so sensible. But is it enough?'

'Is anything ever enough?' asks Juno, less wistful than pragmatic. 'I've just about got to the stage in my life where I no longer feel that the great love of my life is still to come. It may. But it's got to get moving if it's going to get to me in time.'

'I thought you'd had several great loves,' says Claudia, who can't quite see Juno as Mariana pining in the moated grange.

'Mostly unrequited,' sighs Juno. 'Mostly unconsummated.'

Claudia forbears to say that this is not the impression given her by Juno while the love affairs were in progress. 'And Rupert?' she asks instead.

'Half consummated,' Juno says mysteriously and with another sigh, this time one of pleasure. But they have reached Harrod's where Juno intends to look for wallpaper patterns. 'Call me!' she yells, throwing a couple of pound notes in Claudia's direction as she struggles her way out of the taxi.

Claudia checks her briefcase again. She checked it before she left the house, the desk sergeant's voice repeating itself: we can't release him except to a parent. She checked it on the bus on the way to the police station. She checked it as she stood at the bus stop with Josh, waiting for the 73 to take him home. And of course she checked it the moment she arrived at the restaurant. The contents are still there. The class register. The marked and graded papers. The pad with the notes on Women and the Novel. And a paperback copy of *Mrs Dalloway*. That's the lot, isn't it?

But she has prepared nothing for this class. That's what comes of leaving everything to the last minute – as her father always used to say. That's what comes of not getting up till half-past eleven. She got up for the first time at eight o'clock and had her breakfast – a cup of tea, a valium and three cigarettes – with Joshua and Matilda. They were both sluggish, and she had to hurry them. For reasons best known to themselves, they left the house separately, quite as if they didn't belong to the same family. And for the last few days they have also arrived home separately. Each, on being questioned, has professed ignorance of the other's whereabouts or activities. It is only at mealtimes that they have remained in the same room for more than a few seconds. Instead of being at her desk by nine-thirty as usual on teaching days, Claudia went back to bed. And slept. And slept until the phone call from the police station woke her.

Until now nothing much has changed. Claudia and Dorian have been in touch every day by phone. He will take them all out at the weekend. He and Ron O'Brien are trying to get a band together again; now that the panto has finished and there is nothing on the horizon apart from an episode of 'Watchdogs', there should be plenty of time to rethink and rehearse. It is too noisy and crowded at the Freeburgs', so Dorian has moved in with Ron and his new, young wife. It is almost as though he were away on tour again. Almost, but not quite. Nothing is taken for granted in those conversations which seem to Claudia to have been framed on purpose to corner her. Dorian's reports on his doings tell her what a fine, conscientious fellow is, well worth the having, whatever the price. And his anxious enquiries about his children (unexpressed whenever he has been on tour) rebuke her, accusing her of not caring enough, of not coping well enough. It is this feeling of being cornered that has prevented her from asking him, as every night she feels she must, to come back. Every day the horrors of the night recede, and she is glad she hasn't spoken.

Until now. Josh pleaded guilty as charged: what else could he do with the evidence stacked there in front of him? Besides the cassettes there was a polythene bag which the sergeant emptied in front of her, asking her if she could identify the contents as her lad's property. A front-door key, a biro, half a dozen plastic soldiers, an empty tube of glue, a packet of cigarette papers, a peseta and seven and a half pence. What a pathetic little collection. Claudia wanted to cry. The sergeant held up the tube of glue, examining it as if ruminatively. He wanted to know what Josh used it for, how often he bought glue, and was she satisfied that he wasn't sniffing the stuff? Of course she was satisfied. She spoke coldly, describing Josh's war games with airfix models. The sergeant said that they had taken a voluntary statement and asked her if she would read it. It seemed bland enough and no more incriminatory than was justified. The constable then explained, the sergeant sitting sternly by, that Josh should return to the police station in two weeks' time; meanwhile he would be visited in his home by a representative of the Juvenile Board, who would file a report; it is this report which will decide whether or not Josh is to go to court; but the most usual penalty for a first offence is to be let off with a caution. Papers had to be signed. Josh's property was returned to him and the property of Rama Records kept by the police.

There has been no time to think about Clarissa or Septimus or Dr Bradshaw. Proportion . . . human nature is on you . . . the birds singing in Greek. And Rezia, whose wedding ring has become too loose, sitting in the park and asking why should she suffer? Why indeed? Convinced that she is late, Claudia hopes that no one will see her arrive – least of all in a taxi, a mode of transport which a member of the part-time faculty (currently campaigning for higher rates of pay) should be seen to be unable

A.—3

to afford. But she is out of luck. There, standing on the steps and leaning with his hands in his pockets against the notice proclaiming St Alban's Hall, The College for Americans in London, is Boris Phipps, Dean of Humanities. Claudia pretends not to have seen him, which is rather absurd of her because Boris is well over six feet tall, even with his kindly stoop. She rummages in her briefcase. Boris has no difficulty in intercepting her.

'Hi, Claudia,' he greets her with his usual avuncular smile. 'We're right on time today, I see.'

Claudia is about to reply that she has never been late when she realizes that she has not yet adjusted to the St Alban's idiom. Boris's remark is one of the harmless and meaningless sort repeatedly trotted out by Americans who have a horror of appearing to be taciturn. She returns his greeting in a friendly manner, but without pausing to give the opportunity for a chat – however friendly – about the progress of her class. To her dismay, Boris leaps up the rest of the steps ahead of her to open the swing doors, and waves her through. Somehow this unwonted courtesy puts her more firmly in the wrong than did her minimal greeting. Boris walks along the corridor with her.

'Would you mind very much,' he asks, 'if I drop by your classroom later on and sit in for a few minutes?'

She can't very well say no, can she? 'Not at all,' she says brightly, silently cursing him: he might have given her more notice.

'How are they coming along?' he pursues.

At least he hasn't asked how she is coming along. 'They don't seem to say very much,' she says cautiously.

'They tend to need bringing out a little,' he says. 'I'm afraid you have to be very firm with them over the matter of participation.'

'Are they shy?' asks Claudia, suppressing the impulse to utter a plaintive, *how*? 'Or are they just dumb?' Or is it just me?

Boris laughs nervously. 'We do get some dumb ones,' he admits, 'but most students will respond to stimulating teaching – or that's what we generally find.'

'This is a self-selected group, though, isn't it?' she asks, marshalling her command of the jargon. 'I'd have thought they'd be more highly motivated.'

Boris is approached at this opportune moment by a tanned and stocky young man in a tracksuit. 'Excuse me, Claudia,' he says with a wave of his hand, 'I'll try and get to you in about forty minutes.'

Ms Hughes, sometimes erroneously known as Doctor or even Professor Hughes, finds Room 42 occupied by four students. Of these only little Marie acknowledges her entrance with a murmured, 'Hi!' Karima in her elegant fur coat, the antithesis of Claudia's and considerably grander than Sonia's, is reading an airmail letter. Judy and Shula are whispering together. As usual, Shula is chewing gum and has brought a can of coke into the classroom, breaking the rules which faculty members have been urged, in Boris's weekly memos, to enforce with the utmost strictness. This time she also has a polythene bag full of carrots on her desk. Claudia makes a mental note to warn her of the dangers of vitamin A poisoning: that should scare the spoiled brat.

They are all spoiled brats, of course, the daughters of rich Americans sent off to London for a sabbatical semester or two in order to see Europe rather than learn about British women writers and their work. During the Easter break they will visit Paris, Zurich, Rome. They will not read books. Claudia takes out the register and marks the names of those present. Rebecca and Susanna bounce in, both wearing tracksuits, a kind of uniform which seems to have taken over from blue jeans. Robyn, the loner with the incomprehensible accent, waddles in after them. The class was due to begin five minutes ago, and less than half the students have turned up.

'Why,' Claudia asks of no one in particular, 'are there so few of us today?'

Glances are exchanged, and Shula volunteers, 'I guess the others have all gone on the demo.'

'Dawn is babysitting,' says Susanna.

'Babysitting?' Claudia repeats. 'You don't cut class in order to babysit. What is this demo, anyway?'

Again it is Shula who volunteers. 'It's against the government's proposals to cut grants to foreign students.'

Claudia sighs. 'Dr Phipps has decided to grace us with his presence today,' she says, hoping for some sort of reaction, and preferably one which will evince a promise of support, however tacit, for her own precarious position. But there is none. 'You do know who he is, don't you?'

Oh yes, they know. But they don't care. Claudia hands out the papers: this is the easy bit. Shula's is the best, Claudia reluctantly and privately concedes, so she asks her to read it to the rest of the class. She has tried this device in other establishments with some success. Mutual criticism. Get them to participate. But Shula refuses, on account of she has an infected throat. Exasperated, Claudia reads the paper herself. A half-hearted discussion follows. Marie's, which is middling, follows that, and there is a rather more animated discussion. Robyn's paper is the worst: ill-organized and mistaken, but full of deeply felt sentiments struggling towards coherence. Claudia has hoped that Robyn, having learned from the previous two papers, will be able to express herself more lucidly in class, and that the other students will help her to do so.

But Boris is already in the room, rubbing his hands, nodding and smiling. He signals that Robyn should continue reading, then finds himself a desk at the side of the room, where he sits down and immediately begins to write. Robyn reaches the end of her paper. Claudia invites questions and comments. There are none. She opens *Mrs Dalloway*. Boris stops writing. He and the students are looking expectantly at her. But she says nothing: her mind is a complete blank.

'Weren't we talking about Dr Savage?' asks Shula.

'Dr Bradshaw,' Claudia corrects her.

Shula is unabashed. 'Why have I got Dr Savage written here, then?'

'Because he was a savage?' Rebecca suggests.

Marie wriggles in her seat and, blushing, puts up her hand. 'Savage was the name of Woolf's real doctor when she freaked out and heard the birds chanting in Latin.'

'Greek,' says Claudia, letting the rest of it pass. 'Ah yes, the attitude of the medical profession towards those in their power. We were talking about power and powerlessness. We were relating the powerlessness of the patient to the powerlessness of women. Given that Septimus is a man, why were we doing that?' Get them to participate. She looks hopefully round the room at seven bent heads. 'Why is Septimus a man?' Six faces look blankly back at her; Shula is staring out of the window. 'At an early stage of writing the novel, Virginia Woolf intended to have Mrs Dalloway commit suicide. Why do you think she changed her mind?'

Marie tries to be helpful. 'She wasn't the suicidal type – Clarissa, I mean.'

'Let me put it another way,' says Claudia. 'One of the ideas I asked you to bear in mind at the beginning of the course was that of the surrogate for certain aspects of the author's personality or experience. We should be particularly interested, I said, in finding out if women writers used this device any differently or more frequently than men writers.'

How can you tell? What does it matter? And yet it does. The students wait. Boris waits. It is no good: she will have to go on talking because no one else is going to, and they can't all very well sit in silence for the next three-quarters of an hour, or however much is left of the class. Claudia directs the students' attention to the appropriate page of the text, and reads out the passage she has marked. However, it seems to have nothing to do with the medical profession, or the powerlessness of the patient, or indeed the use of the surrogate. She must change the subject. A few explanatory remarks. Get them to participate. Turn over a few pages. Find another passage – something that will stimulate them. Another few pages. Boris is tapping his fingers on his desk, unaware that he is making the loudest noise in the room.

Claudia's mouth is dry (the valium!), her voice thin. She must go on. Page after page, passage after passage, on and on so that there is never any silence in which the sound of Boris's tapping fingers gets the chance to drive all thought away. If she sticks to the text, she can't go wrong. She becomes sick of the sound of her own voice, but she blunders on, seemingly so intent on putting forward her own interpretations that no one else gets a chance to participate. Distaste for what she is doing spreads itself to cover the characters in the novel: how repulsively empty and self-satisfied they are, their gropings towards honest doubt scarcely more than token gestures.

'But Lucrezia is different,' she hears herself say. 'She is not one of the English upper class, and her endurance springs from devotion to her husband rather than to the ethos of the stiff upper lip.' Surprisingly, this gets a laugh – or at least, a ripple. 'She alone can ask herself, why should I suffer?'

But she has forgotten what is so singular about the question. She looks at her watch, as if to indicate that an important topic is about to be broached, so important that it requires more time than is presently available. Five minutes left. Boris stops tapping and clears his throat. This is signal enough for Claudia, who calls the class to a halt. The students troop out, more stunned than stimulated. She fumbles with her papers, hardly daring to look at Boris.

'Well,' he says at last, 'do you have time for a coffee?'

'Yes, of course,' says Claudia, having dismissed the possibility of telling Boris that she must call her estranged husband to tell him that their son has been arrested for theft. Much less that her daily dose of valium prevents her from thinking clearly.

The cafeteria is warm and steamy and noisy. Two of Claudia's missing students are being chatted up by a couple of youths in front of the coffee urn. She pretends not to have seen them, and finds a table in the corner while Boris fetches himself a bowl of chilli. Staring at the stained formica, she feels suddenly old and tired. The faces of Josh, the policemen, Juno, Sonia, Boris and the students seem to melt into one critical – even censorious – blur.

'Sure you don't want to eat?' Boris asks her. She shakes her head and, shaking his, he continues, 'It's not the sort of approach I would have chosen myself.'

'Approach?' Claudia repeats, understanding only that she has failed to make the grade. 'Do you mean approach to the novel or approach to the students?'

'Well . . . ' Boris smiles disarmingly at her. 'Both, really, to be frank. What made you choose *Mrs Dalloway*?'

Claudia tries to indicate with a wave of her hand that the answer must be obvious. What did make her choose *Mrs Dalloway*? Her unconscious? 'It seemed relevant,' she says. Relevant to what?

But Boris doesn't ask this question. 'It's not my favourite Woolf. I find it difficult to sympathize with any of the characters.'

'Don't you think they provide an illustration of the English class system, and women's place within that system?' Claudia's tone implies that it would be sexist of him to demur.

Boris says, 'Do you find anything in the novel which challenges the class system?'

'Not exactly,' Claudia says, as if judiciously, 'or, at least, not in any sustained fashion. But that's what's so interesting. I mean, Virginia Woolf was so much more trenchant in her journalism than she seems to have found it possible to be in her fiction. And so much franker.'

'Hmmm . . . ' Boris remains unconvinced. 'I can see that you have evolved your own teaching method. Each to his own.'

Claudia reaches for a cigarette, only to remember that smoking is forbidden in the cafeteria. Her weariness increases, tempered by a sense of injustice. She knows that Boris knows that she has no teaching method, that indeed she has never taught university students before. She told him so herself; she warned him; he said not to worry; he said it would be easy. He was desperate, having been let down by someone more competent than herself. Oh, but anyone would have been more competent than she is. How was Boris to know?

'Do you think I should be tougher on them?' she asks humbly.

'Yes, I do,' says Boris.

Claudia wants to ask him how, but Boris has finished eating and it is clear that the interview – because that is what it was – is at an end. With a promise to attend the faculty meeting next week, she says goodbye to Boris, who insists on shaking hands, and walks stumblingly along the corridor through a crowd of oncoming students. What an incongruous place St Alban's is. If they want properly qualified teachers, then they should employ them and pay them accordingly instead of cut-price native labour. Claudia is angry with Boris, angry with the college, and angry with Americans in general. But she is also angry with – and disappointed in – herself.

The 73 is only going as far as King's Cross and is quite full: a bad sign. There seem to be plenty of 9s around, all of them empty. Can't they see, the powers-that-be, that people don't want 9s? They want 73s. As it is, examples of the genre are so rare that there ought to be prizes for spotting them. What a strange, shy creature it is, despite its gaudy plumage which proclaims the exhibitionist. The stress of modern life has evidently been too much for it. Snug in its famous habitat and breeding-ground, Tottenham Garage, it scarcely dares venture out alone, but needs must be accompanied on its foraging expeditions to Hammersmith Broadway by at least one other of its own kind. Perhaps paranoia would be an appropriate diagnosis. This creature sees its fellows – cars, lorries, motorbikes and above all human beings – as predators. Poor creature. If it were rational, it would know that it has no natural predator but time.

Claudia knows that she is on the verge of transportation hysteria, an endemic malady for Londoners, and one whose chief symptom is the anthropomorphization of dead entities. But how else to bear it all?

V

Armageddon, Gotterdämmerung and the fucking Apocalypse all rolled into one. That's what it was like the first time I supposedly stayed out all night. At least that's what it was like as far as they were concerned. She was in hysterics and he went and called the law. I ask you. I don't know which was worse. For a long time I couldn't get over the shock of my own father actually calling out the Pigs to look for me. I mean, suppose they'd found me! What the hell did he think would have happened then? Me and Emma crashed out in front of the telly with a quarter of an ounce of Red Leb clutched in her hot little hand and half a dozen of Mum's valium stashed in my jeans pocket. Jesus H. Christ, he should have known better.

I was the one who should have been hysterical. But the calmer I stayed, the more worked up she seemed to get. Anything could have happened to me, according to her. But it didn't, did it, so why all the fuss? I mean, I really couldn't understand what I'd done that was so terrible. All I'd actually done was to stop over at Emma's, not repeat *not*, stay out all night. I called Mum several times, but the fucking phone was always engaged. Of course it shitting pissing was. She was on it. She was rabbiting away as usual to Dad or Claire or Juno or Sonia or some other boring old friend of hers. Christ alone knows what they find to talk about for all those hours on end – and I mean *hours*. Anyway, after a joint or two or three, me and Emma just dozed off. Is that some kind of a crime? (Don't answer that.)

Anyone would think we'd been creeping round Clissold Park mugging little old ladies and raping them with the railings. Or worse: asking for some crazed kerb-crawler to rape us. What made it all the more sickening was that it was Josh who was the sodding criminal – not me. And what happened to him? He got a raise in his pocket money. (Mind you, mine was raised too, so perhaps I shouldn't complain.) He was let off homework – not that he ever did any anyway. And Dad lent him an old electric guitar of his. Mum even stopped yelling at him for a week or two. And I got sick to death of fish pie. Everything seemed to revolve around Josh: Josh bunking off (yes, they found out at last); Josh's interview with the Juvenile Board; Josh's O-levels; Josh's misery. What about my fucking misery? Nobody gave a damn.

Apart from getting him all this attention so that the stupid wanker actually thought he was some kind of hero, Josh's crime had other repercussions. Not least for me and Nat. It practically ruined our relationship. For starters, there was no hope of bunking off, so no more nicking. As far as Fleet Valley were concerned, poor little Joshie and his innocent little sister (ha, ha!) were both under the evil influence of Nat Masters, the professional delinquent. They had their eye on us, all right. We had to sign the register for *every lesson*, not just at the beginning of the morning and afternoon sessions. Nat played along. He said it was best to keep a low profile for a bit, and they'd soon forget about us. So I didn't see that much of him. They kept us apart at school, and when he came round the house he always asked, is Josh in? (I could *hear* him!) If I went to Josh's room when he was there, he'd say hi, and that was about it. If I didn't join them (and what was the point, just to be ignored?) the two of them would go off somewhere together without even telling me. Sometimes Josh would stay the night at Nat's house.

I suppose I must admit that Nat and me had been drifting apart before, but all the same I couldn't help feeling . . . well, cast aside. Then Emma invited me to her birthday party. And she didn't invite Nat or Josh. You wouldn't have thought they'd have minded. But they were green. They kept threatening to gatecrash it. Emma was worried, but I said they wouldn't have the nerve. And I was right. All they did was walk up and down outside, singing 'Happy Birthday to You' in what they thought were girls' voices and making farting noises. Utterly childish. We just turned the volume up and blasted them with Adam and the Ants.

So when the copper from the Juvenile Board came round to put the screws on Josh, and everyone seemed to want me out of the way, I went to Emma's. At least there was no one there to keep needling you. Emma's Mum works at all hours of the day and night at Metropolitan Radio, so she's never around. There's just an au pair, some goofy Dutch girl – to look after Ben, her spoiled brat of a brother, or step-brother. Or is it half-brother? Anyway, Emma and Ben have got different Dads and they're both divorced from Emma's Mum. We could do more or less what we liked. Annika never took any notice of us. Sometimes she went out of an evening with other Dutch people and Emma and I had to babysit. Those were the best times. We'd talk and talk about all the things I couldn't talk to anyone else about. When I told her about Nat she said I was silly and I should go on the pill. She was between boyfriends at the time, but she still went on taking it because you never knew. Her Mum told her on her fifteenth birthday (the one Josh and Nat weren't invited to) that if she was having it off with boys, she should take the necessary precautions. She arranged it all for Emma, ringing up the doctor and whatnot, just to make sure.

But after the so-called staying-out-all-night episode, Mum wasn't too keen on Emma. It was obvious she thought her a Bad Influence and she would contrive all sorts of excuses to make me stay at home. Then, for no reason at all, she didn't seem to mind any more. It was about the time Josh had to go back to the Pig-pen to be told his fate. He said it was all a laugh. This sergeant or whatever he was read out some long-winded spiel about the dire tortures that lay in wait for him if he dared to break the law a second time. Josh had to say he was sorry and that he wouldn't do it again, (Come on, let's hear you, lad) and call the bastard sir. Then he asked him to apologize to Mum for all the worry he had caused her. (Dad wasn't there, of course.) Try and stay out of trouble, sonny. That was his parting advice. So there Josh was – another teenage psychopath let loose to wreck the lives of ordinary decent people like you and me.

Nat was right. After half-term the heat was off or, rather, only warm. During the holiday Josh and me were supposed to be going away with Dad for a couple of days to give Mum a break (from us!) but at the last minute he said something had come up and he couldn't make it. I spent most of the week round at Emma's. It seemed best to keep out of Mum's way for a bit. Anyway I'd been getting pissed off with coming home from school to find her and Clive sitting at the kitchen table drinking whisky for all the world as if they hadn't just spent the afternoon in bed together. Mum was only pretending to drink whisky, of course. It was Clive who was pissed out of his mind, as usual. And if it wasn't Clive, it was Claire or Juno or the Psychiatric Social Worker. There was always someone, especially after half-term. I couldn't walk into the kitchen for a cup of tea without finding some sodding stranger in our midst. Oh, they were all perfectly friendly. But somehow that didn't make it any better. Worse, if anything, because I was supposed to answer their nurdish questions politely and pretend to believe they really meant it when they said how much they liked the pretty colours in my hair.

Emma and me did each other's hair. Hers was easier because it's kind of springy but mine's all floppy, which is why I like it kept short. First we cut it all ragged with Emma's Mum's nail scissors so as to make it stick up. Then we bleached it as white as we dared without it all falling out. It looked kind of funny with our young faces, especially when we sprayed it with silver lacquer, so we put on lots of make-up to get a witchlike effect. Masses of black eye-liner all nice and thick and sweeping upwards and kind of rays underneath so that our eyes looked like hellish carnivorous flowers. *Fleurs du mal*, Emma said. It was terrific! We even wore black clothes and painted our fingernails black. I thought Mum would have a fit, but she seemed more inclined to laugh. First she said what a pity it was for me of all people to dye my hair when I was a natural strawberry blonde. Then she said it was funny but I now looked more like Claire than ever. (Claire is Mum's youngest sister. We never see Chloe, the middle one, because she lives in South Africa with her engineer husband and four kids and thinks White is might is right.) Talk about put-downs. My Mum's an expert at them. Who wants to look like a thirty-five-year-old hippie who thinks it's still the Swinging Sixties?

We started experimenting with different colours after that. Well, it really started when Slime came round with some burgundy Krazy Kolor he'd got left over from streaking his own greasy nit-infested locks. Then we went on to blue, green, pink, yellow. The fluffier the colour the better it looked, if you see what I mean. We wore the fluffiest clothes we could find, things we'd scorned to wear a few months before because they were too girlie-girlie. It was such fun – like a kind of parody. The only thing Mum objected to was me and Emma swopping clothes. I couldn't understand why. Did she think my friend had fleas or something? We hardly knew what belonged to who any more. I suppose that was it. We were violating the sacred rights of property. We even started wearing Slime's clothes. Once we stripped him naked and shared his clothes between us so we looked like something out of *Oliver*. He didn't seem to mind. He didn't seem to mind anything, just stood there smiling in his usual vacant fashion as if he was part of it all. No matter how unmercifully we teased him, he still stuck around. What for?

Well, I was soon to find out the answer to that. One Saturday afternoon I went round to Emma's as usual so that we could do our English homework. (Yes, we *were* virtuous sometimes) and anyway she still had my copy of *Jane Eyre* because she'd lost hers. Annika answered the door and said that Emma wasn't in. So I said, could I go in and wait? She said I'd have to wait a long time because Emma had gone to the football with Simon. I didn't believe her. I laughed. I really thought she was joking. She said she wasn't joking and I could wait if I wanted to. Of course I didn't. I wandered off into the park, shaking all over. I was shocked out of my tiny trusting apology of a mind. What the shitting hell did Emma care about football? What did she care about Slime? She despised him. We both did. I thought she was the one sane person in this fucked-up world and there she was behaving like any other preppy little ponce with a brain the size of a dried pea so as you could hear it rattle every time she moved. It couldn't be true. Of course it wasn't. It was just what she'd told Annika. She was probably doing something fantastically interesting like . . . like . . . But I couldn't think of anything fantastically interesting she'd want to do without me.

And it was true. Eventually – *two whole days* later! – she told me herself that she was going out with Slime. It needn't make any difference to our friendship, she said. The way she said it, she sounded so fucking prissy. I just said, what friendship? And walked off. Some girls just have to have a boyfriend – any boyfriend – because they think they must be failures without one. Fucking brainwashing. That's what it is. I couldn't believe she actually *felt* anything for that toe-rag, Slime, who was in every way our inferior.

I didn't have a friend in the world. I might just as well not have existed, for all the interest anyone took in me. Sometimes I felt positively fucking invisible. Nat and Josh were always tripping on something or other, either zonked out like zombies or else laughing their empty heads off like a couple of sodding hyenas. Mostly it was glue, which I can't stomach. The very smell of it makes me heave. Mum asked why Josh had developed this sudden passion for cleaning his teeth, but I said nothing. Even I wouldn't sink that low. As for Mum herself, she always seemed to be somewhere else, even when she was sitting there right opposite you. She didn't fly off the handle much any more, but she seemed kind of downtrodden and martyrish, which in a way was worse. Half the time she didn't even notice me coming into the room. Even when I spoke to her, she didn't seem to hear me. We seemed to see less and less of Dad, and whenever we did, we always went to a movie, so as he didn't have to talk to us.

What a pair of walking fucking clichés! All they cared about was their own stupid pride, or whatever is was. Why did they have to make such a big deal out of everything? Why couldn't they either stay married or get divorced instead of all this constant agonizing over the past and the future? What about the present? It exists too. What about me? I exist too. It wasn't my fucking fault that they couldn't get it together any more, was it? Why should I have to be punished for something I didn't even do? Or, if I did, I didn't know what it was. How could I know? There wasn't anything, was there? Was there?

Every time I looked in the mirror and saw my hair, I thought about what life could have been like. (You've no idea how important hair is in this story of my short life.) It seemed to belong to another time and another person. I didn't like it. I didn't like that person. Then I knew what to do. One Saturday afternoon when Mum had gone off to see Claire's new baby and Josh and Nat had gone to see some Communist friend of Nat's and I was left alone as usual, inspiration came to me. I cut the whole fucking lot off. Then I found an old electric shaver of Dad's in the bathroom cupboard, so I shaved off what was left. The batteries were a bit run down so there were a few stubborn tufts here and there, but all in all the effect was stunning. Did I feel good? Did I feel fanfuckingtastic? It was like shedding some horrible outworn, outmoded skin and emerging into the light of day like a new self. My real self. Strong, true and dynamic. Unafraid. Self-sufficient. Not the sort of person to be taken for a ride. The sort of person to make you sit up and take notice.

I needed a new wardrobe. No more pastel blues and pinks for me. I bundled up all Emma's things, put them in a plastic rubbish bag and called Annika to leave a message for Emma (who was out, of course) to come and collect them. Next, I raided Josh's room. There I found a purple vest which made my shoulders look broader and my scarcely swelling tits stand out a little; some leather trousers (well, they were plastic, really) he'd grown out of; and a Levi's jacket, also too small for him, with holes at the elbows. In Mum's room I found some black suede stiletto-heeled sandals left over from her youth and a pair of huge loopy clip-on earrings which she hasn't worn since she had her ears pierced, and a deep-blue velvet cravat of Dad's. I put on some mascara to match the cravat, blusher to hollow out my cheeks and bright-red lipstick and nail varnish. *Cabaret*. Jail-bait.

It was worth it all for the look of horror on Mum's face. But my euphoria was, as they say, short-lived. It began to ebb when she put her arms round me: I could feel myself shrinking into a little girl again in her embrace. When she ran her hand over my head there were tears in her eyes. All at once I felt tearful too. She touched my rouged cheekbones, my earrings, the trailing down at the back of my neck, saying, oh Matty, Matty. I was totally unprepared for her tenderness towards me. Had I got everything wrong? I felt about a millimetre high.

And then we both started laughing. Or something. I don't think either of us knew if we were laughing or crying. She gave me a kleenex for my sniffles and asked if I'd thought about what was going to happen when I went to school on Monday. I hadn't, of course, beyond some vague notion of knocking 'em all dead in the aisles. She said she was horribly afraid that people would laugh at me. Laugh at me? Laugh at *me*? Matilda Hughes? No one has ever laughed at Matilda Hughes and got away with it, and no one ever will. Mum said she had a wig she used to wear in the sixties when everyone did. It was all tangled up but we could cut it and even dye it, if I wanted. I shook my head. It felt free. I didn't want anything false and foreign on it. What was so terrible about not having any hair? She said she didn't think there was anything terrible about it, but other people might. Fuck other people! Why think about them? Why couldn't they – she – anyone – accept me as I really was?

And I stormed out of the room. Don't ask me why. Don't ask me what more I wanted from her. I didn't know myself. But I'd have recognized it if she'd given it to me. As it was, I stomped up the stairs, hardly knowing what I was saying and yet knowing all too well, yelling, I want my Dad! Why isn't he here? And all that crap. Mum didn't follow me upstairs, didn't even plead with me, didn't even call to me. Perhaps she was crying too. I didn't want to know. You may think that means I didn't give a damn about my Mum, but the truth is I was shit-scared. Of what? I didn't know. That's why I was shit-scared.

I could hear her down in the kitchen getting the supper ready and I began to feel hungry. Then I could hear Josh and Nat. I could hear them both shriek in their idiotic breaking voices and her shushing them, and I felt sure they were talking about me. How could I face going down to supper? If only Nat would piss off home. But I knew he wouldn't. He always stuck around on Saturdays, especially if Mum was cooking. It looked like I might starve to death, like one of those nuns who shut themselves up in the walls of their convents. Didn't they have shaved heads too? I could smell something good, all meaty and garlicky. My stomach rumbled fit to bust. They were all yattering downstairs. Perhaps they weren't talking about me after all. Perhaps they'd forgotten my existence. They sounded so jolly. I wanted to die.

Mum came up and fetched me. She led me into the kitchen by the hand. The boys stared at me, of course, and Josh started sniggering. But I held my head high, just like she said, pretending I was an actress and playing my part as if my life depended on it. Nat got the point. He applauded. He almost spoiled it by calling me Kojak, but he said at once that I was a right little punkette, which was praise indeed. Not Josh, though. He said, of course we all know why she's done it. Mum said, ssh! But Josh went on, Her girlfriend's gone and got herself a boyfriend, so Matilda's trying to provide some competition by turning herself into Matt.

I could have killed him. How could he be so pissing shitting moronic? He really surpassed his own dismally low standards of wit. I seized the nearest object, which happened to be a bread knife, but Nat's hand was over mine. He gripped my wrist and said, treat that with the contempt it deserves. He squeezed my hand so I was forced to drop the knife. Otherwise I might now be in the nut-house serving my time for fratricide. Then he patted me on the shoulder and said, there's a good girl. Who did he think he was? My father? As we sat down in our places, he looked at Mum, half in triumph, half seeking her approval. Which she gave. Only by a flicker, but she gave, she gave.

VI

'I love your body,' says Clive, rolling onto his back again, 'and I love your cunt.'

Claudia manages to stretch and straighten her leg while still lying on her side, her arm trailing across his chest. There is no need for her to say anything: Clive no longer expects it. A loquacious lover himself, he has learned to come to terms with her silences. As she has with his whisperings. They make her smile, they make her move, and they, as much as anything else, make her come. However the plot may vary, he always has the speaking, she the non-speaking role in the drama. After all those years of waning marital sex, how sweet it is to have a role at all. How gratifying to be translated from the audience at an anxious performance to star status, participating right through to the final scene. How liberating not to have to worry about Clive's worries. Because he has none. To him, sex is no big deal: neither a right nor a duty but a form of communication: lyric, comic, tragic, ironic. Time, place (and sometimes even person) don't matter. There is only one precondition: secrecy.

'You know,' he says, reaching for his pack of Marlboro among the empty mugs and glasses on the bedside table, 'it's Greta's birthday next week. Has she invited you?'

'Not yet. She generally tends to leave it, or me, to the last moment.'

'She wants to finish my portrait before then.' Clive's voice is gloomy as he lights their cigarettes. 'Then she can display me in the altogether to all her guests as her prize possession.'

'Serve you right,' says Claudia.

She reaches for the already overflowing ashtray and places it on her stomach. Greta is Clive's problem, not hers. The afternoon light is fading and is thickened in the low-ceilinged room by two spreading spirals of smoke. The stain in the corner, which has often resembled a leering old man, seems to have spread itself into the avuncular features of Father Christmas. Does that mean that the roof is leaking again? There is a sprinkling of rain visible at the window in the light from the street lamp. She should check the landing outside the bathroom where it always comes flooding in. But not now. Not yet.

She was standing on layers of soggy newspaper with a bucket in each hand when the doorbell rang. Her supposition was that it was one of the children's friends and, because they were out, she was disinclined to answer the summons. But the bell stuck, as it sometimes did. Claudia cursed it and ran down the sodden stairs. A dark, slightly bedraggled figure in an old raincoat was leaning, head bent, knees bent, against the bell. As she opened the door wider it stumbled inside, mumbling and waving its arms. Only when it straightened up and smiled mischievously at her did she recognize Clive. Kicking the door shut, he announced that he had heard about her recent misfortune and had come to comfort her. Just to prove it, he had liberated a bottle of whisky from the Queen's Arms when the landlord had left him in charge of the Snug at lunchtime (it being the day of the Grand National) and moreover he had only consumed half of it himself: the rest was for her. No use her saying she didn't need comforting. She did. So did he. Such joys were in store for them both. He didn't have to be back at work till half-past five, so there was plenty of time for a drink first.

Clive had many disadvantages. He was the sort of drunk who seems to thrive on alcohol, staying lean and healthy, his spirits rising as the level of those in the bottle goes down – the tireless sort of drunk who never gives up and is therefore tiring. He was Australian, contemptuous of the Brits and unrepentantly iconoclastic towards all their shibboleths except those pertaining to sport and, concomitantly, gambling. He lived with Junkie June and her three children, who made his life a misery, driving him to seek the company of other women for solace. He was Greta's lover. And besides, Claudia didn't fancy him – not one little bit. He needn't think she was available just because Dorian had left. But she was. She had no intention of getting involved with Clive. But she did.

She puts the ashtray back on the table and turns towards Clive again. Groaning in mock resignation, he pulls her over on top of him. The hairs on his chest tickle her nipples and she laughs, nuzzling into his neck: the odour contains soap, whisky, tobacco and something indefinable which is Clive's alone. But he doesn't respond. Indeed, she can feel him detumesce beneath her.

'There's someone in the house,' he says.

'Nonsense.'

'There is, Claudia.'

'Joshua and Matilda have gone to meet Dorian. I told you.'

'Then it's a burglar.'

They both lie perfectly still. There is only the sound of rain, then the swish of tyres as a paler light cuts through the orange glow which has warmed the walls from milk to cream. And then, again, the mingled impact, slide and acceptance of liquid from slates into guttering. That's what's wrong: the guttering is blocked. Claudia and Clive sit up simultaneously. There is no doubt about it: someone is coming upstairs.

'It's Dorian,' Clive whispers in an alarm which is only half-feigned.

'No, it's Josh,' Claudia whispers. 'What the hell is going on?'

The footsteps arc slow, heavy, despondent. Josh's leather jacket creaks as he moves, the studs clinking against the banisters. The bathroom door gets slammed and is locked. Claudia attempts to get up, but Clive won't let her go. Matilda yells to Josh not to be long. Claudia gets out bed. Clive whimpers. Matilda is coming up the stairs. Claudia can't find her bra and pulls on her sweater before looking under the bed for her jeans. Matilda is rattling the handle of the bathroom door. Josh yells at her to piss off. As Claudia is struggling into her jeans Clive grabs her by the arm.

'Ignore them,' he says. 'Do them good.'

'Don't be silly, Clive. Something's happened.'

'They sound all right to me.'

'Something's upset them.'

'What about me?'

Claudia doesn't answer him. She zips up her jeans with some ferocity and goes out on to the landing. Josh is trudging his way downstairs. His face, glimpsed from above, looks pained, which is nothing unusual, and weary – which is. He doesn't see his mother and, because he is muttering to himself, doesn't hear her either. She walks across the landing to inspect the flood target area before confronting him. The carpet is no damper than it was yesterday and there appears to be no water coming in from above. Perhaps she needn't call the roof people after all. If she does, she won't be able to pay them. The bank manager informed her by letter this morning that the joint account was overdrawn by £63 and would she kindly refrain from writing cheques until sufficient funds were available to meet them. (You wouldn't think, would you, that with all their millions they'd make a fuss about a mere sixty-three quid? It must be recession jitters, or something.) She intended to ask Dorian for some cash when he brought the children back from the cinema. Creative Commercials always paid in cash and he has just done a jingle session for Mrs B's TV Dinners.

Josh is standing at the sink, idly swivelling the tap, a finger almost covering the outlet so that the water can spray out in all directions. He is eating a thick slice of bread and peanut butter and is waiting for the kettle to boil. He ignores his mother until she actually speaks to him.

'What happened?'

'Why can't she pissing well use the downstairs loo?' he replies through a mouthful of bread. 'She just goes out of her way to annoy me.'

'I don't mean now. I mean, with Dorian.'

'Oh, he wasn't there.'

'Wasn't *there*? Where was he?'

'How should I know?'

'You mean Ron wasn't there either?'

'No Dad, no Ron, no nobody.'

'How very strange,' says Claudia. 'I checked with him yesterday morning. Perhaps he had to fill in for someone on a session.'

'Perhaps.' Josh takes his mug of coffee to the table and sits down. His expression hasn't changed. 'He could have phoned.'

'Oh Josh, anything could have happened.'

'He could have left a message.'

Claudia busies herself in making another cup of coffee. Trying to keep calm (an easier exercise now that she has cut her daily dosage of valium to one first thing in the morning) she rehearses the possibilities one by one. The time was wrong. The day was wrong. The place was wrong. She and Josh are able to dismiss those easily enough. Ron's doorbell wasn't working. It was. Dorian was on the phone or in the lavatory and they hadn't given him time to extricate himself. They had waited for ten minutes. He was asleep. They had thrown stones at the window of his room; they might even have cracked one of the panes. Josh stares murkily into his coffee. Claudia feels a presentiment of . . . what? Sickness? Or death? She tries to react in a wifely fashion but a small inner voice says spitefully, I don't care. Then another, quieter, stronger, corrects if: I am too hurt to care; I am too hurt to care about anyone except my children, who share my hurt.

Josh takes an Old Holborn tin from his pocket and begins to roll a cigarette. He is not very good at it yet. Shreds of tobacco fall on the table and floor. Claudia watches him, realizing that she would once have been irritated by the mess: now she sees it as part of Josh's vulnerability. His face beneath the dirt and the acne is so like his father's in both outline and feature. But Josh holds his mouth tight and hard, his eyes half hidden, fugitive. Claudia wants to tell him that everything is going to be all right. But how, in all honesty, in all fairness to him, can she? How can she lie to a person she loves? She remembers that she has left her cigarettes in the bedroom and she asks him for a roll-up instead. He pushes the tin across the table, not looking at her.

'Why,' he asks, 'do people have children?'

Claudia's hand, poised above the tobacco tin, is arrested, shaking slightly. 'All sorts of reasons,' she says carefully.

'Why did you – you and Dad?'

Claudia experiences a moment of panic. 'Because,' she says slowly, 'we loved each other and we *wanted* to have children.' But of course it was she who wanted to have children. 'Oh Josh, did you think we didn't?' Perhaps Dorian never really did. If so, both he and Josh must be protected from this knowledge.

'I think that if people have children, they ought to see it through till they're grown up, and not go fucking about or fucking off whenever they feel like it.'

'Sometimes . . .' Claudia hesitates. Her impulse to protect Josh from the truth which he has recognized is too strong for her. 'Sometimes it can't be helped. We can't always foresee what's going to happen to us.'

He concedes this with a shrug but his gesture as he flicks the ash from his cigarette onto the floor is angry. 'Why me? What am I supposed to have done? I mean, why walk out on me?'

'You haven't done anything, Josh. You mustn't blame yourself for –'

'Who am I supposed to blame, then?'

When the door opens, Claudia supposes that Matilda (who hates to be left out) has come to join them, and that she must now attempt the difficult task of restoring the children's self-esteem without destroying their need to trust both their parents, their need to possess both a mother and a father. But it is Clive who comes into the room. Claudia is relieved to see that he has dressed. All the same, Josh blushes fiercely at the sight of his mother's lover. Clive hesitates but eventually sits down at the table and greets Josh in a friendly manner. Josh returns the greeting sullenly.

'Cheer up,' says Clive. 'I'm not the monster from the black lagoon, you know.'

'What more do you want?' Josh asks him as he reclaims his tobacco tin. 'A kiss?'

And with that, he makes his exit, flushed now with at least a temporary triumph as well. Clive shrugs, rolling his eyes melodramatically – a gesture to which Claudia does not respond – and lights a cigarette of his own.

'What am I supposed to have done?' he asks. 'Violated the Oedipal triangle?'

'Oh, piss off, Clive.' Claudia abandons her soggy roll-up and takes one of Clive's cigarettes. 'Isn't it time you were wending your way to the Queen's Arms?'

'Haven't I just left them?' Clive sighs romantically. 'Seriously, Claudia, that kid always looks at me as though he'd like to knife me.'

'It's nothing to do with you,' Claudia says wearily. Is there no end to the egocentricity of the adult male? 'Dorian stood them up.'

'So would I.'

'Why don't you go to work?'

'Where's the other one?'

'Her name's Matilda. I suppose I'd better go up to her room and try to comfort her.'

'Don't be an over-anxious Mum.' Clive attempts to take her hand. 'It's such a bore.'

'So are you.' Claudia evades him.

Clive stands up, as if stiffly. 'Well, I'm off to earn a dishonest living, then. See you at the Freeburgs'.'

Claudia, who knows that this is Clive's way of telling her that he will see her sooner, doesn't bother to reply. Neither does she bother to see him out. Indeed, his dejected mien affords some passing satisfaction. As soon as the door slams shut she dials Dorian's number and lets the phone ring fifty times before deciding that there is no one at home. Then, just in case she got the number wrong, she dials again. But the result is the same. She goes upstairs to find Matilda.

But Matilda is not in her room. The window sash is broken and the bottom half propped open crookedly with a splayed copy of *The Physical Geography of the British Isles*. The walls, once pristine white with a Kate Greenaway frieze, are daubed with ill-executed caricatures, some of them obscene, and graffiti in various hands: Punk Rules, OK; Siouxsie; Education is the opium of the middle classes, dope is the opium of the people; Jesus sucks; Life is a venereally contracted terminal disease. There is no sheet on the bed: just a tumbled sleeping-bag, a pillow in a torn and grimy case and a bowl of congealed Weetabix. The mattress is covered in stains of assorted colours and sizes. On the broken-backed chair which serves as a bedside table stand five mugs, two of them empty, two half-full of coffee spattered with mould and one housing a decayed apple core. Hardly a square inch of carpet is visible beneath the scattered magazines, clothes, records and other necessities of adolescent life. The smell is indescribable.

Claudia backs out and crosses the landing to Josh's room. Matilda has never been orderly, but at least she used to make some pretence of tidying her room every Saturday – if only to merit her pocket money. The last time she cleaned it, she'd left it for two weeks and then demanded two weeks' money. This Claudia refused on the grounds that it wasn't fair on Josh who tidied his room on a weekly basis. Matilda received one week's pocket money but hasn't cleaned her room now for four weeks. Josh is slightly more scrupulous. He needs floor space to set up his war games and money to add to his collection of combatants. The Battle of Waterloo has remained in position now for two weeks. Wellington's men have yet to have their uniforms painted on.

'Don't make vibrations,' he says, not looking up from his delicate paint-work as his mother opens the door – without knocking, as usual. 'I don't want my scum of the earth smudged.'

'Is Matilda with you?'

'Yes, she's under the bed.' He indicates the mattress on the floor.

'Where is she?'

'How should I know?'

Claudia stands at the door, holding the knob which has come away in her hand. 'How did this happen? I didn't hear her go out. Perhaps she's gone to Emma's. She might have said.'

Josh makes no acknowledgement of any of this. She pushes the knob more or less into position and pulls the door to behind her. As she reaches the top of the stairs Josh pushes the door shut from inside and the knob falls off. A sense of emptiness overtakes her as she walks downstairs. It is waiting for her in the kitchen with the empty coffee cups and the demerara sugar Josh has spilled along the worktop and hob. It is waiting for her in the sitting-room where he has left the television switched on. It is waiting most insidiously in the study in a file marked 'Women and the Novel: Mid-Semester Examination'. And it will be waiting for her in the bedroom between the rumpled sheets.

She collects the dirty dishes from all over the house – even from Matilda's room, where she has vowed not to intervene – and stacks them in the dish-washer. There is still no reply from Dorian's number. Someone on Radio 4 is talking indignantly about crypto-Communist trade unions holding the country to ransom. Radio 3 offers Mendelssohn's violin concerto. Life goes on – somewhere. She turns to LBC, hoping to get the news headlines. Perhaps there has been a disaster of some sort in which Dorian could have been involved. She must find some reason for his behaviour, however cataclysmic. But the main item is the announcement of a General Election on 3 May, closely followed by a catalogue of the horrors taking place in Iran.

She will cook supper for Josh and herself, hoping that Matilda will appear in time to join them. The semblance at least of structure must be maintained. That's what mothers are for. Meals are now the only occasions on which the three of them are together, the only opportunity for conversation or discussion – unless Nat happens to be around. It is easier to talk to the children in his presence because he will act as an interpreter, translating her anxious, probing questions into blunt, everyday queries unfraught with covert meaning or intention. He has the knack of stripping her clumsy expressions of concern or the possibility of implied criticism. Nat is her ally, but he is also theirs. That they are not each other's is made plain by their joint unresponsiveness to their

A.—4

mother's increasingly desperate attempts to make conversation across the dining-table as if they were still a normal family. Even her anecdotes about her own social or working life (which she now offers as she might to friends of her own age, pointing no moral, claiming no credit) are met with resolute silence from Josh and a polite little laugh from Matilda. Alone with Claudia, Matilda will chatter freely enough if her mother indicates that she is prepared to listen. Alone with Claudia, Josh seeks companionable silence and will work on his project, which the school has long since ceased to expect, while she reads one of her books. Every so often he will ask a devastating question, as he has done this afternoon and which she will do her over-zealous best to answer.

But at their supper *à deux* Josh has no questions to ask. And he evades hers. He leaves his omelette half-eaten, ignores the green salad and retires to watch television after approximately ten minutes. Claudia tries to tell herself that she is not hurt, any more than she is by Matilda's non-appearance. When she has cleared away the supper things she calls Dorian again. Ron answers the phone: no, he doesn't know where Dorian is; no, he didn't know that Dorian had arranged to meet the children; yes, he will tell Dorian that she has called. There is hostility in his voice. Claudia sits at her desk, reading *Frost in May* for her next class and listening to Radio 3. Mahler's Resurrection Symphony. When the soprano sings, '*O glaube, mein herz, O glaube*,' she can read no longer, chilled all at once and goose-pimply as she is from head to foot. And when the chorus sings, '*Aufersteh'n*,' she thinks she might weep. But before she can summon up the will to stop herself the phone rings in front of her. She switches off the radio and picks up the receiver.

'Your voice sounds awfully thin and far away,' says Claire. 'Are you all right?'

Claudia laughs shakily. 'I thought you were going to be Dorian.'

'Sorry,' says Claire. 'I'm only me. Has some new disaster happened, or are you just in the throes of common or garden existential agony?'

Claudia explains hesitantly, inviting Claire's commentary, Claire's assessment of the situation. It seems as though recently their roles have been reversed, Claire assuming a nurturative serenity which befits her newly acquired status as a mother, and Claudia regressing into wayward little-sisterhood, restless and uncertain. If only their own mother were still alive! Their father, four years a widower, lives alone in a remote cottage in Cornwall. He watches the sea. He walks along the shore, collecting driftwood and *objets trouvés*. He neither sings nor weeps and his use of language is spare. His possessions, like his wants, are few. A combination of asceticism and mysticism helps him to keep the material world in its proper place, that is, firmly under his own control. What need has he of daughters?

'Poor little beasts,' Claire says. 'But they must know that there's been some kind of mistake.'

'Josh perhaps. I'm not so sure about Matilda.'

'Oh, I'm sure she'll turn up later.' Claire hesitates. 'Listen, I really called to ask you if you'd seen today's *Evening Globe*. I thought not. Well, the news is out. There's a piece in Yatterbox's column about you and Dorian.'

'Read it to me, will you?' Claudia asks faintly.

'Are you sure?' But Claire knows her sister well enough to proceed. 'The ever-youthful Dorian Grey, erstwhile lead singer with the sixties supergroup, Asteroid, has split with his wife of sixteen years, the former Claudia Farquharson, once a member of the *Globe*'s own staff. "I'm heartbroken," said a friend of Mrs Grey's; Claudia is such a sweet, sympathetic, supportive person.'

'Is that all?'

'Well, there's a photograph. Years old, by the look of it. You're both dressed to kill.'

'Well, it could have been worse, I suppose.'

'At least it's complimentary about you. Who's this friend?'

'I wish I knew.'

'Oh Christ,' says Claire as she and Claudia both listen to the sound of a baby wailing. 'Junior is screaming for his din-dins again. Listen, call me if you need me. Or just to talk, if you want. Promise.'

Claudia promises. As she puts the phone down, she experiences a pang of envy for Claire who is necessary to her offspring, Claire who can hold her baby at her breast and cuddle him. She recalls the weight of Matilda's downy head against her own breast and almost immediately sees her daughter shorn and painted like a victim prepared for some arcane sacrifice. Radio 3 is now playing Schubert's A minor quartet. Form and order, even in the presence of emotion. The piece of plastic protecting the spokes of her typewriter bears the message: *Nicht wegwerren nach dem Schreiben wieder einlegen.* The advice is repeated in English, French and Spanish, but it is the German that holds her attention. It seems appropriate. The language of the Romantic Agony, of *Sturm und Drang*, of rage and tears. The language of psychoanalysis, of the anima and the id. The language of Expressionism, where everything means something and the nature of reality is essentially metaphorical. The language of nineteenth-century music. But her father, in his Cornish cloister, listens only to Bach, especially the organ works, which the BBC is broadcasting in their entirety. He tapes them all on the Hitachi radio-cassette recorder which Claudia and Dorian gave him two Christmases ago. If a man cannot aspire beyond reality, then how can be call himself a man rather than a beast? In the absence of emotion, the transcendence of emotion becomes meaningless and metaphor is rendered inessential. There is only God. Nothing else is worthy of consideration.

When the music comes to a stop and Radio 3 closes down, Claudia calls Emma. The au pair tells her that Emma has gone to stay with a friend in Islington and hasn't been seen since school; she has not seen Matilda. Ron says yes, as a matter of fact he was just about to go to bed because he has a recording session early tomorrow; he agrees reluctantly to leave a note for Dorian. Josh says Matilda is bound to be with Emma because she hasn't got any other friends. Claudia calls Emma's mother at Metropolitan Radio to ask for the number of Emma's friend in Islington. Emma says that Matilda is probably with Sharon, but it's too late to call her because she has to be in bed by ten. Claudia calls Sharon's parents, who rouse their daughter and relay the message that Matilda could be with Cheryl. There is no reply from Cheryl's number. The only people left to call are the police.

Josh says that if Claudia calls the police, Matilda will never forgive her. His argument, expressed with brotherly bluntness, is that if Matilda's absence is due to her having been either raped or murdered, then it is too late to do anything about it; otherwise, she will come home when she feels like it. When Claudia asks him if he thinks Matilda will do anything silly, he looks blankly at her. She persists: anything self-destructive? Josh volunteers to call Nat. Nat says that Claudia is not to worry; he will make a few discreet but exhaustive enquiries and call her back as soon as he has learned anything. It is half-past one.

Claudia unplugs the telephone extension from the study and takes it up to the bedroom. She lies fully clothed on top of the blankets, wrapped in her thin fur coat. If she undresses and gets into bed, it will be like giving up on Matilda. It would be an act of callousness for which she will surely be punished by the realization of her worst fears for her daughter's safety. She feels nauseous and feverish, can't lie still. After an hour she takes a valium. After another hour Nat calls her. He hasn't been able to get in touch with everyone, but he thinks that Matilda is probably with Cheryl because Simon said he thought he saw them together at Punks' Palace around eleven o'clock. Meanwhile he is going to get some sleep and advises Claudia to do the same. She thanks him and blesses him. Gradually and with several fits and starts, she dozes off.

She wakes at seven, panic-stricken that her lapse into oblivion could have put her daughter's life in jeopardy. The day is calm and clear and bright. People are walking in the street, getting into their cars, opening their front doors for their cats, as if nothing has happened. Perhaps they are right. She will have a bath and change her clothes. By the time she is through it will be eight o'clock and she can call Cheryl. She may even be able to catch Dorian before he leaves with Ron for their recording session. No rain has fallen during the night but the door to the linen cupboard on the landing outside the bathroom is jammed. It must have become swollen and warped after the last soaking. Should she force it open? Later. She will have to make do with the rather skimpy towel she has been using for the past week. Let it rain. Let the cupboard door be jammed. Let a leaking roof be the worst calamity that will befall her (and those she loves) today.

Cheryl's mother goes to look in her daughter's room and reports back to Claudia that Matilda has not been seen. Ron says that Dorian didn't come back last night. Claudia's breakfast consists of three cups of tea, a valium and five cigarettes. The mail is mainly for Dorian and looks like bills. But there is one envelope addressed to her in green ink and backward-sloping capitals. It contains the cutting from yesterday's *Globe*. The caption underneath the photograph, 'Dorian and Claudia – is this the end?', has been underlined in green and a tick added as if to answer the question in the affirmative. Nat calls to say that he will be round in an hour to collect Josh: they can look for Matilda together at a couple of squats in the area. Claudia wakes Josh, who promises to get up. The milkman says that he is owed two weeks' money but that he'll let Claudia off this time because she looks so miserable. Emma calls to ask if Matilda has been found. Josh gets up. Claudia goes out to buy some cigarettes and a loaf of bread. The woman in the newsagent tells her that the bill is four weeks overdue. Claudia says she will come back with her cheque book. A note on the kitchen table reads, 'Mum – gone with Nat – luv, Josh.'

Having smoked another two cigarettes in succession, Mum is just wondering whether to clean the house or to hell with it and get on with her reading, when the phone rings. When she hears the pips Claudia assumes that one of the children is calling.

'You wanted to speak to me.' Dorian sounds as if he is addressing a business acquaintance in a rival company.

'Of course I wanted to speak to you,' says Claudia. 'Where have you been?'

'I was routining at Barry Willard's and they asked me to stay because we didn't start dinner till ten. Didn't Ron tell you?'

'No, he did not.' Ron wouldn't tell her the time of day, if he could help it. 'Had you forgotten that you were supposed to be meeting the children after school? Yesterday? Friday?'

She can hear Dorian draw breath, hesitate. His voice is colder than ever when he says, 'I suppose I have you to thank for the exposure in the *Globe*?'

'No, you do not,' Claudia says sharply, fazed by this change of tack into answering him. 'Answer my question, will you, please?'

'Not until you answer mine.'

'Stop playing games, will you? Matilda has disappeared again.'

'Is that supposed to be my fault?'

Again, she is fazed into answering him. 'Of course it's your bloody fault. Are you seriously suggesting that there's no connection between her disappearance and your non-appearance?'

'It's you who's doing all the claiming.'

'Dorian, will you please tell me what's going on?'

During the distracted few seconds in which the pips go again, she registers: Dorian has not expressed any concern for Matilda's safety or state of mind; he must feel guilty about something because he seems so intent on accusing her of some imagined felony; perhaps, like the husband in *Gaslight*, he is deliberately trying to drive her out of her mind.

'I want your solemn assurance,' says Dorian, 'that you haven't been talking to Yatterbox.'

Claudia is tempted to laugh; really, there is something inherently absurd about this conversation. 'Of course I haven't been talking to Yatterbox. I don't know him. Or her. And I don't know anyone who does.'

'They mentioned that you used to work there.'

'Dorian, that was seventeen years ago.'

'Then who told them?'

'How should I know? Look, this really isn't important.'

'Isn't important? I have just been maligned in public, and you say it isn't important!'

'You . . . have just been . . . maligned . . . ' Claudia repeats. Either he is trying to drive her out of her mind or he is completely round the twist himself. Or both. 'What on earth are you talking about?'

'That item was clearly on your side.'

'And who wouldn't be?' Claudia has lost all patience with him.

'Can't you stop thinking about yourself for five seconds and give some thought to your children?'

'Don't shout at me, Claudia.'

'Then don't goad me.'

'You swear you weren't responsible – even indirectly?'

How much longer is this going to go on? 'I swear.'

'Then I'm sorry about the children.'

It takes Claudia a second or two to understand what has been going on. Even then, she can't believe that her understanding is correct. 'Are you trying to tell me that you didn't meet Josh and Matilda out of . . . pique? Out of revenge?'

'I felt too angry to face them.'

'It's incredible!'

'I'm sorry. It was a misunderstanding.'

'How could they possibly have been to blame? Why take it out on them?'

'I said I was sorry.'

'What are you going to say to them?'

'I'll think of something.'

Of course – some lie. 'What are we going to do about Matilda?' Get him to participate.

'I can't get away from here till five. You know how expensive studio time is.'

'I'll expect you at about a quarter to six, then.'

'It may be nearer six.' Again, she can hear him hesitate. 'I'm sorry, Claudia.'

Claudia checks her automatic impulse to say it's all right. 'Six o'clock,' she says firmly. 'Goodbye.' She is shaking so violently all over that she can hardly reach the table, open the cigarette packet, strike a light, draw breath. 'I married a monster,' she says out loud. 'I've been living in some creaking, pathetic B-movie for sixteen years!'

Is any other interpretation of Dorian's action – or rather, lack of action – possible? Is she being unfair? Has she got it all wrong? She doesn't see how. Perhaps it would be a good idea after all to attack the housework. And attack is the right word. There is plenty of scope for violence, for ruthlessness, in the processes of hoovering, scrubbing and the throwing out of rubbish. Dirt, mess, chaos – get rid of it all. Matilda's room alone takes two and a half hours, the task a self-imposed punishment for every word or deed of unmotherliness and an act of propitiation to the Eumenides, who seem to have it in for Claudia Farquharson and her offspring. By five o'clock the whole house, apart from Josh's room, whose sacrosanctity even the Eumenides must respect, is grimly spotless.

By a quarter to seven, when Dorian's key turns in the lock, it is beginning to rain again.

'Josh and Nat have gone to look for her,' says Claudia, moving the desk lamp so that she can see Dorian standing in the doorway. 'But so far they've had no luck.'

'Oh, Nat,' Dorian says dismissively. 'He would have to interfere.'

Claudia is having as much difficulty in keeping her temper as Dorian seems to be having in entering this room which is her own special domain, the room in which she was sleeping until he moved out of the house. 'On the contrary, he's been very helpful and considerate. I like him.'

'Well, I don't.'

'I'm sure the feeling is mutual.'

'That suits me. Anything to drink in this house?'

'There's some plonk in the fridge as usual.'

Dorian makes a face. 'Do you want some?'

'I'll come through and get it in a moment.'

Having put Marie's paper back in the folder with the others, Claudia marks a B+ on the grading sheet, which she then places face downwards beneath a glass paperweight. She finds Dorian sitting at the kitchen table, reading his mail. He has poured out a glass of wine for her, and she sits down in her allotted place at the far end of the table.

'How about this, Claudie?' he asks with boyish excitement, 'Sid Ryder is doing a series of portraits of distinguished people of our time, and he wants me to go to Suffolk and sit for him.'

'Then he'll try to sell you the portrait.'

'Why not?' Dorian leans back in his chair, his hands clasped behind his head. 'It would be a good investment.'

'What about those?' she asks, indicating the pile of buff envelopes.

'Oh, they're just bills.'

'Why don't you open them?'

'Oh, not now. They'll keep.'

The rain is getting heavier and a northerly wind is driving it against the back window above the sink. Claudia tries not to think about the roof. But she finds herself thinking about Dorian instead. Has he always been like this: so self-absorbed, so irresponsible? Surely not. She would have noticed it before now. Then she remembers the Mustang and Mrs Perrins. Two years ago, when Claudia was working with Professor Bernard at reducing his unwieldy memoirs to some sort of acceptable shape and the Hugheses were, if anything, more deeply in debt that they are now, Dorian bought a second-hand Mustang. He had to have it to show people that he wasn't living in poverty, that his career was still flourishing. She understood: in show business appearances are all, and to them that have shall be given. But something had to go. Dorian suggested Mrs Perrins: she was far too old and inefficient to keep the house clean and Claudia herself had often complained about her work and her constant interruption of the editing of the memoirs. Claudia was persuaded. It would be less easy to persuade her now. Dorian is thinking how much she has changed. Surely she hasn't always been so aggressive, such a wet blanket, so charmless? Women ought to learn to approach middle age gracefully instead of punishing everyone else around them for the loss of their own youth. You work for them for sixteen years and then they treat you like dirt, just because you step out of line a little every now and then. And now she is grinding on about Matilda again – as if the girl won't turn up when she feels like it – just as she did last time.

'You really shouldn't treat her and Josh like this,' says Claudia. 'You mustn't break promises. Don't you understand that it's important?'

'Don't talk to me in that schoolma'amy way.'

'I'm just trying to stress the importance of honesty.'

'Not for the first time.'

'Truth is precious, you know – especially as something adults give to their children.'

'You're a hypocrite, Claudia. Ron was right. They all say they want the truth, he said, and when they get it, they don't like it.'

'Who's *they*?'

'Women, of course.'

'I'm not *women*!' She is shouting at him now. 'I'm Claudia! Can't you tell the difference? Can't you tell the fucking difference after sixteen years?'

'Oh yes, you're special!' Dorian sneers as Claudia jumps up from the table. 'You're so special that – what the hell are you doing?'

Claudia has taken two plastic buckets from the broom cupboard. 'The roof is leaking – in case you hadn't noticed.'

The water is pouring in again, just outside the bathroom door. As soon as Claudia has positioned the buckets strategically it diminishes to a trickle again. But she doesn't trust it. She stands, hands on hips, daring the flow to increase. The rusty stain on the ceiling has spread along to the edge of the linen cupboard. Does this mean that everything inside is getting soaked? She tries the door again in a futile sort of way. Then mechanically she bends down to pick up a protruding scrap of paper which she must have missed in the course of her hoovering.

It is not a scrap, after all, but an A4 sheet torn from one of her own notebooks and folded into four. It is a note addressed in red ink to Mum and Dad. Still uncomprehending enough to be wondering only when it dates from, Claudia opens it. It reads:

> You bastards! You really are a pair of platitudes personified. All you care about is saving your own faces. The way you carry on makes me vomit. Corny stereotyped emotions and your own honour mean more to you than I do. I don't feel you have anything to offer me.
>
> I don't know where I'll go or who will help me, but that's not important. All I know is I have to go away for a while. I'M NOT FUCKING LIVING LIKE THIS !!
>
> You'll probably think my sentiments are 'ridiculous', meaning that 'I don't know my place'. Me? 'In my place'? Never !!!
>
> Ta ra, Matilda.
>
> PS. If I'm coming back you'll have to give me £4 for any Clash gig in the near future. At least that!
>
> PPS. As for Josh, he has no regard for me whatsoever.

'Dorian!' Claudia shrieks as she tugs at the door again. 'Quickly! Bring the big screwdriver or something. Matilda's locked herself in the linen cupboard!'

VII

They only thought I'd gone and taken a sodding overdose. What an anti-climax it must have been for the pair of them. No dashing Sir Dorian, screwdriver in hand, saving the life of his desperate only daughter. No ambulance, no flashing lights, no stomach pump, no intensive care. Nothing in the papers to say what a great guy he was. And no Claudia, draped in black and heavily veiled, weeping at the graveside as the coffin is lowered and she flings in one white fragile flower. No opportunity for her friends to gather round and tell her what a suffering saint she is. No big drama. No nothing. Just boring little Matilda with a couple of Mogadons in her bloodstream, rolling out of the linen cupboard and falling in a filthy, smelly heap at their feet.

Mum did cry, though. At first I couldn't tell that that was what she was doing because she wasn't having hysterics or anything, like the night I stayed at Emma's. She was just talking in this funny little voice, far, far away and shaking me back and forth, saying, Matilda can you hear me? Please, Matty, please, please wake up. I didn't even know who she was. I didn't want to know. I didn't want to know anything at all except peace and oblivion. Which is just what mothers are always trying to deprive you of. I might have known. I might have known that there she'd be, kneeling at my side, clasping me to her shrinking bosom, patting my cheeks like some frenzied hen flapping her wings. I tried hard to stay asleep. But then *he* started yelling and I couldn't. That's when I opened my eyes. The first thing I saw was Mum's face staring up at him all wide-eyed and the tears rolling down her cheeks.

I said, What's the matter, Mum? At least I could have sworn that's what I said. But she didn't hear me. She just kept asking me if I was all right. So I smiled and said yes and shut my eyes again. She was stroking my head and it was kind of nice and soothing. Then Dad started shaking me by the arm and yelling at me to stop fooling and sit up. He sounded angry, so I pretended to be dead. But that only made him yell all the more. The more he yelled, the more Mum screamed at him to go away and leave me alone and the tighter she held on to me. I began to wish I had taken an overdose. It would have served them both right. All I could do was gulp and try not to gulp. Fuck it! The tears were forcing themselves out of my eyes, no matter how hard I tried to keep them screwed up tight. So it was obvious that I wasn't dead.

Mum's brilliant idea was that I should wash my face, and I could see that Dad was as disgusted as I was by this obsessive need of hers for cleanliness. Next to Godliness, I suppose. You'd never think my Mum was an atheist, she's that keen on everyone being so pure and holy. And yet there she was screwing Clive in the afternoons when we were supposed to be in school. She really believed that we didn't know about it. Grown-ups are so pissing, shitting naive! They think we're all still living in fairyland with Noddy and Pooh-Bear. Not that me and Josh would ever have mentioned it to each other, if it hadn't been for Nat. How can she – with that wally, he asked us, doesn't it make you puke? It didn't particularly. We didn't answer him. I mean, it wasn't any of his business, was it?

Anyway, back to the melodrama. There was Mum trying to get me to stand up like some staggering day-old chick, and Dad insisting that he wanted to get to the root of the matter, whatever that was supposed to mean. What had I taken? How much? Why had I done it? What was I trying to prove? It was easier in the end to let Mum help me into the bathroom. She wiped me all over my face and neck with a warm cloth. It was amazing to see my own face in the mirror. I mean, I looked so young and so sodding innocent. Really, I did! Just as if nothing terrible had ever happened to me. I couldn't believe it. I should have been covered in wrinkles and my half-inch of hair gone white overnight. Mum was frowning away behind me, concentrating. I couldn't help laughing. She looked surprised, then started laughing too. I told you you'd feel better, she said, all pleased. And I had to admit that she was right. Got to give the old dear her due, I suppose.

She wasn't angry with me at all. That's what I found so difficult to take in. I'd been expecting her to fly off the handle, as usual, so her downbeat attitude kind of fazed me. In a way I was disappointed because it meant she wasn't really taking me seriously. But in another way I was relieved we didn't have to get into some kind of argument about how inconsiderate and ungrateful I was and all that shit. In fact, she seemed angrier with Dad. And he seemed angrier with *me*. I thought he was going to hit me, though he's never done anything like that, not even to Josh. Mum has, but not him. When I shrank away from him he looked kind of scared as if he thought I was going to claw his eyes out. Somehow that frightened me more than if he actually had walloped me. My Dad has this talent for making you feel like you're perched on this lovely sandcastle he's built for you – only you can feel it all crumbling away underneath and you don't like to tell him but at the same time you don't know how to stop yourself falling.

Falling . . . falling . . . falling . . . That's what I was always dreaming about. Like that time I heard Mum screaming. I was crossing over this old wooden bridge, like the one near Grand-dad's cottage that we weren't supposed to put one foot on to because it was dangerous. (Josh said he dreamed about that bridge too!) Only it wasn't the *same* bridge, exactly. Some of the slats were missing and some were rotten and I could see the water foaming away among the rocks at the bottom of the ravine. I mean, I knew it was dangerous. I couldn't understand what I was doing there. But for some reason I didn't want to turn back. I stood there sizing the thing up, picking out the safest bits to tread on and making sure they didn't lead to some dead end – a bit like playing chess. I was putting on some kind of show of bravery because they were watching me, although I couldn't see them. And I didn't even know who they were! Then they started laughing as if they knew I was really dead scared. It riled me. I yelled, what's the fucking joke? But that only made them worse and they started shrieking and shrieking till they were hysterical. I knew then that the only way out was to wake myself up. Don't ask me how I knew I was dreaming – I just did. So I tried and tried and I couldn't. And then I didn't know if I wanted to anyway because there was this sodding great rat on my pillow, nibbling my ear.

But I woke up and it had gone. At first I thought the shrieking had gone too. I couldn't make out where it was coming from, thought it was someone out in the street having some kind of a barney. When I recognized Mum's voice I thought I must still be dreaming after all. There were these horrible sobs, one after the other, monotonous, so they didn't even sound human. I didn't understand how any human could keep it up, again and again, over and over, like some record that's got stuck. When it stopped, her voice was very clear: you've taken my life from me and turned it into a lie – just like your own! I thought I was going to have a heart attack or something. I just couldn't breathe. Then Dad said, for Christ's sake, shut up, do you want the children to hear you? I pulled the pillow over my head and round my ears. I didn't want to know. And I pretended not to. I didn't even think about it again until Dad said he was leaving.

Leaving me! Because Mum said so! Why couldn't he refuse? They sat down one on each side of me and watched me eat my scrambled eggs. Mum had done them just the way I like them with a thick sprinkling of Parmesan on top. She said I must be starving after twenty-four hours in the cupboard. I said, twenty-eight. And we both laughed. And Dad didn't. And I could see he thought we were ganging up on him, so I stopped laughing. It was then he started asking me what I meant by what I'd said in my letter. I couldn't even remember what I'd put. Mum said, let her eat. Dad sat there, grimly waiting for me to finish and I kept thinking the food was going to choke me. But I didn't want to leave it because Mum had cooked it specially. And I *was* starving.

It seemed that whatever I did they would still hate each other. Whatever I did was still of no importance. Dad asked me to explain why I'd called them both platitudes personified. He just couldn't see! Mum thought she knew and started to tell him, but she used so many long words that I couldn't tell if she was right or not. It went on like that, with me saying hardly anything, except to agree with Mum every so often, which got Dad more riled up than ever. She kept saying I didn't have to explain, the point being I'd let them both know how unhappy I was. Was that the point? When she said so, I started to cry again and she said it was time for me to go to bed. Dad accused her of trying to cover things up. Then she did get angry in that steely way of hers which can cut right through your flesh. That's *your* speciality, she said to him. Couldn't he see that I was tired and confused? He said she wasn't to underestimate me. So I yelled, why don't you both shut up? And they did.

Just as well, probably, because at that very moment Josh came into the room. For once I was actually glad to clap my eyes on his moronic features. Seeing us all sitting there in rigid silence, he tried to be jaunty. So the prodigal has returned, quoth he (meaning me, I suppose), do I get a slice off the fatted calf? Mum and Dad turned to him with identical weak smiles on their faces. All Josh meant was that he wanted something to eat. Dad said, look, sorry about the mix-up yesterday, old son. Josh blushed and muttered that it was all right. Silence. We were both waiting for Dad to explain, but he just put on his pleading look so neither of us liked to ask him. I knew Josh wanted to because he was still blushing like a flaming Arsenal shirt. But I've noticed he can't bring himself to make demands, probably thinks it's unmanly, or something. And I wanted to, but I was damned if I was going to give Dad the satisfaction of thinking the episode was of any importance to me whatsoever, because he hadn't offered *me* an apology. And to this day I don't know what the fuck is supposed to have happened.

Dad left soon after that. Mum went to the front door with him and they had words. Not loud enough for me to hear, but words all the same. Then Josh asked for his pocket money, said he'd done his room, which was enough to make a cat laugh because all he ever does is shove all the rubbish under an old blanket in the middle of the floor and pretend the whole thing is part of his Waterloo set-up. Mum said she'd forgotten to ask Dad for any money. All she had was enough for bread and coffee for tomorrow. What she meant was, enough for cigarettes. The way that woman smokes is enough to give the whole street lung cancer. She started rabbiting on about how we'd have to take sandwiches to school on Monday because the Post Office didn't open till nine-thirty. I began to fear for her sanity till she explained that she was talking about collecting her Child Benefit. Her pay cheque was due at the end of the week but it went straight into the bank and would get swallowed up by the overdraft. We knew she was thinking aloud, so we didn't say anything. I mean, what were we supposed to do about it? Josh made himself a peanut-butter sandwich. When she said perhaps she should ask the college to pay the cheque into Claire's account, he said, wouldn't it be simpler to ask Dad? She looked at him like he'd just hit her. He hugged her then and said he could wait for his pocket money. Knowing the state of my room, I said nothing. Josh the beloved son. The sight of the two of them made me sick to my stomach.

And to think that all my nurdish so-called friends used to tease me about my rich and famous Dad. Even Kevin and Bernadette Kelly got more pocket money than I did, and there were nine of them in their family and they lived in a council flat which I thought was supposed to be for poor people. Mum said it was all a question of priorities. That's what she always says when things don't fit in with her own ideas. Did the Kellys take their lot to New York or Yugoslavia? Did they take them to the theatre or to restaurants? Did they have a cottage in the country? Seeing as how I couldn't remember a pissing thing about New York or Yugoslavia and the country cottage could have been a figment of her imagination, for all I knew, I didn't see the point of her argument. Everyone treated the Kellys like some kind of outcasts, but I rather envied them. No one ever nagged them to go to bed at nine o'clock. They all stuck together and didn't give a sod what other people thought of them. Whenever they got into trouble, their Mum told them to stay away from school until everyone had forgotten about it. Of course everyone wanted to forget it because it was such a hassle having to deal with the Kellys and their Mum who was always swearing at the staff and saying she was going to report them to higher authorities. Everyone let them get away with murder. But me? No such sodding luck.

It was all a matter of middle-class morality, Nat said. That's what his Communist friend Rodge had told him. Actually Rodge wasn't a Communist at all, it turned out, but an International Socialist. (Don't ask me what the difference is!) Anyway, middle-class morality, according to Rodge, was what was fucking up all our lives. I must say it was a relief to find out there was a name for it, even if I didn't know *exactly* what it meant. Nat and Josh seemed to spend a lot of time with Rodge, but at this point in the ever-unfolding saga I hadn't met the great hero. Mere females weren't permitted to take part in setting the world to rights. All I knew about Rodge was that he was twenty-five, worked as a milkman though he had a degree in sociology and lived in Finsbury Park with a lot of other International Socialists. Nat and Josh said he had nothing against girls: it was just that girls had never taken any interest in grass-roots politics and he'd given up on them. So, naturally, I asked if Rodge was gay. This hadn't even occurred to the stupid wankers! But then Nat said, so what if he was? Heterosexuality was just another aspect of middle-class morality. We were back where we started.

As far as I could make out it meant doing what your parents expected you to. Like going to school, O-levels and A-levels and on to university. Then a steady job, getting married, having babies. In other words, being normal. Only they seemed to think it wasn't normal. And I was beginning to have my doubts. I mean, it all seemed so flesh-creepingly boring all of a sudden. Look at Mum! She did all the so-called normal bit, and is she happy? Is she hell! Sometimes I think she wants me to go through it all just so I can end up as unhappy as she is. But I'm fucked from here to eternity if I'm going to spend my life having babies and going spare about what's happening to them. Why should I? If that's what it means being grown-up, then I want to stay the way I am. Not that there's anything so sodding marvellous in that. It's just that everything else seems even worse.

Perhaps I was happy when I was a little kid. If so, I don't remember anything about it. Mum keeps telling me little stories about it. I like that, but I often wonder if she's making them all up. I mean, *why* can't I remember? I can't remember living anywhere but here in this house although we've only been here for six years – less than half my life. I can vaguely remember the school in New York because you could do whatever you liked there and everyone laughed at me when I asked for permission to go to the loo. I remember the Statue of Liberty and then seeing it buried up to the neck in *Planet of the Apes*. We went on a boat in Central Park. We tobogganed, we swam, we went to Buster Keaton movies. We ate Japanese food. And in the holidays I had to look after a little turtle which kept making horrible squeaking noises. But I don't remember the show Dad was in or anything like that. When he got back to London I couldn't believe I'd ever been there before. Everything before New York was a complete blank. It still is.

Not much point in having a rich and famous Dad if you can't remember a sodding thing about it. Here I am, supposedly brought up in the lap of luxury, and all I feel is ripped off. The big joke around here for the past five years or so has been the time I supposedly asked, Dad, was you ever really on 'Top of the Pops'? As if I could have said anything so pissing moronic. Even if I did, what's so pissing funny about it? But Mum and Dad would tell *everyone* and then they'd all fall about. How was I supposed to know he was on the telly practically every sodding week throughout the oh-so-mind-blowing sixties? It's all ancient history. You've got to have one foot in the grave even to have heard of Asteroid. And I'm sick to a thousand deaths of hearing how marvellously inspiring and liberating the sixties were and why isn't it like that any more? It's not my fucking fault I wasn't around till 1966. If it had all been so inspiring and liberating for babies, I'm sure I should have remembered.

There's nothing more pathetic than a left-over hippie. I've even seen a photograph of my Dad in a kaftan. But I can't imagine him dropping acid or giving flowers to the Pigs (of all the wet, pointless things!) or freaking out and floating downstream, or whatever you were supposed to do. He's much too uptight, as they themselves would say. I mean, if you're that cool and laid-back, you don't stick gold discs and giant photographs of yourself all over your work-room, do you? No, you give the gold away to be melted down for fillings for old-age pensioners. Or something like that. What you do with the photographs I don't know. But you don't sit and *look* at them all day, do you? I mean, that's not decent. But then there is something indecent about the way middle-aged people cling on to the past.

And the way the girls looked then! Dolly birds! Can you imagine, even in your wettest, silliest moments, allowing yourself to be called a dolly bird? Wouldn't you just rather die? There they are with their mouths hanging open and their eyes all kind of dim and flickering, which is supposed to be sexy, but which looks to me that the most birdlike thing about them is their brains. More than anything else in the world it gets on my wick the way girls are supposed to be stupid. I mean, I didn't *know*. I didn't know till I went to Fleet Valley. I couldn't understand why nobody liked me the way they did at the Montessori. I thought it was because of Josh, because nobody liked him either. Whenever I answered a question in class, everybody groaned. And they mimicked me. I thought it was because I talked posh, so I started talking like the rest of them. Mum dragged Dad along to the Parents' Evening that first time (he never went again) and the teachers told them how well I was doing, except that I'd gone rather shy and didn't speak up in class any more. It was after that that the nurds started winding me up about my Dad. It went on for a whole term before Emma arrived and they started picking on her. Only she wouldn't stand for it.

Anyway, going back to the fateful evening when I fell out of the cupboard, all I felt like was doing something mindless like watching telly. I thought Mum would go on about bedtime, so I crept out of the room while she and Josh were locked in their close clinch. They didn't even notice. That's how I knew that everything was back to normal and nobody – not even Dad – was going to change one fucking thing after what I'd said in my farewell note. I'd been forgiven, which meant that what I'd done hadn't made a blind bit of difference to anyone. All that had happened was what always happened. I'd been bashing my head against a brick wall which suddenly turned into a pillow and I woke up and saw the broken window in my room and knew that it would always be like that. Wasn't anything ever going to change?

There was nothing on the telly anyway. Football, Shakespeare and darts. I ask you! What are people like me supposed to do on Saturday nights when our dear parents don't let us out after dark? Stare at our belly-buttons and pick our noses? I flung the *Radio Times* across the room – there's even something smug about the layout – and decided to go to my room after all. At least there would be something comforting in all the grot. And at the very least, it was after all my very own, my one and only creation.

VIII

Clive, as depicted in oils by Greta, is a slim, dark youth with lustrous, if coy, brown eyes, a wide mouth and a firm clean-shaven chin. Naked as he is in the portrait, he should be sporting innocently with his kind on the banks of a willow-girt river, the spire of the village church visible in the background across the slopes of a green and flowery meadow. Clive, as recalled by Claudia, is pushing forty with greying hair and under-nourished from a diet consisting almost exclusively of alcohol. His eyes are close-set and, except in the mornings, before opening time, their gaze tends to be unfocused. His smile is crooked, conveying mirth without joy, pain tempered by wit and wit by pain. Claudia has never known him not to be in need of a shave. In the circumstances she finds it difficult to know what to say.

Not that it matters. Greta is doing all the talking. The two women are lying, propped up, sharing a joint, on Greta's waterbed and facing the spotlit canvas. The studio with its wall-length windows facing north across the square has been built onto the top storey of the Freeburgs' Georgian house. It was Leo's fortieth birthday present to Greta and for the past ten years it has been her special domain. The Victorian screens behind the portrait are hung with some of her more exotic purchases: silks and satins decorated with beads, sequins, feathers, fringes or embroidery. Like Claudia's father, she is a collector of *objets trouvés*, but whereas his are products of nature, hers have been rescued from the obscurity to which a consumer-oriented society assigns the very ephemera which entice or urge towards consumption: wrappers, cartons, posters, free gifts from cereal packets, fabric samples, mirrors, bottles, twisted chunks of half-melted plastic. Some of these, or bits of them, have been incorporated into the collages for which Greta is so justly famous that she has become a heroine of the post-sixties anti-establishment. What others discard, Greta discovers and transforms into ironic artefacts.

'He can't sit still for more than a couple of minutes,' she says, passing the joint to Claudia, 'so I had to do most of him from memory – or photographs.'

'Must have been fun,' Claudia murmurs inanely.

But Greta giggles. 'Oh, it was. I was determined to capture him somehow. The more he tried to elude me, the more determined I was. And the more cunning. Poor Clive!' She sighs. 'He didn't stand a chance.'

'What does he think of it?'

'He hasn't said.' Greta runs her fingers through the pre-Raphaelite cloud of hennaed hair which she likes to wear long and loose. 'Has he said anything to you?'

'I think he's embarrassed by it.'

'Embarrassed? Is that what he said?'

'No.' Claudia waves the joint in a vague gesture and the ash scatters over her cut-velvet dress, narrowly missing Greta's lurex tights. 'Just the impression I got.'

'When did you last see him?'

'Thursday.' No point in lying.

'That figures,' says Claudia. 'We had a bit of an argument on Wednesday. But then I suppose he told you that.'

'He didn't mention it.'

'Our bodies,' Greta sighs again, 'move so beautifully together. It's as though we were made for each other. I've never known anything quite like it.'

'All right,' says Claudia, sitting up, 'I get the message.'

Greta smiles sweetly at her, the silver bangles tinkling as she stretches and lies back. 'Oh, I really love that guy.'

'Look, Greta . . . ' Claudia tries to sound firm but as she stands up she realizes that she is rather stoned. 'Clive isn't that important to me. If you'd rather I didn't see him, then I won't. Just say the word.'

Greta sits up, indignant. 'Oh, I couldn't do that. He'd never forgive me.'

'Next time he turns up on my doorstep, I'll send him away again.'

'It's not that easy. He won't take no for an answer. Not from you.'

'He doesn't love me.'

'He's obsessed by you.'

'I'll tell him I'm getting it together with Dorian again.'

'He won't believe you.'

Claudia has had enough of the conversation. She resents Greta's oblique but transparent attempt to warn her off. She resents the fact that Clive has discussed his intentions towards her, and perhaps more, with Greta. And she resents the possibility that she is being used by the pair of them. If they want to play childish games, let them, but they can't be allowed to involve her. Greta and Clive were made for each other, were they? It would also seem that they deserve each other. As for Claudia, she has other things to do with her life than to fritter it away in some sort of triangular power tussle. This is not the sort of power she wants.

'Why is it,' she asks Greta, 'that every time a woman sleeps with a man, she compromises herself in one way or another?'

Greta looks startled. 'I never feel compromised.'

'Lucky you,' says Claudia. 'Lucky Clive. You can both fuck and feel free.'

'All you need is practice.'

'But not with Clive?'

'You know how I feel about him,' says Greta. 'He knows how I feel. There's nothing else I can say. And there's certainly nothing else I can do.'

'No,' says Claudia. 'You've done all you can.'

She leaves Greta and wanders downstairs to find the rest of the party, cursing her own susceptibility to moral pressure. It is not that she particularly wants the affair with Clive to continue. But neither does she particularly want it to end. The decision to end it, if and when it comes, should be hers, or even Clive's, but not Greta's. It is none of Greta's business. And yet, poor Greta! Her only child is incarcerated in an institution; her husband is always occupied with some new business venture, some new mistress; her work does not absorb her, but is merely a means to the sweet end of unthinking admiration; she is menopausal and, although considered by many to be beautiful still, as terrified as any spoilt actress of the ageing process. Claudia shudders. How horrible to be like Greta. She should be showing her some compassion instead of setting up in competition with her. The contest will be all too easily won: a cheap victory. And the prize, though pleasing enough, is hardly worth the hassle of either Greta's veiled reproaches or Clive's deliberate provocation of them.

Once upon a time, when she was a girl, Claudia would to to parties hoping to meet someone who would personify that submerged, wonderful part of herself. Wasn't that, after all, how she met Dorian? She approached him, in her role as editor of the college magazine, to ask him for an interview. How charming he was to her, this freakish creature who had dropped out of university life, preferring rock and roll to European history, the vital present to the dead and unlamented past. In 1960, among ex-public-school boys, such preferences were novel, if not unprecedented. Neither the Beatles nor the Rolling Stones had yet been heard of. Undergraduates listened to jazz or folk music and didn't deign to study the charts in the *Melody Maker*. But Dorian was different. Right from the moment she met him she knew that. The charm she might have expected, but not the intelligence with which it seemed to be informed. And not – oh, headiest of all! – the keen and evident interest which this dazzling creature displayed in her own dull-plumaged little person. In short, Claudia fell in love. She can even remember what she was wearing: a pencil-slim skirt, a black sweater with batwing sleeves and a plunging neckline, clinched at the waist by a broad elastic belt; underneath, a padded bra with circular stitching and a girdle fitted with suspenders; sheer nylon stockings and black patent-leather shoes with ankle straps and stiletto heels. Her long straight hair was dyed (to her parents' horror) a deep mahogany, her eyes heavily ringed with kohl. She was practising being brittle, which is what real journalists were supposed to be. Perhaps the plumage wasn't so dull, after all. Perhaps it proclaimed the selfsame voracious and uncertain personality which it hoped to clothe.

Later Claudia went to parties hoping to meet interesting people. It was as though, no longer a unit of one herself, she sought the other in the plural to confirm her own status. Single people were dangerous by virtue of their very singularity. The unit of two is prey to its own narcissism and, like seeking like, meets, receives, and is absorbed by it. What was all that stuff about opposites attracting? The parties became smaller; you sat down and ate; conversation was open and general; niceties were observed. Wasn't that, after all, how the Hugheses had met the Freeburgs? Both couples were friends of the Hadleighs who were perfectly sure that they would get on because they had so much in common. What that 'so much' was Claudia now cannot recall. But she supposes that it must have been both recognizable and welcome.

Leo and Sonia are standing together on the stairs, she two steps higher, so that they are almost the same height. Leo is leaning towards her, talking in his rapid, confidential way, gesticulating, nudging her every so often and laughing at her brief, deadpan replies. He looks persuasive, Sonia doubtful. You, you, he keeps saying. His latest enthusiasm is pub theatre, his latest mistress the

A.—5

beautiful Belinda who was at drama school with Vida the Vamp. It is not difficult for Claudia to draw the conclusion that Leo wants Sonia to enter into some sort of partnership which will culminate in a dramatic performance starring his protégé. She tries to suppress an unhidden start of envy. What she herself wants from this party is the offer of a job. She wishes – no longer hopes – that she can meet someone who will offer her neither love nor friendship but employment. The last would be an act of the first and second combined. So, farewell romance and with it farewell the sweetly shared moment of self-revelation. The bond she seeks now is of another, perhaps older, order: that of barter.

'But I don't write that sort of thing,' Sonia is saying. 'My talents lie in other directions.'

'Your talents lie in every direction,' says Leo. 'Forget those tight-assed little novels of yours and . . . here, you tell her, Claudia.'

Claudia stalls as Leo grabs her by the arm. 'Tell her what?'

Leo's battered face assumes an exasperated astonishment. 'Tell her how wonderful she is. Isn't that what you girls are supposed to be doing these days?'

'Girls!' Sonia is scornful.

'She doesn't trust me,' Leo wails, his arm around Claudia's waist. 'I've loved that fucking little bitch for twelve years and she treats me like shit. Do you know, she's never even given me the taste of her tongue in my mouth?'

'Leave it out, Leo,' says Sonia. 'We've been through all that a hundred times.'

'A hundred!' Leo gasps and his knees buckle at this latest injustice. 'If that were all. Notice the use of the subjunctive, Sonia, and love me for that alone.'

'And besides,' says Sonia, 'Claudia doesn't want to know.'

Claudia does want to know but, taking Sonia's cue, she pretends not to and attempts instead to divert the conversation into what she supposes to be its original course. 'How are you expected to deploy your talents?' she asks Sonia.

'Leo,' says Sonia, 'wants me to write a two-hander for Vida and Belinda, to be performed at the Queen's Arms.'

'Women's problems,' says Leo. 'You can't miss with that shit nowadays. Claudia, I am offering to make this obscure little flower of academe a star, and all she can do is accuse me of trying to get into her knickers.'

'Aren't you?' Sonia asks coolly as she contemplates her empty glass. 'I need a refill.'

'Drinks like a fucking fish.' Leo shakes his head as Sonia picks her dainty way down to the ground floor. 'And never loses control. Do you think she's ever had an orgasm?'

Claudia, who has not failed to note Sonia's capacity for self-control, is unreasonably irritated by Leo's directness. She shrugs. 'Why don't you ask her?'

'I'm sorry, Claudia.' As Leo's expression sobers his face seems to age into defeat, so that she wants in some undefined way to reassure him. 'I keep forgetting you're not one of these women who get turned on by talking dirty.'

This has not been the ground of Claudia's irritation. It was, rather, an instinctive reaction against Leo's male assumption as to what is most interesting about Sonia. But try explaining that to Leo. 'How's Barnaby?' she asks instead.

'Much the same.' Leo sighs. 'Lost to our world or any other but his own. They're trying some new drug on him, but his mother and I don't hold out much hope, as I'm sure she told you.'

'I don't think Greta likes to talk about Barnaby,' says Claudia.

'Would you?' Leo sighs again. 'How's your kids?'

'Joshua's taken to shoplifting.' Claudia tries to make light of it. 'And Matilda seems to have embarked on a series of self-destructive strategies.'

Leo laughs. 'So they're both quite normal.'

'If it's normal to be unhappy.'

'It is at their age.'

'And there's nothing I can do about it?'

'They want their father.'

'You mean I'm not enough?'

'Well, it certainly shook Greta and me,' says Leo. 'You and Dorian of all people. We both thought there was something so strong in that marriage. He thinks the world of you, Claudia. He needs you. He's not going to be able to survive without you.'

To her annoyance, Claudia finds herself pushed near to tears. 'Don't you believe it.'

Oblivious to her distress, Leo laughs again. 'So you really have got rid of him, have you? I don't know what's got into women these days.'

'Women?' she asks forlornly. 'I'm Claudia. Aren't I, Leo?'

'Hey, hey,' he remonstrates. 'Dorian's the one we ought to be feeling sorry for. After all, he's lost you, hasn't he? Where's your drink?'

Claudia explains that she was on her way to fetch one. As Leo follows her downstairs, she tries to dismiss all obtrusive considerations of either Dorian or the children. Causes for grief must give way to cause for hope, however tenuous. And hasn't she been thinking independent thoughts about earning a living? Three hours' teaching (which in practice amounts to three days' work) per week is hardly going to keep her in cigarettes and tights, let alone pay the mortgage. Her qualifications and experience as an employed person are both minimal. As for talent, how (hating herself for it!) she envies Sonia. Claudia's one talent, according to both her tutor at college and her editor at the *Globe* all those incredibly many years ago, is for précis. Where is the prolix frog prince awaiting transformation into manhood by the snipping kiss of Ms Farquharson's incisive little scissors? Probably not at the Freeburgs'. This much has to be admitted. Does the mythical beast indeed exist at all, except within the wish-fulfilling confines of her own imagination?

The mistress of précis pushes her way among the warm bodies inhabiting the Freeburgs' living-room towards the kitchen extension. Only four months ago it would have been unthinkable that she and Dorian should quarrel about money. Now the possibility becomes more thinkable every day. Neither the mortgage nor the rates have been paid. Claudia has paid the telephone bill with the cash gained from the sale of a snakeskin coat made for her in 1965 and now too redolent of thoughtless affluence to be wearable. Or so, in her horror of being cut off from communication, she has persuaded herself. But the final demand from the Gas Board arrived this morning and the Electricity Board has threatened disconnection. Dorian claims to be earning no money, and yet on Monday he was wearing a new silk shirt. This, he claimed, was a necessity: stage gear. He gave her a wad of notes and she took it without comment. Her humiliation was so acute that she forbore to sharpen it by pointing out that the sum was only three-quarters of her customary housekeeping allowance. To do so would have been, in more senses than one, to cut her own throat.

'Claudia!' Belinda's baby-blue eyes are wide with cordiality as she pours a generous portion of Italian white wine into the proffered plastic cup. 'How are you? You're looking great!'

'So are you!' says Claudia, including Vida in the returned politeness.

Belinda and Vida are both dressed, up-to-the-minute fashion, in layers of loose-fitting clothes adorned with bows and glitter. They look as though they are having a good time and, as they gaze benignly at Claudia from behind the improvised bar, it is clear to her that they are anxious for her to feel the same. This concern surprises her. She has previously had the impression that both women considered her to be a boring little housewife, lucky enough to be married to such a fascinating man. The last time she saw Vida, the Vamp was sitting beside Dorian on the Freeburgs' chaise longue, her arms around his neck and one leg draped over his at the thigh. Belinda's line has been to protest poutingly about how difficult it is to be taken seriously as an actress, once you have bared your tits in public. Dorian, who has had a similar problem for different reasons, has always been sympathetic. But now the two women are standing with their arms around each other's waists, inviting her into some sort of sisterly complicity.

'So you've had the guts to get rid of Dorian at last,' says Vida. 'How are you enjoying your freedom?'

'Freedom?' Claudia is doubtful. 'Is that what you call it?'

'What you need is a sugar-daddy.' Belinda giggles. 'Honestly, Claudia, it's much more fun being a mistress.'

'Then you're the boss,' says Vida. 'None of us could ever understand why you took so much shit from Dorian.'

'I suppose I loved him,' Claudia says grimly.

'That's no excuse,' says Vida.

'Love is always a mistake,' says Belinda. 'It puts you at a disadvantage.'

'What is he, after all?' Vida asks. 'A nice voice and a pretty face. That's all. You've got so much more going for you.'

Claudia stares uncomprehendingly at the pair of them. She is stung, quite against her will, by Vida's summation of Dorian's character. How can either Vida or Belinda speak so confidently of her husband's minimal virtues when they themselves are both incapable of seeing beyond the superficialities of appearances? And yet they are not the first people to speak so plainly of Dorian's shortcomings since the separation. The complaints have mainly been about his inaccessibility: he is always acting; his warmth is forced; he will never allow a ripple of pain or anger to disturb the pleasant surface of his personality. In short, he neither reveals himself nor welcomes self-revelation in others. Claudia has always flattered herself that she alone has been the repository of his confidences, that she alone has been capable of understanding the very special problems encountered by those who are forced to match up and yet keep separate their public and private personae. The private persona was for her and the children, the public for everyone else. What private persona? The attempt to answer this question chills her. Suppose there wasn't, isn't, one for anyone? It has long since become a cliché that popular entertainers believe their own publicity. But that's the trouble with clichés: they have an irritating habit of proving true.

'It's not that simple,' she tells Vida and Belinda, believing as she must that Dorian has a lost self to find. Haven't we all? 'Nothing ever is.'

'Dorian is,' Vida insists. 'You're the complicated one, isn't she, Belinda?'

'Not like us!' Belinda giggles again as she replenishes the cup extended to her by a clean-looking youngish man wearing an open-necked shirt and a blazer.

'Nothing's quite like you, darling,' he says. 'Not that I've ever seen.'

Claudia begins to drift away from the crowd gathering round the bar. The conversation has disturbed her more than she cares to admit, and she suspects that its import is currently beyond her grasp. Her judgement, not only of Dorian but also of herself, has been questioned. And in marriage, where the humdrum business of keeping the show on the road takes precedence, judgements as basic as these are rarely questioned. Even now she believes, in a stubbornly sensible and optimistic recess of her being, that sooner or later, when Dorian is able to distinguish the worthwhile (Claudia, Joshua, Matilda) from the worthless (groupies, scrubbers) the status quo will be restored. He is not unintelligent and is surely suffering from temporary moral myopia rather than total blindness. It is just a matter of time.

The lights in the living-room are dimmer than the spots in the kitchen. The shutters are closed and a log fire burns in the grate in the front fireplace. Shadows of flame illumine and then teasingly withdraw from the Mexican hangings on the opposite wall. Sticks of incense are smouldering in brass holders on the mantelpiece. Their perfume and the muted trumpet of Miles Davis slither in and out of monologue and dialogue as the volume of human voices rises and falls. Claudia stands at the door, only partly listening, savouring the surreal quality of overheard conversation.

Someone unrecognizable waves in her direction and she stares blankly at a well-built man of about her own age before turning round to find the blazer-wearer standing behind her. And yet there is something familiar about the stranger in an ill-fitting suit. As he walks towards her, she notes the self-conscious swagger of one who would rather disown his clothes, the fingering of what seems to a newly acquired moustache, and finally the eyes, as blue as Belinda's, in an otherwise strongly angular face.

'Claudia, isn't it?' he asks. 'Notice how I said that. Isn't it. Not innit.'

'Steady on, my dear chap,' says the man in the blazer. 'No need to overdo it. There's no premium in a Standard English accent these days.'

'She doesn't recognize me,' says the other man.

'I'm sorry,' says Claudia.

'Chaz thinks he's famous,' says the man in the blazer, 'now that his photo has appeared in *TV Times*.'

'Chaz?' Claudia begins to remember. 'Weren't you the stuntman when Dorian was filming in Brighton?'

'And I was his stand-in,' Chaz says proudly. 'How are you, Claud? And how's the old man?'

'I don't see much of him these days,' says Claudia. 'We're separated.'

'Come on, girl,' says Chaz. 'Be serious.'

'I am,' says Claudia.

'Oh dear,' says the man in the blazer. 'I feel this is where I should take my leave.'

'This geezer's a doctor,' says Chaz. 'Can't stand the sight of blood. Or the smell or . . . er . . . unpleasantness. Isn't that what you'd call it, Gerry?'

'Gerald.' The doctor corrects Chaz. 'I thought I'd just go and chat up that little number over there. Does either of you know who she is?'

'Sonia Ravel,' says Claudia. 'She's a novelist.'

'Fascinating,' says the doctor.

Claudia is glad enough to turn the attention from herself to Sonia, who is leaning against the mantelpiece, silhouetted in the firelight. She is wearing a black vest and, regardless of fashion, black satin flared trousers which emphasize the slenderness of her hips. She is talking animatedly, using her hands to construct a parallel conversation. The rest of her body seems, by contrast, curiously immobile.

'A bit on the skinny side,' Chaz says doubtfully. 'She looks half-starved to me.'

'But that's just it, don't you see?' Gerald is breathless with enthusiasm. 'That's a perfect example of a controlled and functioning anorectic. I've never seen anything quite like it. How long has she been like that?'

Claudia stares coldly at him. 'Like what?'

The doctor mistakes her hostility for ignorance. 'How old is she?'

'Thirty-three,' Chaz guesses wrongly.

'Why don't you ask her?' Claudia's voice is contemptuous.

'Ask her what?' asks Leo from behind them, as he slips one arm around Claudia's shoulders, the other around Gerald's waist. 'Not a chance, Gerald old buddy. Seal it, save it, double glaze it, that's our Sonia.'

'I think you're all shits,' says Claudia.

The three men look at her in what seems to be genuine astonishment. They look at one another and now again at her, each disowning the other two and rebuking her for her unjustified condemnation of innocent remarks affectionately intended. Claudia reads all this and says nothing. Leo drifts off again, having given her an absent-minded pat on the bottom. Chaz winks at her. Gerald asks sarcastically if he has her permission to talk to Sonia.

She smiles at him, still saying nothing.

'Never did like him,' says Chaz as Gerald slouches off.

'He speaks awfully well of you,' Claudia says at once, remembering the call and response of catch-phrases from their days of filming.

They both laugh. But it is seven years since she last saw Chaz. He looks older of course and has put on a bit of weight – neither of which is necessarily a change for the worse. He was fit to the point of fanaticism then, forever demonstrating his prowess. Once he asked her to punch him in the stomach. When she refused, he insisted: go on, go on, punch me as hard as you can! He stood there, facing her, his arms raised and flexed, his head nodding faster as his urging became more passionate. She laughed. At once he crumpled, physically and morally, became defensive and self-denigratory at the same time. Horrified to see how easily she had wounded him, she kept apologizing. He began to tell her about his childhood in Poplar: what a hell-hole the place was and how there were only three ways to escape: sport, show business and villainy. He had had a go at all three. At first, as the tale of poverty and deprivation unfolded, he sounded ashamed and kept looking defiantly into her eyes as if to anticipate some critical and/or patronizing response. But when he spoke of his parents, 'as good as gold they was, Claud', he could keep neither warmth nor pride from the telling. And as member after member of his extended family was named and described in all the richness of his or her eccentricity, he grew more relaxed, enjoying the telling for its own sake. Strangely enough, it was the treats rather than the traumas of his early years which moved her most to pity: the smell of the hops in the summer rather than the pain of hand-me-down boots which pinched and let in water; the day a cured ham fell off the back of a lorry rather than the weeks of the dock strike. She wanted to touch his hand or his face, to kiss him gently, just to tell him it was all right now, that he himself was all right, that he had always been all right. But she was too shy.

It is she who has changed. She no longer needs looking after as Chaz looked after her at Brighton, always seeing to it that she was warm enough or cool enough or adequately supplied with coffee, sandwiches, cigarettes and conversation. She is embarrassed to recall how easily she allowed him to wait upon her, asked him to drive her to and from the set, accepted gifts on her own or her children's behalf, shared only his apparent devotion to the cause of furthering Dorian's career.

'Did you know all along,' she asks, 'that Dorian was having an affair with Gloria Crabbe?'

Chaz looks hurt again. 'I told him what a stupid cunt he was, if you'll excuse the language.'

'Was that why you were so kind to me?'

'Me? Kind to you?'

'You know you were. Did you feel sorry for me?'

'All men are the same, Claud,' says Chaz. 'Face it, girl. They all want their homes and their wives and their kids. And they all want a bit on the side as well.'

'Is that what you're like, Chaz?' asks Claudia, who knows very well that it is.

'My old girl, my Rosie, she's a good old girl really.' Chaz is trying to be fair, but his voice is impatient. 'Only sometimes I can't stand the sight of her. I look at her and she looks at me and I know that I'm nobody.'

Claudia is distracted from replying by the sound of Clive's voice in the hall. So it must be well after closing-time. It is indeed a quarter-past midnight. That is what Greta is telling Clive. Her voice, rising, is not yet audible to the whole room as she accuses him of trying to humiliate her. Clive's answer, though slurred when he tells her that he doesn't know what she is talking about, is. As is his laugh. Across the room, Juno waves, trying to attract Claudia's attention. Claudia waves back, thus indicating to Juno that she too has heard the altercation in the hall. Chaz takes her cup and offers to fetch her a drink, just like old times. Juno's wave has frozen, become imperious, as it is when she beckons waiters. Smiling, as if to offset any impression that she is obedient to Juno's every summons, Claudia edges her way across the room. Her greeting to Juno is graciously returned. But Juno's companion, a young man with wild hair and the broad, placid smile which is only seen outside of infancy on the faces of those stoned out of their minds, just sways gently back and forth on his bare feet, his hands clasped round his empty cup as if it were a talisman.

'This is Justin,' says Juno. 'He's a brilliant mathematician and says that Einstein was right about everything after all, although everyone else seems to think that he's discredited nowadays. He's also an extremely gifted organist and has written a symphony based on the equations in the theory of relativity.' Juno pauses for breath and Justin raises his eyelids for the fraction necessary to acknowledge Claudia's presence. 'Isn't that exciting? Claudia is a very accomplished scholar in the field of women's studies and is married to – wait for it – Dorian Grey. So there you are, the two of you.'

Justin's expression doesn't change and Claudia assumes that his biography has been inflated to dimensions similar to her own. Sharing neither Juno's relish nor her talent for monologue, she sees no point in addressing herself to Justin. 'Sooner or later,' she says instead with a vague wave of her hand, 'you meet everyone who's anyone at the Freeburgs'.'

'I haven't even seen Greta,' says Juno. 'Has she been upstairs all evening waiting for Clive?'

'She's had his portrait to keep her company.'

'Do you think she ought to paint Justin?'

'Why not?'

'You know why not.' Juno leans forward and whispers in Claudia's ear. 'She'll simply add him to her list of conquests. Oh, why don't I have any artistic talent?'

'Is that what it takes?' Claudia asks innocently.

The party is beginning to thin. People are leaving in twos and threes, apparently unconcerned that they have not been granted the opportunity to wish their hostess a happy birthday. The fire is dying down and the log basket is empty. Claudia must start to think about how she is to get home. As far as she knows, none of the guests live in her area, but perhaps some sober married couple can be prevailed upon to make a detour and drive the poor little deserted wife back to her former matrimonial home. But how many of the Freeburgs' circle are either sober or married – let alone both? She looks round for Leo and instead finds Chaz approaching with two cups of red wine.

'They'd run out of white,' he explains. 'Do you think those two are lesbians?'

'Which two?' Juno asks.

'The double act at the bar,' says Chaz. 'Blimey O'Riley, what a waste!'

'Oh, I shouldn't let it worry you,' Juno says, looking him up and down with evident interest. 'I'm sure they're open to offers from all sexes. I'm sorry, I don't know your name. Claudia is so bad at introducing people.'

'Chaz,' Claudia says heavily, 'is an ex-wrestler, ex-tea-leaf, current stuntman of amazingly versatile talents, friend of the famous, and star of stage, screen, Grisly Risley and the Scrubs.'

'Oh, come on, Claud.' Chaz sounds pained.

'She doesn't know what I'm talking about,' says Claudia. 'She's American.'

'Now, Claudia,' says Juno. 'I'm sure that's not all you've got to say about me.'

'Juno,' says Claudia, 'is a goddess. She exists and has always existed far above the everyday concerns of earning a living or begetting progeny. She brings people together or forces them apart, rewards or punishes them, changes their lives.'

'You'll pass,' Juno assures her. 'Now, Chaz, do tell me, what's a tea-leaf? It sounds absolutely intriguing.'

Claudia leaves them to it, intending to look for Sonia, whom she suspects of being the one sanely sympathetic person at the gathering. Or, failing Sonia, Leo can be her quarry and designated the task of finding her a lift home. But neither Sonia nor Leo is in the kitchen. Vida and Belinda are holding court, their admirers legion. At least two cameras are focused on them, flashing not quite synchronously as each new pose is struck. Vida is informing the assembled company (as if at a press conference) that she intends to vote for Mrs Thatcher in next month's election because she thinks it's time we had a woman Prime Minister in this country. When a small grey-haired woman standing next to Claudia objects to this intention as a short-sighted and unintelligent political act, Belinda says there is no difference between the two main parties anyway, so why not vote for the one which has had the gumption to choose a woman as its leader? Unable to make herself heard above the ensuing argument, the grey-haired woman turns to Claudia.

'What a pair of numskulls,' she says. 'They'll know the difference all right, if the Tories are elected.'

'They won't be, though, will they?' Claudia is doubtful. 'Isn't this one of the few occasions when we have to be thankful for the prevalent misogyny?'

'Don't you believe it,' says the woman. 'Class is still what counts in this country, not gender. Privilege may be sexist by nature, but one of its tenets is that the exception proves the rule. That's how it manages to maintain the appearance of flexibility.'

Claudia would like her to elucidate; but the group around the bar is breaking up (who, after all, wants to talk politics at a party?) and the two women are separated by the general movement through to the hall and living-room. It looks as though the drink has run out. Vida is making coffee for the photographers and Belinda is searching the fridge for a second bowl of hummus. The front door is open, the hall full of the chill night air. Greta, wrapped in her multi-coloured Shetland shawl, embraces guest after departing guest, exchanging promises of imminent meetings. Clive is sitting on the stairs, smiling to himself. Sonia, already wearing her musquash coat, is talking to him over the banisters. When he sees Claudia, he holds out his hand, inviting her to sit next to him.

'Oh, are you going?' she says disappointedly to Sonia, as Clive pulls her to his side.

'Aren't you?' Sonia asks her. 'I make it a rule never to stay more than two and a half hours at any party.'

'Sonia's life is full of rules,' says Clive. 'That's why she's so miserable.'

'And why you're so radiantly happy, I suppose,' says Sonia. 'Oh, where the hell is Justin?'

'I'm *here*,' Justin says from the front door. He has recovered his shoes and with them his voice. His eyes, strangely like Sonia's from a distance, are candid and bright as he adds, 'Goodnight, Claudia.'

'Goodnight, you two,' says Sonia. 'Be kind to Greta, won't you?'

'Be kind to Greta!' Clive repeats in disgust as Sonia and Justin descend the front steps arm-in-arm.

'What a strange couple,' says Claudia.

Clive laughs. 'Stranger than you think.' He takes her hand and kisses it. 'Even stranger than us.'

Greta is watching them as she slams the front door shut and leans against it. 'Why don't we go into the living-room?' she asks with a motherly smile. 'It's warmer.'

'The fire's nearly out,' Clive says sourly.

'Then I'll put some more logs on.'

'There aren't any.'

'Then I'll ask Leo to fetch some.'

'He's gone upstairs with Belinda.'

'He hasn't,' says Claudia. 'Belinda's in the kitchen.'

'Oh, wasn't it Belinda?' Clive asks, all spiteful innocence.

'If you were a gentleman,' says Greta, 'you'd get up off your butt and fetch those logs without being asked.'

'I'm no gentleman, baby doll.'

'Let's you and me go, Claudia.'

'Let's you go, Greta,' says Clive.

'I'll come with you,' Claudia says. 'Just let go of me, will you, Clive?'

She follows Greta through to the fire and the two women walk solemnly towards the kitchen, carrying the basket between them. Chaz, who has been sitting on the chaise longue with Juno, offers to help them, but Greta rejects him, saying she wants to talk to Claudia. He follows them into the kitchen, all the same, and opens the back door for them. Claudia wishes that she had put her coat on before venturing out into the garden. The night is clear and starlit and, uninhabited by human passion as it is, immediately beautiful. Greta, knowing the path, moves briskly, but Claudia has to watch where she places her sandalled feet along the crazy paving. The basket jerks back and forth between them, arhythmically. The woodshed smells damp and sawdusty, intimating a rural otherwhere which is also lodged somewhere in the past. The logs are divided into three piles, according to size. As Greta begins to heave some of the largest ones into the basket, Claudia notes abstractedly that this is the first time she has ever seen Greta lift anything heavier than a paintbrush.

'How could he do it to me?' Greta is now flinging the logs towards the basket – and Claudia – from a distance. 'And on my birthday too!'

'But surely,' says Claudia, 'you don't expect Clive to do as he says. He's totally unreliable.'

'And then to sit there on the stairs with you like that!'

Claudia takes a deep breath. 'Do you know if anyone can give me a lift home?'

'I'll call you a cab.'

'I can't afford taxis, Greta.'

'It's all right – you can put it on my account.'

Claudia stifles an impulse to laugh: how novel to be bought off! 'All right. Thanks, Greta.'

Their progress back to the house is steadier, mainly because Greta's anger seems to have died down and she walks at a pace more suited to Claudia's. From somewhere among the chimneys an owl hoots and the Freeburgs' cat runs crookedly, as if at a signal, across their path. The light is on in Leo's den, the curtains pulled across. It occurs to Claudia that she could walk the two or three miles home: she doesn't want to stay at the Freeburgs' a moment longer. She wouldn't care if she never saw Greta or Leo or Clive again. There must be more absorbing pursuits to be followed than the manipulation of erotic intrigues. And it would indeed seem that the eroticism lies in the manipulation and the intrigue rather than in the satisfaction of anything as basic as sexual impulse. Claudia feels suddenly depressed, as she used to on coming home from school to be told by her mother that supper was going to be late and, no, she couldn't have some bread and jam because it would spoil her appetite; hunger was to be ignored in the name of ceremony. All she wants to do now is to go to bed, alone, and to sleep.

The cat is waiting for them on the back step. Chaz opens the door for them and lets it in before Greta can stop him. Vida is sitting at the kitchen table eating muesli. Chaz carries the basket effortlessly through to the living-room where Juno and Gerald are sitting at opposite ends of the chaise longue, and Clive on the fender seat, staring moodily into the embers. Claudia sits between Juno and Gerald and lights a cigarette while Greta calls a cab and Chaz attempts to rescue the fire.

'How wonderful,' Juno sighs, 'to have a real man about the house.'

'Five minutes,' Greta tells Claudia.

'I can take you home,' says Gerald. 'Where do you live?'

'Are you going my way, Chaz?' asks Juno.

'You don't all have to go,' says Greta, 'just because Claudia's leaving.'

'Are you sure you want a fire?' Chaz asks.

Greta sits on the fender beside Clive and slips her arm through his as she advises Chaz on the art of fire-coaxing. Claudia ascertains that Gerald and Juno live in the same part of town. She tells Juno that Chaz lives in Kent. Juno doesn't want to know. Neither does Gerald. The fire is out. Chaz apologizes to Greta and sits down on the floor at her feet, leaning against the fender. Juno crosses the room and, taking a cushion with her, sits down next to him.

'I'm sure it's no slur on your virility,' she tells him. 'Wouldn't you agree, Greta?'

'If lighting fires was a sign of virility,' says Greta, 'I'd be the most butch of the lot of you.'

'What makes you think you aren't?' Clive asks.

'I know it's none of my business,' says Chaz, 'but if I were you, Greta, I wouldn't let him talk to me like that.'

'Clive and I understand each other,' says Greta, looking at her watch. 'Where's that cab of yours got to, Claudia?'

'Fucked if I do,' Chaz says, shaking his head. 'I don't understand you people at all.'

'How do you know the Freeburgs?' Juno asks him.

'How does anyone know the Freeburgs?' Clive laughs. 'Through the mafia of radical chic. He's their token working-class hero.' He crosses the room gropingly and sits in Juno's place on the chaise longue. Putting an arm round Claudia and burying his face in her neck, he says, 'I'm coming with you.'

'You are not,' she says.

'Please, Claudie.'

'No, Clive.'

'I need you, Claudie. I need you to save me from myself.'

'Clive, I'm trying to save myself from yourself.'

'Let's just fuck and forget the lot of them.' Clive's tongue is in her ear, his hand gentle underneath her hair. 'Just fuck . . . Just you and me . . . darling . . . '

The doorbell rings and Greta, smiling her sweet smile in Claudia's direction, goes to answer the summons. Claudia follows her into the hall, and finds her coat. The door is opened. Greta hugs and kisses her. The cab is warm and smells of fish and chips generously sprinkled with vinegar. As Claudia leans forward to give the address to the driver, the Freeburgs' door opens again. Perhaps she has left something behind. Perhaps her reactions are rather slow, because before she knows what is happening, the cab is moving off with herself and Clive as its passengers, thrown hastily together on the back seat. It is a moment of release. Claudia starts laughing and, once Clive has joined in, it seems that neither of them knows how to stop.

'Greta –' Claudia manages to gasp the words out, '– is paying for this cab.'

'Whoever said,' Clive gasps, 'that money can't buy happiness?'

'Oh but Clive,' Claudia wails, trying to be serious, 'she loves you. You shouldn't be so cruel.'

'Be kind to Greta.' Clive uses the same disgusted tone as before. 'That's supposed to be my mission in life.'

'She's in love with you. She told me.'

'She's in love with the idea of being in love with me. The ageing beauty who gives her all for passion.'

'It'll happen to us one day.'

'It happens to me all the time,' he says, snuggling up to her. 'Greta thinks she's the Queen Bee and all the rest of us are fit for is buzzing around her.'

'Don't you care about her at all?'

'Of course I do, Claudia. But, fuck it, what does she think I am? Her property?'

'So that's my function, is it, to prove to Greta that you're not her property?'

'To prove to myself that I can make my own choices, you stupid irresistible little cow.'

'At Greta's expense?'

'Greta delights in suffering,' Clive says, his voice suddenly weary. 'A Catholic married to a Jew with a schizophrenic son. What else has she got? It's her *raison d'être*. Christ, what a fucking bore!'

The taxi stops at the traffic lights where Essex Road crosses the New North Road. A police notice asks for witnesses to an accident last Saturday night. There on the far corner is the Health Centre where Josh attended Child Guidance for a whole year without ever saying anything more than yes or no and, in the winter months, even failing to take his gloves off. And so it became Mum Guidance: Claudia spent an hour each week with the psychiatric social worker while Josh saw the psychotherapist. What was his problem? He stole money. He had set fire to his bedroom. When his father refused to increase his pocket money, he climbed onto the roof and threatened to jump. He must have been unhappy, in need of help. But Josh reserved his inalienable right to the pursuit of unhappiness: this was something no one – not even a psychotherapist and a weekly game of chess – could take away from him.

There was nothing to worry about. Indeed, it was all easily identifiable and predictable. It's known as the absent father syndrome, Mrs Hughes. Claudia herself represented the depressed mother syndrome. How did Josh stand a chance? They were a problem family. They would be helped. That's what the social services were for. Surveillance for Josh, anti-depressants for Claudia – and for Dorian, exemption. You mustn't worry, Mrs Hughes. Oh, I'll worry, worry, worry: that's what mothers are for.

'You seem determined,' says Claudia, 'to bring out the masochist in her.'

'That's what she seems to want.'

'I don't.'

'I know, I know.' Clive kisses her cheek. 'Don't you see now why I need you?'

The cab crosses the Ball's Pond Road, carrying its passengers beyond the pale. Once it really was the pale, marking the north-eastern limits of London. And here the Nonconformists moved to escape the jurisdiction of the city authorities: Mary Wollstonecraft set up her nursery at Newington Green, alongside the Unitarian Church, which still proclaims its tortuous texts from its Wayside Pulpit for the edification of the traveller or the customers of Barclays Bank. Public transport is represented by the temperamental 73 bus. Dorian promised Claudia that he would drive her to Sainsbury's once a week, drive her anywhere she wanted, if only she would agree to move into that lovely double-fronted villa with its broad, jungly garden. But Dorian was always somewhere else. Juno insisted that he was keeping Claudia in purdah. And why has Claudia never learned to drive? Because Dorian has persuaded her that there is no need for her to go through such a nerve-racking exercise: like all the most sensitive people, she would find it excruciating. Ah, how he has protected her from her own inadequacies.

'I don't know, Clive,' she says. 'I really don't think there's any future in our relationship, do you?'

'Our relationship!' Clive repeats scornfully.

'Don't we have one?'

'Don't think about it.'

'Why not?'

'You're hung up on meaning,' Clive tells her as the cab pulls up outside the house. 'Don't you know yet that the meaning of meaning is meaningless?'

IX

At last I was granted the honour of an audience with His Supreme Holiness, Rodge, the guru of Finsbury Park. Don't ask me what I'd done to deserve it all of a sudden. Perhaps locking myself in the linen cupboard, bombed out on Mogadon, qualified me for membership of the oppressed subculture. Perhaps I was the only bald-headed girl he'd ever heard of. Perhaps he thought anyone with a wanker like Josh for a brother deserved some sort of medal for martyrdom. Which of us can truly say? Anyway, I was just coming out of school one day when there were Josh and Nat sitting on the wall, smoking, like they'd been doing practically all afternoon, in full view of the library. I was going to ignore the pair of them, but they kind of slid off the wall and started walking along the street with me. Nat said, trying to sound all casual, that they were just pissing off to Rodge's and how about it?

Of course I pretended that was the last thing I wanted to do and that I wasn't curious in the slightest about their mysterious meetings. I was above such boyish pleasures as bringing about the socialist millennium. I'd been getting sick to death of the way the boys were so patronizing about everything, as if they had the key to all knowledge and nobody else had ever been pissed off with school or parents or whatever in the whole history of the world. Every time I said anything half-way decent about anyone over the age of thirty (except Mum, who was supposed to be the victim of patriarchal brainwashing) they'd exchange these Significant Glances and accuse me of letting adults get to me. Me, of all

A.—6

people! And them, of all people! When everything they said had been spoonfed to them drop by drop by Rodge! The injustice of it all was driving me round the sodding bend. Especially when they laughed at me for being naive. Me, naive! That's the biggest joke since their moronic voices started breaking.

Not that it was any better being with Emma and Slime, once they'd got over the honeymoon stage and deigned to associate with other human beings again. They would keep rabbiting on about their sex-life. As if anybody wanted to know about their pathetic gropings and grapplings. They both seemed to think it was a subject of earth-shattering importance but to me it was the Number One Bore. Sex is a waste of time, if you ask me. Once you've done it once, you've done it a thousand times. I mean, it's degrading, isn't it? All you do is hang about, waiting for the boy to get it together – just like in every other department of life. If, by any miracle, he does, you're supposed to encourage him and tell him how wonderful he is, so that he gets all worked up and shoots his ten c.c. before you even begin to know what's happening. When he can't get it together, it's even worse. Honestly, you'd think it was the Day of Judgement or something. And you never hear the end of it. Of course it's supposed to be your fault, especially if you don't keep telling him what a superstud he is every other second. All very well for them. What's in it for girls? That's what I'd like to know. I tried to ask Emma what she saw in it, but she went all mysterious on me and said I'd find out for myself in time. In time! She's only three months older than me! People are so shitting unhelpful. Even when she was rabbiting on with Slime, it was all hints and giggles and oohs and ahs. I ask you. Showing off. That's all it was.

Then Josh had the nerve to say I was afraid to go and see Rodge because I would be shown up in all my ignorance. Considering I always got higher marks than him, I thought this the pissing, shitting limit. He *then* had the sodding nerve to say that intelligence couldn't be measured by what schools thought it was, and the only reason girls often got better marks than boys was because they always did as they were told and worked harder. That did it. Take me to your leader, I said, me only ignorant barbarian, want to learn wisdom from Great White Chief. They spent the whole of the way there telling me how I should or shouldn't behave in the august presence. When I asked if I had to walk backwards out of the room, they said there was no need to get stroppy and sarcastic – all I had to do was act natural. Act natural! After the build-up they'd been giving me! I was all butterflies, though I pretended I was suavely condescending and didn't give a toss what they or Rodge thought of me.

And I'd have died rather than admit I was flattered out of my tiny mind at being the only girl ever to penetrate (yes, I know, I'm just as aware of innuendo as you are) the secret cell. Of course I knew it was only my due, but you try convincing people of that. Anyone who's got a brother will know just what I mean. As far as some people are concerned, being a girl is like having some kind of rabid disease. Fuck knows why it's so important. I mean, I don't go walking down the street, thinking every minute of the day, ho, ho, I'm this female creature with a womb and ovaries and a vagina. It's just not something you think about except once a month when you have to. But some people never allow you to forget.

Take school. I was the only girl to volunteer to do metalwork. Even Emma thought it was boring. Even Emma thought I was just trying to be awkward. But how was I to know I was going to be the only one? Then Hazlitt asked me why I wanted to do it. I said I wanted to *make* things. He said I could make things in needlework or cookery. But the point was I could easily have done things like that at home. We didn't have a sodding metal workshop on the premises – a fact which seemed to have escaped his attention. In the end he said it was going to be too difficult to restructure the timetable just for one individual. But I wouldn't have thought it was beyond the wit of man – or woman. When I told Mum, she said why didn't I go to evening classes instead? Which wasn't the point either. The same thing happened in English with the set texts. The boys were given *Lord of the Flies* and the girls had to read *Jane Eyre*. Mum seemed to think *Jane Eyre* was the most wonderful novel ever written and she launched into some great discussion of Charlotte Brontë's tortured life as a woman writer. I've got to admit I ended up agreeing with her, but again, that just wasn't the point. Why couldn't she see it was a Matter of Principle – one of her very own favourite phrases?

All your childhood you're living in some kind of a fool's paradise. No one ever tells you some ghastly accident has befallen you at birth. They all pretend it's wonderful being a girl. And yet you know they're pretending. You know because there's so many things you're just not allowed to do. Like falling over and tearing your clothes. Like kicking a ball around and getting all covered in mud. Like jumping off a bus when it's moving. Like shouting and screaming as loud as your brother. But you don't know *why*. Teachers are worse than parents and other people's parents can be positively diabolical. Anyone would think you had some kind of deformity and it wasn't nice to talk about it in public. Then, when you're thirteen or something, they all start blahing on like Now It

Can Be Told. Then you learn that your life is full of liabilities, that you're a fucking walking liability yourself. Oh, they tell you with such glee. Just like they're saying, now it's *your* turn to suffer! It makes me puke. I mean, I didn't ask to be born female. It's not my fucking fault, is it?

Slime said to me, you know, Matilda, you'll be a lot happier when you get tits. I was so furious all I could think of to say was, and you'll be a lot happier once you get brains, you wanker. Feeble really, because he didn't seem particularly unhappy, worse luck. He should have been. I mean, how can you be happy and be Slime? But I couldn't help wondering if he was right. Perhaps that's what was wrong with me all along. Perhaps I'd been destined to be a titless female. What a fucking joke! Ha, ha, ha! But when I saw that Mum's feminist friend, Sonia, didn't have any tits either, I was cheered up. Not that she's a bundle of laughs, exactly, but she seems to have got it all together and keeps saying all sorts of odd things that somehow make me feel I'm not such a freak after all. And of course Mum's not exactly Raquel Welch, but she says that's because of *us* (Josh and me) and she used to be quite shapely. I don't see how I can ever have any children. I mean, I just don't believe it's possible.

So I suppose I was reconciled to being a kind of perpetual outcast before I met Rodge. At first I didn't know what to make of him – or his grotty basement flat. It looked filthy to me, just like my room before Mum did her blitz on it. I didn't know, you see, that real live grown-ups ever lived in the kind of grot and squalor me and my mates found so cosy and comfortable. His room (because that's all his flat was, really, apart from the kitchen and an outside loo, and he had to share those) was painted black all over, even the ceiling, so that daylight hardly got a chance. Nat said it was like a womb and made you feel safe. It did too. Rodge kept the shutters closed and they were painted white like the doors (one to the hall and one to the kitchen) and the mantelpiece. The floor – where you could actually see it – was bare boards with a few holes and all unvarnished. He didn't have much furniture. Just a huge mattress covered with an Indian bedspread and cushions, a wimpy-bar-type table and two armchairs covered in speckly brown plastic with lumps of horsehair sticking out.

There were posters all over the walls, mostly showing things like red fists and broken chains with slogans in foreign languages (not French or German or I'd have know, wouldn't I?) that conjured up pictures of peasants tramping through the snow with all their worldly goods on their backs. But the one I liked the best was nothing like that. It was mostly bright yellow to the left and then there was a kind of black triangle moving into it from the right, which went into black and white stripes, shading into black and yellow at the top. In the midst of this stripy bit was a blue shape rather like an egg-timer. To its left was a hand holding a camera. Underneath some geezer dressed in black (a robot?) was looking at a lamp. Then, splashed across the top was this girl in a red leotard and running shoes leaping over it all with her arms stretched out in front of her like a diver. She had this fantastic, beatific smile on her face. Oh, I loved it!

Of course I knew it was rude to turn my back on everyone and stare at the walls, a bit like reading someone's diary. But it was less embarrassing than staring at Rodge. Which was what I wanted to do. Not that he was anything to look at. If I'd sat next to him on the bus, I wouldn't even have noticed him, he was that dead ordinary. So what was it? His instant friendliness? Hardly. He never even smiled at me – or my hairless head. His strikingly virile good looks? That even less. He was only about five foot three (five foot seven, it turned out later) and everything about him was soft and mild. His hair was all floppy and clean-looking and he had to keep pushing it out of his eyes, which were soft and grey and serious and searching, without making you feel like you'd done something wrong. His voice was all soft and kind of shy. His hands (yes, we shook hands, fer Chrissake!) were just as soft but dry and firm at the same time. And warm. He was wearing baggy blue jeans just like Slime's step-Dad and a raggedy hand-knitted sweater that could never have fitted anyone.

I was all nonchalant, rather amused. So this was the human dynamo? The shooting star in the firmament of disaffected youth? I asked him, my voice little and brisk like Mum's when Dad's out of the room and she has to make conversation with my Gran, what the poster was. He smiled then – just a little bit – and asked if I liked it. I said, yes. Well, I did, didn't I? So he said it was advertising a Russian film (so the language was Russian!) called *Springtime* and made in 1927. I couldn't believe it. I mean, it looked so modern. Rodge said, would I like it? I didn't know what to say. Somehow I felt mean, as if I'd been hinting, and yet somehow I didn't. Rodge didn't wait for a reply. He took the poster off the wall and rolled it up. Then he fished in his pocket and found an elastic band to go round it. He gave a little bow and presented to to me like a prize. I took it. I wanted it. What else was I supposed to do?

All this time Josh and Nat had been watching us. I'd almost forgotten them, although I knew of course that there was some sort of audience in the room. Josh looked embarrassed. Nat, though, looked rather pleased, like I was his protégé who'd behaved rather better than he'd expected. I'd seen that same look, you see, on Dad's face when we'd been to Gran's and I'd said my pretty little pieces about her dahlias or her apple pie and Josh had just blushed and grunted in his usual totally moronic fashion. Of course she really liked Josh much better than me. On his last birthday he got a radio-cassette recorder (stereo!) but on mine I got a £5 book token. Just shows. I suppose he reminded her of her darling only son. I suppose all only sons were darling as far as she was concerned. Not that I minded. I couldn't have stuck her smarming all over me like she did with Josh. Dad was always telling her how well I was doing at school, etc., but she'd say, her arm round Josh, we can't all be clever. Mum would always be so annoyed with her – afterwards. At the time she just raised her eyebrows to heaven in her usual way or, if she thought Gran wasn't looking, she'd wink at me. And at Josh. As for Dad, he'd always make excuses for Gran. Almost always he and Mum would have a row. Not a proper row with shouting and swearing and all that crap (not their style) but all kind of niggly and tight-lipped and calling each other darling every third word.

I suppose that's why I couldn't believe it when I heard her yelling at him that morning and calling him a fucking pig and saying that he'd turned her life into a lie. Even when my other Gran died, she didn't scream. I couldn't even remember *her* very well though I was nine at the time. Josh did, though. He had nightmares. He used to get into bed with Mum (Dad was away) and I could hear the two of them crying, ever so quietly, together. Hearing them, I'd just cry alone. At first. In a way, the whole carry-on just seemed silly to me. Just like when Mum read *The Call of the Wild* to us and Josh couldn't bear it and hid his face and pretended he wasn't crying. Mum's voice was all dramatic and full of invisible tears. And I didn't feel a fucking thing. And I wondered what was wrong with me. I seem to have spent my whole boring Godawful life wondering what the shit is wrong with me.

I expect it's all because Mum tried to get rid of me before I was born. She did, honestly. Nat wouldn't believe me, but I said how I'd heard her telling Claire about it, so there! I was just going to the downstairs loo when I heard them talking in the study. It was Claire I heard first. She said, I know I should get rid of it, but somehow I can't bear to, not again. Then there was this strange silence which made me realize they were talking about something more important than Claire's Morris Minor which was never going to pass its MOT. I waited for Mum to say something, but it was

Claire again. I'm thirty-five, she said, and I've had three abortions already. This could be my last chance. And besides, I can't stop thinking about those foetuses. She started to cry and said perhaps it was sentimental, but she felt so guilty. That's when Mum said she felt guilty too because she'd tried to get rid of me. It was all to do with something Dr Jaffa said about people never changing. I didn't get it, and I didn't try very hard because I was feeling quite sick. No wonder I kept feeling like I was in the way all the time. I wasn't even supposed to be there in the first place. Nat said none of us was *supposed* to be here and his Mum had told him she wished he'd never been born. So did he, of course. So it could have been worse. Well, that is worse, isn't it? At least Mum said she felt guilty. And so she should.

Rodge made us all some coffee and we sat in a row on his mattress while he asked us all sorts of questions about school. I don't mean the usual sort of questions about which O-levels you're doing and what's your favourite subject and all that shit. I mean, he was talking about things like the core curriculum and corporal punishment and having pupil representation on the Board of Governors. I'd never heard anything like it. Of course we all grumbled all the time about the idiotic things you're supposed to do at school, but it was a kind of ritual, and I for one didn't believe that anyone would take any notice if we said we weren't interested in who was winning what battle when, or the French for Peter and Jane are going to the seaside. When did anyone ever listen to us? But Rodge said it was our education and our future that were at stake. What did we think education was for? Well, to tell you the truth, I never thought it was *for* anything in particular. Nat said it was for getting jobs. What sort of jobs? Boring jobs. Josh said it was for making you a better person. Rodge smiled then, and asked if we thought school was making us better people. Of course we all chorused, no! Josh said it was making him a worse person. I said I didn't think that was possible – especially as he never went to school, anyway. Nat said Josh was still under the influence of school, like the rest of us. We all started arguing then. I suppose I was just arguing for the sake of it, but Josh got all het up and redder and redder and said he wasn't going to let himself be ground down into conformity by petty rules and regulations.

Rodge didn't intervene. He waited till we'd finished, more or less, before asking us about canings. So then we all moaned on about that. When Rodge told us what the rules were, I was pretty well amazed. I mean, I had no idea that they were supposed to use a proper cane like you can buy in porn shops, and not a slipper (Hazlitt's favourite weapon) or a belt. It turned out that Hazlitt was breaking *all* the rules. I'd seen him with my own eyes slipper Darren Baron and Brendan Kelly in front of the whole class *and* it was for a first offence. When I told Rodge, he said I should make a note of it and any other incidents. He asked me if Darren Baron was black. I said he was kind of half-black and Rodge asked if we thought black pupils got beaten more often than white ones. Do you know, it had never occurred to me to wonder. But it was true. They did. Except that the Kellys got beaten more often than anyone else. But then there were more of them than anyone else. Rodge asked if there was a punishment book and where it was kept. We all knew that. In Hazlitt's office. Nat said it would be easy for him to nick it. To my surprise, Rodge thought this was a good idea, but he added that Nat should just take it along to the library and get it photocopied, then put it back before it was missed. What we needed was evidence. Josh and Nat agreed at once, but I said, evidence for what?

It turned out that Rodge's idea was we should try to get a magazine together. Well, it would be more like a fanzine really, only nothing to do with pop music or science fiction. It would be to do with pupil power and we could publish statistics on corporal punishment or whatever else our grievances were, and then distribute the 'zine throughout schools in London. Rodge had a typewriter and said he could easily run off a few hundred copies at the Poly on their paper without anyone finding out. Josh and Nat started ranting on about how they (we?) were going to blast the whole educational system to smithereens. Revolutionary heroes, that's how they saw themselves. As if they could organize a piss-up in a brewery, let alone a magazine. Rodge could, though. I knew that straight away. He knew what he was talking about, all right. In spite of myself, I had to admit that it was a terrific idea. All of a sudden I could see myself as Matilda Hughes, the fearless reporter, refusing to reveal the sources of her information and rallying all those ignorant shits at Fleet Valley (throughout London!) to think seriously about their pointless little lives, for once. This was what I'd been waiting for – probably all my life!

Rodge said he had to go to a meeting, so we all trooped out obediently. My mind was racing. Hadn't I always wanted to be a fighter against injustice? Josh and Nat were whooping and waving their fists and shouting, 'Pupil Power!' as we walked back across Clissold Park. Everyone stared at us. Some skinheads started throwing stones and calling us (well, Josh and Nat) bleeding poofters. I thought, here we go, there's going to be a punch-up. But the boys hardly seemed to notice that we were under attack. They just went on with their double-act. Nat: Bliss was it in that dawn to be alive! Josh: But to be young was shitting pissing heaven! So I supposed they must have learned something at school after all. Needless to say I didn't point this out. I was too busy wondering who would have disapproved of the other more: Rodge or Wordsworth.

Mum was sitting at the kitchen table, trying to do the *Guardian* crossword and listening to the six o'clock news programme at the same time. The very sight of her – all wan and worried and patient – was enough to bring me (and, I suspect, Josh) crashing down instantly. What's another word for obliging? she asked. When we couldn't think of one, she started to work out an anagram while I made some tea. Nat started telling her about the 'zine, which I thought was a bit off, because you never knew how she was going to react, and it was best to keep socks over boots if you had any doubts at all. But she listened properly. Which means she put down her pen and lit a cigarette. Ah, the power of the press, she sighed in that wistful voice she generally uses to moan over her lost youth. Then she asked where the money was going to come from. Nat said we didn't need money because the materials and resources were all *there* (where, he didn't say) and we were going to avail ourselves of them. She said, you mean, steal them? But she laughed, as if she liked the idea. Perhaps she'd have liked it less if it had come from me or Josh. Who can tell? I'll never be able to figure out what makes grown-ups tick, if I live to be a hundred.

X

Everything means something and the body is not an unthinking organism dedicated solely to the satisfaction of biological appetites. The body remembers; the body tries to forget. The body grows, flowers and withers, learning to recognize: this is and is not me. On public holidays the bereaved, the betrayed and all those grief-stricken by other sorts of loss, sit in their ruined gardens, letting the tears flow with the whisky to speak volumes of social analysis, volumes of philosophy. Yes, a tear is an intellectual thing. Who, at such times, can doubt the autonomy of individual consciousness? It feels pain, therefore it exists. I feel pain, therefore it exists. I have been conditioned to feel pain in certain circumstances and the sum of what I am exists in the quality of my pain. The locus of pain is me. Stimulated by memory, it circulates with the blood, each heartbeat keeping it freshly pulsing, every nerve impulse urging it on from synapse to synapse. Perpetuating itself, the body perpetuates pain. Can the skin contain so much? It must; it is the boundary.

It is Easter and yesterday Christ rose from the dead. Gentle Jesus, Our Lord. There was a crown of thorns on His sacred head, nails driven through His feel-of-primrose hands. His rib-cage strained in dubious battle with gravity. Those heavy-lidded eyes, half-shut, proclaimed the ecstasy of passion, which is suffering. Tears of blood, perfectly shaped, rolled, perfectly spaced, down his undistorted face and neck. Oh, but his mien was aristocratic. How those epicene features, the thin line of hair on the upper lip, invited sexual response while contriving to deny sexuality. Suffering is dignified, suffering is holy. It is not.

In class they discussed the crucifixion and the Headmistress (whose subject was Divinity) explained that the posture given to the divine body in most paintings was anatomically impossible. She said that certain organs would have been crushed, others misplaced or torn apart, engendering instant death. She spoke dispassionately and invited questions. Claudia felt sick. Christianity lay revealed in all its pornographic glory. Suffering can be contemplated objectively; suffering can be quantified and subjected to scientific laws. It cannot.

In the middle of the garden stands the purple buddleia, its dark fingers silhouetted against the sky and pointing downwards through the leaves, through the grass, to the dark earth beneath. Never mind the daffodils, brave yellow flags which Matilda planted one November afternoon under threat from Juno of being allotted an even more tedious task. All the spring flowers are white or yellow or mauve, like crocuses. Dorian planted some delicately striped ones below the apple trees at the far end of the garden and beyond the vegetable plot. Claudia planted the cauliflowers which grew tall and thin and – monstrously – without heads. The radishes and carrots too were thin and woody. Only Josh's tomatoes and Dorian's runner beans were successful. And the herb garden – which alone is still flourishing. Dorian planted it next to the rockery one Sunday afternoon when Claudia and Claire went to visit their father for his seventieth birthday. Dorian tended the herbs; she culled them; they all tasted them at meals around the dining-table. Wasn't that co-operation? Coexistence? Family life?

But Claudia, sitting upright on the wooden bench outside the french windows, can only see the buddleia. Her posture, for the whole length of her spine, is rigid, her legs tightly crossed. With one hand she holds a copy of Doris Lessing's *The Summer Before the Dark* balanced on her knee; the other holds a cigarette which she inhales deeply and rapidly. She is trying not to cry. But she must cry. This is an exercise in exorcism. She must sit here in the spring sunshine, surveying the garden which Dorian created and then abandoned. She must face and assess the reality of ruin. All the dead, deserted plants must be mourned along with their cultivator. *Was enstanden ist, das müss vergehen.* Only then can the patient, laborious work of reconstruction begin.

She hadn't intended to cook supper for so many people. As far as she was concerned, she and her flatmate, Beth, and Beth's boyfriend, Steve, would eat spaghetti bolognese and green salad at seven o'clock, after which Claudia had the proofs of the college magazine to correct. When three friends of Beth's dropped by, Claudia was irritated by this disruption and postponed the cooking until they should have the grace to leave. When Dorian dropped by (how sweetly unexpected!) she changed her mind and invited them all to supper, terrified as she was that he would leave with the others. Afterwards Beth and Steve went off to the cinema, taking their friends with them. Claudia was left with Dorian, her proofs and the dirty dishes. Reading the proof copy, Dorian was impressed by her interview with him. It was not as it had happened according to its own disordered sequence, but all the essentials were there. He hadn't realized that so much skill was involved in journalism. What he meant was that he hadn't realized the extent of her skill, her flair. He offered to do the washing up. Claudia demurred. Dorian insisted. Leave it. It won't take a moment. Why should you? Because I love you. Claudia smiled and said nothing although she thought her heart would surely stop. She spread the proofs on the table which Dorian had wiped clean for her. He did the dishes slowly and carefully, even washing the cutlery piece by piece instead of sloshing it around in a bunch as was her (and Beth's) invariable practice. That night they made love for the first time. And it was love. Wasn't it?

It is not the dead plants which are prompting Claudia's tears. It is the new growth of deciduous paler green inching its oblivious way at the ends of the tendrils of ivy and Russian vine. It is the unfolding leaves, the buds which will soon be blossom. My life began when my marriage ended. It is life itself.

Dorian's mother refused to sanction the marriage, so they had to wait until he was twenty-one. She couldn't forgive Claudia for being three years older than Dorian and muttered to him about the abduction of minors. What she really couldn't forgive was the theft of her son. She stood unsmiling throughout the ceremony at St

Pancras Register Office, dressed in powder-blue like a grimmer version of the Queen Mother. Ron and Claire acted as witnesses. Claudia's father refused the invitation because he had a migraine, so her mother came up from Cornwall alone and couldn't stop talking about what a terrible place London was: there was so much of it and it all looked the same. She meant terrifying rather than terrible, but she would never have admitted as much. Both the Farquharson parents believed that attack was the best form of defence, especially for the ego. Claudia wore a bronze corduroy suit, in which she now wouldn't be seen dead, but which she has, superstitiously enough, never thrown away. Straight-skirted, short-jacketed, it was new then. Her shoes were old and she had borrowed a blouse from Claire. But she didn't wear anything blue.

The hyacinths opening underneath the honeysuckle which climbs up the south-facing wall are the colour of fidelity. Their scent is as strong and as pure as faith. Blue is the colour of Our Lady. The Blessed Virgin Mary, Mother of God. Claudia put up her hand in class and asked, what does Immaculate Conception mean? The other children said, ooh, shocked. They were Catholics and knew that you shouldn't ask such (or, indeed, any) questions. But Claudia's parents, being non-Catholics, had never mentioned the Immaculate Conception, let alone instructed her that here was a mystery to be accepted as an Act of Divine Providence. The nun smiled her sweet, forgiving smile and shook her head. Afterwards she took Claudia aside and gave her a catechism, saying that when she had learned it by heart she would get a rosary of her very own. Claudia would stare hard and long at Our Lady's statue in chapel (except during Lent when she was shrouded in purple) trying to unfathom her mystery. She had that same patient, serene expression as the one cultivated by the nuns who were always telling Claudia, oh so gently, as they smoothed her brow, to stop frowning. Like Our Lord, Our Lady had a huge hole in her chest so as to display her outsize heart. See how she points to it with her tapering, translucent fingers. It shone, it bled. Ah, how it bled. As we women must bleed from our own poor wombs which have never received the Son of God. To bleed and bear is our lot. The sweetness of femininity is the sweetness of suffering.

Claudia grinds her cigarette stub beneath the heel of her green suede boot. She has decided: she is going to get pissed out of her mind. Isn't that what redundant middle-aged women are supposed to do: turn to the bottle? There should be quite a bit left in that bottle of whisky Ron gave Dorian for Christmas. Enough, at any rate, to take the edge off things. Enough, with any luck, to blur all the edges. Dorian has gone to Berlin with Ron and their manager, Frank Stein (commonly known as Frankenstein), to take a look at the amenities of a recording studio. Emma is paying an annual visit to her father in Leeds and has taken Matilda along for company. Josh has spent the whole weekend so far at Nat's. They are all doing as they please. It is only Claudia who doesn't know how to please herself, having lost the habit. They have all conspired to cast her in the conventional role of the wife and mother whose services are no longer required. All right, she will build her part and play it to the full. Oh alcohol, friend of the useless and rejected, here I come.

The bottle is about a third full, which should do nicely. Should she dilute it or drink it straight? The latter is more in keeping with her mood but, on reflection, she decides in favour of dilution as a means of prolonging the process. The crystal glasses and decanter were a wedding present from Dorian's mother who had, in turn, inherited them. Her visits are the only occasions on which they have been used. The last time was a year ago – last Easter. Claudia made a simnel cake decorated with marzipan eggs and they all sat in the garden, although it wasn't really warm enough, Dorian being keen to display his handiwork. He cut some golden thyme, some rue and a branch from the bay tree for his mother to take home to Purley. The children became bored with a conversation from which they were largely excluded, centring as it did on property, its upkeep and repair – and disappeared as soon as they had eaten their portions of cake. Only then did Dorian's mother see fit to mention the embarrassingly intimate subject of her health which was failing her organ by organ, muscle by muscle, faculty by faculty. Dorian said it was nonsense: she was going to last for ever. His mother smiled wanly. Claudia said that sixty-two wasn't considered old these days. Her mother-in-law looked wounded. Claudia confined herself to pouring tea and cutting cake. Afterwards Dorian thanked her, with a hug and a kiss, for being so patient.

The tray will not balance on the bench because the seat slopes backwards. Claudia places it on the stone flags of the patio beside the tub with the bay tree. She has a book to read. Although she has read it before she wants it fresh in her mind for the class next Thursday. This is the novel to which all the others have been leading, the novel which will coalesce all the disparate depictions of woman-as-heroine. Reading Kate Brown's story, the students will probably see their mothers rather than themselves. Because they have to see people they can recognize and care nothing for literary form, their criticisms are inevitably couched in terms of whether or not they like the characters, whether or not they find them convincing. They enjoy moral dilemmas, take sides, but persist in demanding solutions. All this Claudia has learned by trial and error. The breakthrough came with *Frost in May*. Having failed to set the book in context by citing other examples of the genre (which no one had read), she asked on impulse how many of the class were Catholics. To her surprise, half the class put up their hands, including Karima whom Claudia had assumed to be a Muslim. They spent the rest of the time discussing their childhood experiences, not only of Catholicism, but of the effect on them of all religious doctrine. The discussion was anecdotal, amusing, argumentative and, for the first time, evinced a need to understand subjective experience in terms other than its own. Claudia went home gratified. Perhaps she wasn't such a hopeless teacher after all. And certainly she now knew all her students better than she could otherwise have hoped.

She doesn't know if she can bear to reread the account of Kate's sojourn in a village in the Spanish interior. She was so stunned, so shocked by it the first time round. Only frivolous or undemanding books should be read on holiday. The Hugheses had rented a villa, complete with maid and swimming-pool, in the Algarve. The whole stretch of coast seemed devoted to the pursuit of pleasure, of sun-worship. Eating, drinking, swimming, sightseeing. All these were novel and absorbing. But Claudia was eventually incapable of lying by pool or sea for hours on end doing nothing. And so she read. She spoke rarely or absently to Dorian and the children, surrendering herself to words as she surrendered to scenery, to architecture, listening, listening so as to catch the faintest murmur from the mysterious otherwhere, worlds upon worlds of it as there was. For the rest of their stay she couldn't rid herself of those images of lives so unimaginably and unchangingly wretched which she knew to exist there at the heart of the Iberian Peninsula. Unimaginably. It was a word she couldn't accept. Her imagination refused to be defeated. And, in doing so, it coloured all actions, all objects, outside the pages of the book with its own clarity of chiaroscuro. Now she hesitates, reluctant to take the same impact again. But she is even more reluctant to face the possible discovery that the impact has become blunted.

Five years ago. The last family holiday – last, in both senses of the word. Josh was eleven, Matilda nine. There are photographs somewhere. There is a whole trunk full of photographs. My little ones when little, my babies, my darlings. In London, in Cornwall, in Edinburgh, in New York. In prams, on trains, exploring ruined castles and autumnal woods. Laughing, crying, self-conscious, bored or indifferent. I am not alone, oh no, I have you still. Claudia has to resist the impulse to go and explore the trunk on the landing outside the bedroom. She will only get sentimental, won't be able to stop the fond maternal tears. The photographs will keep, will keep till she's old and has nothing but the past to contemplate, nowhere but the past to go. She feels a sudden surprised rush of pity for Dorian, who can take it for granted that his children are separate and separable beings; that kids will go their own way whatever you say and there is no point in fussing; that there are no ties of flesh which are indissoluble. Truly, not to care is to be free. Not to love is to be free. Dorian may or may not have reckoned the price of his liberty but it is likely that he has paid it unknowingly and, as is his wont, profligately. What will he do, what can he do, on the day of reckoning?

And yet it is she who has severed the tie of flesh between herself and Dorian. Of course it has been fraying thinner and thinner for years, but all the same she is surprised to find how tenuous it has become. That she should be the one to make the final cut! She can't believe that this is what she has done. She didn't want to end the marriage, just to change the terms of the contract. It should have been possible. It might still be possible. Adapt and survive. Isn't that a law of nature? What is incapable of adaptation condemns itself to extinction. She is not asking so much of Dorian, after all. To trust her enough to be honest with her. Nothing more. And yet this seems to be the very thing he is incapable of doing. She can't understand why.

She is, she recognizes, the sort of person who will always attempt to answer a question, even if it is only with another question. And with what else, indeed, can the most searching questions be answered? The structure of her beliefs, if such it can be called, consists of a progression of questions, each beginning, what is it to be . . .? She has thought that everyone else operated in much the same fashion; that everyone else asked similar questions, wanted to know the meaning of their own and others' behaviour. But it seems that the need to understand is not as widespread as she has supposed. Some people do not want to know, do not want to understand themselves or those around them, prefer not to see or to speak clearly. Why not? The choice is deliberate and must be supposed to have its advantages. Has Dorian never asked himself what it is to be a husband or a father? Has he never asked himself what it is to be a person in whom others can believe on any level other than that of the hyped image? Claudia has to answer herself coldly, uncomfortably, that it seems not. He has assumed that he can fulfil each of those roles simply by putting them on ready-made. He has not cut out the pattern, neither has he sewn the seams: that is the sort of work which can be left to others.

The couple next door are discussing the conversion of their house. They are standing in their garden showing each other where the back elevation needs repointing and agreeing on the necessity to replace all metal pipes with plastic ones. Dorian and the man across the street have objected to the plans for a roof extension: it will spoil the look of the terrace. Claudia can't see the virtue of uniformity but hasn't bothered to argue with her husband. The couple are now discussing the possibility of employing another architect to draw up revised plans. It will be expensive but seems necessary. And besides, he wants a studio window at the back. It will be worth it in the end. Listening, Claudia is moved to compassion for their innocence.

She tries to think of what it was she admired about Dorian. The ease with which he moved through life: the easy charm, the easy success; the easy acceptance of wealth, fame and adulation. Oh, he provided her with her perfect counterpoint. But wasn't it all too easy? There is a thin line between complement and antithesis, an even thinner one between antithesis and antagonism. Dorian's acceptance of the fall from success was not easy. Whereas to Claudia it seemed inevitable, to him it was an unwarranted calamity and, even harder to bear, a failure for which he wasn't prepared to accept any responsibility. Yet, it is pitiful, such a circumstance. To be young is valuable, yes, but its value lies most surely in its brevity: if the commodity were easily and permanently available it would cease to be precious. Eternal youth does not bear contemplation. To be successful is valuable, yes, but not unless that success can be defined according to your own terms. If it depends for its definition on the hard-sell tactics of entrepreneurs, on the adulation of a hard-sold and often hysterical section of the population known as the youth market, it cannot have any lasting value. But then, perhaps, instant value is enough – and all that can be expected. It isn't, though, is it? Human beings last, growing from youth to age, and that sort of success does not: that is the problem. If Dorian wants to be eternally young, eternally at the peak of universal acclaim, and eternally free of the responsibilities of adulthood, then he is doomed. Doomed to disillusion, certainly, but to something worse as well. He is doomed to meaninglessness.

Yes, it is pitiful. Claudia must weep for him. In doing so she weeps also for herself because she has been deprived of meaning. Without entering into a disquisition with herself upon the meaning of meaning, she knows intuitively that it must follow the graph of a human life. Meaning too is the recognition of necessity, but it is more. Meaning is seizing upon that necessity, analysing it, expanding it, improvising on it, and showing it to itself, not as a mirror image but as a translation into something approaching a work of art. To live with it is a moral duty, difficult. To live without it is to assume robotic consciousness, to act upon the unthinking belief that the universe exists to be exploited for gain, and to condone the violations of both community and psyche committed in the name of such a belief as innate to human nature and therefore amoral and unalterable. Meaning knows by learning what is capable of change and what is not. Meaning is bearing and rearing, flowering and fading. But it is also destroying and re-creating, always aware that actions have consequences. It is truth.

How our bodies ache with our children's pain: the cord is never cut quite cleanly. Our bodies don't forget. Josh was sixteen in October, during the week that he, Matilda and Claudia spent in Scotland with Dorian who was on tour in *The Italian Straw Hat*. The three of them arrived in Edinburgh the day before the birthday, Claudia with the Led Zeppelin double album (Josh still being into Heavy Metal then) gift-wrapped and hidden away in her luggage. When she showed it to Dorian, he admitted that he'd forgotten Josh's birthday. At first she was hurt, both for Josh and herself: what, after all, had they both been going through fifteen years before? But Dorian persuaded her that she was attaching too much importance to his omission: he had been so busy; he would get something tomorrow; Josh would understand. Oh yes, Josh would understand. Josh would understand that his father had, once again, been too busy to think of him. What he wouldn't understand was that his father had, once again, been too busy carrying on with a girl, scarcely older than Josh himself, to acknowledge his fatherhood. For Dorian's body there was nothing to remember and therefore nothing to forget. His body chose to disregard meaning. It lied and therefore betrayed.

Who are the betrayed? Are they to be seen in Tottenham Court Road outside the Dominion, waiting to see *Close Encounters*, waiting to be told that they are not alone? Thou knowst 'tis common. That's what the treacherous Gertrude told her son. Human beings are dispensable, Hamlet dear; one of them dies, as we all must, and is replaced; that's life; what are you making such a fuss about? Mother, dear mother, can't you tell the difference between Hyperion and a satyr? Husband, dear husband, can't you tell the difference between a wife who has loved you for so long, bearing your children in love, and any little Page Three substitute who catches your fancy? Claudia could comfort herself, like many another betrayed wife before her, by persuading herself that Dorian can tell the difference. But she knows better than that. Dorian imagines that he is in love with these women and then, just as hotly, repudiates them. If one woman can be repudiated, then so can another. It is not that he has not repudiated Claudia; it is that his repudiation of her takes a different and perhaps more destructive form. What he does is to reduce her to non-womanhood, neuters her. He reduces and at the same time elevates her to the status of the mother: a desexed, authoritarian being, against whom he is bound to rebel, by whom he is bound to be forgiven.

But I'm not that. I'm not like that. I refuse to be. *Non serviam.* Claudia refills her glass and drinks the whisky in absent-minded mouthfuls without benefit of water. She is sitting so still and taut that a sparrow can alight with impunity on the tin tray to ruffle itself in the spilled liquid. One pigeon chases another away from its nest in the lime-tree at the bottom of the next-door garden. The expelled bird squawks and wheels, its feathers falling. The lime tree branches judder, buds and scarcely formed leaves scattering like confetti on the laughing couple beneath. They speculate together about the roosting bird and the predator. Is this a marital squabble? Or the defence of territory, the defence of the young? Their names are Ian and Anne. They are both in their early thirties. (He works at a printing co-operative, she is a mature student, reading for a degree in the social sciences.) Anne and Ian.

Dorian's career is being Dorian Grey. Claudia's career is being wife to Dorian Grey and mother to their children, Joshua and Matilda. It is not being mother to Dorian. He has one of them already and she should be more than enough for anyone. Wife. Mate. Partner. Bride. To be deprived of that career is tantamount to being deprived of her preciously cultivated identity and consigned to oblivion. Baby, it's cold outside. Claudia shivers despite the Scotch fire in her belly, tingeing her skin. Baby, it's gonna be cold for my babies outside. Should she not swallow her pride (wretched, retching phrase) and keep the marriage going for their sakes? She should act as Dorian acts. She too can have affairs. And lie about them? I can't. She is neither Dorian nor his female counterpart. *Non serviam.* But why not? Why not pretend? I can't. Not even for your children, Claudia? I can't. After all, they do need a father. No, I can't.

In December, a week after the end of term, Dorian insisted that Josh cut short his expatiating statement on the nature of the present-day pop scene and go to bed so that he wouldn't be late for school the next day. Josh was startled at this mistake. He was even more startled to hear his father lecture him on his presumption in dismissing the heroes of the sixties as boring old farts. Josh was making a genuine point: that punk music was about his life and the life of his friends and the manifestation of a grass-roots movement, before middle-class management had got its greedy little mitts on it. It spoke directly to him, unlike the music of the sixties, whose performers were more interested in the trappings of success than they were in communicating with the people who bought their records. This is the sort of daily murder that every father, and indeed mother, of adolescents has to suffer. When Josh had gone to bed, his prejudices confirmed by his father's intransigence, Claudia said as much to Dorian. But Dorian refused to admit that he had been harsh with Josh. Why, he asked, did he have to take shit like that from his own son? She failed to convince him that what Josh believed was at least as important as what he himself believed.

In December Claudia went to buy a Christmas present for Dorian. It was raining when she went to Bloomsbury to choose a waistcoat at the Mexican shop. When her umbrella turned inside out as she waited to cross the road opposite Dillon's bookshop, she smoothed the disordered spokes and told them, just aloud: there is no love for him in my heart. But she blamed herself. It couldn't be Dorian's fault. The deadness of feeling was due to depression. And she was a depressive. Dr Jaffa had said so. Your husband is a very nice man. Dr Jaffa had treated her, prescribing anti-depressants which she had duly swallowed for seven years. Perhaps she should never have stopped taking them. It – the Black Dog – was dogging her again. It was rearing on its hind legs, ravening, slavering towards her throat. Well, she knew what to do about it, didn't she? Swallow, swallow, swallow. Take your medicine like a man. Like a *what*? Take it, just take it and don't ask any questions. It's easier.

And of course it was easier than seeing beyond the Black Dog. When your life is under immediate threat, all you can feel is the breath in your face, the spittle spraying into your mouth. You don't pause to wonder who is mastering the beast, whose hand is on the leash. During the panto season there wasn't one night when Dorian came home before one o'clock, although the curtain came down at ten. Often it was nearer four o'clock. He always had some excuse: someone he hadn't seen for years had turned up at the theatre and invited him home for a drink; a film producer had insisted on taking him to dinner and then on to a nightclub; a member of the cast had a birthday party and it would have been construed as snootiness on the part of Dorian, the star, not to have attended.

And always Claudia accepted his excuses, however reluctantly. Not once did she rebuke him, shout at him, tell him she didn't believe him. What a fool she has been! Why didn't she challenge him? Once she said meditatively that she saw so little of him, he could have another wife, other children and allot the same amount of time to them, for all she would know about it. This was as far as she could go towards voicing her doubts. Morbidly jealous himself, Dorian always bridled at the slightest hint of doubt, telling her how unreasonable she was being, somehow making her feel small and dirty. But why should she have allowed him to put her off? Why didn't she trust her intuition? The supposition falls into place with a sickening thud of awareness that her intuition has probably always been right – although she, the rational, tolerant wife has never paused to listen to it properly. On the contrary, she has smothered its insistent cries with all the assiduous pragmatism of a baby-farmer.

I just wanted to get shot of her. That was a phrase apprehensible to her intuitive grasp. That was what Dorian said about Marina Selby, the girl in *The Italian Straw Hat*. When they were on tour together, all right, he was lonely. (And Claudia said, do you think I never feel lonely?) But when they returned to London and he started rehearsing the panto, she pursued him. (And Claudia said, do you think I have never been pursued?) She said she couldn't live without him, and he felt sorry for her, and all right, he wasn't averse. (And Claudia said, do you think I have always been averse?) Yes, he did tell her that he loved her, because at the time he believed it, because at the time he got carried away, needed to be carried away. (And Claudia said, did it never occur to him that she too needed to be carried away?) Every time he thought about Claudia and the children, he thought what a monster he was, so the subject was painfully avoided by himself and Marina. (And Claudia said, how convenient!) He kept trying to break it off, but Marina wouldn't let him, and now felt he'd treated her badly. (And Claudia said, how about how badly you've treated me?)

Dorian smiled through his tears at his waiting wife as he opened the bedroom door. She was lying on her back, her eyes wide and concentrated on the ceiling rather than on him. He asked, how are you? Even in his suffering, she must see, he was giving pride of place to her feelings. At first all Claudia could see was the tenderness in his smile and she wavered, rebuking herself for her own selfishness. But when she saw the tears she guessed that the tenderness was not for her, but had been aroused by a vivid appreciation of his own romantic predicament: the young girl so nobly renounced in order to satisfy the demands of convention, the mundane demands personified by a wife approaching middle age and two adolescent children. His duty done, he was waiting to be congratulated, to be comforted for its painful execution. Claudia couldn't believe his callousness in making such an entrance, crying over the loss of some other woman whom he had known for perhaps five months. Dorian couldn't believe her callousness in thinking only of herself at such a juncture. Marina had lost, and Claudia should have shown some compassion for the loser. I just wanted to get shot of her. So what are the tears for? To impress me? Well, I'm not impressed: the stupid little scrubber has only got what's coming to her. Dorian's tears dried into anger. And now are you satisfied? Oh, sure, sure – I've only got what was coming to me too. What about me? Fuck you. Fuck you too.

The level of whisky in the bottle is dropping at what should be an alarming rate. But it is not alarming: it is exhilarating. The fronds of ivy around the french window are stirring, feeling their blind, weightless way towards her solidity. A solitary bee explores the whisky stain on the open pages of her book, then buzzes merrily away. The grasses, overgrown and unheeded, whisper together. She can watch, she can listen: she will be tolerated. In the paradisal dream, she lies under the spatulate green leaves, her arms around the tiger's neck, while he purrs, purrs, lazily flicking his tail. And the little creatures, many-legged, pick their fastidious way over bestial fur and human skin. Ah, in the dream there is no mistrust and species shall lie down in peace with species. Fruits will reach themselves into their paws and hands. Claws will be sheathed, and teeth bared only to run with the sweetness of scented juices. And then I wake up. And then the day reverberates with what might have been, sustained and yet shadowed by it. No matter what happens to us, no matter how much we are abused, still in the unconscious paradise persists.

The edges are getting nicely blurry now. Ian is stirring a mug of tea and asking Anne if she has put sugar in it. The buddleia, viewed through tears, points less decisively downwards, wavers from side to side like the rest of the garden. This is less real than a dream. This is a picture on a screen with the horizontal hold gone. Neither was there a hint of paradise in last night's dream. On the contrary, it issued an invitation which led straight to hell.

She thought she wasn't dreaming and could feel Dorian in the bed beside her. It was very physical – the warmth and weight of his body. She turned to him, his arms were round her, and he said, yes, before you ask, I love you. Then it seemed to her that the embrace was real and the rest had all been some hideous nightmare. She felt so safe and so loved. And yet she didn't quite believe it. She asked him, are you real or are you a dream? If you're a dream, you must go away again. Otherwise, it's too cruel. And he answered, I am a dream. Until then it had been dark, but now it was light and he was sitting up. Now she could see his face, the face of a stranger. At first she thought that, with the beard and flowing locks, it must be that of Jesus Christ, but when she saw the snub nose and the blue eyes, she knew that this person was only an actor playing the part of Christ. He then said, when you wake up, you will sing a little song.

At that moment the door opened and the children came into the bedroom. They were little children, and Josh wasn't taller than her, as he was in real life. When she looked more closely she could see that they weren't children, her children, at all, but wizened old men dressed as choirboys and with knowing looks on their faces. Each of them was carrying a quantity of white garments of some religious significance. Or were they shrouds? And had they come to bury her? Almost at once she woke up, as she thought, to find all of them vanished. The bed was covered in cat litter. There was also a packet of Nymph razor blades – for ladies' razors, so she knew they were for her. But the blades were about six times their normal size. The top one in the pack had been unwrapped and lay there, unused, temptingly . . .

Then she really did wake up. But there was no little song to be sung. *O glaube, mein herz, O glaube*. I said to my soul, be still and wait without hope. *Dein ist, ja, dien, was du gesehnt*. For hope would be hope for the wrong thing. Be still. It means, remain motionless. *Be* still. It means, continue to exist. Why? The canon 'gainst self-slaughter. Thou Lord seest me. Just suppose it's true. Just suppose she is mistaken, has failed to read her situation, her very life, aright. Perhaps where she has seen meaning and purpose, or sought to find them, there has in reality been randomness, chaos, matter colliding with matter at the whim of an arbitrary God against whom the individual consciousness doesn't stand a chance? What the hammer? What the chain? To doubt your own doubt is to fall into a pit of snakes, but curving bend after bend, like Alice down the rabbit-hole. And at the bottom, the razor blade says, use me; it's quicker and cleaner. Help the poor forked animal out of its agony.

Gethsemane in Hackney, Claudia? It just isn't on. Why not in Hackney as well as anywhere else? My pain is as real as anyone else's and I refuse to deny it. I feel pain, therefore I am.

Remember? I refuse to diminish the extent of my suffering and confusion in order to satisfy the demands of good taste. By such circuitous and casuistric paths is the self, the true self, deceived and appeased. For in truth we cannot love those who reject and betray us, unless we also reject and betray ourselves. The child of unloving parents knows this and cannot bear to know it: unloving parents are parents still and better than none at all. Once we accept the rejector's or betrayer's estimation of ourselves, we sacrifice self-knowledge to a life of easy or uneasy hypocrisy, with no questions asked. Until the true self, battered for so long and catching some intimation of what it is or might have been, wreaks an often terrible vengeance on that second betrayer. Or dies.

The bottle is empty and there is only one cigarette left in the packet. Claudia has smoked the other nineteen almost without pause. She cannot remember when she last ate, but it must have been with Matilda. They had a take-away Chinese together before Matilda left to spend the night with Emma, so as to make an early start for Leeds in the morning. What has Claudia eaten since? A bottle of valium. Her clothes don't fit her any more and her wedding ring drops off her finger every time she undresses. Perhaps now is the time to give up wearing it. *Das müss vergehen*. Perhaps, perhaps. If only she knew what to do. If only there were someone to advise her. But it has always been Dorian who has advised her in times of indecision. It is he who has called the Black Dog to heel. Of course. It was his animal.

All she has ever asked of him is that he should not lie to her. Has that been too much to ask? Why should he need to lie to her? What makes a man want a dupe for a wife? He said he lied in order not to hurt her, but she knows he has lied in order not to hurt himself, in order not to lose her. He wants her, the children, and a secret life. This is what he asks of her: that he should be allowed his secret life. That he should have everything; not to have to make choices; to have all the sweets in the shop window, all the choccies, soft- and hard-centred, in the box. And to his naughty-boy greed she must sacrifice her moral universe. Why the hell should she? The crux of the matter is that she rejects the role of deceived and deserted wife as one unsuitable to her talents. It is an insult to her intelligence. And more: it is an insult to her integrity.

A fly is crawling on her neck, the paperback has fallen from her lap, and the phone is ringing. Claudia has fallen asleep sitting straight and upright on the bench. The phone is ringing. Let it be Sonia. Or Claire. When an unfamiliar voice asks for Mrs Hughes, she almost puts the receiver down again. But what can shock or hurt her now? Now she knows all there is to know. Emma's stepmother is trying to explain that Matilda is on her way home. Or, at least, this is what the stepmother hopes. She reads the note Matilda left: thank you for everything, but I must go home because my mother is ill, and I think she needs me. Is Claudia ill? Claudia tries to explain what she has read into the note: that Matilda needs her. The stepmother, who has spoken briskly, now sounds doubtful. It is plain that she thinks Matilda to be an ungrateful little liar. Claudia is diplomatic, reassuring: she will call back when Matilda arrives.

Meanwhile she must wash her face, lie down with teabags on her eyes to reduce the swelling, sober up. Black coffee. Perhaps even something to eat. Back to normal, to motherhood, to self-control. When the phone rings again she is trying to eat an apple and a lump of cheese.

'Claudia? How are you, girl?'

'Oh, Chaz, hullo.'

'What you doing with yourself?'

'Waiting for Matilda to come home from Leeds.'

'How about coming out for a little drinkie-poo with yours truly?'

'I can't, she'll expect me to be here.'

'Well, I'll pop over with a bottle of champers, then, and wait with you. I haven't seen Matilda for years.' And before Claudia can demur with any conviction, he says decisively, 'See you in about an hour, then.'

XI

Leeds was shit. The whole Easter holidays were shit, but Leeds was the shittiest bit. Who would have thought that Emma would have such a nurd for a father? I mean, her Mum's all right. Admittedly she's not around very much (no bad thing?) but when she is, she at least listens to what Emma has to say and, considering her age, she's surprisingly street-wise. But, Jesus H. Christ, you should have seen her Dad! More to the point, you should have heard him. He's a solicitor and looks like one – never a hair out of place – not that he's got many. Never use one word when half a dozen will do. That's his motto. As for the step-Mum – a twittering little blob of cotton-wool agreeing with everything he said. Yes, Henry. No, Henry. Your father's quite right, Emma. I bet if he hit her (which he wouldn't, of course) she'd say, I'm sorry, Henry. She used to be his secretary.

Breakfast was at eight-thirty sharp (yes, in the holidays!) and if you weren't there, you didn't get any. It was all proper china and cups and saucers and bacon and eggs. The Dad read bits of *The Times* to us, especially the Law Reports. We were supposed to make intelligent comments. When I asked him when the law was going to make up its mind about what an adult was, he said, whatever do you mean, young lady? So I explained that when you were fourteen you had to pay full fare on buses and trains, but you weren't allowed into X-films. You could get married when you were sixteen, but you couldn't vote or go into a pub till you were eighteen. He smiled in his patronizing sort of way and said, oh well, the law does have its minor vagaries, you know. And that's all he would say. I could tell he thought I was just another minor vagary.

We had to say what we intended to do with ourselves for the rest of the day. Of course we never *intended* anything, but Emma was good at inventing schedules to satisfy the most eager culture-vulture. Not that there was much culture to be found. Or much anything else. Emma said she knew where some punks lived, so we took a bus to the other side of town, only to find the house all boarded up and a bunch of black kids sitting on the steps, stoned out of their minds and pretending they'd never heard of Punk. They kept mimicking the way we talked, and of course you can't say anything to blacks because they immediately accuse you of being a racist. So we went into the city centre and trudged round the record shops looking for punks. We never found any. Sodding depressing, it was. Everyone was still into Heavy Metal, years behind the times. Emma said what they needed was a bit of consciousness-raising.

I thought the North was where it was all supposed to be happening. Glorious working-class warmth and all that crap. Bollocks! They're all a right load of wallies. I thought Punk was supposed to be a grass-roots movement, invented by us for us. We have to watch it in London because now that the boring old farts at the *Melody Maker* etc. have actually deigned to acknowledge its existence, they're starting to trendify it for the middle classes. After all, it's already started with Zuzu Rakoff (who the fuck does she think she is?) selling silk dresses tied up with gold safety pins for rich twits who shop at Harrods. Can't those shitting idiots understand that Punk is about being young and working-class and oppressed, and not just another fab craze for the middle-aged bourgeoisie? Only thing being, the young oppressed working class of Leeds never even seemed to have heard of it! Having so many illusions shattered in one short week was too much for my sensitive young soul. My expectations of a nationwide Punk network were all blown to buggery. But Emma said what the sod else could you expect from a bunch of peasants?

I didn't even tell her I was going home. I knew she'd just try to persuade me to stay because she didn't want to be alone with her Dad and step-Mum. Not that I could blame her for that. But she didn't have to stay any more than what I did. She could have come and stayed with me, seeing as how her Mum and little brother had gone away. But she said no, she'd promised her Mum, and besides Josh gave her the pip. So that was that. When they were all going off to visit some auntie or other on Easter Monday, I said (whisper, whisper) I had my period and wanted to lie down. The rest was easy. I wrote a note saying I'd been called away by my Mum's sudden illness and took a taxi to the station. I had plenty of pocket money left because there was nothing except bus fares and sweets to spend it on. And of course I had my return ticket which Mum had paid for in advance with her credit card before it ran out at the end of April when Dad could well refuse to renew it.

I had ages to wait at the station so I went into Menzies and read my horoscope in all the glossy mags like *Harper's* and *Cosmopolitan*. I'm Leo and they're always telling me how bright and sunny I am, which gets on my wick. This time they said I was going to have partnership or financial or emotional problems (it varied) but that my usual optimism would see me through. I ask you. My usual optimism wouldn't see me through a paper bag. But one of them (can't remember which) promised a romantic encounter around the middle of the month. That'll be the day. I bought a packet of Polos and a Peanuts book instead.

The train seemed to be full of screaming babies, harassed Mums, old-age pensioners and youths with rucksacks and glowing cheeks. Everybody stared at my hair, of course, and there was some subdued jeering, but no one said anything to my face. They wouldn't dare. I ignored them all, in any case, and spent most of the time staring out of the window, pretending to be preoccupied with some secret sorrow. You know, I half-convinced myself that I really was rushing home to Mum's sickbed. When the guard told me to cheer up, it may never happen, as he punched my ticket, I tried to make my eyes well with tears. But it was no good. He just thought I was sulking, and said to the woman next to me, I don't know what's the matter with kids today, I'm sure – not a please or a thank you between the lot of them. I despised him, the self-righteous git. Even I knew he should have said *among*, not *between*.

Blimey O'Riley, was I glad to see Kings Cross Station. It was like a return to civilization after a long sojourn in the wilderness. Even waiting for the 73 (twenty minutes) didn't piss me off as usual. I knew Mum hadn't gone away anywhere (she never does) but I kept worrying that she might be out when I got back. I don't know why. I mean, I don't know why I was worrying. I had my own key and could cook my own food (always supposing there was any) but somehow I didn't like the idea of letting myself into an empty house and not knowing where anyone was. Even the thought of Josh sitting slumped in front of the telly picking his nose and farting in his usual disgusting manner cheered me up a little. Which only goes to show the Godawful state I must have been in.

Ever since our visit to Rodge he'd been slightly less unbearable than usual. When Nat said in front of him how Rodge had said I was remarkably intelligent (ha, ha!) he didn't even flinch. Somehow or other, our plans for the magazine never quite seemed to get off the ground (who would have thought it?) and had to be postponed to next term. If Josh and Nat and Slime (whose idea was it that *he* should be involved?) hadn't spent so much time arguing over who was going to do what, we might have got somewhere. Entirely typical of the male of the species! Each one just had to prove (prove? that's a pissing laugh) that he knew better than anyone else. If you ask me, Rodge was patient with them far beyond the demands of normal humanity. Me and him – we could have had the whole thing wrapped up and in circulation by the end of term. The trouble with the boys was they never did what they said they would – apart from Nat getting photocopies from the Punishment Book.

Seeing as how it was Hazlitt's bright idea that I should be class rep (keep her out of mischief?) it was down to me to raise the matter of pupil representation on the Board of Governors at the next School Council. Jesus H. Christ, was I puking nervous? Was I? I was shaking so much I could hardly stand up, and I didn't know what the fuck to do with my hands. Then I thought I'd gone and lost my sodding voice. When I finished there was absolute silence. I began to wonder if I'd really spoken at all or just dreamed it, like you dream you're screaming and you wonder why nobody's heard you, and all the time you haven't uttered a sound. Then Fairfax said that was indeed a radical suggestion and it would have to be put to the whole board, but meanwhile what did anybody else think? Not much, it seemed. Of course I didn't expect the staff to agree with me. And they didn't. Venables shook his head and Hazlitt said it was quite out of the question and that I was under the influence of Trotskyist troublemakers. That last bit got everybody supporting him, even the other class reps – except for Ben Cobbing, whose Dad once got chucked out of the Communist Part for saying Stalin was a shit, or words to that effect, and nobody ever took any notice of *him*. I couldn't bleeding well believe it, just couldn't believe my burning little ears. I felt like a pariah. The only thing that made it worthwhile was Rodge telling me that now I'd lost my political virginity.

Next day Fairfax asked to see me. Naturally I thought she was going to bawl me out, or even suspend me, but she turned out to be all sugary-sweet and asked if anybody had been trying to influence me. Of course I pretended not to know what she was talking about. All I could think, sitting there opposite her and muttering yes, miss, no, miss, with my eyes downcast so as I could see under the desk, was what enormous feet she had. She then asked me if I knew what the letters IMG stood for. That was easy. International Marxist Group, I said brightly. She seemed to brighten up too. Did I know what SWP stood for? Socialist Workers' Party. And WRP? Workers' Revolutionary Party. I thought I'd done rather well, but she looked suddenly all serious and pious. She wanted me to listen very carefully to what she had to say. Those organizations we'd been discussing (discussing?) were dedicated to the violent overthrow of society. I said I knew that. She said, doesn't it perturb you, Matilda? I said, not really. She asked if I wanted to see blood flowing in the streets. I said (Christ knows how I found the bottle) it depended whose blood it was. She pushed her chair back and said, I see, in a grim sort of voice. But of course she didn't see at all. The next thing was, I shall have to have a word with your parents. Something prompted me to say, you can't have a word with my Dad – he's pissed off. Well, blow me to buggery, if she didn't do a complete turnaround. Oh my dear, said she, I'm so sorry. Let's forget the whole business, said she, until next term when things might have simmered down a bit. I mean, I didn't have the faintest idea what she was talking about, but it seemed politic (oops!) to agree.

When I saw the lights on in the kitchen and the shutters closed, I knew there was a good chance that Mum was in. Josh would never have bothered to close the shutters. But of course Mum could have closed them and then gone out. As I opened the front door I could hear this strange voice – all urgent and cockney – and Mum shrieking with laughter. Oh no, I thought, not another sodding lover! How many did that make? I didn't want to know, although Nat kept a list. He said he had proof that flash Brendan with the tight jeans was Mum's lover. But Brendan was the psychiatric social worker who was writing a report on Josh to present to the school. I told Nat to mind his own fucking beeswax. Just because he's always fighting with *his* Mum's lover, there's no need for him to go on about *my* Mum as if she was exactly the same. So I was quite relieved really to find Chaz sitting there at the table with Mum. I mean, I didn't know who he was, but I knew I'd seen him somewhere before with Dad. And if he was a friend of Dad's he couldn't be Mum's lover, could he? So I said hullo, all cheerful, and asked if I could join in the celebration. Well, there was this bottle of champagne sitting there between them and another full one and another empty one. I knew they were totally pissed by their glazed eyes, so I thought it was worth the risk.

And it was. Mum hardly asked me any questions, said what about a kiss, and asked was I hungry. Chaz said why didn't we all go out somewhere to eat. Mum said everywhere was shut. Chaz said no, it wasn't. Mum said only expensive places were open at that time of the night. Chaz said, so, he had plenty of cash and three credit cards besides. I said the Chinese take-away was still open when I'd passed it, and they both seemed to think that this was hysterical. So I said, the kebab place is open too. This apparently was even funnier. Then Chaz started asking me if I remembered going to his caravan at Eastbourne and how we'd built a sandcastle and Josh had put his plastic soldiers all over it. He kept calling me Tilly, said that's what I used to be called. Silly Tilly. I pretended not to remember. He kept looking at me and saying he couldn't believe it. I can't believe it, Claud. I just can't believe it, girl! And Mum smirked and looked all sentimental. Fanfuckingtastic, said Chaz. (And apologized to me for his language.) Exfuckingcruciating, I thought.

And, believe it or not, it got muchfuckingworse. For a start, he was flashing his money about. Two tenners. That's what he thought a Chinese meal for three would cost! He gave them to me and said I could exercise my ingenuity or ingeniousness or whatever it was called in planning a menu of my own choice. I actually had the bread in my hot little hand but Mum said, don't be ridiculous, Chaz, it won't even come to half that. And she snatched one of the notes away from me and gave it back to him. I could have hit her, I mean, what difference would it have made to Chaz? Short on pragmatics, my Mum, and long on principles. That's what Rodge said when I told him about it.

Chaz said he'd walk me round to the Chinese, and Mum said *she* would. They started arguing. I said I'd go on my own. They they started arguing with me. I said if I couldn't go on my own I wasn't going to go at all. That silenced them. I got prawns with peppers in black bean sauce for Mum (because that's what she always has), sweet and sour pork for Chaz (because I reckoned he'd be conventional) and chicken chow mein for me (because I'm even more conventional). What with rice and prawn crackers and spring rolls I hardly had any change. Mum had laid the table with Chinese bowls and chopsticks and shoyu and chilli sauce. And Chaz had poured me a glass of champagne. He said he didn't know how to use chopsticks, and Mum said, shame on you, coming from the East End. Matilda will show you, she said. He was hopeless. Mum handed out bright-red napkins from a Sainsbury's pack. Chaz poured more champagne and ate with a Chinese spoon. He kept telling me not to worry about nothing, I was a good girl, as good as gold. I felt like telling him I was a revolutionary, dedicated to the violent overthrow of society, but instead I smiled and held my peace. The Duke of Edinburgh had been going on about how poor the royal family were, so at Chaz's local they'd got up a collection and sent him £550. Can you believe it? No, neither could I.

Chaz kept trying to make me laugh. After a couple of glasses of champagne that wasn't too difficult. Mum laughed a lot too and talked a lot, getting manic, like she always does when she's pissed. It was after midnight when Josh and Nat came in. Nat took one look at the remains of food and drink on the table and said, I see, I see, like he suspected us of having some kind of orgy. But I could tell he felt left out. Not so with Josh who blushed his usual mottled colour and said nothing. When Chaz asked them if they wanted any food, Josh said the Chinese was shut and he wasn't hungry anyway. They wouldn't sit down with us but slunk off to Josh's room – sulking, no doubt.

A few minutes later Nat stuck his head round the door and beckoned to me. I was in the middle of asking Chaz how the working class could possibly support the royal family against their own interests, so I told him to fuck off. Chaz said, Matilda, a nice girl like you! Mum said, I'm so used to it I just don't notice any more. Chaz said, I hate to hear a woman swear. Nat groaned in the doorway. Chaz said, got anything to say, mate? Nat said, only to Matilda. I groaned and followed him upstairs to Josh's room. It turned out he didn't have a sodding thing to say. He just wanted to know what was going on between Mum and Chaz and why I wasn't in Leeds. I didn't answer him, even when he tried to bribe me by saying didn't I want to hear the latest about Slime. I knew he'd tell me anyway. Josh said I'd run away from Leeds. I said I'd walked out, not run away. After that I had to tell them what a shitty farce it had been. They weren't exactly sympathetic, said I might have known. But how *was* I to know?

Nat rolled a joint and Josh put on a Stranglers LP. It turned out that Rodge had gone away too – to see his Mum in Glasgow, and he'd said to the boys that he bet he'd last longer than I would. A friend of Rodge's called Ros was going to do an article with lots of pictures about contraceptives for the 'zine. And Slime (this was the latest!) was going to write about wanking, telling everybody it didn't make you go blind or grow hairs on the palms of your hands after all. Slime of all people! Well, I suppose he should know. I said, what about girls? Josh said girls didn't wank. Nat said they did but it was called frigging. This was news to me. I wanted to ask Nat what they did, but to tell you the truth I was too embarrassed with Josh sitting there, so I asked about Ros instead. You should have heard those sexist morons. Ooh, she was a right little cracker with legs all the way up to her armpits and great big knockers. I told them to shut their shitridden faces. Josh said I was jealous. I said I didn't give a soggy tampon what boys thought of me. Josh said ah, but Rodge is a *man*! But he shut up and left me alone when Nat passed him the joint.

When we went down to the kitchen to make some tea, Mum and Chaz had disappeared and the dishes had been cleared away. Nat of course said they'd gone to bed. Josh said he was going to bed himself and he didn't want any tea anyway. Nat made the tea and helped himself to some bread and apricot jam. We sat down at the table like an old married couple with nothing to say to each other. But of course we were both wondering about Mum and Chaz. I thought he was an improvement on Clive, and said so. Nat shrugged and said there was nothing to choose between them. I could never understand why he and Josh would go all sombre whenever the subject of Mum's lovers cropped up. I suppose they thought it was OK for men to fuck about, but women should stay at home and wait for their husbands. I was just figuring out how to put this in words when an almighty crash came from upstairs. It was Mum's bedroom door slamming. Nat and me stared at each other in expectant silence, listening to the footsteps coming down the stairs. Then Chaz came in, looking all bleary and wearing Mum's towelling bathrobe.

I was shit-scared. I admit it. He looked at us like he wanted to kill us, and I wondered if he'd murdered my Mum. Then he smiled at me and said he was sorry for the racket, so I knew it was all right. Nat – the nurd! – asked, what happened? Chaz looked furious again and shook his shoulders in a funny sort of way. I wanted to laugh but I didn't dare. Nat said, kind of muttered really, all right, don't fucking answer me, then. Chaz said, what did you say? Nat shrugged. Chaz walked towards him. Then before I knew what was happening, Chaz grabbed Nat's collar,

Nat took a swipe at Chaz, and there they were – fighting! Of all the sodding stupid things! I shrieked, stop it, stop it! But they took no notice. It was really horrible, the expression on their faces. Like animals. You could almost believe they were growling. And it wasn't fair because Nat's a bit of a weakling really though he's big. So I shrieked, don't hurt him! Chaz looked at me then and kind of pinned Nat back in his chair again. That's enough of that, he said. He let Nat go and said, sorry, girl, it's just a natural reaction when somebody lands me one.

Mum was standing in the doorway wearing her jeans and sweater and looking horrified. Out of my house, she said, out of my house, the pair of you. Nat started laughing hysterically and saying that Chaz was a fucking madman and ought to be locked up. Mum asked him if he was all right and said he could sleep in the study. She asked me what had happened, but I didn't know what to say. Chaz and Nat both tried to tell her, contradicting each other. Mum yelled at them to shut up. She told (yes, told, not asked) me to go to bed. So Nat and I left them to it. I could hear Chaz ask Mum, is he your lover? And Mum saying, don't be silly, he's only fifteen. And Chaz carrying on, I don't care how old he is, is he your lover? Josh was hanging over the banisters, but when he saw me he pretended he hadn't been listening and crept back to his room. The kitchen door shut and I couldn't hear any more. By the time I got up next morning, Nat and Chaz had both gone home.

XII

'Mrs Hughes?'

'Yes?' Eyes still shut against the bedside light, Claudia gropes for her watch on the table.

'This is Detective Sergeant Baines from Fleet Valley Police Station.'

'Police?' she repeats stupidly. It is five-past three.

'You have a son, Joshua?'

'Has anything happened to him?'

'That depends what you mean, Mrs Hughes.' The sergeant's voice is severe. 'Have you any idea where the lad is now?'

'In bed. It's the middle of the night, you know.'

'Are you sure he's in bed?'

'He went to bed at half-past ten.'

'Would you just check that he's still there, please?'

Still more irritated at being woken up than alarmed for Josh, Claudia crosses the landing and gently opens the door of her son's room. He is not there. She was so sure that he would be that for a moment she doesn't react. Then she is frightened: something terrible has happened to Josh. She rushes back to the telephone and Sergeant Baines. 'You're right. He's not here.'

'No, Mrs Hughes, he's here.'

'Why? What's happened?'

'We've had to arrest him and his pal, Nathaniel Masters. Good friends, are they?'

'Very good friends.'

'I'd be worried about that, if I was you, Mrs Hughes. That boy's a mental case.'

'You have no right to say that,' Claudia says in cold exasperation. 'Will you please tell me why you've arrested them?'

'They were breaking into parking meters and vending machines down by Fleet Valley School. They've damaged a great deal of property. Moreover,' the sergeant's voice gets heavier, 'they both resisted arrest, so there will probably be a charge of assaulting a police officer.'

'My God . . . ' Claudia can't think. All she can remember is the sergeant at West End Central saying that no one ever got cautioned twice. 'What will happen to them?'

'That will depend on the magistrate, Mrs Hughes.' Sergeant Baines sounds brisker now, washing his hands of the matter. 'How soon can you get down here?'

'I'll try and get a lift with Mrs Masters.'

'If you must. But if I was you, I wouldn't get mixed up with those people, and I wouldn't let my lad have anything to do with their lad.'

'You're not me, Sergeant,' says Claudia.

She sits down on the bed, takes a valium and lights a cigarette. Try to think lucidly, Claudia. How could Josh and Nat have been such silly idiots? They will surely be charged and prosecuted, and Josh will have a criminal record. Why couldn't he have thought of that? Why couldn't Nat? He may have a criminal record already, but he should have thought about his friend. It is all so wearing, so depressing. She must call Dorian. Perhaps he will be able to get over there before Dorothy Masters. But no one answers Ron's phone, and the Master's number is engaged. Dorothy is probably arguing with the police. Not for the first time, Claudia curses herself for never having learned to drive. She could get a cab, of course, but she would prefer not to have to go to the police station

A.—8

alone. Eventually she gets through to Dorothy, who, sighing and speaking as if out of some incurable lethargy, says that she and Cormack will be over as soon as they can get themselves together.

It is an hour before they arrive. For half that time Claudia has let Ron's phone ring constantly. Leaning back in his seat, Cormack opens the back door of the new Volvo for her. Automatically sociable, Claudia admires the comfort of the upholstery before realizing the futility, in this context, of everyday conversation. Cormack Batchelor, similarly well-trained in the niceties of social intercourse, proceeds to list for her the reasons for his loyalty to this particular model. As he anatomizes the virtues of the suspension and God knows that else – she isn't really listening – in that level, kindly voice of his, Claudia is seized by a kind of panic. She wants to hit him or to cry. Cormack drives on as steadily as he speaks, quite as if there were no urgency to the journey. He looks like a respectable hippie, balding, neatly bearded and well-disposed towards his fellow-creatures. Dorothy is a large, pretty, short-sighted woman with a blonde urchin cut. From the distance and without her glasses, she looks about seventeen. She speaks as if the very act were a physical effort, as if the weight, either of her body or of life itself, were altogether too much for her.

'Of course,' she tells Claudia, 'we've been though all this before. Oh dear, oh dear, if only they knew, these boys, how unimpressed we are, how boring it all is.'

'Boring?' Claudia is startled. 'Aren't you worried?'

'Oh, I've given up *worrying*,' says Dorothy. 'That's just what Nathaniel wants me to do, isn't it? I'm not supposed to have a life of my own, but spend every second worrying about him.'

'Of course you're worried.' Cormack puts a hand briefly on her knee. 'We both are.'

'What I want to know,' says Dorothy, 'is when is it all going to end?'

'How long has it been going on?' Claudia asks.

'We've had two years of sheer hell,' says Dorothy, 'haven't we, Cormack? And Barney's no help whatsoever. He's off on holiday now with his girlfriend. When do I ever get a holiday?'

'Well, he wasn't to know, I suppose,' Claudia says doubtfully. It is difficult to picture Barney, all Irish charm and sudden Irish invective, in the role of consistently caring father. At least Dorian has never hit Josh – or Claudia herself. At least! Perhaps Barney is simply more honest in expressing his emotions. 'Do you think it's inevitable, Dorothy? That men lose interest in their children, once they reach adolescence?'

'Oh no.' Dorothy's voice is wearily sarcastic. 'It's you and me, Claudia. We've been unlucky. We picked wrong 'uns.' She smiles at Cormack. 'Better luck next time.'

'Next time?' Claudia says bleakly. 'I'm still trying to salvage this time. God knows why. I don't think I'm going to make it.'

'What do you actually think of Dorian?' Dorothy asks.

'I think he's a shit.'

'You don't really, do you?'

'Sometimes I want to kill him.'

'Poor Claudia.' Dorothy sighs. 'You're still in love with him.'

Claudia is surprised by this assertion and starts to deny it, but they have now arrived at the police station. Cormack tells the two women that he will drop them off while he parks the Volvo in a side road out of harm's way. As they walk up the steps, Claudia's impulse to refute Dorothy becomes dissipated, first by self-doubt, and then by the general sense of uneasiness which attends all encounters with the agencies of law enforcement, however innocent the participants. The desk sergeant asks them to wait and they smoke a furtive cigarette, like schoolgirls, but in silence. And Claudia feels old, tired, far from giggling. The police-station floor is covered in a mottled green linoleum which reminds her of the school corridors, now buried a quarter of a century (can it be so long?) in the past. There is the same smell of institutional food mingled with disinfectant and stale sweat. A poster proclaiming Wanted For Robbery shows a photofit picture made up of pieces so disparate as to evoke the assumption that some sinister mutation has occurred; another photograph, this time of a woman and clearly taken from a corpse, asks for a murder victim to be identified. Cormack joins Claudia and Dorothy just as two uniformed policemen, laughing together, emerge from the swing doors behind them.

'Which one of you is Mrs Masters?' the older one asks in a voice recognizable to Claudia as that of Sergeant Baines.

Dorothy puts up her hand, looking as if guiltily at him from under her long lashes. She looks just like Nat. 'I have that misfortune.'

The sergeant shakes his head. 'That's a very disturbed boy you've got there, Mrs Masters. Pathological, I'd say myself.'

'Oh, you don't have to tell me,' says Dorothy. 'That's what I've been saying for years. But no one ever takes any notice of me. I'm just his mother.'

'You know he threatened one of our officers with a claw hammer?'

'And a Stanley knife,' adds the younger man, a constable.

'He was extremely abusive,' the sergeant continues, sounding surprisingly emotional. 'Calling our men all sorts of names. Hitler's bastards and Fascist pigs. We shouldn't have to take that sort of thing, you know. We're only human.'

Dorothy, however, is not surprised. 'Was anyone injured?' she asks with another sigh.

'Two of our men managed to overpower him,' says the constable, 'before he could do any permanent damage.'

'We've had to put him in a cell,' the sergeant says. 'Let him calm down a bit. By the way, he's had a medical examination. We thought the violence might be due to the ingestion of certain substances. We found some tissue paper stuffed up his back passage. When questioned about this, he told us he was bisexual. However, there was no evidence that anal intercourse had taken place.'

Claudia has been listening to the conversation, if such it can be called, with mounting horror. None of it sounds the least like Nat. He is never violent unless grievously provoked and his refusal to retaliate against gangs of skinheads and other bullies has often left him badly beaten up. Why doesn't Dorothy say so? As to the bisexuality, it must be some kind of ploy to provoke the police. Even they must be able to see that. And why has no one mentioned Josh?

'What about my son?' she asks. 'Have you locked him up too?'

'We haven't been able to get a word out of him, Mrs Hughes,' says the sergeant, 'beyond his name and address. He gave us the correct ones, which is more than the other fellow did.'

'When can I see him?'

'You can see your lad right away, Mrs Hughes. Just go along to the charge room with the constable.'

Claudia follows the constable through the swing doors, which he holds open for her. She tries to persuade herself that she is still dreaming, that nothing from the phone call on New Year's Day through to the present moment has actually happened. She would like to believe that all of it is a nightmare which must only be ridden out and into exhaustion for it to be finished. But it would seem that she has been hauled instead into an awakening which stinks of reality and which promises to be prolonged. There is no doubt in her mind that the boys' actions have been prompted by the sort of anger which arises from despair. And how else but with a mirroring despair can she respond? How else? With patience, with supportive care. That's what mothers are for. But there isn't enough of me left! Unbidden and unspoken comes the cry from the heart. It must go unheeded too. Unlike Dorothy, she will not allow herself to lose faith, either in herself or her son.

In the charge room everything becomes confused. There are some half dozen police present, assorted men and women. Josh is sitting huddled on a bench at a table in the far corner. He gives no indication that he has seen his mother come in. Claudia is prevented from approaching him by further questioning. It is only when she is giving his full name to one of the policewomen that he looks up and she can smile and wave at him. He nods at her with the flicker of a smile and she is instantly comforted.

'The lad tells us,' says the policewoman, 'that he lives with you and his sister and that there is no father present. Is that correct?'

'We're separated,' says Claudia, wondering whether the question is routine or one of major sociological significance. 'Temporarily.'

'How long have you been separated?'

'Four months.'

'Has your son been in trouble before?'

'Yes – for shoplifting.'

'When was that?'

'Just under four months ago.'

The policewoman looks up at her for the first time. *Post hoc, ergo propter hoc*. Draw your own conclusions. Claudia wishes she knew whether the broken-home syndrome is in Josh's favour (poor kid, he's had a rough time) or tells against him (another problem family, hopeless case). If only she could think clearly, assess the meanings of which her mechanical replies are capable, and choose among them the ones most advantageous to her wayward (no, not criminal) son. When she is ignorant of the parameters of the situation (now she's beginning to *think* in the language of officialdom) how can she hope to control it? The policewoman is questioning her about Matilda.

'Has she ever been in trouble?'

'No – not with the police.'

The policewoman smiles unexpectedly. 'Yes, girls tend to take it out on themselves rather than other people.'

Taken unawares, Claudia exclaims, '*You* know that?'

The policewoman looks at her reproachfully but still good-humouredly. 'Perhaps we're not all as thick as we look, Mrs Hughes.'

'No,' says Claudia, seeing perhaps a nurse or an infants' teacher beyond the ugly uniform, 'I'm sure you're not.'

The policewoman folds her arms and leans on them across the table towards Claudia. 'I know what you're thinking, Mrs Hughes. What's a nice girl like me doing in a place like this? Well, you see, we haven't all had your educational advantages. I went to a secondary modern and there was no hope of me getting to university. It was either the services or the force. And I thought the force would give me more scope.'

'I see,' says Claudia.

'I look on this job as a form of social work. You know, it really isn't about wanting to dominate people and kick them around, as your youngsters seem to think. They don't know how privileged they are.'

'I see,' says Claudia.

'Well . . . ' The policewoman stands up, the sermon over, smoothing down her skirt. 'Let's have a chat with that lad of yours, shall we?'

Following her through the desks and across the room, Claudia finds herself wondering at the general air of defensiveness she has met since entering the building. Sergeant Baines seemed to accept that being attacked with a hammer or a knife was part of a policeman's lot, but he drew the line at verbal abuse. Who would have thought that language was so powerful? Or rather, that the police should find it so? Nat will not be forgiven for his words but Josh's silence, which has in its stubbornness so often infuriated his teachers and herself, is endowed by contrast with something approaching the golden. Clearly to be articulate is a crime in itself. And especially to those who have not had our educational advantages. It is after all the duty of the criminal classes to become tongue-tied in the face of authority, thus demonstrating that they know their place among the ranks of the disadvantaged from which that very authority has arisen. The distinction must be maintained between those of the disadvantaged who have made good and those who have not.

'I thought I was never going to get to talk to you,' Claudia tells Josh when the policewoman has left them.

He grins. 'So did I.'

'So tell me, please, what is all this about?'

He shrugs. 'They hit me.'

'Who hit you? Where?'

'Here.' His lower lip is slightly swollen and he pulls it down to show where he has bled. 'That bastard Bulldog hit me. And I hadn't done anything.' His voice trembles. 'You're not supposed to hit people for nothing.'

'What do you mean, bulldog?'

'That's his name. That one over there talking to Dorothy and Cormack.'

'You mean Sergeant Baines?'

'The big one with the ugly face.'

'Sergeant Baines. Are you sure, Josh?'

'I'm sure, Mum. He said, this should take care of you, sonny Jim.'

'He said you were resisting arrest.'

Josh's voice is near to tears and full of indignation as he speaks. 'They all ganged up on Nat. I thought they were going to pound him to a pulp, the fucking bastards.'

'So what did you do?'

'I can't remember.'

'You must, People are going to ask you all sorts of questions. Listen, did you attack any of them?'

Josh nods, not looking at her. 'I think I jumped on this geezer's back and locked my arm round his neck – like this.'

'And that's when Sergeant Baines hit you?'

'Yes.'

Across the room Dorothy is making a phone call. Claudia remembers that in theory Josh is permitted to call his solicitor. But she doesn't know any solicitors. The charges against Josh are theft, attempted theft, criminal damage and assaulting a police officer. It all sounds so dreadfully villainous. Perhaps she should call Chaz: he has had as many dealings with the police as any solicitor. And Chaz will be only too glad to help. He will sweep up ostentatiously in his Rolls, swagger into the station, address the policeman as 'my good man', and, like an avenging angel, bear Claudia and her wronged son away. Alternatively, he will stalk through the corridors, demanding to see 'your superiors' and, when frustrated, start a punch-up. No. Both Josh and Claudia are better off without any help from Chaz. Dorothy is weeping into the phone: you're a shit, Barney, a prize shit! Is she still in love with him? Cormack puts an arm round her, takes the receiver gently from her and replaces it. Barney is refusing to be a father. And Dorian? Dorian is refusing to wake up.

Policemen are whispering together in twos and threes. Policewomen are moving from group to group, fluttering pieces of paper. The room seems to be filling up. Two of the men walk firmly towards Claudia and Josh, only to leave the room again by a door to the right of their corner. It is Sergeant Baines who joins them at their table. Josh is instantly on his guard, edging closer to Claudia and yet at the same time seeming to switch off, looking expressionlessly at the floor. Claudia recognizes this stance. It says: I refuse to participate in this drama any longer; my part is played out; if you want it to continue, you will have to take over the action yourselves. Sergeant Baines looks at him with a kindly half-smile, trying to shame him into looking up. Claudia could tell him: there is no point in entering into a battle of wills with Josh; attrition is his speciality. Only a Trojan horse could penetrate his state of siege.

'How's that lip, then, son?' the sergeant asks.

'All right,' Josh murmurs, not looking up.

'You hit him?' Claudia asks, barely a question.

The sergeant laughs. 'There was a bit of a scuffle, Mrs Hughes, during the course of which I was called upon to defend my colleague.'

'And Josh, it seems, was defending his friend.'

'That's one way of putting it.'

'How would you put it?'

The sergeant draws breath to answer, but he is looking at the door in front of him. It opens and Nat comes in, flanked by the two policemen. Immediately Sergeant Baines stands up. A voice from across the room yells, keep them apart! His escorts grip Nat's arms, twisting them back. He blinks, as short-sighted as his mother without his spectacles, his mild, blank eyes searching in vain for some familiar face. The sergeant, feet apart, arms stretched and flexed, is blocking his view of Claudia and Josh. The room is hushed as Nat is led, limping, across to his mother and Cormack.

'Let that be a lesson to you,' the sergeant says to Josh, who, without raising his head, flashes him a look of pure hatred. 'You behave nicely and you get treated nicely.'

'What's that supposed to mean?' asks Claudia.

The sergeant sighs. 'This is not a bad lad, Mrs Hughes. This is a lad who's been led astray by an older lad. All he's really guilty of is a severe case of hero-worship.'

Taking her cue from Josh, who is looking at the sergeant in the same expressive way as before, Claudia says, 'I think you've misinterpreted the situation. The two boys are in the same year at school.'

'Come on, Josh,' says the sergeant, 'it was all Nat's idea, wasn't it?' Josh says nothing. 'Did Nat suggest to you that you went to the school and broke into the parking meters?' Again, Josh says nothing. 'Perhaps your mother can persuade you to make a statement.'

'Does he have any choice?' Claudia asks.

'It seems he's known to the Juvenile Board,' says Sergeant Baines, 'and I don't think it would go down particularly well with them if they found out he'd been unwilling to co-operate with us.'

'Well, Josh?' Claudia asks. He shakes his head. 'It might be better, you know.'

'We can go into the next room,' says the sergeant, 'just you and me and your mother.'

'All you have to do is tell the truth,' says Claudia.

'I've been telling the truth,' Josh says to her, 'and no one's believed me,'

'You've told us nothing, son,' says Sergeant Baines. 'That's just the problem. We want to know your story.'

Josh looks at Claudia. 'If you come with me.'

Sergeant Baines drops his persuasive manner and adopts a brisker one as he stands up and snaps his fingers in the direction of the nearest policewoman. Hurrying over at once, she is directed to take Claudia and Josh to an interview room. It is colder there. Huddling into her coat, Claudia lights a cigarette. Josh sits as before, still, unmoved. Was it thus he sat, his gloves on, with his psychotherapist? Perhaps they both sat in silence throughout the session. Perhaps she made pleasant conversation, pretending not to notice that she was engaged in monologue rather than dialogue. If so, did she ever wonder, as Claudia has often done, whether she was actually speaking out loud at all? Did she lose the ability to distinguish between what she had said and what merely thought?

When he was nine Josh walked a mile and a half home from the adventure playground with his shoulder dislocated and the bone fractured. His friend, Mark Ferris, did all the talking. They had crept in, after hours, through a hole in the fence and were mucking about on the big boys' climbing-frame. Instead of swinging by his arms from the top rungs, Josh had walked along as if the log had been a tight-rope. He didn't scream when he fell. He just lay there. Mark thought he might be dead. Mark was shaking all over, as pale as Josh. Dr Jaffa called an ambulance and went to the hospital with them. They had to wait two hours before anyone saw Josh, who lay on his trolley staring at the ceiling, as still and as seemingly unconcerned as an effigy. Two more hours passed while Josh was X-rayed and manipulated. It was no good: he would have to stay in overnight, and they would try to set the bone in the morning. After that, he'd be out in a week. But Josh was in hospital for five weeks.

Claudia visited Josh twice a day, once at lunchtime and once in the evening, bringing him fruit and books and games. He was so brave and patient. The nurses all thought him so well-behaved – not like the fat little girl in the next bed who screamed and screamed every time she had to have an injection, and it took two of them to hold her down, as well as one to administer it. Wasn't Claudia lucky to have such a good, such a lovely little boy? She nodded, choking back her tears. He's going to be all right, love.

Lucky it wasn't you or me – our bones wouldn't heal like that. But Claudia had never doubted that Josh was going to be all right. It was less his pain that prompted her grief than his bravery, his patience, his very goodness. Why couldn't the nurses see how unnatural it all was? Why shouldn't anyone except herself see that something was wrong with Josh beyond the physical effects of the accident?

He didn't eat, didn't read, didn't smile. And he didn't talk to his mother, seemed indifferent to her presence. She tried not to show how frightened she was. Occasionally, especially when Dorian could spare the time to join them, they played a series of board games – all dice and counters and flashing lights – which Josh always won. It was better when Dorian was there. Beating Claudia was no fun because she never seemed to try, never seemed to mind losing. Dorian would curse his luck or his stupidity, make a drama of it. And Matilda would gratifyingly lose her temper and throw things on the floor. Josh smiled then. He laughed loudly enough to attract the attention of the nurses. But his smile was no more than a stretching of his lips, and his laughter was forced and empty, forced out of emptiness and despair. For Claudia the nightmare element consisted in Josh's indifference, Dorian's indifference to Josh's indifference, and the nurses who, fussing over Josh, asked for Dorian's autograph. It wasn't just Josh's shoulder that was dislocated: the world was dissolving and, her mother dying of cancer in another hospital, she couldn't find any pieces to pick up. Josh was no longer Josh. Two weeks after he got out of hospital he set fire to the house.

Claudia too can sit still now, without speaking, without asking any questions. There is no struggle to prevent herself from weeping over her son's misdeeds, weeping for his inarticulate despair. The introjection of his pain is no longer an automatic process. Pain exists out there somewhere. It is all around, no longer specific, no longer subjective, but part of some vast, meaningless network binding us all together in our common anaesthesia. That's what valium does for you. It kills your appetite, makes your hands shake and removes any inhibitions you might have about being rudely truthful to people, but oh how it protects you from the impinging world. Sometimes you can even see yourself from the outside. Claudia sees Claudia now, a dot disappearing with increasing speed into the far-flung reaches of infinity. Quick. Catch her before she is snuffed out.

'Perhaps,' she says, 'you'd better tell me what happened.'

'Nothing much.'

'Quite a lot of damage.'

'We couldn't get into the parking meters,' Josh explains with a sigh, 'so we got fed up and got some chocolate out of a machine. We were just sitting there in this shop doorway eating it when suddenly all those Pigs appeared from nowhere with screaming sirens and flashing lights. Anyone would think we'd ripped off the Crown jewels.'

'Are you trying to tell me that all you've actually done is steal a couple of bars of chocolate?'

'Yes!'

'The police say Nat threatened them with a hammer and a knife.'

'He didn't, Mum!'

'Then what happened?'

'Six of the bastards started giving Nat a going-over.'

'Because he threatened them?'

'No, Mum!' Josh is impatient with her stupidity. 'We just came out of the doorway like they told us, and Nat held out the hammer and gave it to them.'

'You're sure he wasn't waving the hammer at them?'

'Mum, he was holding it by the sodding head.'

'And then they laid into him?'

'Yes!'

Claudia is about to question him on his own actions when Sergeant Baines comes into the room, pad of official paper in hand. He smiles at her in a conspiratorial way and she immediately mistrusts him. But such is her habit of conciliation that she would have returned his smile, had Josh's sullen observation of the scene not deterred her. Thus, it crosses her mind, is paranoia instigated in the young. She feels very much on her guard as the sergeant settles himself at the table opposite Josh. Always on his guard in the presence of adult authority, Josh himself maintains his sullen expression, his face closing into the sort of passive hostility which is perceived by the insecurely powerful as insolent. Yes or no (and that grudgingly) is all the information he is prepared to give, until the sergeant repeats a previous question.

'Whose idea was it?'

Josh gives one of his shrugs. 'Mine.'

The sergeant puts down his pen. 'Are you sure?' Josh nods. 'Are you sure it wasn't Nat's?' Josh nods, but the sergeant makes no record of his reply. 'What did you hope to achieve by it?'

Josh grins. 'Money.'

'And all you got was chocolate,' says the sergeant. 'Hardly worth it, was it?' Josh makes no reply. 'If you think it was worth the worry you've caused your mother, you've got to be joking, son.'

This is an implication which Claudia must refuse. The feelings of frustration and indeed rage which she assumes to be the basis of Josh's conduct are not so far removed from her own. She has often wished in the past few months that she could be afforded some sort of similar release. All she has smashed is one wine glass, her own property, and within the confines of her own kitchen. She knows the anger of the provoked and cornered animal who growls, waits, springs and destroys. She knows how the organism rallies itself to the threat of destruction. Attack may not be the best form of defence, but it is surely one of the most common and goes all too often and disastrously unrecognized for what it is. At least Nat and Josh have not elected to go mugging old ladies. At least they have damaged property rather than people. The ostensible target, inanimate and arbitrary, felt no pain. The real target, their parents, whom they cannot help loving as well as hating, cannot be acknowledged as such. If unassailable, they will be perceived as unloving, and there is terror there. If assailable, they will terrify through their very vulnerability and the offspring will have no choice but to assume, however guiltily, the mantle of the parricide. Let the parking meters, arch symbols of needless authority, take the brunt. And have they not withstood? That is more than Claudia can say for herself.

She takes the written statement from the sergeant and begins to read it. 'I met Nathaniel Masters by prearrangement at 1.00 a.m. in Cloister Street outside Fleet Valley School. No one else knew of our arrangement. I took with me a claw hammer from my father's tool-box, and Nathaniel had a knife which he had stolen from the school art room.' (But the sergeant is asking her questions. Does he or does he not want her to read the statement?) 'Our intention was to break into parking meters and appropriate the money therein. However, we found this impossible. As we were hungry by this time, we smashed a chocolate-vending machine instead.' (Now he is telling Claudia that the Juvenile Board must be informed. They will want to interview Josh.) 'We were sitting in the doorway of S.J. Patel, tobacconists and stationers in South Row, when we were apprehended. A struggle ensued, during the course of which my lip was cut. I could not see what was happening to Nathaniel.' (Did Josh say that? Is Claudia too getting paranoid?) 'We were taken to Fleet Valley police station for questioning in separate cars. This statement was made voluntarily by me . . .'

'Shall I sign this?' she asks Josh.

'And you, Josh,' says the sergeant. 'Well, that's it, Mrs Hughes. You're both free to go home.'

'I came here with Mrs Masters,' says Claudia, 'and I was rather hoping that she and Mr Batchelor would give me a lift back.'

'Oh, they'll be some time yet,' he assures her. 'One of our lads will take you in the squad car.'

'Thank you,' Claudia says politely. 'I'd just like to tell Mrs Masters we're going.'

'That's all right. I'll get the message to her.' Sergeant Baines pauses at the door. 'I think you've made a wise decision.'

He has gone before Claudia can ask him what he means. She lights another cigarette, using the metal bin as an ashtray. Josh looks pale with fatigue. Outside the light is delicately blue, but steely rather than pastel. Another day. What promise can that hold? Claudia is familiar with the dawn: it is when she wakes and takes a valium, unable otherwise to contemplate the possible horrors of the waking hours ahead. It is the time of the upsurge of birdsong, now clear and blithe in the plane tree whose branches just touch the ribbed-glass window and then move away again, an intimation from some long-forgotten world of spontaneous ease. It is as obtrusive as the light, and clearer. Josh yawns. Claudia sighs. Sergeant Baines comes back into the room and says that Mrs Masters would like to speak to her.

Dorothy wastes no time. 'Did you say that you'd rather you got a lift home from the police because you didn't want Josh to associate with Nat?'

Claudia looks from her to Sergeant Baines and back again. 'No, I did not.'

'It's up to you,' the sergeant says. 'But you didn't disagree with me, did you?'

'You hardly gave me time.'

'As I said, it's up to you.'

Defeated, he leaves them standing in the corridor, leaves Claudia to explain. 'He said you were going to be some time.'

'They'd just said we could go,' says Cormack.

'Bloody nerve,' says Dorothy.

'Did Nat make a statement?' Claudia asks.

'No,' says Dorothy. 'Did Josh?'

'Yes. Do you think that was a mistake?'

'It's all a mistake.'

Claudia sits in the back of the Volvo, wedged between Josh and Nat. Even without the valium she would be shaking with fatigue. Even the suspension, so dear to Cormack, cannot stay wave after wave of nausea which accompanies the turning of each corner, each bend in the road. Nat winces as he is swayed from side to side. He says his leg has been injured and is giving him hell.

Dorothy and Cormack question him about the going-over he has received. They have decided to press charges against the police. Cormack says they must get Nat to a doctor while the evidence is still fresh. Nat says he's too tired. Dorothy insists. Nat says nobody is going to believe him, anyway. Cormack insists. Their voices rise and fall, weaving in and out of one another, the words of strangers overheard and only dimly understood, tangential. It is very warm in the car. Josh is silent. Claudia, to her dismay, is falling asleep.

XIII

It was Slime's rotten idea in the first place. I mean, I thought the little wanker was joking. I thought Josh and Nat did too. Any git with half a per cent of a brain could have told you Slime was just being his usual flash self, all mouth and no action. Us three were having quite a reasonable conversation about the morality of theft before he swaggered in and started rabbiting on about how we should rob a bank. Josh was just saying what a laugh it was he should be thought some kind of loony just because he ripped off a few cassettes. I said I didn't see what was wrong with nicking from rip-off merchants like Rama anyway, when we knew they were making a fat profit from talented kids who didn't know better than to get mixed up with a bunch of creeps like them. Nat said that all property was theft. It was then that Slime brought up the subject of banks. And somehow we got on to parking meters – all that lovely lolly just stacked up there in the street, our very own territory, and ours for the taking.

OK, so we all got carried away. But I assumed it was a series of improvisations on a theme, riff after riff, just for the sheer joy of it. I mean, we often went on like that when we elaborated on ways of overthrowing the capitalist system. Nobody *really* thought it was down to us. Slime least of all. He didn't even have the guts to bunk off, let alone get into real trouble. Oh no, his speciality was egging on everybody else and watching them carry the can.

Rodge said we weren't to trust Slime. His Mum was a parent-governor and ever so matey with Fairfax. I think they went to Oxford together, or something nepotistic and élitist like that. They called each other Joan and Heather and invited each other to dinner. Slime's Mum would always invite some spare male (usually gay or retarded or both) just so's poor old Fairfax wouldn't feel the odd one out. Why there's supposed to be something odd about not being attached to some male or other I've never been able to figure out. I mean, I don't want to attach myself to anybody. Why should I? Fat lot of fucking good it does you, anyway, always having to pretend you're stupider than they are. Rodge says that pair-bonding is part of bourgeois mythology and monogamy its moral manifestation designed to keep women in slavery. Wow! When he explained what he meant, I realized it was what I'd been thinking all along without being able to put it into words. Right on, Rodge! The first sensible thing I've heard any grown-up say on the subject. After all, it's always women who are supposed to be poor old sex-starved crones if they're not married, but men can do as they sodding well please without being criticized and other people envy them their freedom. It's so unfair!

Take Mum's feminist friend, Sonia, for instance. Claire always calls her poor Sonia, like she had some terrible affliction it wasn't quite nice to mention. I kept asking, why is she poor? Mum said she wasn't, and Claire just shook her head. I asked if there was anything wrong with Sonia, and Claire said it must be dreadful to live all alone like that. There she was with this snotty, smelly baby bawling away on her knee and she was thinking herself lucky! Or perhaps she meant she was lucky because of Stan, which is even more of a joke, because he's always beating her up, and she comes running here to Mum, moaning and wailing that she's never going to go back. But she always does. Once I asked Mum why, and she said the thing to remember was that Claire was in love with Stan. I would understand one day. I should bleeding well hope not! Rodge says people are always saying they're in love when they want to make excuses for themselves for behaving like creeps. He says it's the one excuse bourgeois morality will accept for every form of bad behaviour – even murder. Now that I *can* understand.

Anyway, back to Slime – if I must. The general idea was that he should be treated like a mole in our ranks and fed useless pieces of information which he could then blab freely to his Mum or Fairfax or any other potential enemy. We kept trying to sneak off to Rodge's without him, but like as not he followed us, showing off the whole way about how Rodge was going to be knocked out by his (Slime's) latest brilliant idea, which he wasn't about to divulge for the benefit of the likes of us. Of course when we got there he didn't have any ideas at all except idiotic ones like why didn't we get Marks and Spencers to advertise in the 'zine. Durex, more likely, said Nat. Nat could stand Slime even less than me and Josh could. I think Slime had once gone out with some girlfriend of Nat's (before my time!) behind his back. Slime couldn't take a hint, like all Mummy's boys, and was impervious to sarcasm. So one day Nat just told him to piss off because Rodge thought he was a nurd anyway. It was a mistake. Slime only went off to Rodge's on his own and asked straight out if Rodge thought he was a nurd. Of course Rodge wasn't at all pleased with Nat. But what he actually said to Slime was nurd? turd? what does it matter? Slime thought this was hilarious and after that there was no hope of getting rid of him.

We had to have our editorial meetings in secret, preferably when Slime was having his guitar lessons. We got our statistics together and Nat took his cassette recorder to school and interviewed some pupils whose names were in the Punishment Book. Ros typed a transcript, leaving in all the swear words and putting laughs in brackets. I never read anything so funny in all my life and ended up on Rodge's floor helpless with hiccups. Josh did some little strip-cartoons, which he thought were brill, about a monster. And I must admit it wasn't half bad. I wrote an article about girls not being allowed to do boys' subjects, which Josh and Nat said was boring, but Rodge said other girls would be interested. *And* he said I needn't only cover girls' interests in future. So that was one in the eye for the boys. He showed us how to mark up copy discreetly without bothering too much about punctuation or spelling (just as well!) so as to maintain the integrity of individual style. Well, that's what he said. We experimented with layout, getting columns all askew, sometimes going up and down the page and sometimes across. Josh said it would be difficult to read, but Rodge said people *would* read it because it looked different from anything else and it was a kind of challenge.

Then Rodge got caught. At the Poly, I mean. He was just taking the key to the copy room from the hook in the secretary's office when she came back early from lunch and asked to see his ID card. Of course he had one, with his photograph and everything from the time he used to teach there, but it was years out of date. So then she looked him up in the files and discovered he was this notorious radical who'd been given the boot for attempting to corrupt their innocent youth. The bleeding bat only went and called the Principal and he, being new, had only heard vaguely of Rodge and didn't believe a word he said. Probably thought he was an IRA bomber or something, seeing as how his last name is Flanagan. But poor old Rodge has never set foot in Ireland in his whole life. He said it was a total fucking farce the panic they got into, even threatening to call the police. Rodge's turn to panic. He said the Principal could search him and his briefcase. So the

Principal took Rodge and the secretary took the briefcase. That's when she found the so-called subversive literature. Not that she bothered to read it. The illustrations of sheaths and diaphragms were enough to send her into a fit. She kept screaming that Rodge was going to spread filth around the Poly and that there were girls from good Catholic homes there. That did it. The Principal (a Methodist, it seems) said Rodge could do what he liked with his sordid little tracts as long as he made no attempt to distribute them on those hallowed premises.

It was a near-run thing. And of course we had to find other ways of getting the 'zine printed. Rodge said not to worry. The Poly wasn't the only place with the necessary equipment – just the most obvious. But Josh got into one of his horrible sulks about it. He kept saying things like he might have known that anything he got involved in would turn out to be a flop. Nat grumbled too because he told everyone (except Slime) that *Pupil Power* would be out before half-term and now there wasn't a cat in hell's chance. I think they both thought they were going to look fools, but I couldn't see what the fuss was about. If Rodge didn't mind waiting another week or two, why should anyone else? When I said it wasn't the end of the world, they groaned and said no, it just felt like it. Now, I'm not saying that there's any connection between the 'zine incident and the parking-meter incident, but one did happen shortly after the other.

In the end it might have been more sensible to rob a bank. No kidding. At least, with a bit of bluff, masks and toy guns, they might have had a chance. Of course you couldn't expect anything from Josh after the Rama incident, but I was really surprised at Nat. What did the prize pissing moron think he was into? He knew the Pigs would pick on him. They always did. And this time they had a wonderful excuse. In the dark, they said, they couldn't tell he was a juvenile because all they could see was this six-foot geezer brandishing some weapon. If you believe that, you'll believe anything. And anything is just what they wanted to believe. They even accused Josh and Nat of having a homosexual relationship so as they had some excuse for prosecuting them. It seems they looked up their arses but couldn't find anything. (What did they expect to find, for Chrissake?) I thought they only did that when they were looking for dope. Of course Nat went along with it all and told them he was bisexual. That put them into a right old tizzy. One of them asked him how much he usually charged and what sort of drugs he bought with the proceeds. Nat said heroin, thinking that was what they wanted to hear. But they couldn't find any needle-marks on his arms. Blimey O'Riley, how disappointed they must have been.

Nat told it all like it was some sort of battle between him and the Pigs and that he was the winner. He seemed to forget that they'd practically broken his leg and done it in such a way that there was hardly any bruising or anything to show for it. But then he never admitted that anything actually hurt for long, unless it was something silly like me tapping his wrists with a ruler and then he'd moan all day. His Mum and Cormack took him along to Casualty at the North London. He couldn't understand why the sudden interest in his welfare, said it must have been because they thought *their* property had been damaged. So this doctor takes a look at him and asks him all sorts of questions about what he'd done and what the Pigs had done. By this time Nat was practically dead on his feet (or on his arse) and kept getting into a muddle and contradicting himself. He said he thought the doctor kept trying to trap him. Suddenly Nat felt he'd had enough and started claiming that the Pigs had made a sexual assault. He was just being his usual sarcastic self, but the doctor wasn't to know that. He said he thought Nat was in need of psychiatric treatment and should be kept in hospital for forty-eight hours for observation. His Mum made no objection, and nobody actually consulted *him*, so there he was – in shtuck.

Then the silly sod went and took an overdose, didn't he? I couldn't believe it. I mean, I thought the Pigs had murdered him and were trying to cover up. With the help of the hospital, of course. Authorities always stick together. Jesus H. Christ, the place was like a morgue anyway. All those corridors going on and on like something out of some film from Eastern Europe. And all those human bodies lying around like bits of garbage so as you couldn't tell whether they were alive or dead. Remind me never to be ill. Or grow old. Some of the zombies perked up a bit when they saw Josh and me and one or two looked truly horrified, like they suspected they might have actually gone to hell for all the poor little sins they thought they'd committed. The nurses were kind of horrified too, tried to shoo us away and keep us out of sight, like we were representatives of the ugly underbelly of society and would cause offence to all the ordinary decent people who preferred to believe that we were just a creation of the media. But there we were. In the flesh. Young and healthy. We couldn't help that, could we? And yet everyone seemed to think we should have been ashamed.

At last, after hanging about for hours and depriving the poor patients of their right to be bored rigid, we got to see the ward sister. Oh my God, she said when she saw us. Oh, my God! Just like that. She didn't seem to have a clue that she was being rude, seemed to think she could say whatever she liked as if we didn't have any right to a bit of respect from her. Typical fucking adults – parents, teachers, whoever they are. They're always going on about respect and how important it is. But do they ever show any? Oh, no! Not to us. You can't see Nathaniel Masters, she says, he's in intensive care. I mean, I thought that's what happened to people who had heart attacks. Well, Josh and I knew he'd been beaten up, but that was all, so we just stood there. Off you go, she said, and started to go on about how busy she was. So I asked why Nat was in intensive care. She said she couldn't tell us that, so I asked if his Mum knew, and she said next-of-kin had been informed. And then she walked off, leaving us standing there in the corridor like a couple of idiots who should have known better than to ask such silly questions. There was nothing for it but to go and see Nat's Mum.

Josh wouldn't talk to me on the way back. I started eating Nat's grapes because the paper bag was getting all soggy. But when I offered some to Josh, he just stared at me like I'd just crawled out from under something. It wasn't my fucking fault, was it? He wouldn't even sit next to me on the bus. And all I'd said was, did he think Nat had been murdered? It seemed like a possibility to me. I mean, suppose the Pigs had kicked him in the wrong place and something had ruptured inside of him where no one could see it . . . and then . . . kind of spread. The more I thought about it, the more I believed it, and soon I'd made myself feel really sick. I felt like killing every Pig in London with my own bare hands. Whatever happened afterwards would have been worth it because it would have given me such pleasure. Who the fucking hell do they think they are, anyway? They put on a uniform and think they're little tin gods. But you can't go around beating up teenage boys just because you don't like the look of them. I mean, *can* you? I don't like the look of a lot of people, but then I just look the other way.

It hadn't occurred to us that Nat's Mum would be at the hospital, but that's where his sister said she was. Cormack was there, though, because he'd just come back from work. He said Nat had nicked a whole load of sleeping-pills off a trolley and then swallowed the lot. He seemed angry, said the nurses should have had more sense than to leave dangerous drugs lying around. Then he said that Nat was just trying to draw attention to himself. I said, what for? He said, well, I knew Nat as well as he did and surely I couldn't have failed to notice his attention-seeking behaviour. I didn't really know what the sod he was talking about. And I didn't care. Cormack gets on my wick. Self-important. That's what he is. When he said Nat was going to be all right, he kind of sighed as if he thought that was a pity. All he could think of was poor old Dorothy and how could Nat do this to his mother, hadn't she suffered enough, and so on and so forth. It didn't seem to have occurred to him that Nat had suffered enough, and that was why he took an overdose. It didn't seem to have occurred to him that Nat had suffered at all. But fifteen-year-old boys aren't supposed to have any feelings, are they? How dare they mention suffering at their age! Didn't they know that life is supposed to be hell for kids, which is good for them anyway, and only when you're grown up are you entitled to any pleasure (or pain) in life? End of sarcasm. But it really made me pissing puke to listen to Cormack.

It was another three days before we got to see Nat. Slime and Emma came along with Josh and me. The ward sister ignored us all except Slime who she clearly recognized as another of her own kind – upright and moronic. And there was Nat, sitting up in bed smiling, just like nothing had happened! I thought he'd be all tragic and feeble and talking in a whisper, but he was his same old self, except a bit cleaner than usual. He asked me why I was looking so fucking miserable. I told him what I'd thought about the Pigs murdering him and he said, not a chance, they know better than that. I wanted to ask him if he was really trying to kill himself, but I didn't like to with all the others around. He said he'd seen all the pills on the trolley and was seized by this idea to take the whole lot and see what happened. It was all very disappointing, he said. No hallucinations or anything. He just fell asleep and the next thing he knew he was puking away like Niagara Falls and there was this ruddy great tube down his throat. It all sounded disgusting and Nat said the stomach pump was the worst thing that ever happened to him. We just stood round the bed horrified out of our tiny minds, and I for one didn't see what he had to be so cheerful about.

Well, if Cormack was right, Nat certainly got his way after that. Enough attention to satisfy a sodding film star. Social workers, psychiatrists, doctors, teachers – the lot. Suddenly everybody wanted to talk to him about his problems. He said he didn't have any, except life, and everybody seemed to think this was terrible. Especially his Mum. She had a fight with his Dad and then the Dad moved out, taking the girlfriend with him. Nat spent most of his time at our house and his Mum didn't seem to give a toss, even when he stayed away from home for three nights in a row. He never told her where he was (though he told Mum he had) and she never tried to find out. Unless Mum told her, of course, but I don't think she did because Nat asked her not to talk to Dorothy about anything they'd said in their many little chats over the kitchen table. And Mum said, no, of course not, all worried, like she always does. She loves secrets almost as much as she loves problems – which is saying something. Give her a problem and she practically loves it to death.

As for Dad, he was called in to give one of his man-to-man talks to Josh. But he was going off to Germany the next day with Ron so we didn't see much of him for a couple of weeks. And he missed the whole drama with Nat. Boys will be boys. That's what he told Mum. She nearly hit the roof, said why couldn't he take anything seriously, just for a change? I thought they were going to have another row, but Dad was all calm and refused to be riled, although I could see he was angry. He said he had to go and rehearse with his band because, as he was sure she knew, he took his career very seriously indeed. She said, yes, it was the only thing he did take seriously. So he said he didn't want to discuss Josh with her until she was capable of being objective and he hoped she'd be more rational by the time he got back from Berlin. I was sitting on the stairs and at this point he opened the kitchen door, so I shot up to my room and didn't hear what she said to that. And Dad went off without saying goodbye.

XIV

'It's not your problem,' says Chaz, 'and it's not mine. Why don't you just leave it out, Claud?'

'Wouldn't you feel dreadful, though,' says Claudia, 'if your mother had had you taken into care?'

'Not really . . . It might have done me some good.'

'Well, it's not going to do Nat any good.'

'Fuck Nat.' Chaz pulls up suddenly at a zebra crossing for two little girls who seemed to be on the verge of running unheedingly on to the road. 'But then I suppose you've done that already.'

'Oh, don't be ridiculous,' Claudia says wearily.

Chaz's face is clamped and shut as the Rolls glides on, seemingly of its own volition. The driver's window slides down and he leans his forearm across the opening. His arm, the shirt-sleeve rolled up to the elbow, is muscular and as rigid as the line of his jaw. His fist is clenched, the veins on the back of his hand prominent. The hairs at his wrist are reddish in the late afternoon sun. Claudia sits upright in the leather upholstery at his side, further constricted by her seat-belt. She too is tense, but determined not to get into an argument with Chaz. It never does any good. Her comparative verbal dexterity, which she is powerless to check, demoralizes him. Thus, in being disadvantaged, he disadvantages her too: whatever she says is perceived as rhetoric, redolent with ulterior motivation. Even the simplest of her statements is capable of being interpreted as an attempt to humiliate him. So she will say nothing. She resolves to say nothing. The traffic thickens as they approach the Angel intersection. Chaz, frowning, draws breath to speak.

'What's so ridiculous about it?' he demands at last. 'He's a man, isn't he – physically?'

'Lots of people are men physically,' she says patiently. 'That doesn't mean to say I'm screwing them.'

'Doesn't it? What about Clive?'

'I haven't seen Clive for two months.' She sighs. Why should she have to justify herself? 'I told him I was getting it together with Dorian again, and he went back to Greta – not that he'd ever actually left her.'

'Good job I came along, then,' says Chaz, turning sharply into Pentonville Road on an amber light. 'I mean, you couldn't have done without it for two months, could you?'

'I've changed my mind, Chaz. I'll get the tube.'

'I know, you know.'

'What do you know?'

'I know you love it, girl. I've felt you spunking away at the end of my cock, you fine educated lady, and I know you love it.'

'Just because your wife is frigid –'

'I never said my Rosie was frigid.'

'You don't have to. She must be, if you think I'm some kind of nymphomaniac.'

'She's a bag, for fuck's sake.' Chaz is on the verge of tears. The traffic is at a standstill. 'She's only ruined my fucking life, hasn't she?'

'Listen, Chaz.' Claudia puts a hand on his arm, wondering at the same time if it is wise to touch him. 'I really don't want to go on with this conversation. Would you drop me off at Kings Cross, please?'

'She's a bag,' Chaz repeats, ignoring her touch. 'But what can I do? She's good as gold really, a wonderful mother.'

Claudia is suddenly impatient. 'Just because you feel guilty about deceiving your wife, there's no need to take it out on me.'

'Women like you,' says Chaz, 'are enough to drive an ordinary bloke like me screaming round the twist. You give yourself. Again and again. But you're not giving nothing, really. You could be at it with a different bloke every night, and I'd be none the wiser.'

'So what?'

'I'll tell you so fucking what. It's breaking me up. It's destroying me. That's what.'

'Your jealousy is destroying you.'

'Yes!'

'Don't you realize how boring it is for me?'

'Boring!' Chaz sounds contemptuous. 'Is that all you've got to say when I'm going fucking spare about you?'

The traffic is moving more freely now that they have crossed the Penton Street junction. To their left, the grey tower blocks, to their rights, St James's in its greenly anachronistic churchyard. The road slopes downwards to Kings Cross where, behind barriers, the new Jubilee Line (formerly known as the Fleet Line) is being built. There are more traffic lights at the cinema. Chaz must let Claudia out there. But the lights are green and they drive without hindrance round the corner into Gray's Inn Road and from there into the broad thoroughfare which passes the station. The next lot of lights is red. Claudia unfastens her seat-belt.

'Just drop me off at the underground entrance,' she tells Chaz, 'and I'll get the tube.'

'I said I'd take you, Claud.' Chaz changes deliberately into the middle lane. 'And I'll fucking take you.'

'I don't want you to take me.'

'Don't be daft. You'll be late for your meeting.'

'Screw my meeting. I'm not going.'

'I'll take you home, then.'

'I'm not going home.'

'Where are you going, then?'

But the traffic has halted and Claudia is out of the Rolls in an instant. She threads her way dangerously among the stationary but impatient cars, nearly choking on the fumes, and runs down the steps to the tube station, quite as if she believed Chaz to be in pursuit. Managing to avoid most of the passengers emerging into the street, she collides nevertheless with a balding, middle-aged man, who takes the opportunity to squeeze her breast through the thin cotton of her sweat shirt. It is only with difficulty that she suppresses the impulse to kick him down the remainder of the concrete steps. Instead she wrenches herself free with a wordless yell of anger, and stumbles into a run again as she reaches the bottom of the steps. Arriving breathless at the ticket machines, she can't remember where she is supposed to be going.

She will be late for the faculty meeting. There is no doubt about that, because there is a ten-minute walk at the other end of the tube journey. Better late than never, perhaps. Probably. Faculty meetings are not well-attended, and decisions are inevitably taken by some five or six people who deem it politic, in terms of job security or furtherance, to let Boris see the extent of their commitment to college affairs. Trivialities are disputed, but in major matters Dr Phipps is always deferred to, despite his honest efforts to involve his colleagues in the democratic process. Thus, at the last meeting, there was a heated argument about the advisability of faculty members smoking in class – an indulgence forbidden to the students – while a proposal from Angus Baker of Creative Writing that part-time faculty should be paid for setting and marking papers was vitiated by a counter-proposal from Boris himself to the effect that part-timers be sent a questionnaire about their working hours. Claudia's one contribution was to complain that Boris's suggestion was, like a Royal Commission, tantamount to shelving the question. But Boris promised her earnestly that this would not be so, and that the results of the questionnaire would be followed up with all possible speed. Everyone else, including Angus, agreed with him: they should be sure of their facts before making any recommendations. Claudia felt powerless and frustrated, but said nothing. She has nothing to say now. Then why is she bothering to attend the meeting? To ensure that she is re-employed by the college in September? But the prospect of another year at St Alban's is daunting rather than inviting. Curiosity? It has faded. A chance to get away from home and offspring, to forget the role of deceived wife and inadequate mother?

Yes. That's it. That's what she wants. The chance to feel effective, the chance to deal with that which can be dealt with, rather than the imponderables of highly fraught relationships among those who are bound together all the way through the frangible spectrum of human emotion. Oh, for an arena in which protagonist, antagonist and chorus are all easily identifiable by virtue of their formal garb and groupings! Oh, to be enabled to believe that some problems at least are solvable! Claudia has to laugh at her own foolishness. A mere faculty meeting, at which all the dreary moves are known in advance, is capable of providing her with only the most superficial of certainties.

She will go and see Sonia. The notion comes happily, as if only waiting somewhere in the wings to be recognized. But first she must telephone. She makes her way back up to the main concourse with a lighter step. Chaz is impossible. Dorian is impossible. Josh and Nat are impossible. Claudia is altogether out of love with the male of the species. What she needs is some cool, frank, feminine conversation. Let's just hope that Sonia is at home and not too deeply immersed in the demands of her routine to allow an hour or two to friendship. Sonia is neither cold nor fierce, never openly rude or rejecting, but in her presence you are cautious, almost afraid. Of what? That she will find you out. But, if Sonia is your friend, she will not use any such information against you, either at once and face to face or later with a third party. You will see her register it, whatever it may be, and file it away without comment. She judges but she doesn't condemn. She judges and she remembers. Your weakness becomes her strength, which she will never use. It serves to maintain her as Sonia, a being apart from you, a being eternally apart from everyone. This is a circumstance she seems to need so badly that you feel she must be terrified of losing it. Then Sonia too is afraid. Of what? That you will find her out. Are not all the best friendships balanced nicely between the preservation and surrender of the inviolate self?

On form, Sonia is all warmth and self-revelation. Her novels too are (so they say) all self-revelation: passion laid bare and analysed under her supreme control. Thus she will communicate with you in everyday life – if she chooses to communicate with you at all. And yet who is Sonia, what is she? You feel that there is always more to be revealed: the self is endless. When Claudia is with Sonia she can believe that she too, the essential Claudia, is endless, layer upon layer of selfhood which, though stripped successively away, never succeeds in uncovering its own core because that is still growing and regrowing, constantly renewing itself. Claudia suspects that for Sonia life is primarily research for fiction, which in turn is life itself, but life converted to form, order, and meaning. The process is not a matter of calculation but springs from a basic need for transcendence. Isn't that what we all need – a bit of transcendence? Oh yes, that's why we seize upon the tiniest pieces of it we are offered. That's why we get into bed with men like Clive and Chaz. Sex, which can liberate the soul, as well as the body, is available to all for free, the poor person's trip towards union with the other in which the self is lost and found. And resurrected.

Why, then, does it always turn out to be such a sordid mess? Claudia's vehement finger has contrived to misdial Sonia's number, and at first she fails to recognize the number-unobtainable signal. The ten-pence piece still perched in the slot, she redials carefully, trying not to let her impatience with Chaz distract her. Why the hell can't he just accept their relationship for what it is, instead of polluting it with class and class-ridden notions of ideal womanhood? The number is ringing. And of course she cannot expect Chaz to ignore the mores and barriers of class. It is only the free-floating professional classes who can do as much.

'Claudia!' Sonia sounds pleased. 'I was just thinking about you, wondering how you were coping with the teenage fiends.'

'Are you busy?'

'Right now I'm on my way to a meeting . . .'

'So was I but I decided not to go.'

'Well, I must go to this one because I called it. But I'll be back around nine. Why don't you come over then and have some supper?'

'Love to. I'll bring some wine.'

Claudia looks at her watch. The faculty meeting is beginning. It will take half an hour to get to Sonia's. That means she has another two hours to kill. She walks aimlessly past the queues waiting at each set of platform gates. She could go home. But that means two separate sessions of waiting for the 73, and in between the possible horror of walking unexpectedly into the middle of some teenage event to which she might prefer to turn a blind eye, and thus avoid another familial confrontation. She could go to the bar and have a drink. But a woman sitting alone in a bar, while not necessarily identifying herself as being on the game, is bound to attract unwelcome attention. She could have a cup of coffee, but she doesn't want a cup of what British Rail chooses to pass off under that name. No, she will buy a book or a magazine and sit in the bar and to hell with it. The lighted windows of Smith's draw her to her left. In one narrow room all Britain's printed wealth! Romances, Thrillers, Science Fiction, Memoirs, Do-It-Yourself . . . To her dismay, Claudia cannot summon up interest in any of them. The act of reading requires a certain inwardness coupled with a willing surrender: together those requirements add up to the very state from which she wishes to escape. She wants to talk, to spill, to impose herself on others who will respond, favourably or not, to the fact of her existence, the fact of her uniquely felt consciousness.

She will go and see Juno. Sonia lives in Notting Hill and Juno in Knightsbridge, nearly on the way. Juno has a new flat, which she is in the process of decorating and which Claudia has only seen in its undecorated state. Problems of design and decor will divert Claudia from her own less tractable ones: she and Juno can give each other advice, which need or need not be taken, in a series of acts of mutual trust. Neither will condemn the other's weaknesses, but look on them rather in a spirit of affection, tempered with commonsense caution. Let's just hope that Juno is at home studying her wallpaper patterns or stripping the panelling which encases her staircase.

'Juno Smithson.' This manner of answering the telephone has been acquired with the flat. 'Oh, Claudia, how unlike you to invite yourself! What's come over you?'

'I just felt like seeing you.'

'How delightful! Come right on over.'

As Claudia puts the phone down, she is struck by the thought that although there are several women in her life to whom she can say, with equanimity, I just felt like seeing you, there is not one man. This must be wrong. She makes her way back through the crowds to the ticket office, glumly wondering if the sexes are not perhaps incompatible and, were it not for the demands of procreation, better able to function in a state of apartheid.

The advertisements, as she descends in the escalator, do nothing to alleviate such reluctantly cynical musings. There is a smirking male in a nicely laundered shirt, a pair of beautifully manicured female hands caressing his shoulders from behind. She does his shirts and he gets admired for her labour. Here are three women standing on an escalator, wearing London Transport T-shirts, which emphasize the shape of their breasts. The caption reads: Shirts that Go Down Well. The implication is quite clear: the purpose of women is to service men sexually. Blow-jobs: that's what we really want, girls; none of this face-to-face between-equals nonsense. On the platform, the advertisements are larger – larger, indeed, than life. Claudia sits on a wooden bench aligned with the spot where she knows the smoking compartment will pull up. Opposite her, some three yards high, is a photograph of a pair of female legs, cut off at the crotch by a frill of black lace, and tapering downwards to impossibly high-heeled sandals. Beats the pants off trousers any day. Of course it does. No point in walking through life in trousers like a man. Why hide your real assets? After all, your legs and your crotch are all you've got. A little to the right is another enlarged photograph of a portion of the female body – this time a torso which is being unveiled to reveal an immaculate set of underwear. Underneath they're all lovable. Underneath, women are all the same. But I'm not women. I'm Claudia. Underneath they're all whores who will sell their bodies for commercial gain. Don't be put off by the pristine white of their bras and panties. Rip 'em off, lads! It's what they all want, you know.

The smoking compartment, where the addicts gather to light up as soon as the train moves off, if not before, is less crowded but dirtier than the non-smoking strongholds. Grinding her cigarette, half-smoked, where it has fallen between two slats of the wooden floor, Claudia experiences a sadistic urge to grind the faces of the advertisers beneath the abrasive heel of reality. How is it possible not to be affronted by their products? And yet, if you complain, you are accused of overreacting, as if each offering were merely an arrangement of line, colour and shape, devoid of ulterior meaning: not Whistler's mother after all, but a study in grey. The only ulterior meaning allowed by your ordinary decent adman is that of making money. No doubt Josh, Matilda and their mysterious friend Rodge would label the whole business a capitalist plot. And for once they would be right. Everything means something. But what shall it profit a man to recognize as much? In acknowledging layer upon layer of meaning, he might be forced to recognize himself. And that's an exercise fit only for women, foreigners and lunatics.

The streets behind Harrods are deserted except for the occasional knot of people in Arab dress outside expensive restaurants. It is beginning to rain in large occasional splodges which presage thunder. Claudia hurries on, impeded slightly by the spindly sandals she put on in the belief that she would neither have to walk far nor climb the stairs to the top deck of a bus. And now she will have to do both. Why ever did she buy such impractical footwear? Because her husband thought red high-heeled sandals were sexy. Because her husband drove her from place to place in his car. And today her lover offered to perform that same protective service. From his mansion in Tenterden he called his ex-colleague's estranged wife and offered to take her to a new French restaurant in Richmond where only those in the know were admitted and served. When Claudia explained about the faculty meeting, Chaz was neither impressed nor acquiescent. He told her to leave all that sort of thing to frustrated middle-aged women and earnest little men who had nothing better to do with their lives. Claudia put the phone down. Chaz called again, all apology: would she at least allow him to drive her to her meeting? She asked him if he had nothing better to do with his life. He swore he had not. After some protestation on both sides, she agreed that his Roller was a more pleasant form of transport than the 73 bus and that she was not deliberately trying to make him feel useless and inferior. What else could she do? What else has she ever done? Poor Chaz. Poor Clive. Poor Dorian. How frail is the male of the species. What chance of survival has it without the benefit of female compassion? Only a bitch would withhold what is so easily given and so gratefully received.

A drunk in a gaberdine coat lurches out of the shadows behind the church, muttering to himself. When he reaches the zebra crossing at the corner he takes hold of the Belisha beacon with both hands and, knocking his head against its column, begins to yell in a voice as full of despair as anger, Fenian scum! Thinking it politic to avoid him, Claudia runs across the road at once. But he has seen her. Recovering his equilibrium with surprising alacrity, he strides over the crossing to intercept her. His face is young, bloated, unshaven. His eyes are red and rheumy and he stinks of vomit as well as whisky. The hand on her arm pleads before it grips.

'Here's a pretty girl, now. How about a little kiss?'

'No!' Claudia pulls herself free and walks on.

'Fenian bitch!' he yells after her. 'Up yours! Up your tight little Fenian cunt!'

Juno is wearing a kimono and fluffy mules. She is holding a paint-pot in one hand and a glass of gin in the other. The furniture is shrouded in dust-sheets and the living-room walls are pink where freshly plastered, white where the undercoat has been applied. She invites Claudia to admire her industry rather than her handiwork. Here is no difficulty for Claudia, who wonders in addition whether Juno has abandoned her plan to wallpaper the room. Having explained in the patient tones of one who has done so several times before that the wallpaper was intended for her bedroom, Juno salvages two cushions, which she calls pillows, from behind a dust-sheet and invites Claudia to sit down.

'If you must walk the streets alone at night,' she says, sitting down rather heavily herself, 'you must expect to be pestered.'

Claudia is irritated by this assumption, all the more so because she knows it to be true. 'But what the hell else am I supposed to do?'

'Learn to drive,' Juno says in her cheerful way. 'Or else take taxis everywhere. It's probably cheaper anyway.'

'Not cheap enough for me.'

'So, open an account.'

'But I'd still have to pay.'

'Not yet, though.' Juno sighs. 'Really, Claudia, I sometimes think you create your own difficulties. There is no problem that's incapable of solution, so long as you don't play by the rules.'

'Isn't there? What about Chaz?'

'What you've got to ask yourself is what you want from him.'

Claudia shrugs. 'Nothing.'

'Then why don't you tell him to piss off?'

Claudia stares up at Juno's newly painted ceiling. 'I see you chose the plainer type of moulding for the light fitting, after all that.'

'I figured it would look better on a low ceiling,' says Juno. 'Now, answer my question, Claudia.'

'Oh, I will. Tell him to piss off, I mean. Chaz is only the least of my problems.'

'So what's Dorian done now?'

'God knows. I haven't seen him since the day after the crime. I suppose he's still in Berlin.

'Don't you know where he is?'

'He's not going to tell me, is he?'

'And you two used to be so close.' Juno sighs again. 'I'll never forget the first time I met the both of you. So many married people have a kind of basic contempt for each other. But you two seemed to have the utmost respect for each other's opinions. I thought you'd got it all worked out. Very impressive.'

'Dorian's an actor.'

'And Claudia?'

'Claudia rises to the occasion. She's a real little Angela Brazil heroine. Or don't you read school stories in America?'

'I know the sort of thing,' says Juno. 'Now, I can see you're depressed, so let me show you around. The kitchen's come on something unbelievable since you were last here.'

Claudia trails after Juno through the unlit basement hall to the long narrow kitchen, formerly a store room containing little besides the central-heating boiler, and now equipped with a row of streamlined units in stainless steel and red enamel. It must have cost a pretty penny. The spectre of poverty joining hands with that of loneliness ahead of her, Claudia shivers as they step lightly and lovingly over her grave. And there, lining Juno's walls above the waist-high cupboards, are the very same red-and-white, Italian tiles which Claudia and Dorian chose together for the house in Colehan Road, which took a whole year and as many thousands of pounds as the original price to renovate. Infuriatingly, her eyes fill with tears and she turns away from Juno, opening and shutting doors of cupboards overhead. They had bought that house in hope after the business with Crabbe had come to an end. They lavished their hope on it, as if hope were something which could be bought. It was a gift they made to themselves for coming through. And then, one day when the house was finished and the people from *Beautiful Homes* had come to take pictures, Claudia and Dorian laughed and laughed at what a delightful farce it all had been, and Dorian said to Claudia, I've fallen in love with you – permanently. She cannot stop the tears now and, fumbling in her pocket for the grubby kleenex which she knows must be there somewhere, she walks quickly back to the sitting-room to find a cigarette.

Juno, in front of whom she must not allow herself to weep, follows her at once. 'Can't you go for ten minutes without smoking?'

'I'm sorry.' Claudia is surprised at the steadiness of her own voice and the dryness of the eyes with which she gazes back at Juno. 'You're right. I am depressed. I don't seem to be able to cope with my life at all.'

'You've been spoiled for so long, Claudia,' says Juno, 'and now you're just getting your dusty answer like the rest of us.'

'Well, try not to sound so pleased about it.'

'Claudia!' Juno lays a hand on her chest as if on heart. 'I'm as shattered as you are.'

'And if you think being married to someone whose total life is lived in public means being spoiled, you've got a funny idea of what constitutes happiness.'

'Claudia, please! Don't let's fight. All I'm saying, my dear, is that you've just got to grin and bear it.'

'Oh, I'll bear it. But I'm damned if I'm going to grin. My teeth are permanently gritted.'

'Here am I,' says Juno, 'showing you my new flat and trying to demonstrate in the most basic fashion that life must go on, and you're simply not responding.'

'I'm sorry.'

'So am I. Let me get you another drink.'

Juno takes their glasses back to the kitchen and Claudia sits down forlornly in her allotted place. She has not come to Juno for comfort and yet, now that it is being withheld, she is disappointed. She knows that by all apparent standards Juno is right: she, Claudia, has been lucky. But she also knows that, according to some standard which is so deeply a part of her moral nature that it is scarcely accessible to consciousness, Juno is fatally wrong. However, she finds it impossible to voice this knowledge, let alone justify it, and is glad that Juno has not expected her to do so. Such an exercise would entail a catalogue of Dorian's faults, each one seemingly petty, unworthy of condemnation and indeed even unworthy of her attention. It must be admitted that his chief fault is that he has hurt her. He has hurt her more than she supposed she could ever be hurt again. And what hurts most of all is his wilful refusal to acknowledge as much. In doing so, he might be forced to recognize himself: a man who treats women with contempt and children with the indifference born only of self-love. As if every act of coition were onanistic and its issue a series of mirror-images.

'How's Josh?' Juno asks, sitting down beside her.

'I wish I knew. He doesn't talk to me any more. Not that he ever did – much.'

'Is he worried about the court case?'

'He pretends not to be. I suspect that he's truanting all the time. Martin Hazlitt thinks he ought to go away to school.'

'Of course he ought.' Juno's voice is triumphant. 'That's what I've been telling you for years.'

'It seems like giving up.'

'If you can't cope, you've got to give up.'

'But it's like getting rid of him. Like Nat's mother having him taken into care.'

'Come on, Claudia, we know it's not like that.'

'But does Josh? He hasn't got a father who's any use to him. He ought to be able to feel that at least he's got a mother.'

'He'll still have a mother.'

'And, besides, who's going to pay the fees?'

'I will,' says Juno.

Claudia stares at her: this is the last thing she has expected. 'Oh, Juno, that's wonderful of you. But why should you?'

'I have my reasons,' says Juno. 'You know I'm fond of Josh. I've made worse investments in my time, believe me. What I mean, of course, is that I'll lend you and Dorian the money. You talk it over with him and see what he thinks.'

'He won't give a damn what I do. The person to talk to is Josh.'

'Oh no, you don't,' says Juno. 'You just tell him.'

Claudia smiles. 'That's not the way I operate, Juno. Remember, I was sent away to school against my will.'

'It didn't do you any harm, did it?'

'Yes, it did.'

'Oh nonsense, Claudia. You always think the worst. You're a survivor – and so is Josh.'

Claudia smiles again. 'I don't feel like a survivor. I feel like a total failure.'

'You'll get over it,' says Juno with the briskness she habitually uses to obviate self-pity. 'Now, let's go eat.'

'I promised Sonia,' says Claudia. 'I'm due at her place at nine. In fact, I'd better get going.'

Standing with her hands on her hips, her face flushed, Juno pronounces, 'Sonia is a rat.'

'Sonia is my friend,' Claudia says sharply.

But Juno persists. 'That's because you haven't done anything to offend her – yet. But watch your step, Claudia. The way she's behaved over the whole business with Justin is . . . is repulsive. She doesn't own him, after all.'

Claudia makes no comment, stands up unsteadily on her sexy heels, smooths her skirt down, zips up her bag. She is not used to drinking gin but, in much the same way as she didn't want Juno to see her weep, she cannot bring herself to confess that she had no idea how she is going to make her way to Sonia's. Smile and say nothing. Thus you avoid giving yourself away. Thank Juno. Kiss her goodbye. Then walk with all the dignity you can muster out into the street. Never let it be said that you have lost control. If you can get as far as the main road without either falling over or being molested, you can hail a taxi. But Juno is already at the telephone.

'I'm calling a cab for you,' she says. 'I can't let you out on your own in those shoes. It's on my account, so you needn't worry about breaking the bank.'

'Oh thanks, Juno,' Claudia says, wondering whether to risk sitting down again. 'But I'll pay for it. Don't worry.'

'Forget it,' Juno says as she puts the phone down. 'Invest your money in a pair of sensible shoes.'

'Oh, I'll be sensible,' says Claudia. 'And practical. I'll buy some sneakers and a tracksuit and look just like my students, wonderfully liberated women that they all are. I hate these things anyway. Do you know anyone who takes size three?'

'Sonia,' Juno says promptly. 'But I don't think she'd be seen dead in those. They really are cheap and nasty. Now, there's the cab. Have a lovely time.'

'A lovely time with a rat?' Claudia murmurs as she takes her leave.

In the cab Claudia stretches her legs and examines her shoes. They are not as high as the ones on the poster in the underground. You have to have big feet to wear six-inch heels. Nevertheless, Claudia's heels are about three inches high and very narrow. They are imitation patent leather with a metal-chain T-strap. Yes, they are a symbol of slavery, no less than the bound feet of Chinese women. She takes them off and, as the cab moves speedily west along Kensington Gore, she opens the window and throws one sandal in the direction of the Albert Hall. The other she deposits at the corner of Church Street and in the direction of St Alban's College. The taxi-driver doesn't seem to notice that she has shrunk. The pavement is wet and cool, unyielding but at the same time promising intimacy. It recognizes the shape of the foot.

Sonia's flat is as high as Juno's is low. Her roof terrace faces

A.—10

south and overlooks some wooded private gardens to which she has a key. The heavy door swings open as Claudia announces her presence. There are sixty-seven steps to climb, all stone and uncarpeted. Standing in her doorway, Sonia is startled by Claudia's noiseless appearance.

'I've been drinking gin with Juno,' Claudia says, as if by way of explanation, 'and then I threw away my shoes.'

Sonia laughs. 'I'll lend you some, if you like. Come in.'

Sonia's carpets are beige and thick-piled, tender to the feet. She leads Claudia into her living-room which, by virtue of its height and its long windows, bears some resemblance to Greta's studio. But whereas Greta lives in what she herself would doubtless consider delightfully artistic chaos, Sonia's surroundings are almost Spartan. A huge desk, occupying a position similar to that of Greta's waterbed, dominates the room. The furniture is sparse and beige. But Sonia has been lavish with brightly coloured cushions and rugs, and her plain walls are hung with clusters of inscribed and richly decorated plates. Books and papers are stacked in neat piles around the foot of her desk like so many offerings to a god who demands constant propitiation.

'Juno is a shit,' she says, handing Claudia a glass of chilled white wine.

'Juno is my friend,' Claudia says weakly.

'So far,' Sonia says emphatically. 'As long as you're poor little Claudia. Don't give her the opportunity to demand gratitude from you – that's all.'

'Strange you should say that. She's just offered to lend me the money to send Josh away to school.'

'And have you eternally in her debt?'

'Not eternally. Dorian keeps telling me how well he's going to do with this band of his.'

'And you think he'll repay Juno?'

'Well, I can't. And why shouldn't he?'

'Maybe to spite you?'

Claudia groans: there is a dire ring of truth to Sonia's suggestion. 'It's Josh I have to think about. It's Josh we both have to think about. Dorian and I, I mean.'

Sonia looks sceptically at her. 'Well,' she says with a little shrug, 'at least Josh is too young to merit Juno's amorous intentions – though I wouldn't be too sure even of that. I really draw the line at her attempting to seduce Justin.'

'Justin?'

'My son. I think you met him at the Freeburgs'.'

'Justin is your son?'

'What else did you think he was? My lover? You wouldn't be the first.'

Claudia feels herself blush. 'Oh no,' she lies. 'I thought Juno said you didn't have any children.'

'Justin is my son by my first marriage. The GI. Warren Wolynski. He now runs a funeral parlour in Salt Lake City. Though, God knows, business can hardly be brisk with all those Mormons around.'

Claudia laughs. 'I can't imagine you being married to an undertaker. I can't really imagine you being married to anyone.'

'Neither can I,' says Sonia, 'now. Though it seemed quite natural at the time.'

'You mean the feeling doesn't last?' Claudia asks wistfully. 'I'm not at all sure that I'm adequate to being alone in the world.'

'You mean you're afraid of being lonely?'

'Aren't you?'

'It's the worst possible reason for staying married,' says Sonia, ignoring the question. 'Come on, let's eat. I put the quiche in the oven when you rang the doorbell. Meanwhile, I hope you like artichokes.'

'Love them,' says Claudia, following her into the kitchen. 'Oh, Sonia, I'm sorry, I forgot the wine.'

'I'll never forgive you,' says Sonia, setting two plates of artichokes, their flower-heads forced open and spread, on the unvarnished pine table. 'If I hadn't been afraid of being lonely, I'd never have remarried. I didn't know then, you see, that being lonely and living alone are not the same thing. The latter is not as terrible as you may suppose.'

'I can see that,' says Claudia, looking round the room.

Sonia's kitchen is comfortable and cluttered, but nevertheless neat. The fittings and furniture are of plain wood and look worn. Everywhere there are tidy rows of jars, bottles and tins. At the far end of the table a radio-cassette recorder is flanked by two pyramids of plastic cubes displaying photographs, mainly of children, the young Justin recognizably prominent among them. The unoccupied chairs are piled with newspapers. Claudia sits down opposite Sonia. Her place is set with heavy silver cutlery, to the left a finger bowl of water with a slice of lemon floating on top, to the right a majestic wine glass. The artichoke is arranged invitingly, the choke removed and the centre sodden with melted butter. Claudia notes that for Sonia eating is more of a ritual than a mere quenching of appetite. There is something deliciously cruel in the way the two of them are dismembering the sacrificial vegetable petal by petal and chewing their relentless way toward its very heart. As if conscious of sharing a sacrament, neither of them speaks. Sonia refills their glasses. The discarded leaves are built into circular walls around the edges of their plates. Claudia experiences an unfamiliar sensation. Dare she call it happiness?

'Ah, bliss!' says Sonia, spearing the butter-soaked heart with her fork. 'I'm sure there must be some Freudian symbolism involved in all this. Should we go into it?'

Claudia is surprised to hear herself reply, 'Sex and eating are both cruel, aggressive activities.'

Sonia too is surprised. 'Do you really think so?'

'I don't know. I spoke without thinking.'

'But I agree with you.' Sonia looks steadily at her for a moment before removing their plates. 'So pretty,' she says with a sigh, looking at them. 'And of course, Claudia, you and I have both been brought up to be good little girls and nice young ladies, with nothing cruel or aggressive about us.'

'I'm always nice to people,' says Claudia, watching Sonia take the steaming quiche from the oven and set it on a mat between them. 'It's not that I don't want them to think ill of me. Often, in fact, I don't give a damn what they think. It's that I can't bear to think of *myself* as an unkind person.'

Sonia gives her a quick look of comprehension as she refills her glass. 'Go on.'

'Is there any more?' Claudia takes a meditative mouthful of wine while Sonia waits, one hand still gloved in an oven mitt, standing opposite her. 'Oh, yes. If I can think of myself as being married, I feel safe. Single, I seem to fall to pieces. Just a girl who can't say no. I keep feeling sorry for people – men, I mean – and that it's my duty to comfort them. As far as they're concerned, of course, that means sex.'

'I know this is supposed to be eaten warm,' says Sonia, as she takes a couple of hot plates from the oven and sets them in their places, 'but I like really hot food, don't you?' She cuts into the quiche with practised deftness. 'I take it this isn't just a simple matter of feeling guilty about being, in quotes, promiscuous?'

Claudia shakes her head. 'More a matter of worrying about things getting out of control.'

Again that quick look from Sonia. 'You feel quilty about being emotionally dishonest.'

'Of course,' Claudia says in some relief. 'In a way I offer comfort in the hope of getting some myself. But it's more a matter of principle, almost impersonal. People always know at some level. They resent it.'

'Like Chaz?'

'Like Chaz. But not like Clive. He never seems to resent anything.' Claudia cuts into her quiche. 'This is delicious, Sonia . . .'

'Didn't Juno remember to tell you what a good cook I was?' Having eaten only half her portion of quiche, Sonia is opening another bottle of wine. 'If she forgot to plug my chief virtue, she must be annoyed with me.'

'She said you didn't eat much,' Claudia concedes. 'Oh well, I suppose I'm just a total incompetent at dealing with men.'

'Not specially.' Sonia is almost as brisk as Juno. 'No more than anyone else. Just an ordinary, fallible human being, like the rest of us.'

'Is that really how you think of yourself?'

'I try to.' Sonia's smile is mysterious as she pours the wine. 'So now you're feeling about a millimetre high because you imagine you've been unkind to both Dorian and Chaz.'

Claudia smiles too: put like that, it sounds absurd. 'And Clive.'

'Oh, I'd forgotten Clive.' Sonia pushes the quiche across so that Claudia can now help herself. 'You've sent him back to Greta. Never mind. I'm sure he enjoys his martyrdom.'

'And Dorian?'

'Dorian, by the sound of it, has needed a good kick up the arse once a week for the past sixteen years. All you've done is to give him the lot in one go.'

'That's what he couldn't take . . .'

'Oh come on, Claudia, you know damn well he's got what was coming to him at last.'

Claudia laughs uncertainly. 'You're wonderful, Sonia.'

'Of course I'm wonderful.' A third of her portion still remaining on her plate, Sonia lights a cigarette. 'I'm a ordinary, fallible, wonderful human being. Just like you.'

It is only now that Claudia can admit to herself how highly she values Sonia's opinion of her. 'Do you think so?'

'The trouble with you and me, dear Claudia,' says Sonia, leaning back and looking at her through a haze of smoke, 'is that we can never be good enough for ourselves. So it's little wonder that other people fail to measure up to our standards.'

'But that's so bleak!'

'Except for our children, of course.' Sonia glances towards the photographs. 'They alone deserve our unconditional love.'

Claudia deliberately lights a cigarette before asking, 'Don't you ever fall in love?'

Again the mysterious smile. 'Not exactly. Do you?'

Claudia sighs. 'I wonder if I ever will again.'

'Chaz is in love with you.'

'Infatuated, maybe. He certainly doesn't love me.'

'He sees you as some symbol of the privileged classes. That's what he's in love with.'

'How do you know?'

'He more or less told me.'

'Oh.' Claudia doesn't ask where or when this conversation has taken place.

'What's he like in bed?'

'What do you think?'

'Clumsy.'

Claudia laughs. 'Poor Chaz. But you're right, of course. The first time he couldn't get it together at all. He got so angry with himself. That's when he had the fight with Nat. And he was so persistent about seeing me again. But I knew it was nothing to do with me. He just wanted to prove himself the second time around.'

'And did he?'

'To his own satisfaction, yes.'

'And then?'

'That's all. I've managed to evade him ever since.'

Sonia laughs. 'Yes, poor Chaz. But hardly your scene, Claudia.'

'What *is*?'

'Forget about men. Concentrate on your work.'

'Like you, you mean?'

'Like me, among others.'

'I don't have any work, Sonia.'

'What about the college?'

'It's May. I'm just setting the final exams. After that, I'm unemployed. And besides, I loathe teaching.'

'Then we'll have to think of something else.'

'What else?'

'I said we'll have to think.' Sonia begins to clear the table. 'I'll make some coffee.'

Claudia gets up to help with clearing away. Sonia scatters coffee beans into the electric grinder, judging the correct amount precisely by eye. The noise of the grinder, vibrantly in need of repair, makes conversation impossible. A ceramic text hangs above the sink: Behold GOD will not cast away a perfect man; neither will HE help evil-doers. The words are garlanded prettily in black-and-white leaves and framed squarely in pink lustre. Just the thing to make you feel virtuous with your hands in dirty dish water. Claudia sits down again, rebuked. She can't remember how much money she has in her purse, whether it will cover the taxi-fare back to Hackney.

'Why don't you stay the night?' Sonia asks, as if on cue, handing her a cup of coffee. 'I'll give you a nightie and you can stay in Justin's room.'

'Justin lives here?'

'No, alas!' Sonia sighs. 'He lives with his boyfriend in Brighton. But he sometimes comes to stay when Ralph is otherwise occupied. I'm still waiting for the day when he feels they can both come and stay here together.'

'Doesn't Juno know that Justin is gay?'

'Juno thinks it's a youthful aberration.'

'What do you think?'

'Oh, what's the point in pretending? I can tell you, can't I, Claudia?' Sonia glances towards the photograph again. 'When he told me, I felt this tremendous sense of relief. It seemed to explain so much about Justin. And of course it meant that no other woman could come between us – ever.' Sonia's voice becomes steely as she continues. 'Justin is all I've got. A poor thing, but mine own. A failure, but my son.'

Claudia doesn't quite know what to make of this. She asks tentatively, 'Did he find it difficult to tell you?'

'Oh yes.' Sonia covers her face momentarily with her hands. 'He had to get drunk. Well, we both were. Everything was fine and dandy between us – for once. Then he told me how he'd been assaulted by the babysitter when he was eight. That seemed to explain even more.' Sonia covers her face with her hands again: they are shaking. 'It was Barnaby Freeburg.'

It takes Claudia a few moments to absorb this information. 'Greta's darling son.'

Sonia nods solemnly. 'Greta's darling son. Not that she knows anything about it, of course.'

'But you don't think Barnaby *caused* Justin to become gay?'

'Oh no, nothing is ever that simple.' Sonia lights another cigarette. 'But I think Barnaby clinched something. That the act of penetration is cruel and aggressive, as you implied, and something from which Justin has wanted to dissociate himself ever since.'

'I've often wondered,' Claudia says, though in truth at a loss for words, 'how men felt about that.'

'The next morning . . .' Sonia pauses to inhale several times on her cigarette. ' . . . I felt so hungry after all that drinking, and I decided to cook us some fried eggs for breakfast. Justin was still in bed. But when I broke them into the pan, the yolks were split with gashes of blood. You know, I screamed, Claudia. I screamed and screamed. I threw them away. I couldn't stop crying.'

'Oh Sonia . . . ' Claudia is as perilously near to tears as Sonia herself. 'I can see. You felt you'd failed to protect him.'

Sonia's face is once again devoid of all expression of emotion as she answers, 'It's the least he could have expected of me, isn't it?'

'The Freeburgs were your friends,' Claudia murmurs. 'How were you to know?'

'Of course.' Sonia's voice is light and brisk again. 'It happens all the time, doesn't it? Let's leave the washing-up, shall we? I'll show you your room.'

Sonia's nightie is coral-pink wincyette, embroidered at the yoke with forget-me-nots – not at all the style that Claudia would have expected. Wearing it, she feels strangely abstracted from her own body, a thing no longer in her possession. Sonia has cut short the conversation, but Sonia has given her a nightie, a towel and a toothbrush, wishing her a peaceful sleep unperturbed by dreams of cruelty and aggression. Claudia runs her hands over her body through the nightie from neck to groin, as if making sure that it is still there. She doesn't want to experience Sonia's dreams. It is as if Sonia has said to her, I am the future, put me on. She doesn't know whether to tear the nightie off again or to clasp it all the more closely around her. Sonia can function alone and independently. Can Claudia? And how, if through weakness, she allows the marriage to continue, can she ever face Sonia again?

XV

I really am brill, you know. I mean, I'm a fucking genius. We were sitting around in Rodge's room, him and me and Josh and Nat, and nobody was saying anything much. I was chewing at my broken thumbnail and the boys seemed to be occupied with picking their spots in an absent sort of way. Rodge was watching them. Suddenly I caught his eye, and it was like we were both thinking the same thing, whatever that might be. I burst out laughing. I just couldn't help it. Then it came to me. You know, I said, I think we should call the magazine *Zitz*. (Yes, with a z. A touch of class, that, don't you think?) Josh and Nat looked at me in disgust, waiting for me to stop laughing. Rodge was smiling (he never really laughs) and this confused them some. He said, I think that's a brilliant idea, Matilda, really grass-roots. Jesus H. Christ, did I glow? I glowed like a thousand-watt neon bulb. Slowly, the expressions on the boys' faces began to change (you could hear the sodding wheels turn) until they were both smiling too in a smug sort of way, like I'd paid them some sort of compliment. Once they'd seen the funny side of it, they thought it was a great idea too. As for me, I got quite carried away by my own brilliance and suggested we have a cover-boy, a spotty adolescent, instead of the usual glamour-girl. The boys loved that. Nat even said it was real Punk thinking on my part.

Well, that cheered us all up. What with one thing and another, we'd all been down and depressed and quarrelsome since the crime and Nat's suicide attempt. Rodge kept saying that Dorothy and Barney should go ahead and sue the Pigs for assault. For some reason, Nat wasn't very keen on this. I don't know whether he felt reluctant to ally himself with his parents or whether he'd just had enough of the whole hassle and wanted to forget it. Josh agreed with Rodge that the Pigs shouldn't be allowed to get away with it. He wanted Mum and Dad to sue for what happened to him, but they said they couldn't because he had no wounds or bruises to show for it. It turned out that Hazlitt (who was a magistrate in his spare time) had told Mum (who told me, swearing me to secrecy) that parents who made allegations against the police were rarely considering the well-being of their child, but just wanted to defend themselves against accusations of negligent parenting. Didn't make much sense to me, but at the same time it seemed typical of the sort of twisted adult thinking magistrates might go in for, and then automatically assume they were dealing with some kind of incurable delinquent. In other words, I could see that Mum wanted to present Josh to the court as some kid from a good home who'd unfortunately gone astray as a one-off. I could see too why Josh didn't like this. He didn't want to be thought of as some wally who'd been led astray by the notorious Nat Masters. So he and Rodge went around muttering, remember Liddell Towers, and suchlike phrases. Result: mild dissension in the ranks.

I don't think Josh and Nat were ever in school very much for the rest of that summer term. Well, Nat was actually suspended for two weeks. Poor old Fairfax: her naive assumptions about the adolescent male responding to sweetness and light were severely challenged by Nat's attempted suicide. And then she found out that him and me and Josh had gone to Blair Peach's funeral. Not exactly a crime, as Rodge said. But to her it was just another sign of our general evilness, especially Nat's. Of course it was supposed to be his doing. No more sweetness and light for him, but the usual dollop for me. And for Josh, well, seeing as how he was never there for her to fasten her fangs on him, he got away unscathed. Anyway, how could she suspend someone who'd already suspended himself?

As Rodge pointed out, no amount of sweetness and light can make up for the deprivation of freedom. If you feel hemmed in and patronized by petty rules and officious teachers, you're hardly going to thank someone who goes on about the sweetness of your slavery, now, are you? Fairfax decided that Nat's presence would be disruptive and asked his parents to send him away somewhere for a holiday. So off he pissed to Wolverhampton to stay with his Dad's parents. I know for a fact that Josh didn't even go anywhere near the school all the time Nat was away. Perhaps he didn't feel safe without Nat. Anyway, he spent most of his time wandering around the streets or sitting in the library pretending to read *Das Kapital* or sitting in the park actually reading Olaf Stapledon's *Last and First Men* (which seemed to last him forever) or talking to Rodge after he'd finished his milk round.

Things weren't quite the same for me either. I don't really know how to explain what was going on inside me because it felt like nothing actually *was*. Emma said, how come I'd turned into such a puke-making bore when I used to be the chief life-brightener? I knew I should have been offended, felt hurt, but somehow I didn't. I could see that from her point of view I'd let her down and I expect she thought I was still jealous of her and Slime. But it wasn't that. It really wasn't. It was just that I couldn't get off on spending hours on my hair or clothes or giggling with Emma any more. To tell you the truth, I began to wonder what I ever saw in her in the first place. I think it must have been to do with getting involved with *Zitz* as well as the crime and what was happening to Josh and Nat. I just gradually began to see everything in a different light. I couldn't help it. I mean, she couldn't expect me to *close* my mind, could she? Oh yes, she could. She did. She just refused to understand. I felt sorry for her.

When Nat came back from Wolverhampton, his Mum had him taken into care. She told his social worker that he was beyond her control. What an idiotic thing to say! What sort of pissing control did she pissing want? To keep him under lock and key? Of course we all knew that Cormack was behind it. We knew (because Nat had told us) just the sort of thing he was always saying to Dorothy. Why should he have to be *your* responsibility? He's got a father, hasn't he? Why shouldn't Barney shoulder some of the burdens? But Barney wasn't having any. Any fool could have seen that. He thought that mothers should look after their children, and any attempt to get him to change his mind was just fucking pointless. Might as well get the Pope to start advertising condoms. But Cormack and Dorothy were too busy waging their own war with

Barney to see that. And which of them all gave a toss about Nat? That's what I'd like to know. When they had a family therapy session, the geezer in charge asked Cormack what he would have felt if Nat had succeeded in bumping himself off. And do you know what the bastard said? He said – with Nat sitting right there beside him – that he would have been relieved. Relieved! What kind of a human being could say a thing like that? When Nat told Mum she was horrified. Then she said that Cormack's remark should be seen in its therapeutic context where everyone is supposed to be honest, otherwise there's no point to the exercise. I mean, she actually tried to get us to admire Cormack for his honesty! If I'd thought she really meant it (and she said she was just putting it forward for our consideration), I'd have left home there and then.

Anyway, Nat was packed off to live in this hostel, where he had to be in at half-past ten every night. I ask you! While the rest of us could hang around outside the Grope and Wanker till closing time, poor old Nat had to piss off at ten, even on a Saturday night. Needless to say, this didn't last long and he'd come home and stay with us most weekends. They didn't like it too much at the hostel, of course, but they weren't that bothered either. I mean, in the death, there wasn't much they could do about it, was there? The only advantage to the hostel was that it was quite near Rodge, so Nat could go round there whenever he wanted to escape. And of course he didn't have to put up with all the nagging from Dorothy, Barney and Cormack. If you ask me, he was better off without the lot of them. And – believe it or not – that's exactly what the social worker said to him.

It was then that Mum had her brainwave (!) of sending Josh away to school. At first I couldn't believe it. I mean, we'd all expected Dorothy and Co. to do their best to get rid of Nat. But I never expected Mum and Dad to try to get rid of Josh. For starters, I'd always thought he was their favourite – well, Mum's anyway. But it was Mum who was keener on the idea than Dad was. Her rich American friend Juno, who lives in Knightsbridge, said she would pay. Not that Dad had any objections to that. I think he thought, like Barney, that mothers should look after their children and stop pestering other people about them. Anyway, somehow or other, Mum managed to talk him into it, as she usually does, and we all went out for an Indian meal to have a family discussion.

I was crawling with embarrassment, I can tell you. There was Mum, all anxiety and good intentions, trying to get me and Josh to say what we really thought, like we too were all in her beloved therapeutic context. And there was Dad, bright and breezy and cracking jokes, as if nothing had happened, as if nothing ever happened. The same old story. Mum taking everything too seriously. Dad not taking anything seriously enough. I say the same old story, but that's not strictly honest of me, because to tell you the truth I'd never actually seen it like that before. I'd known that they'd sometimes disagreed, of course – I wasn't that thick. But this was the first time I'd seen the difference between them so clearly and I began to wonder how they could ever have been married to each other in the first place, let alone for sixteen sodding years. This was kind of frightening. But not as much as it would have been a few months earlier. In fact in many ways the thought came as a kind of relief. Somehow it made me feel that I didn't have to go on fighting the separation. What happened in the end wasn't really down to me at all, and whether I behaved well or badly didn't have anything to do with it.

Well, I thought Josh would be horrified out of his tiny stagnant mind. But he just refused quite calmly and went on eating his chicken biriani. When Dad asked why, he said he didn't want to go to any sort of school. Mum said how about if she found somewhere small and non-authoritarian, where pupils made their own rules and chose their own lessons. Josh said there was no such place. It turned out that she'd actually found somewhere down in the depths of the country in Devon and not too far from Grandad. It was called Abbot's Combe and had about sixty pupils. There was no Head, just a staff co-operative, no corporal punishment, no uniform, and attendance at lessons was voluntary. Josh was eating more slowly and I could see he was interested, though all he did was shrug and say he didn't want to leave London. I knew this was a lie because he was always saying how he wanted to live in the country with lots of animals, which is more than I can say for myself. I loathe the country and as far as I'm concerned all animals are totally boring. I couldn't live without human conversation.

Anyway, Mum didn't press the point. When we got home she gave Josh this brochure with a picture of a sodding great mansion on the cover. She sent off for it after seeing an advertisement in the *Guardian* saying, Comprehensive School Stresses? We offer a peaceful alternative. Nonconformist individuals especially welcome. Or some such crap. But Josh really fell for that bit. For days afterwards he went around referring to himself as a nonconformist individual. Nat said it sounded like someone from the Salvation Army. I thought Rodge would be dead against it all, seeing as how he doesn't believe in private education, but he said Josh should think himself lucky to be offered such an opportunity. So I said, why? And Rodge went into a great long spiel about what was wrong with education as offered in comprehensives, which weren't really comprehensive at all, seeing as how the rich sent their offspring elsewhere or lived in posh places (all of which we agreed with) and that he'd heard about Abbot's Combe from a friend of his who used to teach pottery there until she had twins and had to give up teaching for a few years. He said there was no coercion and no hierarchy, and pupils could learn about what really interested them, which was the true meaning of education.

We were all a bit stunned by this and didn't know what to say in reply. That's when I started chewing my nail and the boys picking their spots. Nat said Josh's spots were worse than his and so Josh's picture should be on the cover of *Zitz*. Josh said his might be worse today but, generally speaking, Nat had more than he did. So then they started arguing over what did and what didn't qualify as a spot. Rodge settled the matter by saying they should both be on the cover and that he would take the photograph himself, if Ros would lend him her camera. Slime was the only person we knew with a camera, and nobody wanted to ask him. Rodge did tell the boys that they were sticking their necks out, probably only to have their heads chopped off by the authorities and were they sure about it? Were they sure! They were delighted and nothing and nobody could have stopped them. Rodge said what a lucky accident it had been he was caught at the Poly and it was an ill wind. Ros now had free access to a copier because she'd just joined a feminist publishing collective which was run from some rich journalist's house in Barnsbury. Can you believe it? Suddenly everything looked at least half-way hopeful.

Meanwhile there was school itself to be reckoned with – at least for me. It was all very well for Josh and Nat to keep bunking off all the time, but I got as bored as all hell just wandering about all day with nothing to do. I'm sure Hazlitt and Venables and the rest were only too glad to see the back of them because not having those two around made their job that much easier, the lazy sods. But, as luck would have it, old Fairfax herself had her eye on me. I suppose you could call it taking a special interest. For some reason I was moved into her history class, which was the top set. I was a bit suspicious and I never liked history anyway. But then it turned out they were doing the Suffragettes and, quite against my will, I got really interested and began to look things up in the library and ask Mum questions, etc. Then, when I wrote a paper on the Federation of Women Workers, Fairfax said it was brilliantly original work and read it out to the class, which I don't remember anyone ever doing before. Afterwards she called me to her office and we had another of our little talks. She told me I had a good mind and a nice historical sense, which I must learn to direct to the proper channels. Christ alone knows what she meant by that, but the words, *proper channels*, made me feel kind of wary, so when she asked me if I'd thought about going to university, I said I wanted to be a journalist. It was the first thing that came into my head. But she only smiled and said a university education was no handicap to a journalist. She was always nice to me after that. I began to get teased, especially by Slime. He said that Fairfax had been talking to his Mum about me! It seems she called me Oxbridge material. So that became my sodding nickname. Even Emma started yelling, Hi, there, Oxmat, whenever I walked into a room.

Home wasn't exactly a bed of roses either. Every so often Dad would turn up without warning and expect us to stick around and eat a proper meal with him and Mum. It didn't seem to occur to him that we might have better things to do, especially Sunday lunchtimes when we usually went to Rodge's and ate fish and chips from the Chinese. We were supposed to talk to Dad about our lives and what we'd been doing. Somehow, none of us – not even Mum – saw fit to mention Rodge and *Zitz*. It was like some kind of unspoken agreement among us. And of course we couldn't mention Nat either, because Dad said he didn't want to hear any more about him or his family. He didn't seem to realize that Josh had more or less lost interest in football, or that I didn't actually worship the ground Adam Ant trod on. He kept referring to himself and his band in a jokey sort of way as boring old farts, as if this couldn't possibly be a true description of them. Everything he said seemed to make the distance between us and him bigger than ever. And less and less possible to bridge. It was agony because half of me wanted to tell my dear old Dad that he was approaching us in the wrong way, seeing as how our lives had changed so much, and half of me wanted to fucking well shut him out forever. After all, he fucking well deserved it, didn't he?

Zitz got off the ground with a whopping great bang. Naturally we'd all thought the 'zine was stupendous, sensational and so forth. But I don't think any of us (except perhaps Rodge) was prepared for the sensation that followed its publication. Rodge and Ros had organized it so that every school in the area was covered on the same day. We worked like sodding slaves, I can tell you. Nat and I did three different schools in the lunch break besides our own dear Fleet Valley at the end of the afternoon session. We just stood at the gates handing out copies and asking people to subscribe what they felt they could afford. We actually collected £7.76! Most people took the copies from us, with only the most conventional types or those who probably didn't speak English refusing. I expected lots of people to throw it away, outraged when they saw the cover, and in fact some did, but only a handful. Most people thought the whole thing a big joke, so I kept saying, read it, *read* it. When we saw any staff coming in our direction, we put *Zitz* behind our backs and looked innocent. This wasn't because we were being cowardly, but because we wanted to cover as many people as possible before getting stopped. Rodge's very sound advice, that. At other schools it was no sweat, of course, because nobody knew who we were. Not that they all did at Fleet Valley, but there was enough of them did to make our little subterfuge worthwhile. Afterwards we all gathered at Rodge's for a party. Our work was done. All we had to do was sit and wait.

And we didn't have to wait long. As far as I was concerned, it all started happening the next afternoon when (you've guessed it!) Fairfax called me into her office. The kindly liberal Head smiling on her Oxbridge Material protégé had vanished and there instead sat this positive Gorgon who didn't even speak at first, let alone smile, and motioned me to sit down, like she was the Queen, or at least Maggie Thatcher. Blimey O'Riley, was she shattered? (No more than what I was, between you and me.) Here was her sweet little favourite slapping her in her affronted hatchet face. Shit-scared as I was, you know I also felt this amazing sense of power. How can I describe it? Heady. Zing-a-ding, zap-between-the-eyes heady. There was a copy of *Zitz* on her desk. Do you know anything about this, Matilda? I nodded. Are you in any way responsible? I nodded. You, of all people, she said. Me of all people, I said to myself, little sister Matilda of all people. Heady, yes, heady. Not only have you let me down, she said, you've let yourself down. More in sorrow than in anger by now, you understand. Trying to make me feel guilty. Not that I didn't, in a funny sort of way. I kind of muttered, I don't agree, Miss Fairfax. Then she exploded. This is not worthy of your intelligence, Matilda, you should be ashamed of yourself. At that some kind of hidden voice in me demanded to be heard. I looked her straight in the eye and said in this calm, clear voice which (I must admit) took me by surprise, I'm not ashamed, Miss Fairfax. I'm proud.

Honestly, I thought she was going to burst into tears. Her face kind of twitched into a grimace and she shut her eyes as if the sight of me was altogether too much for her to bear. Then she laughed. She actually laughed, dabbing at her eyes with the back of her hand. I held my breath. Then I laughed nervously myself. She said, all right, I think I understand. Then she said she wanted me to understand her position too. Didn't I realize that she wasn't exactly popular with the old guard in the teaching profession? I must say this was news to me. I mean, as far as I was concerned, teachers were teachers, all the same, a little lower on the scale of evolution than your average human being. At the same time I wasn't dumb enough not to see that this was prejudice on my part. After all, my own Mum was a sort of teacher. Nor was I dumb enough to think, like Nat did, that teachers were actually Pigs in plain clothes. Anyway, Fairfax went on to say she'd had all these outraged phone calls from parents who objected to their offspring being contaminated by filth and pornography. Now, Matilda, says she, I'm sure you don't think of yourself as a pornographer . . . Well, we both had to laugh at that. It seemed it was all the stuff about wanking that people were getting worked up about. Especially the fathers, she said. And of course the Catholics (including Mrs Kelly) were getting into a frothy lather about contraception.

Of course it had never occurred to me that Fairfax would see *Zitz* as a personal attack on herself. Of course that wasn't the way it was intended. Of course I never meant to get at *her*. I mean, I'm not that much of a shit, am I? She gave me the impression that she didn't actually agree with all the complaints, but that she had to pretend she did for one reason or another. So I asked her why she couldn't just ignore the whole thing. She said, oh my dear Matilda, I only wish I could! An outbreak of morality, she said, is one of the most difficult epidemics to deal with. She was responsible to the parents; she was responsible to the school; she was responsible to the teaching profession and to comprehensive education. I could see that she meant what she said, but at the same time I felt this was yet another example of twisted adult thinking. I mean, people should say what they really think, shouldn't they? I don't see why it's so difficult. It's like some kind of disease that gets hold of you once you reach the age of majority. Why? What's the point of pretending? What you think is what you think, and nobody should be able to take that away from you.

I wanted to say all this to Fairfax. I mean, I really want to know what she thought, but I just couldn't put my feelings into words. Fucking frustrating, it was. Especially as she seemed to take my silence for some sort of consent, and went on to say she would have to consult her staff before deciding on any disciplinary action. And then she kind of dismissed me.

As I walked back to my class I was kicking myself. Why hadn't I asked her about uniforms and corporal punishment and school democracy and so on? I'd just been so carried away by seeing her all vulnerable that I'd lost sight of the real questions. So I had nothing much to report to Josh and Nat (who of course weren't in school that day), let alone Rodge. My feelings about Fairfax's feelings were so mixed up that I didn't know how I was going to give them an accurate assessment of the situation. All I could tell them was that we had succeeded in our immediate aim. We'd shaken up the whole fucking establishment. What I didn't say was I had my doubts as to the ultimate value of it all.

When, the next day, Fairfax announced that she and her fellow-Heads had decided on an inter-school PTA meeting, my worst fears were confirmed. But the boys were jubilant. Rodge said we should organize as many of our people as possible to attend the meeting. We shan't win, Matilda, he said, but at least we'll let them fucking well know we're out there someplace. It was the first time I'd heard him swear.

XVI

'I can't believe it,' says Claire. 'It's totally against all our principles.'

Nursing and rocking her baby at her breast, she looks with tragic eyes at her sister across the width of the mahogany table. But Claudia, who has just shared a bottle of Beaujolais and a cheese omelette with her, doesn't even look in her direction. Instead, she is gazing up at the chandelier which is shuddering under the impact of Josh's footsteps overhead. Claudia is indeed irritated by Claire's blithe assumption that in this matter there is still a number of choices to be made. Has she not supported Claire through all the vicissitudes of her emotional and sexual entanglements? When Claire was broke and feeling rejected, she lived with Claudia and Dorian for seven months, and was supported by them psychologically and financially. Claudia has found Claire jobs, doctors, referees, therapists, and even lovers. It is not that she expects to be repaid. But she certainly doesn't expect to meet criticism where surely some sort of reciprocal support should be rendered – if only as a sisterly due.

'Principles hardly come into it,' says Claudia. 'This is a matter of life and death.'

'I thought you believed in State education.'

'Believed? Of course I believed.'

'So why are beliefs so unimportant, all of a sudden?'

'It's not that they're not important,' Claudia says with the sort of impatience that she would hesitate to display to anyone who wasn't family. 'Look, there's no way Josh is ever going to go to Fleet Valley again. He's made up his mind. He's voting with his feet. What am I supposed to do? Drag him there by the scruff of the neck? For pity's sake, Claire, he's bigger than I am.'

Claire smiles down at her own son. 'I'm talking about gentle persuasion, not physical coercion.'

Restraining the impulse to shriek against Claire's complacent motherhood, Claudia reiterates, 'Nothing on earth will induce him to go to that school again. I really think he'd rather die. Do you know what that means?'

'It means he's making a mistake which he's got to live with for the rest of his life.'

'It means he's on strike. An unbreakable strike.'

'Unbreakable by you, you mean.'

'I'm not even going to try to break it any more. It's his life, you know.'

'He's still a child, Claudia. You're responsible for him until he's eighteen.'

'Of course I'm bloody responsible.' Does she really need Claire to teach her her responsibilities? 'Why do you think I've gone to such pains to find an alternative education for him?'

'The more that people like us opt out of the State system,' says Claire, holding young Luke over her shoulder and gently patting his back, 'the more likely that system is to collapse.'

'Fuck the system,' says Claudia, recalling that Josh wears a badge bearing that very phrase. 'This is a real live human being I'm talking about. Whom I love. You don't stop loving them, you know, because they're huge and spotty and have minds of their own.'

'Of course not,' Claire says, frowing, affronted.

'And I suppose that when Luke's ten or eleven, you'll make sure you're living in Hampstead and not Brixton.'

'No, I'll live in the country.'

'Same thing.'

'You know,' Claire says, lowering Luke tenderly on to her lap again, 'I think you're secretly rather proud of Josh.'

'I'm not making a secret of it.' Claudia looks up again as the chandelier stops rattling and footsteps can be heard on the landing. 'Josh can think for himself. That's rare, you know.'

'I thought you said he was being got at by some Trotskyite.'

'So? Let him be a Trot, if that's what he wants.'

'Even if it lands him in more trouble again and again, like this business with the magazine?'

'Even if it lands him in gaol.'

'Claudia!'

'I mean it, Claire. What's so terrible about having passionate political convictions? You've just been telling me how important they are.'

'I bet you wouldn't feel the same if he joined the National Front.'

'He wouldn't, would he? No son of mine could possibly do anything like that.'

'No doubt the Yorkshire Ripper's mother said the same.'

'Oh, really!' Claudia sighs, the ready riposte stilled as the footsteps are heard to descend the stairs. 'I'd really like to have this conversation with you again in ten to fifteen years' time.'

Josh comes hesitantly into the room, closely followed by Nat. Both boys are wearing jeans and studded leather jackets, but whereas Josh still has on the ripped T-shirt he has been wearing for the past week, Nat sports a white shirt open to the waist so as to reveal the sprouting hairs on his chest. His hair is dyed pink to match his jeans, while Josh's is a spiked mixture of red and black. Their fingernails are varnished alternately pink and maroon. Claire's horrified eyes take in every detail as she clutches Luke more closely to the bosom which she has covered with the same hasty, protective gesture.

'Boozing again, I see, Claudia.' Nat's voice is studiedly airy as he and Josh pass through to the kitchen end of the room.

Claudia avoids her sister's wide-eyed and wordless stare. 'Actually, we've run out. Perhaps you'll condescend to get us another bottle. That is, if they'll serve you.'

'Of course they'll serve me,' Nat says in his wounded voice. 'Anything to oblige.'

'Well, get one of those large bottles of Frascati.' Claudia reaches for her purse in the bag which she keeps hanging on the back of her chair and carries with her from room to room, just in case Josh starts stealing from her again. 'And twenty Silk Cut King Size. Here's a fiver. That should keep us all going.'

'Ta.' Nat folds the note and puts it in his jeans pocket. 'Come with us, Josh?'

'My God, Claudia,' Claire says as the front door shuts behind the boys. 'What the hell is going on here?'

'Don't you start.' Claudia begins to clear the dirty dishes from the table, fetching two glasses on the way back. 'I had enough of that from Chaz. The plain fact of the matter is that Josh only talks to me when Nat's around.'

'So you're getting them well oiled?'

'If you like. I do enjoy talking to them, though, you know.'

Claire sighs. 'I hadn't realized you were that lonely.'

'It's a sign of loneliness to want to talk to my son and his friends?'

'In the circumstances . . . ' Claire pauses as Luke begins to wriggle and then wail. 'Look, I'd better change him.'

'Try the bathroom. There's a table there.'

There is no point in arguing with Claire, whose opinions are formed from prior conviction rather than from experience. Indeed, Claudia wonders now if experience will ever lay siege to the citadel of Claire's principles. In this the younger woman resembles their father – a comparison which causes Claudia to sigh with weariness, finding in it as she does no small reason for believing in the fixity of human character. Why don't you divorce him? He won't change. Stubbornly, perhaps in the face of all reason, she cannot bring herself to believe in any such things. As far as she is concerned, there is something terrible in her father's inability to recognize that perhaps some things have changed for the better since 1939 – the very year in which she herself was born, two months after Yeats's death (which he mourned) and six months before Freud's (which he perceived as no loss). Twenty days later there was ample cause for grief: Britain's declaration of war on Germany. Her father's rigidity, his cynical rejection of what amounts to her period of history, frightens her, repudiates her. Did she not marry Dorian because (among other reasons) he seemed so unlike her father? You're an idealist. Her father is an idealist. Dorian is not. His moral ambience is at variance with that of the Farquharson family! Claudia shudders to think that there is such a thing, and moreover that she is part of it. Which, after all, is the more reprehensible: pride (hers) or vanity (Dorian's)? Each, you may be sure, exacts its own peculiar price. Now, that's Farquharson thinking for you. Baby, it's cold outside. That is not. But it's cold not to love. It's cold to be free.

'Mum!' Matilda has come silent and shoeless into the room. 'Are you in some kind of a trance or something?'

'Matilda.' Claudia looks at her daughter as though she has forgotten her existence. 'No, I was just thinking.'

'What about?'

Claudia hesitates. 'Your father and me.'

'Oh, I forgot,' Matilda says, sitting down in Claire's place. 'Grandad rang up the other night when you were out. He said he had to go into hospital for a minor operation.'

'What sort of minor operation?'

Matilda shrugs. 'He didn't say.'

'Why didn't you tell me before?'

'I'm sorry, I forgot.'

'Really, Matilda!'

'I said I was sorry.'

'What's all this,' Claudia asks as Claire reappears, a clean and contented Luke in her arms, 'about Father going into hospital?'

Claire looks uncomfortable. 'It's just a small hernia. Nothing to worry about.'

'Or so he says. Why didn't you tell me?'

'He was only there for two or three days,' Claire says in a manner which her sister finds evasive. 'I sent him a card from both of us.'

'I'm not a child,' Claudia says crossly. 'Why the hell didn't you tell me?'

'Because I knew you'd get all worked up about it,' says Claire. 'And I was right.'

'It had to be Soave,' says Nat, barging into the room ahead of Josh and waving a large bottle wrapped in lurid pink tissue paper. 'They'd run out of Frascati. I hope this is in accordance with Madame's wishes.'

'Thanks, Nat,' Claudia says vaguely, looking round for a corkscrew. 'We need another glass, Matilda.'

'I want to open it,' says Josh. 'Let me.'

'I'll wait until after six o'clock and then phone,' says Claire, her father's daughter in this practicality too. 'He was due home this morning.'

Claudia watches Josh raise and lower the heavy bottle to fill five glasses, her unseeing gaze unnerving him. Tutting with a housewifely shake of his head, Nat mops up the spillage with a piece of kitchen paper, glancing at Claudia for some sign of approval. But she is thinking about her father, admitting to herself how she is dreading the illness which will prove to be his final one. He is seventy-five and the hernia must only be the beginning of a series of breakdowns, bearing witness to the body's unstoppable decay. For some reason, the thought that he may die alone and without her knowledge fills her with a kind of panic. Can't Claire see that? Doesn't she feel the same? When their mother was ill, Claire kept talking cheerfully about mastectomies, instancing various women in public life who had survived them. She bought brave books about the will to live, books which were too heavy for her mother to hold up as she lay wasting alone in her marriage-bed, scarcely able to speak. Claire wanted to spare them all the necessity of recognizing that their mother was dying. She and her father entered some sort of unacknowledged complicity which Claudia couldn't share. And now it looks as though they are repeating that behaviour. Enmeshed together within the family circuit, they share the supreme secret: that there is a secret to be shared. Why should they relinquish the sweetness of such a bond? Why should they change?

'Aunt Hester is with him,' says Claire. 'I told her I'd call today. Really, Claudia, you worry too much.'

'That's what I'm always telling her,' says Nat, offering Claudia one of his cigarettes.

'If Mum didn't worry,' Matilda tells Claire, 'she wouldn't be Mum.'

'You're all ganging up on me,' Claudia says before Josh can add his mite of wisdom.

'Never mind, Claudia,' says Nat, 'we all love you, really.'

'How very heartening,' says Claire, raising her glass. 'Here's to you all, then.'

'You mean I've got to drink to Josh?' Matilda asks disgustedly. 'When he's just gone and trodden on my glass beads!'

'It wasn't my sodding fault,' Josh mutters.

'Are you doing beadwork, then, Matilda?' Claire asks brightly. 'What are you making?'

'A choker,' says Matilda.

'And I hope it does,' says Josh.

'Now, now, Joshua,' says Nat. 'Drink up your wine like a good little boy. It'll make you feel better.'

Josh blushes angrily. 'Patronizing git!'

'Just a joke.' Nat offers him a cigarette. 'Honestly, old chap.'

'What do you think of your new school?' Claire asks Josh. Josh shrugs. 'Are you looking forward to it?'

Josh glances, perhaps defiantly, at both Nat and Matilda before replying. 'I suppose so.'

'All schools are the same,' says Nat. 'Just factories of the capitalist State, churning out more good little capitalists.'

'That hardly applies to comprehensives,' Claire says with a frigid smile.

'You've got to be joking,' says Nat. 'They're agents of the State much more than private schools.'

'They want us all to be policemen or join the army,' says Josh.

'Nonsense,' says Claire.

'It's not nonsense,' says Nat. 'I've been to five and I ought to know. Every one of them got the warmongers or the Pigs along to talk to us and say what fun it was killing people or bullying them to death.'

'Perhaps they're anticipating high unemployment,' says Claire, 'now that the Tories are in power.'

'Who cares about unemployment?' says Josh.

'Who wants their lousy jobs anyway?' Nat asks.

'Why should people have to have jobs?' asks Matilda. 'There are better things to do with your life.'

'It's just the Protestant work ethic,' says Nat.

'What better things?' Claire asks Matilda. 'Do you mean having babies?'

'No, I do not mean having babies,' Matilda says scornfully. 'They don't take up your whole life.'

'She means better things than being regimented,' Nat explains in a kindly voice. 'Having a job. Having a baby. What's the difference? They're both just what other people expect of you.'

'Like getting married,' Matilda adds.

'Or getting your O-levels,' says Josh.

'Or wearing school uniform.'

'People yelling at you all over the place . . . '

'Treating you like idiots . . . '

'Telling you when to breathe.'

'Never listening.'

'Compulsory RE is the worst,' says Josh. 'That really is brainwashing from the Christian establishment. Especially if your teacher is a Fascist, racist pig.'

'And ours is,' says Nat. 'Do you know he told us how God created black and white people different, and we each had different parts to play in the Great Plan. About half our class is black, for fuck's sake.'

'You should report him,' says Claire, looking at Claudia.

'Do you think anyone's going to listen to us?' asks Matilda. 'That's why we had to start *Zitz*.'

'Whose idea was that?' Claire asks.

The three teenagers look at one another, but say nothing. Nat refills all the glasses, not spilling any more wine. Claire's question is not going to be answered, and she looks with some exasperation at her sister, inviting her to intervene. But Claudia evades the invitation, as she has learned to evade so many others of its kind, by lighting a cigarette. She will not enter into some sort of adult complicity with Claire. The list of complaints has been a performance staged for Claire's benefit: Claudia's role has been to admit and perhaps even endorse through silence. What she is in fact endorsing is the validity of feeling which accompanies the complaints rather than the complaints themselves. The wearing of uniform, for example, would not be perceived as an infringement of individual identity, did it not proceed from an authority whose overall demands were perceived as both arbitrary and hypocritical. Do they not wear a kind of uniform anyway? Yes, but it is a uniform of their own choosing. Clothes are expressive. That is why they anger authority. How much more angry, then, does it become when the means of expression is authority's own: words and pictures. *Zitz* has acted like a goad. The power of language, the power of the image: these are power indeed, and a power which adult authority is reluctant to grant to the adolescent.

'What do you think of our modest little magazine?' Nat asks Claire.

'I liked the picture of you and Josh on the cover,' Claire says cautiously.

'Is that all?'

'Well, you might have known,' Claire says with a sigh, 'that anything to do with sex is bound to get people all worked up.'

'So?' asks Josh. 'What harm does it do?'

'We wanted to get them worked up,' says Matilda.

'We're interested in sex,' says Nat. 'Why shouldn't we write about it in words we can all understand?'

'People are worried about wanking,' says Josh.

'And about getting pregnant,' says Matilda.

'Adults never tell you the truth,' says Nat. 'They think you're too young to understand – like sex was their property and "kids" like us should lay off it till we get mortgages, or something.'

'We don't all think that,' says Claire. 'Why don't you campaign for proper sex-education classes?'

'Nobody takes any notice of us,' Matilda says again.

'But have you tried?'

'There's no point.'

The boys agree with Matilda and Claire shakes her head. 'I don't see what it is you want.'

'Nothing much,' says Nat. 'Just to be treated like human beings.'

'Oh come on,' says Claire. 'Don't try and tell me you're not treated like human beings. You belong to the privileged classes, you lot. If you were living in Bangladesh, your lives would be very different – if, indeed, you'd survived to the ripe old age of fifteen, or whatever, at all.'

'We never said we liked what's going on in Bangladesh or wherever,' Josh says with hoarse indignation. 'That's typical adult logic for you.'

'And of course our lives are bloody marvellous,' says Nat. 'Golden opportunities stretching from here to eternity. Which is just round the corner, of course, in the shape of a sodding great mushroom cloud.'

'Oh well.' Claire shifts the sleeping Luke gently on to her other arm. 'I suppose we all have to go through some sort of teenage rebellion. I mean, I did myself, of course. Tearing up cinema seats and rocking and rolling in the aisles . . .'

'Poor little sod,' says Josh, regarding his cousin with a mixture of compassion and maliciousness.

'Why?' asks Claire.

'Years of brainwashing ahead of him.'

'Years of school,' says Nat.

'At least he's not a girl,' says Matilda.

'Don't you like being a girl?' Claire asks, but Matilda's disgusted look is answer enough. 'By the way, I thought your piece on opportunities for girls the best thing in the whole magazine. If only the rest of it had been so literate, and so well argued, it wouldn't have been so easy to get it banned.'

'Thanks,' Matilda says uncomfortably.

'Why shouldn't the illiterate have freedom of expression?' asks Nat. 'The tyranny of the word doesn't exist in Bangladesh.'

'Nonsense,' says Claire. 'Literacy is power.'

'Knowledge is power,' says Josh.

'*Zitz*,' says Nat. 'Let's have that on the next cover.'

At once the question arises as to whether there will be any more editions of the magazine. It emerges that its editorial board is determined to defy the ban imposed by the educational authorities. In addition, it has every intention of massing support to disrupt the inter-school meeting the following Monday. Intentions may be made clear, but tactics are not discussed. When the doorbell rings, Claudia, who alone is not participating in the somewhat rowdy conversation, takes it upon herself to answer it. My children, she tells herself, including the adopted Nat in the description, may be stubborn, exasperating, or even criminal, but at least they're not boring little prigs, like Claire and I probably were at their age. Glowing with the maternal pride which is the permanent obverse of her anxiety, she opens the front door with a welcoming smile. To her consternation, which she immediately does her best to conceal by continuing to smile, it is Dorian who is standing on the doorstep, encouraged by her demeanour into smiling in return.

'You look nice,' he says.

Claudia is wearing some pink dungarees which used to make her look fat. 'Do I?' She stands confusedly in the doorway. 'Why didn't you use your key?'

'I thought I should announce my presence,' says Dorian, 'seeing as how I usually call first. Are you having a party?'

'Just the usual gang,' she says, holding the door open for him. It is Dorian who looks nice – tanned, lean, handsome and not at all unpleased with himself. But Claudia cannot bring herself to tell him so. Any sort of compliment could lead to misunderstandings. 'We're discussing the future of *Zitz*. Can you come to the meeting on Monday?'

'Well, it's a bit difficult . . . '

And then, as she shuts the door after him, he doesn't look nice any more. Or rather, his carefree looks become capable of another interpretation. Instead of the attractively familiar friend for whom she experienced a momentary spasm of compassion and indeed (how she hates to confess it) a momentary but instantly suppressed spasm of desire, he becomes the equally familiar narcissist, dedicated to the cultivation of self, whether in mind or body, and oblivious to all extraneous demands upon it. She follows him through the hall, not failing to note that his T-shirt, emblazoned back and front with the name of his band, and his white cotton trousers are both new. But she mustn't be so petty-minded, must she? Dorian has just returned from Italy, and the temptation to buy new clothes is always greater in a foreign country. And, besides, you can't go on wearing the same old things when you're appearing on stage every night, can you? A man is entitled to his little pleasures. Perhaps. It would certainly seem that the habit of making excuses for him is hard to break.

'Hi there, you guys!' Dorian announces himself with a flourish, including the assembled females, American-fashion, in his mode of address. 'How about a little drink for dear old Dad?'

There is an edgy pause, during which Claire greets Dorian with brassy affection, Josh looks steadily at the table, and Nat watches Claudia light another cigarette. Dorian smiles down at Luke, clearly searching for some appropriately avuncular phrase. It is Matilda who shows herself prepared to accept responsibility for acknowledging her father's presence. She fetches a glass which she fills with wine and hands to him, indicating at the same time that the chair next to her own is unoccupied. So Dorian sits at the foot of the table opposite Claire and, raising his glass with a smile which seeks to appease in return for his own appeasement, drinks to the health of all those present.

'What about absent friends?' Nat asks slyly, provoking a flicker of amusement from Josh. 'Absent just-good-friends.'

'If you like.' Dorian fails to keep the coldness out of his voice.

'Let's drink to pretty girls,' says Nat. 'Who can resist them?'

'Fuck off, Nat,' says Matilda, barely audible.

'Come on, Josh,' says Nat, pushing his chair back. 'Let's go round to Rodge's.'

As Josh too gets up, Dorian says, 'Wait a minute. I've only just arrived.'

Nat mutters something to Josh and then addresses Dorian in the politest of tones. 'Please excuse us. We have very important editorial matters to discuss. Coming, Matilda?'

Matilda looks apologetically at her father. 'It really is important, Dad.'

'All right, all right,' Dorian says with a shrug, 'I thought the five of us might go out for a meal, that's all.'

Matilda's hesitant expression changes. 'There are six of us.'

'So I see,' Dorian says with a dismissive wave of his hand. 'Well, have a good time changing the world, or whatever it is you get up to.'

No sooner has the front door shut than a concertedly raucous and high-pitched burst of adolescent laughter can be heard on the steps and along the road. It is redolent with a sense of release. The summer evening is xanthous with all the warm shades of the spectrum before the red tones of sunset take over. The benign air invites beginnings, the reaching out, however tentative, of one person towards another. It provokes, young as the day is yet in deed, memories of youth, fragile and golden as the light. Ah yes, it invites sentimentality along with the urge to relive those memories, or at the very least enact some more mature approximation to their intensity. The time of year and the time of day strive together to deny the mundane and to assert the potentiality of the unknown and other. Children are playing football outside in the street, their voices eager and sharp with argument. From the house opposite the reggae music which will continue, with intermittent breaks, over the weekend has already started up. The security guard who lives two doors away has already embarked on the weekly and loving process of working on his motorbike. His Alsatian, tethered to the railings for company, barks in sympathy.

The three around the Hugheses' dining-table sit in silence, an involuntary audience. Claudia is acutely conscious of Dorian's humiliation at the hands of his children and their friend. She is equally conscious of the pain which must have prompted the need for such behaviour. It occurs to her that Nat is using the Hugheses to live out the familial conflicts which he cannot express, being exiled, within his own family. It is hardly surprising that Josh, if not Matilda, should share some of the perspectives of Nat's family romance, along with his reactions to them. Or are these speculations reductive? Of course they are. Every formula, even that of language itself, is reductive when applied to human behaviour. But sometimes one or another is the best that we can do. Even if it is not, it can give the illusion of meaning, and that in itself is illuminating, therefore comforting, however little comfort the apparent meaning may hold of itself.

'So,' says Dorian, 'What was all that about? Am I as much persona non grata with you two as I am with that lot?'

'Of course not, Dorian,' Claire says with a quick glance in Claudia's direction.

'All I wanted to do,' he says with a rueful smile, 'was to take us all out to supper.'

'That dreadful Nat.' Claire sighs. 'I mean, he really is some kind of a nut-case, Claudia.'

Dorian's smile becomes more rueful. 'Mad or bad – that is the question.'

'Slagging off Nat,' says Claudia, impressed despite herself by the way the other two have immediately engaged in their own brand of complicity, 'is not the way to win my sympathy.'

'How unfair you are,' says Dorian.

'We know,' Claire says judiciously, 'that your sympathy is always directed towards the underdog. But are you sure you can always recognize the underdog correctly? Nat strikes me as being grotesquely manipulative.'

Dorian's smile is now as benign as Claire's sisterly words. 'Just because *we* seem to be OK, just because we have learned to adopt all the adult defences, doesn't mean to say that we are any the less vulnerable.'

Claire nods and the two of them continue to smile, now at each other, in perfect agreement. Is there something sexual in the complicity? Oh well, yes, there always is. Claudia remembers how pretty Claire was as a little girl and how protective she felt towards her when she, Claire and Chloe all went to the convent together, Protestants among Catholics in suburban Ealing. All the Farks have little plaits, sticking out behind their hats. The Farks. That was their corporate identity, drawing as much attention to them as if they had been triplets. There was a little boy called Sammy Price who always had a runny nose, didn't belong to any gang and was continually being set upon. Claudia suggested to Sammy that he form his own gang and that she help him. They succeeded and Sammy became a person to be reckoned with. He became Claudia's slave. But he sent a valentine to Claire. He was afraid of

Claudia, but he was in love with Claire. Is this story of any significance? Claudia thinks so. She decided even then, at the age of seven, that some fate was in store for her other than being someone's valentine.

'Nat has never done anything to hurt me,' she says. 'Why should I join in this general condemnation?'

'Meaning that I have hurt you,' says Dorian.

'Meaning precisely that.'

'You know that wasn't my intention.'

'You should have known that I would see it as your intention.'

'I'm not a cruel person. I'm not strong enough.'

'Your weakness makes you cruel.'

'Do you think I'll ever be strong enough to meet your requirements?'

'That's up to you.'

'What if I find them excessive?'

'What if I find yours humiliating?'

Claire looks round-eyed from husband to wife and back again: the conversation is becoming dangerous. 'I think I'll call Aunt Hester, Claudia, if you'll hold Luke for me.'

'Use the extension in the study,' Claudia says, taking the sleeping baby with some trepidation, 'if you prefer. Say I'll call later.'

Luke stirs but snuggles willingly enough against Claudia's milkless breast as she cradles him, her body responsive as she has forgotten it could be. From Sammy she turned to Chris Reed, who was illegitimate, fathered by a GI and very tall for his age. Chris was sullen and violent. The other children had been warned not to play with him. Claudia asked her mother why. When she heard the explanation, that Chris's parents were not married, she said in amazement, is that all? Her mother said, out of the mouth of babes, adding that Chris would surely respond to sweetness and light. And he did. No sooner had Claudia befriended him than all the other children followed suit. Chris's mother thought Claudia quite the nicest little girl she had ever met, kissed her and hugged her as Claudia's own mother never did. As for Chris himself, he was her slave. How he cried when they had to move to the country so as to be with his grandmother. And how bereft Claudia had been with no one to care for, apart from her younger sisters, who were notably unappreciative of her efforts. Oh, this fatal tenderness towards the male of the species, Claudia. Have you never learned to overcome it?

'I brought you a present,' says Dorian, lifting his briefcase on to the table. 'Duty-free, you know.'

'I don't want anything,' Claudia says at once, but he looks so hurt, how can she? She takes the gift-wrapped bottle of Chamade and says on cue, 'My favourite. Thank you.'

'I got one of those spray-on things of Miss Dior for Matilda, and a Swiss knife for Josh.'

'I'm sure they'll be pleased.'

'Are you?' Dorian's eyes are moist. He laughs nervously. 'I got the impression they'd be just as likely to throw them back in my face.'

Claudia is dabbing the perfume on her wrist. 'You don't stop caring about people altogether, just because they've hurt you.'

'Don't you?' Dorian's voice is hopeful. 'Don't you, Claudie?'

'They can't help showing you how hurt they are,' Claudia says, shifting Luke to her right arm and holding her left wrist up to her face. 'You can't expect anything else.'

Dorian moves into the chair to her left and takes her hand, holding it up to his face now so as to inhale the perfume. 'That's it. I don't know what to expect. Can't you tell me?'

Feeling his breath on her skin, Claudia weakens and her answer emerges as a whisper. 'I don't know.'

'We can work it out,' Dorian whispers, holding the back of her hand to his cheek.

'Can we?' Claudia's voice falters.

'I know things have got to change.'

'How?'

'For a start, we can move somewhere more convenient, so that you won't have be be dependent on me or the 73.'

'Do you mean that?'

'Why not? I know this place is a nightmare to run.'

'It's a buyer's market.'

'What the hell?'

'Highbury would be nice.' Claudia allows herself to speculate, regardless of the consequences. 'Near the Victoria line.'

'We're off on tour on Wednesday for three weeks.' Dorian sidles his chair closer to hers. 'But I'll put this place on the market on Monday. We'll start afresh.'

'Like we did before?'

'We can do it again.'

They look at each other. Dorian's eyes are bright with unshed tears. Claudia's are misty, fearful. His smile is as it was when he said, I've fallen in love with you – permanently. All those years ago. They have come thus far. Why should they not go further? Once before, in a new home, they managed to establish a different basis for their marriage. Why should they not be able to do it again? All sorts of reasons. Why should Claudia not be able to dictate her own terms? All sorts of reasons, not least that she doesn't know how Dorian will ever understand their import. If there is to be a marriage it must be a partnership between equals, each dedicated alike to the onerous and complex task of parenting. There will not be the same dependence. There will not be the same closeness. It is only thus that basic trust can be re-established and maintained. No more of that idealistic nonsense, Claudia. A partnership rooted in the reality of imperfection. What's wrong with that? That is what makes sense. That is the only way to proceed with the business.

'I'm sorry,' says Claire, although at first it is not apparent why there is any need for apology. 'I'm afraid Father is still in hospital.'

Claudia attempts to take her hand from Dorian's as Claire reclaims Luke. 'Why? What's happened?'

'All sorts of complications.' Claire hugs the child to her as he begins to fret. 'I know Aunt Hester tends to be alarmist, but she seems to think he's in a pretty bad way.'

'What do you think?'

'I don't know.'

The sisters look bleakly at each other. Claudia is disturbed to see that Claire seems to be as anxious as herself. As if sensing this unease, Luke begins to cry. Claire sits down and with mechanic fingers starts to unfasten her blouse. Dorian's hand clasps Claudia's, prompting her to look at him. And she half-turns towards him, as if for comfort, before remembering that they have not in fact lived as husband and wife for six months. Her gesture arrested, she reaches for her cigarettes, but that comfort too seems inadequate. Wrenching her hand from Dorian's, she covers her face and begins to rock herself back and forth in her chair. Her eyes are dry. She cannot tell which of the many conflicting impulses besetting her deserves precedence of expression. At once Dorian's arm is round her shoulders as he and Claire exchange urgent and indistinguishable words. Claudia can neither hear nor see. For one hideously suspended moment Dorian's arm tightens its hold against her passive resistance.

'How about that, then?' he asks. 'I'll drive the two of you down to Cornwall tomorrow.'

XVII

It seemed to happen quite suddenly, to hit me in the guts, although I suppose the whole thing had been hotting up for some time. I feel almost ashamed to write about it, it's so silly. I've got to nerve myself. One of life's little ironies. Not that there was anything little about it. It seemed huge and fateful. In between the times when I felt a sodding ninny, it was like I was walking on clouds far above the boring, squalid world which everyone else seemed to be living in. All that poncy poetry you're supposed to read at school suddenly made sense. Eternity, infinity, and all that. After everything I'd always said! And, worse, after everything Rodge himself had said on the subject.

It was the meeting that did it, really. It was easy to get carried away. At least it was easy for me, unaccustomed as I was to public glory, etc. Dad said he couldn't come to it because he was working. But Mum came. So did Dorothy, Cormack and Barney. They all sat together at the back and Barney kept yelling things out till Brotherton, who's head of Charles Lamb, asked him if he was actually a parent. As if anybody who wasn't a parent would actually deign to interest himself in the carryings-on of mere teenagers! What the fuck did they think he was? A KGB agent? A reporter from the *News of the World*? As it happens, that's exactly what some of the audience did think. Some of them yelled, go back to Russia. Others wanted to see his press card. It was embarrassing to see grown-ups behave in such a sodding ignorant and juvenile fashion. If it had been us in school, the teachers wouldn't half have given us hell.

We hadn't been invited of course – only sixth-formers. But seeing as how you can't tell people's ages nowadays (we all mature so quickly, ha ha!) and nobody asked to see your birth certificate, the thing was to slip into the hall by one of the doors guarded by the thugs who weren't from your own school. They didn't dare interfere in case they were made to look fools. After that it was a matter of sidling in somewhere behind tall people (bit of a problem for Nat) so as none of the staff could spot you from a distance. Nat and Josh solved the problem of their hair by wearing woolly hats like Rastas. As for me, I'm the sort of person who can always slip in somewhere because no one ever notices my existence (even Mum tends to forget it) unless I draw attention to myself. Which I do all the time, of course. But I know how not to as well. It's a trick all small people learn how to take advantage of. That and an air of innocence. You'd be surprised at how many people are taken in by that. Especially men. But then, if you haven't got tits, they're not distracted, are they, and just think you're some little thing beneath their notice.

The ironic thing is that around this time I did get tits. About sodding time too! I mean, I was *fifteen* for Chrissake! Of course I'd had these kind of lumps since before I started my periods. Frankly, I thought they were a bloody nuisance. They kept itching. Then they'd ache. You couldn't forget about them, even if you wanted to. Then, when I started, I thought they'd grow. Well, they did a bit. But I didn't have proper periods either. I mean, some girls had horrible pains and headaches and swelled up and went on bleeding for five whole days! Me, it was just a couple of days and it seemed to happen any old when. Emma said the pill made everything regular, but I didn't dare mention it to Mum. Not that she'd have been shocked or disapproved of putting chemicals into your body or anything like that, like Claire. I don't even think she'd have laughed: she doesn't have much sense of humour. No, she'd have done another of her heavy trips on me, asked me all sorts of questions about my feelings, which I never seem to be able to answer. She always wants to know what people are feeling, like it was something simple to describe. Then, when you can't, she describes it for you, and half the time she gets it wrong. All right, so half the time she gets it right too. But it's just sodding exhausting because she doesn't give up, even with Josh who's perfectly capable of just sitting there for hours on end, saying nothing at all and just nodding or shaking his head.

So there were these tits at long last. But once I'd got them, they didn't seem such an advantage after all. For one thing, I wasn't allowed to forget them. People stared and made rude remarks like, how about a nice juicy pair, then, or, she'll never fall flat on her face, ha, ha! At first I was kind of flattered and glad that I was like other girls at last, but then I got fucking sick of it. Who wants to walk down the street with people yelling and whistling at you all the time? Who needs it? At the same time I seemed to start bulging out all over the place, and my jeans didn't fit me. Nor did Josh's. I had to ask Mum for some new ones and she was so dense she kept saying the ones I had were in perfect condition, but a bit worn. When I explained that they didn't actually fit me, she said she'd have to ask Dad for some money, and seeing as how he was away, I had to wear skirts all the time, which was all right in hot weather, but seeing as how we didn't have a proper summer, there wasn't much of that, and I had to have tights as well. More expense. That's what Dad said. More pissing embarrassment was the way I saw it. Mum offered me some of her old jeans, which were about the right size, if hardly fashionable, and the legs had to be taken in, otherwise they'd be flapping about around your ankles all the time. Mind you, she did help me with that, so it could have been worse. It was just having to explain everything, to ask for everything, that I objected to.

Dad eventually gave me some money, but only after he and Mum had a row about it. Well, not exactly a row and not exactly about that either. I heard them. They were both talking in cold little voices, even though Dad kept calling Mum darling. At one point she said, my name is Claudia. I just got this horrible sinking feeling in my guts. I mean, I'd just been thinking that they were actually behaving like normal human beings towards each other. When Dad took her and Claire to Cornwall to see Grandad, Josh and Nat and me, fools that we were, began to believe that they might be making the effort to get it together again. Perhaps they would have if Grandad had died. Mum and Claire seemed to think that he might. And then he was OK after all. And then Mum and Dad started arguing again.

But they went on pretending. I mean, Mum said that we were going to sell the house and find somewhere smaller and more convenient. The estate agent came round to value the place. Mum kept getting excited about advertisements she'd seen in the Sunday papers for other houses. In fact, she seemed to spend all her time covered in newsprint, calling this person or that and poring over the *A–Z*. That is, when Dad wasn't taking her somewhere to look at some marvellously suitable place or other, which nearly always turned out to be a complete con, though I couldn't necesarily see why. I went on one or two of these trips with them but, honestly, it got to be such a pissing bore. They all looked the same to me, anyway. Mum said didn't I care where I lived, and I said no, and she got all upset and started choking back the tears like she does. Sodding pathetic, it was.

I could see that Dad was getting fed up too. He kept talking about the cost of moving, and Mum would say it was his idea in the first place, and so on. The thing was that if Mum had had her way, they'd have been traipsing about all over the place twenty-four hours a day. In the end Dad left her to it and she got friendly with the estate agent, who kept giving her lifts in his car. Nat said they were having an affair. If so, they were having it somewhere else, because I never saw any signs of it. Rodge said Mum was full of frantically misdirected energy, and that was what marriage did to women. Josh said he didn't want to move anyway, but seeing as how he was going to boarding-school, nobody took much notice of him. I suppose I didn't want to move either. I didn't see the point of it.

Of course this whole business about moving really started to happen after the night of the meeting, by which time I was into other scenes, which I shall shortly reveal – if I must, and yes, I must. Somehow Rodge had got himself into the hall, though he was too old to be a pupil and too young to be a parent. I suppose it's just possible that someone could have taken him for a sixth-former. After all, some of them, especially the Greek boys, had moustaches, though they were against the rules at Fleet Valley for some obscure sodding reason. Perhaps they thought they would over-excite us girls, though I must say I've never found them particularly sexy myself. Rodge's moustache was gingery, though his hair was a kind of mousy blond. His skin was pale and freckly and kept changing colour and he wore glasses with steel frames. He wasn't very tall, as I said before, and he always wore the same old jeans with some sweater or other which looked like they'd been knitted by his auntie. Not exactly the answer to a maiden's prayer. But then I wasn't exactly a maiden, was I?

As a matter of fact, I didn't know if I was or if I wasn't. I thought perhaps you had to have some kind of orgasm before you could lose your virginity. I also thought you were supposed to bleed, and when I did it with Nat I didn't. Nobody ever tells you these things, let alone what it's supposed to feel like. It's all one big adult secret. Of course Mum talked to me about everything, and of course she asked me to ask her questions. I didn't. Not that I didn't have any. I just didn't know how to put them into words. And of course – I have to admit it – I was afraid of making myself look an idiot.

At school it was even worse. We had these sex-education lessons with all sorts of diagrams, which made everything look like some kind of theorem. The boys looked at pictures of boys and the girls looked at pictures of girls, and never the twain shall meet, which I would have thought was the whole point of the exercise. Unless they were all supposed to be homosexual or something. Not that *that* was mentioned either. Come to think of it, heterosexuality wasn't either. More like a lesson in naming of parts, really. And what names! All kind of Latin and medical-sounding, which made you feel there was something wrong with you, just by existing. I mean, vulva. Like everyone else, I thought it was some kind of car and half-expected to hear an engine starting up between my legs. It was all so complicated and nothing to do with anything so nobody asked any questions. And poor old Gooch, who was supervising it all, seemed rather relieved, stupid cow that she is. Some people giggled and sniggered, others just sat there, looking embarrassed or pretending to take notes. Emma said loudly as we trooped out that the whole thing was a total farce and you'd learn more from reading *Forum* or listening to LBC. Amazingly enough, Gooch agreed with her, and said it should be down to parents and not teachers to explain the facts of life. Facts of life! It was all science fiction, as far as I was concerned. If I wanted to know anything I asked Emma, usually in a veiled sort of way. She always came up with some sort of answer. Only trouble was, I didn't know if she was telling the truth. Take the virginity business, for instance. She was the one who said you always bled. And I didn't. And yet I knew I wasn't a virgin. Just shows you can't trust anyone, really, not even your own best mates.

When Rodge gave us the signal, we were all supposed to stand up and clench our fists and chant Pupil Power three times and then sit down again, at which point we would probably be ejected from the hall. But we would have made our presence felt and our views known. We were in the middle block of the tiered seating, and Rodge was towards the front of the block to our right, near the door so as he could make a quick getaway, if necessary. This wasn't selfishness on his part. It was just that none of us was likely to cop it the way he was, being grown-up and a well-known activist and what have you. The trouble was we had to keep shifting our gaze to the right instead of staring at all the staff massed on the floor behind their barrier of tables. We really must have looked suspicious to anyone who could actually see us. I felt sure that Fairfax had spotted me several times, but I think I must just have been in her line of vision because there was no recognition on her face.

What a lot of moth-eaten old dinosaurs they all looked – not one of them who didn't wear glasses, and some who even had two pairs which they kept swopping over to read their papers or to look round the hall. There seemed to be two types of women. The ones who looked like they'd spent all day with their hair in rollers and wore crimplene dresses. And the younger ones, all with straight hair in a fringe and wearing T-shirts, flowery skirts and espadrilles. The men were no better, most in nondescript suits to match their features, and one or two dashing ones (not from Fleet Valley, worse luck!) in tight jeans and T-shirts and rumpled hair.

Seeing as how we were at Charles Lamb, Brotherton was in charge of the proceedings. Now, let me tell you that Brotherton, who is also a Tory councillor, is well-known for his views on education and especially corporal punishment, which he thinks is a jolly good show and the only language we young thugs understand. He's on the telly almost as often as Fairfax (but not quite, which must peeve him) and sometimes they're both on together, though on different sides, of course. Unlike Fleet Valley, Charles Lamb used to be a grammar school, and Brotherton has never quite got over the shock of letting the riff-raff in. He was a great believer in standards, whatever they might be. Charles Lamb was boys only so at least the poor old sod didn't have to contend with female riff-raff. Standards seemed to mean wearing uniform (even caps, which you raised when a master approached) and passing O-levels.

But these things were well in the past by then. Nat, who'd been chucked out of the place, said that walking down the corridors was like running an obstacle race at the best of times, and at the worst it was like fighting off a wolf pack. A social worker got beaten up there, and nobody ever found out who did it: all boys looked alike to her. Meanwhile Fleet Valley, which used to be a sink school, had this wonderful reputation for tolerance and progressive ideas, thanks to Fairfax, who kept telling everyone how marvellously the whole place was run. What a sodding joke. It was better than Charles Lamb, all right, but that's not saying much. Once you get on the telly you can say what you like and everyone will believe you. When did we ever get to be on the telly and tell people what the place was really like? That's what pissed us off. But no matter how riled we were, you can bet your best pair of trendy Kickers that Brotherton was getting his Y-fronts into a right old twist over it all.

He took the items one by one, droning on in his unbelievable accent, trying to be posh and the champion of the people at the same time. The audience loved him. Ignorant sods that they were, they looked up to him, thought he was some kind of great intellect or something. The way they talked to him when they asked questions was quite disgusting – all humble and full of sirs. Enough to make your flesh crawl into a corner and hibernate. When he went on about uniform and corporal punishment, the same old fucking platitudes you hear every day, they kept saying, we want the sort of school you want, Mr Brotherton, we trust you, Mr Brotherton. Lick your arse for you, Mr Brotherton? But when he talked about *Zitz* and said how filthy it was, people started cheering. One woman with an Irish accent (it wasn't Mrs Kelly) went on about how she didn't want her younger children to be exposed to such corruption.

Then, would you believe it, Mum stood up and said knowledge was power and ignorance led to misery and impotence. People started yelling at her, and the Irish woman said, you dirty woman, you, I feel sorry for your children. Mum had to sit down again because her voice was being drowned out. I saw her blow her nose and wondered if she was crying. I mean, she sounded so nervous. And so posh. It was embarrassing. There was a vote at last, when everyone had calmed down a bit, about whether *Zitz* should be distributed in the schools or not. Only a dozen or so people out of hundreds voted in favour. The rest were *all* against and started clapping when they'd won.

I thought Rodge must surely give the signal at that point, but he didn't. Afterwards I realized why. We hadn't got to the nitty-gritty as far as the teachers were concerned. This was the question of whether there should be pupil representatives on governing bodies. This it seems was what was getting up everybody's nose – having to sit through all those meetings with pupils there and having their own say. *Zitz* they could have laughed off, if the parents had allowed them to, but not this invasion of their sacred rights. Several people in the audience spoke up in favour, which really surprised me after the way the vote had gone. Then some woman said, we support you, Mr Brotherton, you just tell us what you think and we'll support you. So there was bleeding Brotherton, all smiles and rubbing his hands, saying that certain decisions should be taken confidentially, etc., etc. Though why the running of Charles Lamb or Fleet Valley should be considered on a par with State secrets I've never been able to understand, myself. What on earth do they talk about, anyway? Nothing important, I bet. I reckon they just pretend to have all these secrets because that makes them feel important. Brotherton said he'd take a vote, but it was a foregone conclusion really.

It was then that Rodge gave us the signal. So we all stood up and chanted. I hadn't realized that there were so many of us – about fifteen, so some must have been from Charles Lamb and even St Benedict's. Wow, it was impressive, though. Did we give the smug old fuckers a heart attack? You could see their blood pressure shoot up before your very eyes. I thought Brotherton's own eyes were going to pop out. There was this really deathly hush as we all sat down again. Then Brotherton gave this false laugh and said, I see we have rent-a-crowd here tonight. And some man from the audience yelled out, rent-a-cell, more likely. And everyone laughed.

Nobody even bothered to eject us, but Fairfax said to Brotherton that some of us were well-known to her, and he looked pleased, like he might have known such scum as us would have come from Fleet Valley and not his own model establishment. What a sickening sodding farce it was. I wanted to yell too and tell them all what fucking shits they were, but Rodge had said not to and we must resist all temptation. So we sat on through the vote, which of course went against us. Brotherton made a few more supposed jokes and said, God bless you all. And everybody clapped again. Then someone said, three cheers for Mr Brotherton. And, would you believe it, they all cheered. Except for us of course. And Mum. And Dorothy and Barney and Cormack. And a few others. Mass hysteria, that's what it was.

We met Mum in the car park. She said it never did to underestimate the reactionary nature of the British working class, especially in a fit of morality. Rodge agreed with her. She gave him this funny look and said, I suppose you must be Rodge. He just nodded. They didn't seem to like each other. Or at least they didn't seem to trust each other. Then she got into Cormack's flash car with the rest of them, leaving me and Josh and Nat and Rodge to get into Rodge's mini, which was really Ros's mini, but she was looking after her Mum who'd fallen downstairs.

On the way home Rodge said we mustn't be disappointed, we had made our mark. Then he asked us what we wanted to do about *Zitz*. Josh and Nat were both gloomy and discouraged, said there didn't seem to be much point in producing a magazine we couldn't distribute. I said they were a couple of poofs for giving up so easily. They wanted to know in their sarky way what sort of brill ideas I had up my sleeve. I said there wasn't any need for brilliant ideas. We could distribute *Zitz* in the street outside the schools and nobody could stop us. We'd just stopped at a red light, and Rodge turned round and smiled at me like I'd never seen him do before. All radiant and all for me, me, me. You're a brave little creature, Matilda, he said, a girl after my own heart.

Well, my own heart, poor little pump, nearly stopped beating. I thought perhaps I was going to throw up. But my head was clear, so transparently clear and certain-sure. There was no getting away from it. I'd just fallen in love with Rodge.

XVIII

Claudia looks furtively at her watch under the table: a quarter of an hour to go. Jeffrey has whispered that she must stay until midnight when they will all drink Juno's health in pink champagne. Most people will surely be going back to the centre of town from Wimbledon, and one or other of them should be able to give her a lift. Then she can get a taxi. Of course she can. It is all quite simple and straightforward. Then why is she fretting? For one thing, she has forgotten that it is Juno's birthday tomorrow – well, in a few minutes. For another, she has found the evening extraordinarily difficult. Thanks to Juno's financial involvement in a film project initiated by Jeffrey, the other guests are all strangers, all in show business, and therefore all aquainted with Dorian, at least by repute. Claudia has told the man on her right that Dorian is on a provincial tour and that she doesn't want to be cross-questioned about his activities. She has made it plain that she has no wish to talk about Dorian. But the man has taken no notice, has blithely continued to bring the conversation back to the same subject. For most of the evening, the place to her left has been unoccupied, and so it has been difficult to include herself in any alternative conversation. It is now occupied by an actor called Dave whose wife is pregnant and thus too tired to drag herself along to Jeffrey's do. Dave himself is clearly too anxious about her to be able to provide much in the way of companionship.

Jeffrey repeats, for Dave's benefit, a story he has already told earlier in the evening, concerning a well-known elderly actress who, when playing Saint Joan, had to be tied to the stake in order to prevent her from falling down drunk. Dave too has heard the story before: he has indeed often worked with the actress. Undeterred, Jeffrey persists to the end of the anecdote. He laughs but Dave only smiles abstractedly. Not for the first time Claudia wonders why she has bothered to come. Because she has nothing better to do. Because Juno, pitying her loneliness, has asked her from the kindness of her heart, telling her that it would do her good to meet new people. Claudia looks round the table at Jeffrey's ten other guests. There is nothing new about any of them. She has indeed met them all, not individually but as types, on innumerable other occasions for which she was engaged to play the role of Mrs Dorian Grey. She has nothing to say to them and, unless they are asking questions about Dorian, they have nothing to say to her. It's as simple as that. Why does she never learn? Because she always hopes: this time it is going to be different. Because she mistrusts her own intuition: she should try to be rational and tolerant, unprejudiced. Should she? Why should she?

When Jeffrey changed the time from seven-thirty to nine o'clock, she should have demurred, declined, taken that as an excuse. But poor Jeffrey. It wasn't his fault that an Equity meeting had suddenly been called at six-thirty in the hopes of settling the dispute with London Theatres Ltd. And poor Juno. She would feel rejected. She was investing dollars in Jeffrey and his project, so he and his guests were business acquaintances rather than friends. Claudia would be her only real friend at the gathering. Claudia couldn't let her down. And Claudia didn't.

'I really think it was so sweet of Jeffrey,' she is saying. 'I'm always giving parties for people, but no one's given one for me in a long, long time.'

'Oh, he's an angel,' says one of the women. 'We all adore him.'

Balding, bearded and paunchy, Jeffrey blows a kiss in her direction. 'I adore you too, darlings.'

'Of course you do, darling.'

'Remember that time in Cannes, Sabina, when Zara brought her chimp along and Jeffrey insisted —'

'That wasn't Cannes, darling. It was Sorrento. Come down-market a smidgeon.'

'Sabina, dear, it was at the Carlton.'

'Now, now, loves.' Jeffrey stands up with some difficulty. 'It's midnight and time for champers. Have you got the glasses ready, Timbo?'

As Jeffrey and Timbo fill the champagne glasses, the other guests produce gaily wrapped parcels from under their chairs or the folds of their clothing and present them to Juno, who is suitably overwhelmed by their attentions. Sabina starts up a chorus of Happy Birthday as Juno begins to unwrap her prezzies, trifles all of them. But expensive trifles – at least by Claudia's standards. She and Dave alone have nothing to offer. She and Dave alone are not participating in the general hilarity; Dave because he is notably the only sober member of the party, Claudia because she has drunk enough to become morose rather than animated as she might among friends. Her alienation becomes complete when Juno, unwrapping a pair of earrings made from brightly coloured beads and not unlike Claudia's own (a present from Matilda), guesses that they must indeed be a gift from Claudia. She allows Timbo to refill her glass. Perhaps a little more champagne will cheer her up. It is surely not going to make her feel any worse.

'Oh, the phone,' says Jeffrey, as Timbo slips into the hall to answer it. 'Now that's either my New York agent, who has no sense of our time, or it's another birthday greeting for darling Juno.'

'It's for Dave,' said Timbo.

'Oh, not Marigold, I hope,' says Jeffrey. 'She really doesn't want this one to be premature.'

'Poor dear Marigold,' says Sabina. 'I should think she does.

She's as huge as an elephant.'

'You should be so lucky, darling.'

'Serge wouldn't be able to get it up if I put on another ounce, would you, sweetie?'

'It's Marigold,' Dave says from the doorway, his face so pale that it looks almost green. 'There's been some bleeding, so they've taken her to North London General.'

'Oh poor love!'

'Watch him, Timbo. He's going to faint.'

'I'm all right,' says Dave, collecting the leather jacket which he has hung on the back of his chair. 'But I must love you and leave you all.'

'If you're going to North London,' says Juno, 'why don't you take Claudia with you part of the way? She lives in Hackney.'

Dave looks confused rather than unwilling. 'I'm going further west, but of course . . .'

'Kings Cross will do,' says Claudia. 'I'd be very grateful.'

'I'd be delighted,' says Dave, recovering himself somewhat.

Claudia is relieved to find that she can stand up, and indeed as she takes her leave gives every appearance of sobriety. Dave's mini is parked on the other side of the street and he takes her arm – quite unnecessarily – to guide her across. Being tall and long-legged, he fits awkwardly into the driving seat. There is a lingering flowery fragrance in the car, and Claudia suspects that both actually belong to Marigold. She herself feels very small and fragile in the passenger seat as Dave, keeping his eye on the gauge, drives just within the speed-limit but nervously, jumping lights. Attempting to distract him from his wife's possible suffering, Claudia asks him a few mundane questions. Dave's replies are polite and to the point, but arrived at with some difficulty. He has known Jeffrey only since last Christmas; he has been asked to play the lead in the planned production, which will be Jeffrey's first as producer *and* director; he thinks this will probably be his own big break; and no, he doesn't know Juno at all well, but guesses she must be about forty-three.

What he really wants to talk about is Marigold and her propensity for miscarrying. It is clear that he considers Claudia to be an expert on childbirth simply because she herself has borne two children. What he is seeking from her is some kind of reassurance that his wife, now spirited away from him, into a world of feminine mysteries, is going to be all right. Claudia does her best to comply, but she is not in an optimistic frame of mind and, being no actress, she is unable to conceal as much.

And yet there is no need for her to be despondent. Has her life not taken a turn for the better? Josh will go to Abbot's Combe in September. Her father has recovered from his illness. Matilda seems to have matured and quieted down. And of course she and Dorian are going to try to keep the marriage going. At last they have found a house, about which they can agree. It is near Highbury Fields: lots of open space for the children and a short walk to the tube station for Claudia. Everything has been sorted out according to her specifications. What has she got to be depressed about?

The rolling breakers, stony-hearted, widow-making, and yet the widower's only solace as he walks, his galoshes tied up with string, along the resounding shore. Sitting beside Dorian on a damp and mossy rock which stained their blue-jeaned bottoms green, Claudia watched the waves tug, arch, topple and surrender. Dorian was telling her that marriage is a contract which can be renewed, the clauses of which can be altered to suit the contracting parties. We ourselves tug and are tugged. Claudia thought only of her father, snoozing after Aunt Hester's nut-roast, in the sitting-room of the cottage on the other side of the dunes, his pale skin still illuminated by the bluish tinge it had assumed at the time of his wife's death. Oh no, she will not grow old, she will not mourn. The pallor, the transparency, her father's long-suffering smile.Her answering cry: leave me alone; I haven't even begun to live! We ourselves arch, arch and stretch and triumph, glorying in our own strength. Dorian said that any marriage between consenting adults should be able to withstand infidelity. So Claudia told him about Clive and Chaz. She said she was sorry. She said it would never happen again. It was such a relief. But Dorian said he wished that she hadn't told him. We ourselves topple and are toppled before we even know what we have done. Unburdened, Claudia deprecated her inability to deal with her single state, laughed, declared that she had forgotten how to conduct herself in sexual matters outside of marriage, that only within it could she find some sort of code to follow. We ourselves surrender, trickling away into the eroding sands. Life is not chaos after all, but neat and pointed with meaning. Ah, too much meaning.

There was no kiss to seal the compact, not even the pressure of hands. Claudia and Dorian talked of their children and their property: these were what they had in common. They sat for a long time on the rock until they too were chilled. Their voices were neither raised nor hushed, but even and controlled as they discussed their sensible and productive future. Marriage was not a matter of passion but of mutual respect. The gulls screeched, swooping overhead, scavenging. A breeze from the dunes around the curve of the bay blew the sand against them and the air was fizzy with sea-spray. A fishing boat with a red funnel appeared on the horizon: the hunters and gatherers of the deep on their way home to feed their families. This is reality, Claudia. Things are as they are. Husband and wife walked back across the dunes together arm-in-arm. Aunt Hester had made up a bed for herself in her brother's room. Claudia and Claire slept in the double bed in the spare room, Luke in his carry-cot at their side. Dorian slept on the sofa in front of the sitting-room fire. Thus do families accommodate themselves.

Neither she nor Dorian has made any promises. The new house has become the symbol of their renewed alliance. It has been tacitly agreed that once the move has taken place, Dorian will come back and relations will be resumed on the same basis as before – more or less. There have been no declarations of love, remorse or forgiveness. Little by little the breach will heal of its own accord. There is no need to force the issue by establishing rules or guidelines and perhaps not being able to abide by them. The point is to be tolerant and to have come through.

'We'll soon be at Kings Cross,' she says. 'If you drop me at the station, I can join the taxi queue.'

'Are you sure?'

'There are bright lights there and lots of people. I'll be quite safe.'

'I'm sure I can take you further than this,' Dave says as they pass Euston Station. 'How about Highbury Corner?'

'Kings Cross will be fine.'

'It seems ridiculous to drop you off sooner than I need to.'

'I won't hold it against you.'

'It is ridiculous,' Dave insists as they reach Kings Cross and, the light being green, he drives straight on to the Pentonville Road instead of along York Way. 'I'll take you to Highbury corner. I go along the Holloway Road after that. You should be able to pick up a taxi easily enough.'

It is too late to do anything other than acquiesce. After all, Dave is trying to be helpful, even in the midst of his own trouble. There is no point in telling him that she feels safe at Kings Cross because she knows it, whereas Highbury Corner is foreign territory. Oh well, at least the cab fare will cost less. Dave seems to relax. His chivalrous good deed has contributed to allaying any anxiety he may have felt about his powerlessness in the face of Marigold's pain and misfortune. He is still a man who can be of comfort to women. Claudia doesn't argue with the unspoken argument she has perceived. Instead, when Dave offers to wait with her until a taxi appears, she insists that she is perfectly capable of hailing a cab, and that it is Marigold who will benefit from his presence. After some polite demurral, he agrees with her and, giving her a little hug and a peck on the cheek, leaves her standing at a strategic position in the roundabout complex of routes.

The chill night air (it is August, after all, when summer goes into abeyance) takes Claudia by surprise. Walking towards home is out of the question. She is far too unsteady on her feet to attempt any such thing. And besides it would be silly. Much safer to stay where she is, a place which has claims to being public, than wander through the back streets, alone and vulnerable. Not that she doesn't feel vulnerable as it is. Her clothing consists of three layers: a nylon petticoat, the cut-velvet dress she wore to Greta's party, and a second-hand raincoat, much too big for her, which she bought from the Nearly New shop at Newington Green. If only she were at Newington Green now. It would be just as deserted but at least it would tender, however deceptively, the comfort of familiarity. Is it possible that a junction so busy, even congested, by day, should be so quiet by two o'clock in the morning? An urban landscape, devoid of traffic and people alike is an eerie sight, a disjunction like those experienced in dreams and set up by the unconscious to induce you to take a closer look and pay attention to what you have seen. Is she dreaming now? No, the physical discomfort of the wind whistling up her skirt and the pinch of her shoes across the width of her feet are both too localized and arbitrary to merit the attention of the unconscious. She is awake and alone and beginning to feel apprehensive.

But it is all an illusion. There is plenty of traffic after all: a concatenation of red lights along the various routes has probably been responsible for the temporary lull in activity. So many private cars, each apparently inhabited by a couple, male and female after their kind, as if this were the norm. Several heavy lorries, each cab inhabited by a couple, male and male after their kind, ready to wave, shout or whistle at the sight of a lone female figure, swaying slightly, a forced smile on its face, as if to appease. There are no other pedestrians about. But here comes a taxi. Of course Claudia has known that sooner or later one would come along and that everything would be all right. No matter that the For Hire sign is not lit up. The block of flats at the far end of her street houses many taxi-drivers and once before one of them answered her summons and ferried her home free of charge. She hails the taxi. It doesn't stop but almost at once the car behind it pulls up alongside her. The driver, a man of about her own age with a benevolent expression, a droopy moustache and a foreign accent, asks her if she wants a mini-cab. Relieved, she returns his friendly smile and gets into the back seat of his car. Three plastic cubes, miniature versions of the ones on Sonia's kitchen table, dangle on a cord from the roof, containing pictures of his wife and children, smiling, smiling nervously and sweetly at the photographer, perhaps the driver himself. Claudia leans forward to take the nearest one in her hand and asks him about the little girls, who seem to be about seven and nine. They are his pride and joy. He is a family man.

The driver knows his way, so much so that he hardly deems it necessary to keep his eyes on the empty road ahead, but keeps turning round to look at Claudia. Small wonder, then, that he takes a wrong turn. They have entered a cul de sac where most of the houses are empty and by day building work is going on. The driver curses (or seems to) in an unfamiliar language. He stops the car, but instead of backing into the main road again, gets out and, muttering to himself in that same language, lifts the bonnet to take a look at the engine. Claudia is only slightly irritated: if they have run out of fuel, she will simply walk the rest of the way home. It shouldn't take more than twenty minutes – less, if she takes her shoes off. And indeed the driver seems to have come to the same conclusion. Rather than getting back into the driving seat, he is opening her door for her.

It is only when he himself gets into the back of the car, pulling at the same time at his trouser-belt, that she realizes in an instant of the purest clarity what is about to happen. She opens her mouth to scream as she edges away, but no sound comes. Surely she can scream – at least. And then it is too late. His hand is over her mouth and she is being forced down to the floor of the car. All she can register as the belt is pulled round her neck like a noose is that the name of the car is *Avenger.*

It is only a piece of flesh. She is only a piece of flesh. It will not hurt. But it does. Her whole body heaves, arching itself back and away, and she gags as the belt constricts her throat. There is only one thought, one image in her mind: death. If she continues to struggle, to resist, she will be killed. Her body relaxes minimally and involuntarily as it assimilates this realization. Then, as if from another life, it remembers. Passive resistance. The advice given to those on CND demonstrations who were likely to be arrested was: go limp. At first Claudia thinks it has worked. She is allowed to fall backwards away from him against the front seat of the car which lurches forward. Cunning is called for. She will pretend that she has fainted.

The next moment it is clear that her unconsciousness, perhaps even her death, is no deterrent. Her thighs are forced apart and in a sudden stab of pain he is now inside her. The resistance of her vaginal muscles has told him that she is alive and conscious and, as if hoping to provoke some further response, he pulls her head back by the hair so that her throat now lies exposed and curved over the back of the seat. Passive resistance. Easier said than done, when every muscle, every nerve rebels. Try, Claudia, try. You must survive this. Think, think of your broken marriage, of your perhaps fatherless children. There must be no perhaps about their being motherless. All you have to do is tell yourself, this is happening to my body, not to me; I am something other; I am that part of me which cannot be violated. Try, Claudia. Try to dissociate. Passive resistance. The body too can think and foresee its own extinction: let it then put on more cunning. And at once she is all body, a living organism whose element is life and whose every cell asserts its independent claim to go on living. The atavistic impulse towards survival, towards victory. She must win. She will win. In surrendering, in submitting: there is the struggle expressed at its bitterest and most desperate. Just let him get on with it. Pretend to be dead. Then you'll live, you'll live.

When it is over, Claudia scarcely knows whether she is alive or dead. It has, intermittently, ceased to matter. Even her children ceased to matter: all that mattered was that the pain and the violation should stop. If death was the only way, then so be it. As the belt is tugged forward, she tries to look into the eyes of her violator, as if for some explanation, some justification. But he will not look into her face, least of all into her eyes, for fear of a glimpse of the unique individual whose existence he has denied. Perhaps he will kill her now. How can it make any difference if she is indeed dead already? Somewhere in the distance an aria of birdsong is being performed and the sky is paling into tentative light. She can hear and she can see. The belt is removed from her neck and, her tights wet and torn, she is shoved unceremoniously out of the car, manumitted. Before getting back into the driving seat the man flings her little black velvet bag at her, so that its contents spill at her feet.

Poor little thing. Poor pretty little thing to be treated with such contempt. Claudia squats to pick it up and gather its contents. The car drives off and – too late – she tries to read the registration number. All is a blur. There is no one about, no human sound to be heard. The houses to either side of her are dark, as if averting their eyes. She will not disturb them. There is no need now. It's over, Claudia, and what you must do is get home as fast as you can, before it gets light, and without anyone seeing you. She takes off her shoes and then her tights, which she deposits in a builder's skip and, holding her velvet bag against her cheek as an unwitting absorbent for her tears, she begins the walk back to safety and normality.

The alarm clock on the bedside table registers half-past four. Claudia's tears have ceased and she feels no pain, as if anaesthetized. All she feels is cold, a chill which has entered and taken possession of her bones. She crawls under the bedclothes for respite and lies curled upon on her side, her thumb in her mouth. When she has thawed out a little, she will have a bath. But, despite herself, she falls asleep. When she wakes, with a guilty start from a dream which has reminded her that she is still unclean, the sun is shining with an intensity which she cannot bring herself to meet. The house is quiet. Perhaps the children are out. It is twenty-past ten. Perhaps they are still in bed. A sparrow is giving itself a dust-bath in the window-box among the neglected geraniums, now drooping wretchedly, their leaves edged with brown and their brave red subdued into the colour of a stain by thirst.

The bathwater is hot and enriched with Badedas. Claudia's body looks no different: although it aches and is stiff, there are no marks to be seen, apart from the weal on her neck where the belt has bitten into her flesh. Soon perhaps there will be bruising on her face, her arms, her back, but now there is only tenderness which the water, in soothing, exacerbates. It is scarcely credible. But I have that within which passeth show. Let the water enter and cleanse me. That's all we women are: repositories for semen, for another person's lust, another person's anger, frustration and vengeance. How can we ever be clean, be ourselves, our pure selves? The very nature of the sexual act entails contamination, the introjection of what is not ours, what by its very foreignness violates our integrity. Only if I submerge myself completely, only if I sink down, down, down, can I ever be clean, ever be myself again. Purge me with hyssop. Wash me in the blood of the lamb. I shall confess my sins. I shall tell them over one by one, and bewail them with tears of remorse. Forgive me, oh, forgive me!

Watching, listening to herself, Claudia begins to wonder if she is going out of her mind. For a start, the violation she has suffered was not essentially a sexual one: sex was the metaphor for an assault based on aggression and contempt. Try as she might, she cannot see herself in her oversize raincoat, her hair close-cropped and her body endowed with hardly more in the way of womanly contours than that of an adolescent girl, as the object of uncontrollable sexual desire. No, it was not sexuality she exuded as she stood, innocently well disposed towards her fellow-creatures at Highbury Corner. It was vulnerability. Her assailant's desire was not that of a man for a woman, but that of the bully for a sadistic encounter with a victim. In that he could find some release for those impulses of hatred and destruction which might otherwise find no outlet. Except against the self. No, that's what women do. Male narcissism sees to it that the cherished male self, however denigrated and despised within the prevailing culture, goes eventually unscathed. Why shouldn't it? There are other left-luggage lockers for all that junk, for all that is blameworthy and therefore unwanted. That's what women are for.

Claudia gets slowly out of the bath and begins to dry herself, sitting on the edge. How neat and young her body seems to be. Oh, it would fool anyone. But I have that within which passeth show. Look like the innocent flower, but be the serpent under it. He probably drove straight home and got into bed beside his wife. She doesn't know him. No, not any more than she has known Dorian. For each of the men, his wife has been a woman set apart from the rest of her kind, a woman to be openly cherished according to the rules, and yet covertly deceived, even despised. For each man, women are essentially things to be used. For neither can a woman ever be fully human, fully individual. Only women. The other. She who must be appeased with lies and hypocrisy is only the obverse of her who is used and degraded in the service of narcissism. The truth of the matter is that they loathe us. And so we must be violated. The difference between Dorian and the rapist is not one of kind, but of degree.

Her leg begins to tremble. When she tries to stand up, she finds that she is shaking uncontrollably, her teeth chattering. It can't be true. Why not? Life can't be like that. But suppose it is. If so, it's hardly worth the living and she may as well have struggled and been killed. She takes the towelling bathrobe from behind the door and wraps it round her, hugging herself. But her body seems insubstantial, ungraspable, and, worst of all, incapable of warmth. All she wants to do is go back to bed. And sleep. And sleep. And sleep forever.

Matilda is standing hesitantly on the landing outside Claudia's bedroom. 'Oh, there you are, Mum. We thought you must be ill.'

'I am – rather.' Claudia forces a little laugh. 'I think I'll go back to bed.'

'Oh, poor Mum! Can I get you anything?'

Claudia stifles the impulse to hug her daughter: she mustn't touch anyone. 'Just a cup of tea, please, Matty dear. And if you could get me some more cigarettes . . .'

'It stinks of cigarettes in here already,' says Matilda, following her into the bedroom. 'And you really shouldn't be smoking if you've got flu or whatever.'

'I know.' Claudia sits down wearily on the bed. 'If it's against your principles, I'll ask Josh.'

'No, I'll get them,' Matilda says quickly, looking strangely at her. 'I'll even get you a clean ashtray. See how kind I am to you.'

'I know.' Claudia bursts into tears.

'Oh, Mum!' Matilda's arm is round her shoulders. 'What's the matter?'

'I'll be all right,' Claudia says unsteadily, patting her daughter's hand. 'I'll be all right tomorrow.'

But tomorrow is a long way off. Will it ever come? Claudia gets into bed and smokes her last cigarette. She drinks the tea Matilda has brought her and smokes another cigarette. Once upon a time Matilda had no existence outside of her mother's body; she was part of her, as Claudia was in turn part of her mother. Clinging on to this bodily knowledge affords some small comfort: I was conceived and born in love; I conceived and bore in love. That's what women's bodies are for. To give life. That's what pain is for. To give life. That's the answer to hurl forth in the face of violation and destruction. To give life. But it's a losing battle. Her own mother is dead, dead of cancer of the breast at the age of fifty-seven. Claudia curls up sobbing with grief. Oh, mother, mother, I need you. Oh, Claudia, you too are a mother. Remember, remember that. Hold on to it, hold fast.

She must have fallen asleep because the next thing she is conscious of is waking up awash with sweat, and outside it is already dark. She must get up and have a bath. Cleanse herself of dreams. It was all a dream, wasn't it? The whole year, starting with the phone call on New Year's Day, has been nothing but a dream, a nightmare from which she must force herself to awaken. Soon Dorian will be home. He will take her in his arms and they will laugh together over her silly fears. As if he was likely to deceive and betray her! Oh, I'm sorry, Dorian, sorry to have doubted you. As if anyone was likely to rape a forty-year-old married woman with two teenage children! No, no, of course not – silly me!

In the dream the sun was shining, not in the fierce heat of the day but softly in the tenderness before dusk, as if apologizing for its imminent setting. Claudia sat on the verandah in a white dress, looking across the river to the jungly mass of trees beyond, dark, green and impenetrable. There were brightly coloured birds on the roof and perched on the rail of the verandah. Tiny monkeys, bright-eyed and blinking, swung down towards them. A snake slithered across the boards to rub itself at her feet like a cat. And she was not afraid.

After another bath, more tea and even more cigarettes, she lies in her clean nightie, listening to the clatter of dishes in the kitchen below. Either Josh or Matilda switches on the radio and, after a few brief bars of Chopin, turns the dial to some station broadcasting reggae. They mustn't know what has happened to her. They must never find out. No one must ever find out. If anyone asks her any questions about her neck, she will say that she has been mugged and her purse stolen. Her purse, not her body. What an utter fool she has been. Why did she not have the sense to realize that the car was not a mini-cab at all? It didn't even have a radio. Why did she get into it? And, once in, why didn't she get out again? What was she doing anyway all alone at half-past two in the morning? Where was her car? Where was her husband? What else did she expect?

'Greetings from the land of the living.' Josh pokes his head round the door. 'Want anything to eat?'

Claudia shakes her head. 'Just more tea, please, Josh.'

'You look awful, Mum,' he says cheerfully. 'What you need is a hot toddy.'

Claudia nearly bursts into tears again. The hot toddy is an innovation she introduced into the household the last time Josh was ill, offering it not as a medicine but as comfort, as soporific. And thus now it works for Claudia herself. But the night is long. She wakes often. Sometimes she can't tell whether she is awake or asleep. It is just after dawn when she decides with the certainty born of horror that she has contracted syphilis. After that, it is impossible for her to go back to sleep. Instead she spends the morning in a state of paralysis which is both moral and physical, knowing that she must do something, but not knowing what. It is another beautiful day and the street rings with convivially exchanged greetings. She takes the phone off the hook. No one must talk to her. No one must know where she is. No one must know she exists.

As the day drags itself into the afternoon, rationality gradually begins to assert itself. She should report the rape. To the police? To Sergeant Baines? The thought is abhorrent enough to start her shivering again. From somewhere in the recesses of her mind, the name Rape Crisis presents itself. She gets out of bed, fetches the phone book from the empty kitchen, takes it upstairs, looks up the number and dials it. A woman, identifying herself by her first name only, answers the phone. Claudia explains that she has been raped and would like to see a doctor because she feels sure that she has contracted syphilis.

'I think you should see a doctor,' the woman says hesitantly. 'You sound very distressed.'

This surprises Claudia. 'I don't want to go to my GP.'

'Have you been to the police?'

'I don't want to go to the police.'

'Have you talked to anybody?'

'I don't want to talk to anybody.'

'I can understand that,' the woman says in the same hesitant tone. 'But perhaps you should. I think it might help. What about your husband?'

Claudia hears herself explain about her husband, her children, the stark events of the last few months, in answer to the woman's questioning. The voice at the other end of the line is cool but not devoid of sympathy, persistent without probing. Soon Claudia is relating what has happened, piece by piece, almost as if it has happened to someone else. Almost. It has happened to her. It happens to other women too. That is tacitly understood. Although the immediacy of Claudia's own experience is not devalued, she somehow feels less alone. It was an accident. The Fates don't have it in for her, uniquely for her. It has happened. It cannot be undone. It has happened, but she has survived. The woman promises to arrange an appointment for her at the Cavell Clinic and to call her back as soon as this is done. Meanwhile, Claudia should try to talk to her closest friends: she needs support. No one should have to bear what she is bearing alone.

When she puts the phone down, Claudia remains sitting where she is, still and curiously calm. Of course. It has happened, and now the consequences must be faced. She must ease herself, edge herself, back into a world where friendship and reciprocity exist, have meaning. It has happened and it was an accident, a misfortune. She has survived. When the phone rings, she picks it up at once, ready to communicate.

'Claudia?' It is Dorian. 'Have you heard anything from the bank about the transfer of the mortgage?'

Claudia feels she doesn't know how to answer this question. And yet it is quite simple. 'No,' she says.

'Shit, I'll have to call them again. Unless you'd like to.'

Again she pauses. Again she answers, 'No.'

'You sound strange.'

'Something's . . . happened.'

'To the children?'

'To me. I was raped.'

'What did you say?'

'I said I was raped.'

'Oh dear God!' There is nothing more Dorian can say. The silence lengthens. Will he ever speak again? 'Look, would you like me to come over?'

'No. I'm all right.'

'I could come over later – after the gig. We're in Reading tonight.'

'I'm all right.'

'I'll be round tomorrow. I need your signature on these documents from the bank.'

'All right.'

Again, Claudia sits stock-still on the bed. She has managed to evade a confrontation (because that is how she imagines it) with Dorian. She doesn't want to see him. She doesn't want him to see her, humiliated and degraded as she is. He sounded so shocked, too shocked to be able to respond with any sort of spontaneous sympathy. She would not have been able to bear his pity, but even less his incompetence in expressing it. That is too much to ask of her. He must stay away from her, not involve himself. Her body no longer belongs to him and he has no stake in it. She must not lead him to expect or assume otherwise. All the same she is conscious of a vague sense of disappointment at his ready acceptance of her refusal to be comforted.

XIX

Moan, groan. Sigh, sigh. What the hell is the point in writing anything down? I kept trying, of course. I thought it would help. Help what, for Crissake? Help to sort things out. It was because I had no one to talk to. But when I tried to write down my feelings about Rodge, nothing happened. I love Rodge. That's all I could write. Otherwise I just sat and sighed and felt sick. I thought about him *all the time* – at home, at school, on the bus, in the bath – but when I tried to write my thoughts, only one word came: his name. It seemed to say it all. And in a way it didn't seem right, a kind of sacrilege, if you like, to say anything else. It seemed like I was doing him wrong. I can't explain this. Oh, pissing, shitting hell, I can't explain any of it. I only wish I could. It's frustrating to be condemned to silence because of your own inadequacy. And to think I wanted to be a journalist. Oh yes, I thought I was a fucking genius till I fell in love.

And yet in a way I still was. Oh, you'll think I'm getting above myself now, giving myself importance above my puny appearance. That *was* what I felt, you see: important. At the same time I felt like some miserable worm sludging through my existence under other people's feet, and a bird, some soaring kind of bird, soaring and singing, winging my melodious way up and up above the boring everyday world I was forced to live in. Strong, strong and free. What, me? Crazy, wasn't it? And of course I kept thinking maybe I was going round the twist. One moment I was up, the next I'd come crashing down. One moment everything seemed possible and I loved everyone in the whole world, and the next I hated everyone because they were all against me and would see to it that I was doomed to eternal defeat. But those moments – when I seemed not to be myself at all and yet at the same time the essential Matilda, if you see what I mean – were worth all the rest put together. They would hit me suddenly like the sun coming out in a burst. And, you know, the strange thing was that they seemed to come from some other world where I had once used to live a long, long time ago – a world where the sun always shone and people loved each other.

But I couldn't have talked to anyone about that, now, could I? They'd all have thought I was some kind of prize loony. I mean, where was it? Had I made it all up? How I longed to know. There were so many things I wanted to know. And no one to ask. Fairfax said that curiosity was the first sign of a good mind. But what's the point of having a good mind if you can't put it to use? You're supposed to ask your teachers questions. At least, that's what they're always telling you. But how could I have asked Fairfax about that was occupying my thoughts? I shouldn't think she's ever been in love in her whole boring life. She'd just have told me to concentrate on my work. But how can you get interested in the Austro-Hungarian Empire when your whole being, body and soul, is desperately trying to make sense of your own life? And besides, I wouldn't have known what sort of questions to ask. I didn't even know what they were. All I knew was that they were *there*. Oh, why, why, why, don't they ever teach you anything useful at school?

Of course I was never alone with Rodge. Josh and Nat were always there – and, increasingly, Ros. Among others. Rodge's room was the sort of place people drifted in and out of, borrowing milk or books or spoons or whatever they fancied, and sometimes even bringing them back again. Mostly it was the other guys in the house (Ros was the only woman) but sometimes a lot of other strange guys who looked just like them – kind of shabby and earnest – and talked about Thatcher or Brezhnev or Ayatollah Khomeini like they knew them intimately. At first I thought they were all showing off, but soon I caught on that all that stuff, politics, was more real to them than what was happening in the same room. They were always polite to us lot, greeting us by name and asking how the struggle was progressing, before going on to some involved conversation with Rodge about policy statements and who was going to make a speech at which stage of the campaign and so forth. I suppose it was the sort of thing that most people find boring, but to me it was as exciting as learning a foreign language and actually being in that country to do it. It certainly made a change from Mum and Dad going on about mortgages and school fees. And of course I got a series of glimpses into the heart of the beloved, about whom everything was endlessly fascinating, precious and sacred. I listened in awe and learned in love.

Our editorial meetings were still going on, you see, although our plans for getting *Zitz* printed seemed to be running into difficulties. None of the local printers wanted to touch it but Ros was trying to get something fixed up through the collective. I half-wished she wouldn't get it together, which I knew was bad thinking, if not bad behaviour. I mean, I should have been thinking about the magazine and the welfare of all concerned. But I wasn't. I was thinking what a heroine she'd be in Rodge's eyes if she and her sisters got *Zitz* printed. It was our sodding magazine after all, not hers! And I didn't see any reason why she shouldn't just type it and get it run off, like before. But I was outvoted, even without Ros having her say.

I wondered if Rodge thought she was pretty. She was about the same height as him with very yellow-blonde hair, which she wore long and always tied back with an elastic band. You couldn't tell what shape she was because she always wore dungarees or baggy trousers and the same pink quilted jacket, day in, day out. As far as I could tell, she never wore any make-up. Everything about her face was kind of pale and washed out, like she'd been hiding away from the light all her life. She didn't smile much, and when she laughed, her expression hardly changed. There was nothing anxious or awkward about her, though. And that's just what made *me* feel all anxious and awkward. Ros was serene. That was what women were supposed to be, not twitchy little gigglers always making funny faces, like me. Was Ros prettier than me? I didn't know who to ask. I asked Josh if he found her attractive, and he said he'd never thought about it, really. His usual helpful self. When I asked Nat the same question, he said, not as attractive as

Rodge does, nudge, nudge, wink, wink. I kicked him. But was I ever worried? I kept watching every move Rodge and Ros made when they were together. Did their hands touch? Did their eyes meet tenderly? Did they have secrets? I couldn't always tell. But I went on torturing myself.

Now, I don't believe all this propaganda about the female of the species being masochistic, do you? I mean, it's rubbish, isn't it? And yet there I was, actually inviting misery and pain. If I thought Rodge's greeting to me was kind of colder than usual, I'd get this knot in my stomach, like everything was shrinking into a lump of ice. But if he smiled at me, his face lighting up suddenly the way it does, I'd melt. I could feel my body go all liquid like it wanted to sink into an adoring heap at his feet. Have you ever heard of anything so idiotic? How I loathed myself. I loathed myself so much I couldn't imagine that anyone could ever like me, least of all Rodge. What could I expect him to see in me? Nothing. That was the dusty answer I kept giving myself. And yet I knew he must like me. Just a little. I could tell. Couldn't I? Oh, surely I could. Surely I wasn't just imagining it.

I always got into such a state before our meetings. I couldn't eat, couldn't sit still, couldn't concentrate on anything. And I kept sweating. The more I thought about Rodge, the more I sweated, and squirting myself with anti-perspirant didn't seem to make any difference. If you ask me, those things are a complete con. There I was with these soggy armpits, changing my T-shirts umpteen times a day, wondering if I'd got some horrible disease and everybody could smell me a mile off. It was so embarrassing! I must have lost so much weight during those summer holidays. My new jeans that we'd had all the fuss with Dad about had to be taken in all round the crotch because they got so baggy. I did it myself so as Mum wouldn't start asking me all sorts of questions and feeding me large bowls of muesli, which is her answer to all ills. I began to feel disgustingly *visible*, like my body was telling tales, announcing to the world what was going on inside me. I lived in fear of giving myself away by some careless gesture or, worse, some kind of aura which everyone could see at a glance and which I had no control over whatsoever. I could even be unaware of its existence, like some wanker walking down the street with a notice saying 'kick me' stuck on to his back.

I didn't dare say anything to Emma. She hadn't been involved in *Zitz*, and thought Rodge quite beyond the pale. Or pretended to. I think really she was jealous because she hadn't been included in our plans – this because we thought she'd tell everything to Slime. She kept making these lofty remarks about how we were all being brainwashed, and how her Mum had called Rodge an insignificant little man playing at being a revolutionary to get rid of the chip on his shoulder. I mean, what a fucking cheek! She'd never even met him. Why do grown-ups always assume that anyone who thinks differently from them must be insincere and behaving as they do for psychological reasons instead of political ones? It's pissing pathetic of them, imagining they're the only ones capable of rational thought, while the rest of us are full of ulterior motives rumbling up from the unconscious.

Talking to Josh was out of the question. He simply had no interest in what are laughingly called affairs of the heart. He never seemed to notice the way people felt about each other. Bad vibes he seemed to pick up all right, but then that's what he expected out of life – that everybody was going to be against him. And I can't say he was wildly wrong about that. As for Nat, he'd have made a meal of it, really gone to town. Plotting, planning, any kind of intrigue – that's what he thrives on. He'd have told Rodge. Well, perhaps he wouldn't have told him directly, but he'd have made all sorts of sly remarks so as to make it obvious. He might even have been jealous and tried to mess things up between me and Rodge. I wouldn't put anything past Nat. He really likes to manipulate people, and half the time he doesn't even know he's doing it. It's just some kind of habit with him.

At the very least he would have told Mum, which was just what I wanted to avoid. I don't quite know why. I suppose it must have been because she never talked to me about falling in love, like it was something that didn't happen to decent people. We'd had our little talks about sex, all right, and she'd tried to tell me that sex and love were not necessarily the same thing and shouldn't be confused. But seeing as how she said what sex was but not what love was, I couldn't really make out what she was talking about. It was like falling in love was really a matter of no importance. And I suppose that's just what it was, as far as she was concerned. I mean, people of her age must be past all that kind of thing – if they were ever into it in the first place, and that's hard to imagine with some of them. Then she'd said all that about Claire being in love with Stan even though he kept shoving her around and whatnot, and that one day I'd understand. But she'd said, oh she *loves* him, in a silly kind of voice, like it was the silliest thing in the world. I didn't know what to make of it. Did she think it was OK to be in love or didn't she? On balance, I decided not. And yet in a funny sort of way I did want to talk to her. I wanted her to share the burden and to tell me what to do about it. I wanted her to make everything all right. Sodding ridiculous, I know, but sometimes I felt as weak as a baby, and wanted my mama to do everyfink for poor ickle me.

After the sweating came the nose-bleeds. They would just start for no reason at all, without any warning, and then go on and on. The first two times it happened when I was walking through Clissold Park with Josh and Nat on our way back from Rodge's. Each time it happened at just the same place, where the bridge goes over the pond with the ducks in it. Mum said it must be an allergy and were there any trees overhanging the water? There were, but of course I didn't know one sodding tree from another, did I? Nat said there was a weeping willow, and she got it into her head that this was the culprit. Frankly, I thought she'd flipped her lid. The willow was miles away, but she got Nat (Nat, mind you, not me) to promise that we'd take a different route in future. Then it happened when I was sitting in my room, writing my new piece for *Zitz*. There I was, perched on the end of my bed, my spiral-bound exercise book on my lap and one of Mum's precious extra-fine Pentels poised in my right hand, when I felt this kind of buzzing in my head. I took no notice. I was too busy trying to work out why it was no better for boys to be slippered or caned than it was for girls, which was what Rodge wanted me to write about because I always had something fresh and original to say. Up to that point I couldn't think of one pissing, shitting thing that came into that category. Then it hit me (ha, ha!). It went back to what Nat had said about people being brainwashed into heterosexuality. The moment I remembered that, it occurred to me that people (like Stan?) thought there was something sexual in hitting females, but pretended the same didn't apply to hitting males, when we all knew only too sodding well (ha, again, ha!) what went on in public schools. Then – whoomph – there was blood all over my nice clean page.

I just opened my mouth and screamed for Mum. I couldn't move. She came running upstairs and stared in a suitably horrified manner at all the bright-red mess. Then she told me to lie down and hold this wet flannel to my face while she sopped up all the blood. Her next move was to try to shut the window because there was a tree outside, but of course the sash had been broken for yonks and she couldn't get it to stay up. I said I'd stifle to death. Stifle or bleed, says she, take your choice. And she got Josh in to help her so that it was kept shut by the catch between the top and bottom halves. Honestly, Mum, you're giving me tree phobia, I said. Dendrophobia, said she. But she wouldn't let me get up. Well, I must say I didn't feel that wonderful. When Josh said he was going off to Rodge's, she wouldn't let me go!! Screw Josh. The only comfort I got was from thinking about Rodge talking about me with Josh and Nat. If they ever even mentioned me! Josh said afterwards he had told Rodge about the nose-bleed, but when I asked him what Rodge had said, he just gave one of his irritating little shrugs and said, nothing. But at least I'd written my piece for *Zitz*.

About a week later I had another nose-bleed. This time I was actually sitting at the kitchen table with Mum and Josh and Nat, so they could all see I'd done nothing to provoke it. And there weren't any trees within spitting distance. The windows were all shut. I can't even remember what we were talking about. Certainly nothing special. So I went off to bed again, and this time Mum said I had to stay lying on my back and not sit up to read or anything. So I just lay there listening to the radio while it got dark, and Josh and Nat went off to Rodge's taking my *Zitz* piece with them. It was almost as if I was trying *not* to go to Rodge's. And yet how could that be true when it was the one thing I most wanted to do? I kept wondering what they were all talking about, worrying that it was me, worrying that it wasn't me. When Josh came back all he said was that Rodge was going to send me the proof copy when it was ready. I said I wasn't going to stay in bed that long, but Mum said perhaps I was. I felt too tired to argue and fell asleep before they were hardly out of the room.

I stayed in bed all next morning and in the afternoon Mum said it was all right for me to get up and take things quietly. She went off to a dinner-party with some friends of Juno's in the evening, and I knew Josh had gone round to Slime's to collect some tapes, so I thought, ah, here's my chance. I called Rodge to say I wanted to make some urgent changes in my copy and I'd be round in half an hour because I was going to see a friend who lived in the next street to him. But it was Ros who answered the phone. She asked about my nose-bleed, and went into some great thing abut how she used to have them when she was my age, but she never minded because it meant that she didn't have to play hockey. She would have gone rabbiting on about her schooldays all night if I hadn't interrupted her with a sharp question: when's he coming back? She didn't seem to know who I was talking about, so I had to keep saying Rodge, Rodge. It was like some kind of release just to say his name aloud to someone else. With impunity. (I like that word.) Ros said he'd gone to a meeting and usually they all went to the pub afterwards and stayed there till closing time. So that put the kybosh on that one. Not that I'd have minded going round there at half-past eleven. It was just that Rodge would have found it rather odd. Not to mention Ros. And suppose I should find the two of them together? I shuddered at the very thought. As it was, I was asleep before either Mum or Josh got back.

Next morning I felt chipper as a sparrow again, my usual self. I was first up and collected the mail from the mat. To my amazement there was a letter for me! Of course it was my proof copy from Rodge, but I hadn't expected it so soon, and I'd forgotten all about it. I ask you. How could I have forgotten? It must have been because I never took anything Josh told me seriously. But it was beloved Rodge's own beloved handwriting all right, small and neat (a sign of great intellect) in blue ballpoint in the middle of a foolscap manila envelope. My heart lurched. I felt this strange sensation, not pain and not numbness, but a cross between the two, right there behind my ribs. For a moment I thought I was going to have another nose-bleed, but the moment passed. Taking all the mail into the kitchen, I resisted the temptation to tear the envelope apart and instead slit it open with a fruit knife. There was my article. In print!

And there was a letter – well, a note really – from Rodge. Dear Matilda, it said. *Dear* Matilda: the boring old greeting rang true with meaning. Dear Matilda, I do hope you are feeling better. He hoped I was feeling better! Dear Rodge. Darling Rodge. Just look after yourself for a day or two and you should be all right. A day or two. But I'd only looked after myself for a day. I resolved to do the same throughout the rest of the day. Meanwhile, here is your excellent article for you to look over and spot the howlers. Excellent article! Oh Rodge, Rodge, Rodge. Take as long as you like and don't tax yourself. Love, Rodge. Love, Rodge! Love. He wrote it. Love. Rodge. Love, love, love, love, love.

I sat around in a kind of trance while Josh came in and prepared his muesli, scattering it all over the floor as usual to encourage the mice, as Mum would say. He even made me a cup of coffee. The sun was shining and all, all, all was right with the world. Love, Rodge. I took the letter up to my room with me without showing it to Josh. I wanted to hide it away somewhere safe. I sat on the edge of my bed, where I usually sat, holding it to my cheek, my lips. If anybody had seen me! They'd have thought I was a right little nurd. The envelope was coming unstuck where the flap had been glued down. Almost without thinking I licked it to stick it down again. As I did so I realized: Rodge had licked that same piece of flimsy paper. Something extraordinary happened. My whole body kind of shuddered and I wet my knickers. Not much, but they were wet enough for me to have to change them. It was so strange. Not nasty at all. Actually, it was quite the opposite. I felt kind of shocked. And then, to tell you the truth, I burst into tears.

I didn't know what to do with myself. All I wanted to do was be with Rodge. Be near him. Just to be in the same room would have been enough. I felt so happy and yet I couldn't keep myself from the verge of tears. What was going on? The sweating started up again with a vengeance and my knickers seemed to be damp again although I'd only just changed them. Was it my period? No, that wasn't due for another week or so. Perhaps I had a fever. Perhaps I was suffering from some rare disease which made you kind of melt away from all the holes in your body. I'd be getting diarrhoea next at this rate. I tried not to think about my diseased body, tried to think instead about Rodge and me gazing into each other's eyes or locked in some clinch like in all the soppiest magazines. Somehow it always looks so *clean*! Just as if nobody had any hormones. I decided that was what was wrong with me: hormones. But how could it be? Does falling in love do things to your hormones? Why doesn't anybody ever tell you such things? If, however, falling in love had nothing to do with hormones, then I must have some awful disease after all. If only there was somebody I could talk to.

The best thing, I decided in the end, would be to talk to Mum but in some kind of roundabout way so as she couldn't get all worked up about it. It took me practically all day to nerve myself. When I thought I'd go and find her, it occurred to me it was three o'clock and I hadn't seen her all day. I asked Josh if he'd seen her and he said no. She wasn't in the kitchen or the sitting-room. There was no sign of her. Perhaps she hadn't come back last night. Perhaps something had happened to her. Suppose she was dead? I felt horrified at the very thought and rushed upstairs to her bedroom. She wasn't there either, but the blankets were all in a mess and the room was full of smoke, so I knew she must be around somewhere. Jesus H. Christ, was I relieved! Then the bathroom door opened and out she came. I wanted to rush up to her and hug her, but something stopped me. I don't know what it was. Something about the way she was walking. Like an old woman. She looked at me at first like she didn't know who I was and I felt frightened again. But then she said she was ill, so I tried to be the efficient daughter and ordered her back to bed. But she wanted more cigarettes. When she had the flu or whatever! I don't think she'd stop smoking if she had only one per cent of a lung left.

Anyway, she did seem kind of wiped out, so Josh and I looked after her, bringing her cups of tea, etc. I knew I couldn't talk to her. She just didn't seem in the sort of mood where she could understand. It always happens like that, doesn't it? You gear yourself up, searching your soul, to some, well, confrontation, really, where you tell the truth and nothing but the truth, but not necessarily the whole truth, so as to find out more truth in return. You gird your puny loins to break through some seemingly impossible barrier. You're ready to expose yourself, to ask stupid questions, to risk ridicule. And then something totally petty and unexpected and down-to-earth like flu happens and you've lost your chances for ever. The moment has passed.

XX

The room is full of prostitutes. Claudia is sure of that. You can tell, can't you, by the way they're dressed and do their hair, and make themselves up? Look at that one over there: hard-faced and brassy in tight jeans and stiletto heels. Or the one next to her: obviously Irish and considerably down-market in her flowery dress, her calves bulging with varicose veins above her wrinkled ankles and tiny feet. As to their faces, they are blank, unconcerned. They must be prostitutes. Anyone else would be horrified at having to come to such a place. The waiting-room faces south and the sun emphasizes the tawdriness of the brightly coloured carpet, the imitation grain on the table covered with magazines, the irremoveable stains on the orange polypropylene moulded chairs, and the blistering green paintwork. The electric clock on the chimneypiece, where once a fireplace must have stood, registers a quarter-to-three. Claudia's appointment was for two o'clock. So, it seems, was everyone else's. But most of them have had the wit or the experience to wander in at whatever time has seemed most convenient to them. Not so Claudia. And indeed her impulse is to dissociate herself from her fellow-patients, to declare, I'm different, I was raped. But at the same time she recognizes her impulse as yet another symptom of her possible madness. In doing so, she is ashamed of her shame, the shame of being polluted. There is no need to feel shame. And yet she does. There is no need for any other woman in the room to feel shame. And they don't. That's obvious.

The red second hand jerks its way around the flat white face of the clock. The doctors have arrived and gone to their rooms. Nurses visit them with bundles of case-notes, whispering together at corners. Here is a mystery, in both the ancient and modern senses of the word. It seems to Claudia that she has spent the larger part of her life waiting for something or other to happen, someone or other to acknowledge her existence and restore her to her sense of it in the naming of her name. It seems further that this waiting has always had the same feel to it: that of being hollowed out, a vessel. Not an open vessel. Far from it. A vessel like a building, pretending to be a solid block but, as its windows betray, housing innumerable private rooms. The mysterious interior into which you must not pry: there are experts for that. They alone are privy to the arcana of inner space, telling them over by number and by name. They know the language. They have a licence. If my womb was placed in the palms of my hands, would I know what it was, would I recognize it as mine? Doctor, doctor, tell me who I am. My pathology defines me, and you alone are versed in its grammar. Parse me. I am limited to the passive voice.

The Farquharson girls were brought up as vegetarians. The flesh of another creature was not allowed to enter their flesh. Their father read to them from the Bible. This is my body, this is my blood. The idea of communion was disgusting and fearful to them all. They were to speak when they were spoken to, and wipe their noses. Constipation and diarrhoea were disasters alike, and pains were taken to avoid them both. Billy McCann wet the bed and his mother had to wash the sheets every day: there they were, come rain, come shine, flapping away in her back garden, witnesses for the neighbours to the purity of her intentions, an expiation of Billy's disgrace. The body must be controlled, especially at its orifices, where public and private meet. Whatever exudes is nasty. And yet what is within, girls, is precious and must be guarded, even with your lives. None of it made sense. Or, rather, the sense it made was that of horror: the horror of the worthless, which must be disposed of; and the horror or awe of the valuable, which entails the fear of loss. To be human, to exist in a body, is a dangerous business.

Tiger lilies had surprisingly pleasant, freckled faces, but red-hot pokers could singe and sear your flesh, and the sundew ate flies alive. There were more horrors in Kew Gardens than there could have been at the zoo, which the girls were not allowed to visit, because even a robin redbreast in a cage puts all heaven in a rage. Love-lies-bleeding expired in agony over the trellis from Mrs McCann's back garden, and the gaping throats of the gladioli spoke of scarlet fever and passions beyond mere childish understanding. Oh, there was horror in nature. It irrefutably was. Was sure of itself. How was a little girl, made of sugar and spice and all things nice, to liken herself to a flower? Pansies, meadow-sweet, love-in-a-mist, the unfolding rose. Those were the flowers for little girls. Dost thou know who made thee? Little girl, it is not enough to be. You must know, you must learn, who and what you are. I will learn, Daddy, I'll be your good little girl. Screw you, Daddy. I will not. *Non serviam.* Baby, it's cold outside. Baby, it's colder inside, believe me. It is cold with fear. An outside fair, no doubt, and worthy well thy honouring, thy cherishing and thy love. But I have that within which passeth show. These but the trappings, baby, these but the trappings and the suits.

The nurse calls a name which sounds foreign, satirical, and a large black woman who arrived later than Claudia puts down her copy of *Country Life* and walks heavily over to the desk. She is directed towards one of the three doors behind which the doctors await their supplicants. Next to be called are a Mrs Dempster and a Miss Evangeliou. The Irish woman sighs. Perhaps her name begins with O. Claudia lights another cigarette. Smoked lung: isn't that some kind of delicacy for Eskimos? The black woman emerges and, after a brief conversation with the nurse at the desk, returns to her place – a process which dismays Claudia. At this rate, she is going to be here all afternoon. She flips through the pages of a month-old copy of the *Lady*. Once she used it to advertise for a nanny. Is it possible? The Irish woman is identified as Mrs Halloran. Hughes can't be far behind.

Dr Byng is young, tall and balding with a pinkly innocent complexion. His white coat suits him. He inhabits it and his body as if they had been made for him. Look, Claudia, and learn. This is what it is to be at ease in the world, to know your place and who you are. Dr Byng's voice is soft and appropriately sympathetic, his gaze shrewdly professional. He is not really listening. He has heard it all before. His skilled hands toy with his pen, hands which soon, encased in surgical gloves, will enter Claudia's body, probing for injury, collecting evidence on swab after swab.

'There's no need to look so worried,' he says. 'I can't pretend it's going to be a pleasant experience, but at least it will have the virtue of brevity.'

Claudia shakes her head. 'I'm not worried.'

'Are you usually this tense?'

'Tense?'

'Are you normally so . . . shy?'

'Shy?'

'You seem to be having some difficulty in talking to me.'

'I'm not very experienced,' says Claudia, recovering, 'in talking to people about having been raped.'

'Oh, of course not.' Dr Byng agrees readily. 'Of course not. So you're feeling bitter about your experience, are you?'

'Wouldn't you?'

'Oh, quite, quite.' Dr Byng is taking notes. 'It doesn't do, though, bitterness.'

'Doesn't it? I think it has its uses.'

Dr Byng leans back in his chair and looks at her. 'You're an intelligent woman, Mrs Hughes, and if I may say so, an attractive one. It wouldn't do to let this affect your whole life.'

'You mean I should just shrug it off?'

'Of course not.' Dr Byng smiles. 'All men aren't beasts, you know.'

'Aren't they?'

Dr Byng's smile vanishes. 'If you report back to nurse with this piece of paper, she'll tell you what to do next. And, Mrs Hughes . . .'

Claudia turns at the door. 'Yes?'

'It's not that bad, you know. After all, you're still alive.'

It is Claudia's turn to smile. 'Am I?'

The nurse asks her to wait until she is called again. Claudia realizes that all the women in the waiting-room must be seen for a preliminary interview before she herself is examined. She looks at the clock, but fails to register what time it is. What does it matter? Mrs Dempster is eating a chocolate bar. Mrs Halloran takes out her knitting – a baby-blue matinée coat. Miss Evangeliou is cleaning her nails with a corner of her return tube ticket. Outside in the street – another world – a police siren blazes its breathless, aggressive way. Momentarily the walls assume a bluish tinge. Claudia shuts her eyes and finds herself thinking about her children, whom she sees as static, suspended in time, within the matrimonial home, like figures in a doll's house. Josh has been positioned sitting on the floor of his room, one hand posed above the ranks of Wellington's army. Matilda is sitting at the kitchen table, surrounded by history books, sucking the end of her pen as she stares up at the chandelier. If Claudia were to die, they would stay like that for ever. Motherless, they would have no redress against the arrest of time.

Claudia's mother was tense and shy, despite a five-year-long course in the Alexander technique. Her bitterness crouched hidden, scheming and scheming, until it sprang, gathering itself into a knot in her left breast. Gordian, unravellable. But I have that within which passeth show. I love my husband, I love my little girls, my good little girls. What hussies they are. How brash and brazen. How lucky. I never had their opportunities – especially Claudia's. How dare they treat me with contempt because I lack those very skills and advantages I have been at such pains to confer on them? Oh, they're good girls really. They need me still. Chloe has gone to live in South Africa. But she writes. And sends presents at Christmas. They all remember their mother. As for him, where would he be without me? Has he ever been able to made a decision without my help? I am his earth, his anchor, his very stability. The buffer between him and reality. Solid, solid. Oh, to melt, thaw, resolve myself, my flesh, into a dew. Oh to give vent to the grief within me which passeth show. The grief for my lost self. I'm lucky, though. I'm loved and needed. What more can any woman ask?

Claudia draws deeply on her cigarette. If breast cancer is hereditary – and, given that woman's lot is inherited from mother to daughter, from generation to generation, why should it not be? – then it will get to her before the lungs even know what's hit them. You can only die of one disease. You can only die. It may as well be of one disease as of another. The Farquharson girls must have been a disappointment to their mother. Claudia was the bright one. That a daughter of theirs should get to university! But then what did she do? Marry a pop star. Chloe was the pretty one, so feminine, so gentle, so good with children, such a good cook. Mother's favourite. But what did she do? Emigrate, desert. And Claire, Daddy's little girl, his Cordelia, ready to argue staunchly and sweetly with him in the name of truth, in the name of love. But what did she do? Break her father's heart by refusing to do the decent thing and marry her boyfriend. Break her mother's heart by getting rid of a potential grandchild. Such grief, such grief.

Mrs Bolungwela is called for her examination. The nurse explains that she must go into one of the cubicles, undress completely, put on the overall she will find hanging on the back of the door, and lie on the bed to await the doctor's arrival. The waiting-room is filling up with those who have been given appointments for four o'clock. Claudia asks the nurse for a glass of water: she has to take a valium. In the room with the sink, two nurses are talking a blood sample from Mrs Dempster. The water is warm. Claudia takes the plastic cup back to the waiting-room and swallows the pill when she judges that no one is watching her. But what does it matter who sees her? Who is she, anyway? A woman who may or may not have venereal disease. A woman who has been used. In other words, a woman. That is all. No, that is not all. She is a woman who had and is a mother. She is a woman who knows that her body knows.

She knows the arcanum of the arcana, the woman's secret that must never be told, or even whispered, for fear of recrimination and the theft of that very knowledge itself. The female body possesses and encloses a mysterious otherwhere, of which the female mind (such as it is) must be kept in ignorance. But that is not the secret. The burrows and passages know their own layout by intuition and are sentient. But that is not the secret. The female body is capable in its entirety of ecstasy without the intervention of the obtrusive other, opposite, the male. But that is not the secret – not quite. The secret is that the most transcendent bodily experience available to the human animal is childbirth. Because in childbirth we move beyond the pleasure principle and into teleology. The body inhabits the mind – as it always does, of course, but here in the sort of harmony which some may call divine, and is however essentially human, that is, essentially creative. It is within the female body, that well of all dank and maybe dreadful springs, that the essential human aspiration is fulfilled. Unfair, isn't it? Men have suspected as much for centuries, for ever. They have taken control of the mysteries and made God a man. A father. A priest. A doctor.

'We'll take this swab first, nurse,' says Dr Byng. 'Just try to relax, Mrs Hughes.'

Claudia tries. 'I'm sorry.' She is not trying to make things difficult.

'Have you always been afraid of sex?' asks Dr Byng.

Claudia tenses again: the notion is too absurd. 'I'm not afraid of sex,' she says at last.

'Why did your marriage break up?'

'Various reasons.'

'He's obviously an extremely attractive and charming young man. Were there other women?'

'He was persistently unfaithful, if that's what you mean.' Why should she be answering these idiotic questions?

'Because of your aversion to sex?'

Claudia is temporarily speechless. But, spreading her legs wider, as she is told, she asks carefully, 'What makes you think I have an aversion to sex?'

'You're very tense, Mrs Hughes. You shrink away from being touched.'

'I have an aversion to being raped.'

'I am not raping you,' says Dr Byng, his hand inside her.

Over his shoulder, Claudia catches the eye of the nurse. What can she say? The nurse winks at her. She relaxes. 'No,' she says as the swab emerges. 'All right.'

But her thighs are trembling. She is a sacrifice, a sacred object, and she is being desecrated. Don't be silly, Claudia. Dr Byng is only doing his job. It is the job you asked him, or someone like him, to do. What grounds can you have for complaint? Oh, none. In fact, you are learning something new and useful, aren't you? Rape victims are not scarlet women after all, but frigid little snowflakes. Snow-white, rose-red. Either, both. What does it matter? Both are women and therefore, by implication, asking for it.

'Just one more thing,' Dr Byng says cheerfully as he removes his gloves, 'The blood-test for syphilis. But there's nothing to worry about. Syphilis is very rare in this country – except among homosexuals, of course.'

'Why, of course?' Claudia asks, sitting up.

'Promiscuity,' says Dr Byng, shaking his head in a confidential manner, as if she may be unfamiliar with the concept. 'Meanwhile, we should have the results of these tests. But, just to make sure, we'd like you to come back at the same time next week, I'm afraid, for a repetition.'

'Yes, of course.' Claudia has resumed her middle-class, responsible persona.

She is left alone to put her clothes on again, as if this were the private process. She has not been given the opportunity to wash, and she feels sticky, sweaty. But her hands are dry, and the face reflected in her pocket mirror is pale and remote, evincing no signs of warmth. The two nurses are sitting waiting for her, where she last saw them with Mrs Dempster. They sit her down between them, young things that they are, breaking off their easy and intimate dialogue to take her blood. Her unease is partially dissipated. They like her. She can tell. It matters. Isn't that pathetic? The dark one's hands are gentle on her arm while the red-head takes notes.

'We thought there must be some mistake,' the red-head says as her colleage sinks the needle into Claudia's vein. 'It says here you were born in 1939, but that must be 1949, mustn't it?'

'No,' says Claudia, holding the cotton-wool in the crook of her arm. 'That's right.'

'You're forty?' the dark girl asks. 'You don't look it.'

'Yes,' says Claudia, warming to this unexpected flattery. 'I have two teenage children.'

The two nurses exchange a glance, and the red-head says, 'I hope I look like you when I'm your age.'

'Thank you,' Claudia murmurs.

In truth, she can barely reply, unable as she is to adjust to this, a familiar mode of discourse, from that within which she has been operating in relation to Dr Byng. These girls, women, are hardly older than Matilda. She could hug them both. Thanks to them, quite as much as to the results of the tests which declare her to be in unusually unblemished health, she leaves the clinic with a lightened step. From the top deck of the bus, she can read the placards advertising the *Evening Globe*: Rapist Gaoled for Thirteen Years. But the man who raped her is, partially thanks to her silence, still at large. How can she quiet her conscience? There is no way. She must reserve the right to be a self-centred shit, just like anyone else. And if that means growing another skin, she will do her best to acquire one. Or two. The more, in fact, the merrier.

The girl sitting next to Claudia is telling her friend in the seat in front some complicated story involving cold coffee, the torn-off pieces of lavatory paper, with which a colleague is (so disgustingly) inclined to blow her nose, and a boss who sounds as though he deserves to be poisoned with the former or suffocated with the latter. The story is one of bribery and seduction, but the girl seems unaware of either element, her tone of voice flat and relentless, neither bewildered nor indignant. She cannot sift the substance from the detail. Her tale is for her friend's ears alone, and yet it is audible to anyone who, like Claudia, cares to listen. And, listening, Claudia notices that all the talkers seem to have adopted a similar mode of discourse: each is behaving as though the passengers other than the chosen audience have no existence – or at least, no human existence.

It is not possible. The girl's body is wedged against Claudia's, thigh to thigh and, when she leans back, shoulder to shoulder. And yet Claudia is not flesh to her. Is it possible? It is possible, but is it not extraordinary thus to deny the evidence of your senses? Not at all. It is an ordinary convention, a convenience. It is a form of behaviour perfectly adapted to its surroundings. Claudia must learn to adopt it. Meanwhile, her part in the proceedings is to pretend that she is not listening and, indeed, that there is nothing to listen to, that no story is being told. She must look weary and self-absorbed, like a lone drunk in a pub staring into his beer and ignoring the flickering television screen. She does not altogether dislike the role. On the contrary, she finds some respite in it, the kind of respite granted to those who can sit still, keep their own counsel and maintain the dignity of their isolation. They may be invisible on the top of a bus, but – oh, comfort – are they not felt presences in their own domains?

Neither Josh nor Matilda is at home. They have left dirty dishes on the table, dirty pans in the sink. Claudia's fleeting desire for food is extinguished. She will get drunk instead. It's easier. It makes everything easier. It even makes it easier for you to like yourself, to live with yourself. She fills a beer mug with wine and takes it into the study, where at least the mess is her own. On Radio 4 the denizens of Ambridge are living out the everyday story of countryfolk. How Claudia envies them. From swine vesicular disease to sabotage at the village fete, their troubles are easily remediable and arouse no existential angst. How reassuring. If only she could believe it. If only she could believe anything any more. It will all come out in the wash, Claudia. No, it won't. These stains are called experience: indelible. They are called life. Or death. What's the difference? Blood, circulating or spilt, stands for both.

She will have a bath. Another bath. And there she lies in the foamy water, a freshly filled mug of wine beside her as she smokes a cigarette. At school it was considered the height of decadence to eat oranges in the bath. Now she is going two better. Now too the radio (which she takes with her from room to room as a killer of silence) is playing Shostakovich's piano quintet. She takes her cue, her mood from it. Is there anyone in the audience who has ever lived in vain? No, Uncle, I am nervy, bold and grim. Such do you become when you are alone in the world, when you have been abandoned, betrayed and abused. Or go under. Under the water, under the earth, as once under the heart and under the flesh, deaf, blind and dumb, immured and buoyant in an amniotic sea without any thought of land. Baby, it's cold outside. Suppose she just lay down, stretched out, and let the parted bathwater close over her upturned face? What would happen? Her lungs would fill with water. Poor lungs, already so ill-used. Her brain would be deprived of oxygen. Poor brain, already so tortured. How can she mistreat them? They want to live. Let them, Claudia. And from your fair and unpolluted flesh may violets spring.

Nervy, bold and grim, the anti-Venus steps out of the bath and wraps herself in a large towel before she can glimpse her protruding ribs and pelvic bones in the mirror. Perhaps she will now be able to fit into that silly dress she bought for £12 in Camden Passage. It is made of coral-pink crepe, with the skirt cut on the bias and bound with wide bands of satin in the same colour. The shoulders are padded, the sleeves bell-shaped, the collar modestly rounded with a scalloped edge. Its hem touches the floor. But this last is a problem as easily solved as those of the Archers. Claudia puts on a pair of silver sandals with three-inch heels. A silver belt around the waist completes the outfit. What else goes with pink? Red. She finds some red and silver earrings and paints the nails of fingers and toes with scarlet varnish. This is an absorbing process, occupational therapy. Next the face must receive attention. Poor mask: it has been neglected for so long.

Lavish your care on it, Claudia. Give it blusher, mascara and lipstick, the toys it has had to do without. Look how it responds, so gratefully. The eyes are even beginning to sparkle. More blusher. And the reddest lipstick you can find.

Oh, but the result is stunning. Starved, frightened and totally artificial, Claudia is now herself, the only self she can accept. This is the self which proclaims, I am in hell: screw you. She looks like a little girl dressing up in her mother's clothes. She looks grotesque. She doesn't care. From the wardrobe she takes a black velvet cloak with a pink silk lining – Dorian's property – and lets it hang on her. Like the dress, like herself, it is some forty years old and worn, shrunken, in parts. Ah, they are good companions, the three of them, relics as they are of other lives. Nervy, bold and grim, Claudia picks up the phone and asks for a taxi to take her to Twistleton's. After all, Rupert did say, that evening at Juno's, that she was to turn up whenever she felt like it and tell the girl on the door that she was a friend of his. Oh, to be a friend of Rupert's, as rich and mindless as himself.

The taxi-driver is impressed. 'Not often you get anyone from round here going to a classy joint like that.'

Classy. That's what she is in her faded finery. 'Oh, Rupert Twistleton is a friend of mine.'

'What, really?' He tries to catch her eye in the driving-mirror. 'I thought maybe you worked there.'

'Worked?' Claudia endows the word with the horror of the unfamiliar, much as Edith Evans spoke of a handbag.

'Yeah,' the driver says, unabashed. 'Thought maybe you was a croupier or a hostess.'

Claudia laughs, What he means is, she look like a whore. 'That's an idea. Perhaps I'll ask Rupert to give me a job.'

'He could do worse. Topless, are they?'

Claudia doesn't know. 'Why don't you take the wife for a night out and see for yourself?'

'I might, at that.' The driver laughs. 'Don't know about the wife, though.'

Of course not. 'Isn't she broad-minded, then?'

'Nah!' The driver spits out of the window. 'But what the eye doesn't see, eh? Don't get me wrong, I'm a family man myself. But variety is the spice, know what I mean?'

At first Claudia is too enraged to reply. then, with a tinkly laugh, she says, 'Oh, I do.' Indeed, as the driver eventually succeeds in catching her eye, she winks at him.

As she pays him, he looks longingly into her glittering, drunken eyes and sighs, 'If only I was twenty years younger.'

Twistleton's proclaims itself in a discreetly pink neon approximation to Rupert's signature beneath a candy-striped canopy. Claudia teeters into the foyer, as insouciant as any eccentric aristocrat. They always look like whores, don't they? The light is dim and pinkly flattering, the carpets red and the walls luminescent, shot with gilt. Claudia approaches the girl at the desk, affecting to look vaguely around her.

'Is Rupert here?' she asks.

The girl looks at her without interest. 'Don't think he's coming in tonight.'

'Oh, typical.' Claudia sighs. 'He said he'd meet me here.'

'Oh.' The girl summons up a flicker of interest. 'Why don't you wait in the downstairs bar? I'll tell him you're here, if you give me your name.'

'Claudia.'

'Claudia who?'

'Just Claudia.'

It has worked. Claudia leaves her cloak, leaves the disco on the ground floor and trails her way down the spiral staircase, a bottle of wine inside her, her eyes wide and lost. She is not disappointed when everyone in the bar looks up at her entrance. She is only disappointed that there are so few of them. Twistleton's is supposed to be exclusive, which, being interpreted, means that it tends to get crowded with rich yobs and their freeloaders. It is also supposed to be lively. But it looks, in the dim light, like the anonymous lobby of any anonymous hotel in any anonymous city in Europe: full of businessmen in sober suits. At least the waiters are wearing satin shorts – and nothing else, apart from their running-shoes. There are only two women, sitting together in earnest conversation, among the twenty men or so. Claudia's nerve falters as she approaches the bar, twisting a strand of hair around her finger. Perhaps she should go back up to the disco. Or to the gaming-rooms on the first floor. She will have a drink first. The two men nearest her are watching her every move. One is in his mid-forties, overweight with dark greasy hair combed forward unnaturally to conceal his creeping baldness. His companion is about twenty-five and decidedly good-looking: slim, blond and fair-skinned. He'll do. Unless, of course, he's gay. Claudia smiles shyly at him.

'Have you seen Rupert?' she asks.

The younger man looks at the older one before replying. When he smiles his teeth are white and even. 'Who's Rupert?'

'Rupert Twistleton.' Claudia's surprise is unfeigned. 'He owns this place.'

'Never heard of him.' The younger man is amused, interested.

'You mean the poof?' the older man asks.

Well, that's one question answered, anyway. 'Yes.'

'Have some champagne,' the older man offers as Claudia tries in vain to attract the attention of the barman. 'Another glass here, Joe.'

'The name's Ivor,' the barman says sourly. 'And all breakages must be paid for.'

Seen from the other side of the counter, he appears naked apart from his jewellery. Claudia edges herself onto a stool between the two men, while the older one explains that the glass is for their friend. The younger one lights her cigarette with a Gitanes lighter. She can see herself in the mirror among the multi-coloured bottles, a waif in the saloon. And yet, drawing her cheeks in, narrowing her eyes, she doesn't seem out of place. Standing, the men lean on the bar, lean intimately towards her and so towards each other.

'I'm Burt,' says the older one. 'With a u. And that's Bart.'

'It's with an e, really,' says Bart. 'He's my father.'

Claudia looks from one to the other of them, smiling doubtfully. 'Never.'

This pleases them both. Burt says, 'No kidding.'

'Straight up,' says Bart.

'How about you, sunshine?' Burt asks her.

'Claudia.'

Bart's skin is inclined to be freckled. His green eyes are flecked with brown. His grin is boyish, narcissistic, as he asks, 'Come here often?'

Claudia giggles. 'Once in a while.'

'Lucky me, then,' says Bart.

'How old are you, Bart?'

'Twenty-four. How about you, Claudia?'

'You should never ask a lady her age,' says Burt.

'Guess,' says Claudia.

'Twenty-nine,' says Bart.

'Thirty-three,' says Burt.

'Never thirty-three,' says Bart.

Claudia's nerve falters again. Are they winding her up? The face in the mirror tells her nothing. How old is she? Who is she? Does it matter? What matters is that she must be the one to control this situation.

'Sorry to disappoint you both,' she says. 'I'm thirty-four.'

'Could have fooled me,' says Bart. 'Keep yourself in good nick, don't you?'

What he means is that she's thin. Sock it to him, Claudia. 'Ah, well, I'm a dancer.'

'A dancer!' Bart takes her hand. 'Come upstairs and let's have a bop, then.'

'Not that kind of dancer.' Claudia takes her hand from his abruptly. Will she be able to go through with this? 'I have a classical training. Ballet, you know.'

'That explains it,' says Bart, running a finger down her spine.

'Explains what?'

'The way you walked in here – like someone in a mime.'

Claudia turns to Burt. 'What do you do?'

Burt laughs. 'What do I do, Bart?'

'He's a radio-man,' says Bart.

'What's that?'

'And he's a disc jockey,' says Burt. 'You know what that is, don't you?'

Claudia scents danger. This time they are winding her up. The trouble with lying is that you come to suspect everyone else of doing the same. She can no more believe that Bart is a disc jockey than he can surely believe that she is a ballet dancer. And yet he has the right sort of easy charm, the right sort of precocious self-confidence. It is possible. After all, wasn't she married to a pop star, however tenuously? Anything is possible.

'Ever listen to Metro?' Burt asks.

'He owns half of it,' says Bart.

'Ever hear his show?' Burt asks.

'Metropolitan?' Claudia asks. She never listens to it because it plays nothing but pop music. 'I know someone who works there.'

'Who?' Burt asks.

'Me,' says Bart, putting an arm round her shoulders. 'You've heard me. Now you've met me. Aren't you lucky?'

'I haven't heard you,' says Claudia.

'She hasn't heard you.' Burt thinks this very funny. 'She hasn't even heard of you, have you darling?'

'Bart?' Claudia struggles for the right associations. 'Bart Finnegan?'

'Got it in one, darling.' Bart kisses her cheek.

Claudia summons back her little-girl-lost look as Burt calls for more champagne. Gazing from one to the other of her companions, she asks, 'Do you know lots of pop stars?'

Bart laughs. 'Millions, darling.'

'Intimately,' says Burt. 'What's happened to that champers, Joe?'

'Call me Joe once more,' says the barman, 'and I'll pour the fucking lot over your head.'

'Ooh, hark at her,' says Burt. 'No need to get shirty, Gertie.'

'Do you know Dorian Grey?' Claudia asks.

'Dorian?' Bart frowns. 'A bit before my time, darling.'

'I know Dorian,' says Burt. 'Of course I know Dorian. Worked with him often. Temperamental type. Takes himself too seriously.'

'One of the most difficult people I've ever had to interview,' says Bart. 'Never gives anything away.'

'I'm not surprised,' says Claudia.

'Listen, Bart,' says Burt. 'This little girl knows something we don't.'

'Dish the dirt, darling,' says Bart.

'He's my husband,' says Claudia.

Now that she has told the truth, neither of them believes her. Indeed, they both laugh. Claudia sits revealed as a fantasist nurturing a common dream. It emerges that the two men believe her to be too young and too unconventional to be married to Dorian, especially when she lets it slip that they have been married for sixteen years. Their image of Dorian is that of a man who keeps his private life apart, not because he has anything to hide, but precisely because he doesn't: his wife is a boring little housewife; his children must be protected from the glare of publicity. What does it matter? Sooner or later both Burt and Bart will recognize that she has been telling the truth. Bart will be able to boast (a man among men, of course, because he too is married with two children) of how he screwed Dorian Grey's wife. The revenge of property on ownership is to give itself away – and as publicly as possible.

Dorian kept saying, don't. Don't talk about it: it doesn't do any good. Don't dwell on it: the sooner you forget about it, the better. Don't think about it. I don't want to know. I don't want to hear the details. He became very busy because – out of the blue – he was offered a part in a new rock musical. What with that and the band, he didn't have a moment to spare. Life was one long rehearsal. You can say that again, said Claudia. And Dorian said, what's that supposed to mean? It means, said Claudia, when are we going to be granted the privilege of attending the performance? She was referring to moving house. But Dorian was evasive on that matter, hinting that the whole process was an unnecessary expense. There were delays with the building society. There were delays with the bank. There were delays with the solicitor. None of them would tell her anything. They all wanted to speak to Mr Hughes. But the vendor spoke to Claudia. She said she'd had another, higher, offer which she had accepted: she had told Mr Hughes about it a week ago.

Burt and Bart offer her a lift home. It is with some difficulty that she manages to ascend the stairs, and if Burt hadn't reminded her, she would have forgotten her cloak. Chattering still, silly little thing that she is, she leaves the club with Bart's arm round her, Bart's embrace sustaining her. She can talk, oh, she can talk, talk, talk, but can she walk? It is the sudden cold air that provokes the question. Where is she? Who is she? All her body knows is the warmth and strength of another body, younger than hers, male and protective. But that wasn't the point, was it – to be protected? What was the point? She can't remember now. It was something to do with being in control of the situation, something to do with revenge. Control. Revenge. The concepts have become remote, ungraspable. What are they for? They seem so urgent, so wearisomely, ludicrously urgent. They belong to that boring little housewife who was married (oh, enviable her, oh cynosure of glamour-starved eyes!) to Dorian Grey. Who the hell is he? Control, revenge. Such virtues are already available to the powerful. Who are the powerful? Those who know who they are.

Burt's car is large and comfortable, more so than Cormack's. It crosses Claudia's mind as she gets into the back seat that father and son might be in the habit of sharing their women. But when Bart gets in beside her, she dismisses this idea: it is she who is in control, having taken them both by surprise. Bart takes her hand like a young lover. The three of them talk and there is a lot of laughter. Claudia can hear it. She can also hear herself dominate the conversation. At least she supposes that it is herself: there is no other woman present. Is there? Is she present? In a sense. Her underweight body sits perched on the cushioned upholstery, hardly denting it. And yet she is present. Surely there is no denying that. Something present is controlling that animated voice, the words sounding themselves so rapidly, with never a slip or slur. It is an affected voice, that of an actress who has taken elocution lessons. As for what it is saying, it amazes Claudia to hear how knowledgeable it is about recording techniques and the internal affairs of the Musicians' Union. Is she making it all up? Is she writing dialogue for some seedy soap opera? Two men and a girl they have picked up in a bar?

They are in the car. Now they are in the house, in the kitchen. At least, Bart and Claudia are. Burt seems to have disappeared. No loss. What are Bart and Claudia doing? They seem to be drinking coffee. Its heat must have woken her up. She is talking again. Or is she *still* talking? It doesn't seem possible because there doesn't really seem to be that much to talk about – not to a stranger, anyway. Unless she is relating the story of her life:

autobiography of a victim. There are volumes of that. But what a lapse of taste! She keeps saying he, him. Bart listens, smiling, holding her hand across the table. Dorian. She must be talking about Dorian. She was sure she heard herself say his name just then: it was his name that alerted her. What an act of treachery! Serve him right. Dorian. Well, then, she must be Claudia. Claudia, you're being a bore. Why don't you just shut up?

Another interval of consciousness. The coffee is finished. Bart is sitting opposite her, his fly unzipped, stroking his erect penis with one hand while he rolls a joint with the other. He is still smiling. Have they already smoked a joint? Bart keeps telling her to relax. As he hands her the joint, he asks her to open the satin buttons on her dress and caress her own breasts. Automatically her hand begins to unbutton. But then she remembers: she is not going to do what he wants; she is going to do what she wants; he is going to do what she wants. And besides there is nothing to caress. No flesh. There is no flesh left. Bart says again that she must relax, murmuring the word over and over like an incantation, while he continues to stroke his penis. He wants her to touch it. She refuses. He wants her to take it in her mouth. She refuses. Bart is not offended: his smile doesn't change as he rolls another joint. As she begins to relax, either soothed by the dope or hypnotized by his words, he begins his own monologue. What is he talking about? She can't understand a word.

They are in the kitchen. And now they are in the bedroom, in the marital bed. How did they get there? They must have climbed the stairs. Both of them. Surely Bart couldn't have carried Claudia upstairs. He looks too slight. And yet he doesn't feel slight. His body is young and muscular, in its prime. There is hardly any hair on his chest, and round his neck a gold chain with a medallion in the shape of a lion, signifying the astrological sign of Leo. His hair, with the light behind it, looks more like a halo than a mane. Claudia is sitting propped up against the pillows and the brass rails at the head of the bed with Bart moving inside her. Is that what is happening? Does it matter? Bart's smile is becoming beatific. Claudia's body moves in response to his. Is it Claudia's body? It is a body with a will of its own. There is no more Claudia. There is only flesh: opening, closing; clenching, unclenching; back, forth; rhythmically. The defeat of consciousness, the defeat of meaning. The triumph of the body.

'With a climax like that,' says Bart, 'what is there left to say?'

From the bottom of a well, from the other side of the looking-glass, Claudia's eyes meet his. 'Nothing.'

But Bart goes on talking. 'Except to say thank you, Camilla.'

'Thank you, Bernard.'

'Bart.'

'Claudia.'

You can't have everything. Simultaneous orgasm. Isn't that supposed to be what we all want? Don't some people spend a lifetime pursuing this unattainable goal? Lucky Claudia. Lucky Bart. The perfect lovers. Who would have thought that pleasure was so easily available, that ecstasy was to be had for the asking? Bart, perhaps. Most men, perhaps. But not Claudia. My life began when my marriage ended. What a lot you're learning, Claudia. A crash course in the principles of freedom. Not to love: to want and to take, whether by demand or guile: that way fulfilment lies. At this rate you're going to pass with First-Class Honours.

Bart snuggles down under the bedclothes. 'Good night.'

'You're staying?'

'You're not going to throw me out. It's raining.'

'I thought your wife might be expecting you.'

'She's in Gloucester.' Bart pulls her down to lie beside him. 'I only see her at weekends.'

'I see,' says Claudia.

'Let's sleep.' Bart kisses her neck. 'I want to do it again in the morning.'

Claudia kisses his brow. The bed smells of violets. 'So do I.'

XXI

Of course a girl's best friend (if it's not diamonds!) is supposed to be her mother. And there I was, all alone with Mum, once Josh had gone off to school and they finally decided Nat was a nut-case and locked him away in a special unit. Actually he wasn't locked away at all. He was in one of the few adolescent units in the country where they don't shut you away from dawn to dusk to dawn again. It was in a huge hospital in the country – well, it was just outside London, but it had all these grounds with lawns and trees and flowers, so it was almost like being in the country. There was a separate psychiatric wing for nut-cases and part of this wing was the adolescent unit. It was mainly girls, for some reason. (Mum said this was because girls always got treated like nut-cases and boys like criminals. And although there were boys there, I could see what she meant.) Anyway, Nat soon found himself a new girlfriend. Her name was Marika, and she was the thinnest-looking creature I'd ever set eyes on. You should have seen her! She looked like something out of a concentration camp, with her arms and legs like match-sticks, and bandages round her spindly wrists where she'd been slashing herself. But she had those enormous eyes, which she kept rolling around when Nat was rabbiting on about one thing or another. She spoke very fast and kept waving her arms about so that her bandages came unrolled. First time I saw her, she came running towards me and Nat over the lawn in front of Birdwood Wing with the bandages all streamed out behind her like spirally wings. I liked her. She made me laugh.

I suppose it should have made me feel sad going to see Nat. After all, there he was, a criminal lunatic, now that he'd been arrested twice for TDA and shut up out of harm's way before all his cases came to court. Because, you know, by the time Josh went away to school, they'd already adjourned his and Nat's case twice. This was to give the social workers time to get their reports together. And then it was the summer holidays. And then, believe it or not, there was a strike among all the people who worked at magistrates' courts. So off Josh went, not knowing what the hell was going to happen to him. But at least someone (Mum or Juno) had bothered to do something for him and worry about what he was feeling. And the same goes for Nat. Some social worker had seen to it that he was sent off to this open unit where there were all sorts of people to talk to and look after him, and they did psychodrama and all sorts of exciting things like that. But me? I was supposed to carry on like nothing had happened. Nobody ever asked *me* if I wanted to go away to school. (Not that I did – but I should have been given the chance to say no, shouldn't I?) And there were no psychiatrists around to listen to *my* problems for hours on end. Good old Matilda was supposed to be able to cope on her own. Well, almost. All I had was Mum.

She was always being ill. As far as I could make out, she spent most of her time in bed. I'd go into her room, and there she'd be, just lying flat on her back and staring at the ceiling. She'd always look at me as if she'd forgotten who I was. Even then I'd have to attract her attention first. Once I found her lying on Josh's bed in exactly the same position, except that she was clutching his old leather jacket in her arms. She'd tidied his room so that he wouldn't have recognized it, even sorted out his records into alphabetical order. Would you believe it? I began to wonder if she was the one who was going round the twist. I mean, if she wanted her darling Joshie around, why did she send him away in the first place? She didn't have to. And why all this fuss about Josh anyway? She still had me, didn't she? I couldn't help being a girl, if that's what was worrying her. I didn't know what was worrying her. But I can tell you, the atmosphere in that house was so fucking gloomy and bleak, it made me want to scream my head off.

When she wasn't lying on her bed or Josh's, she was pissing off to some library or other. To do research, she said. It seemed her feminist friend, Sonia, had another friend who was writing a book about famous women. Actually, I think it was some sort of encyclopaedia. Anyway, this woman Harriet would send Mum all these lists of names and things and she had to take them off to the Fawcett Library or wherever and look them up in other encyclopaedias. So she wasn't around all the time, Mum. In a way that was a relief. I mean, I could use the stereo in the sitting-room instead of my piddling little portable. I could turn the volume right up and dance around the room or sing along with Blondie or Toyah. I could walk around in bare feet without anyone moaning at me about veruccas. I could eat what I liked when I liked. I could have Weetabix for supper and put masses of sugar on it, which would have given her a fit. And I could ask my friends around. Only trouble was that with Josh and Nat both being away, I didn't seem to have any left.

That's when I started going round to Rodge's on my own. After all, the magazine had to be kept going, didn't it? And who else was going to do it? But I can tell you for nothing that the first time I set off across Clissold Park all on me tod all I wanted to do was run off in the other direction as fast as I sodding well could. Could anything be more ridiculous? This was the person I wanted to see more than anyone else in the world. And yet I was terrified. Of what? Making a fool of myself, probably. Something unworthy like that. I kept planning what I was going to say to him and then telling myself that I mustn't decide anything in advance. But I couldn't help it. These scenarios kept writing themselves in my head. As usual. By the time I actually got to experience anything, it was so chewed over by all my elaborate rewrites that the real thing was always tame by comparison.

In the event it was Ros who opened the door. Like I said, things never turn out the way you expect them to, no matter how many twists and turns your imagination takes. I'd been nurdish enough to have forgotten Ros. I'd been inhabiting a universe where only me and Rodge existed. Ros said, oh, it's you, Matilda. And my heart sank. Wasn't he expecting me? But she let me in and led the way into Rodge's room. At once he asked me what the matter was.

It was because I couldn't look at him. I didn't dare. I don't know why. I just thought something would happen to me if I did. I didn't know what – just that it would be devastating. But devastating-terrible or devastating-wonderful I didn't know. I couldn't tell the difference any more. So there I stood, kind of shaking, avoiding his eye, mumbling, no, no, I was quite all right. He looked at Ros then. That's when I plucked up the courage to look at him. Rodge. Standing in front of me. In the flesh. Oh, Rodge! All I wanted to do was to put my arms around his neck and cover his face with kisses. He looked at me so tenderly then, I nearly died. He said I looked tired and Ros said she'd get some coffee together. And that was the only time we were alone. I sat down on the nearest chair instead of next to him on the bed. I didn't dare. He started asking me questions about Josh and Nat. But I could hardly concentrate. I kept wondering why he'd sat on the bed instead of in his usual chair. Had he wanted me to sit next to him? Had I rebuffed him? Should I get up and walk over to the bed? I didn't dare. The brave little creature didn't dare. Then Ros came back with the coffee and it was too late because *she* went and sat next to him.

Something of the same sort happened with Dad. Not exactly and not the first time I went out alone with him. Oh, it was so sodding embarrassing that first time! I couldn't understand what had happened. It should have been better than usual, not worse. For starters, there was no Josh rabbiting on about football, which he always did to please Dad. Then, Dad actually came to pick me up instead of leaving me hanging about at Oxford Circus outside Peter Robinson's which was where we usually met for some reason. And then it was down to me to choose the movie. But he arrived forty minutes late (Mum was out) and there was nothing I was dying to see anyway. I'd rather have stayed in and watched 'Dallas'. We ended up going to see *Airplane* because he kept insisting I'd said I'd wanted to. But I hadn't! It was Josh, not me! Afterwards we went to McDonald's and I didn't feel hungry, and he kept asking me what the matter was. Christ only knows why I didn't feel hungry. I just didn't. When I said as much, Dad agreed at once and that made things a bit beter. But then he started asking me about school and I couldn't say anything because there wasn't anything to say. When I tried talking about *Zitz* (the next best thing to talking about Rodge) he didn't seem interested. He wasn't disapproving or anything – just kind of distant. The same thing happened when I told him about Nat and Marika, and how they all sat around and acted little plays about each other's lives, and how they could talk to the staff any time of the day or night, whenever they felt like it. When I described Marika, he actually shuddered.

Then he said that she and Nat probably deserved each other. By the end of the meal I was dying to get home. All I wanted to do was to get away from him. Don't get me wrong. I wasn't afraid of him and I didn't hate him or anything like that. It was just that I could hardly believe he was my Dad. He didn't seem like the same person. And yet he did. And he was. It made me feel all churned up inside because I didn't know how to be me if I didn't know that he was my Dad. I wanted to cry. What with all that and being in love with Rodge at the same time, it was no wonder I couldn't eat.

It was nearly half-term before he took me out again. This time he wanted me to meet him at the theatre where he was rehearsing for this musical about the life of Dr Livingstone. (He was Livingstone, but it turned out that Stanley had a bigger part, so he was well pissed off.) To say I was dreading it would be an exaggeration. But I wasn't exactly looking forward to it, especially as he suggested it over the phone just after he'd been having some kind of row with Mum about moving house. There she was crashing about in the background, making a cup of tea or something, while he was asking after my health in that funny voice he always uses when speaking to children or animals. Christ Almighty, he'd just made Mum cry, and there he was carrying on as if he was unaware of this and everything in the garden was lovely. Mum said the woman who was selling the house near Highbury Fields had accepted another offer a week ago and she'd told the solicitor, who'd told Dad, but he hadn't told Mum anything about it. I hope I've got that right. Anyway, what it all added up to was that we weren't going to move after all – at least, not to that particular house. To tell you the truth, I'd forgotten all about moving. We seemed to have been on the point of moving so often I'd lost all faith that it was ever going to happen. But Mum kept saying, why didn't he tell me? What the shit was I supposed to say? Then she said, what's going on, Matilda? Try to find out. I ask you. How was I supposed to find out?

When I got to the theatre, they said Dad was in the bar, so I just kind of stood there, thinking they wouldn't let me in, but some jolly-looking man with a grey moustache just like a walrus said it was OK, he'd take me in himself. Just as well because Dad was hidden away behind a pillar, although I could hear him laughing as soon as I got into the room. And there he was, sitting at a table right next to some ghastly-looking woman with a squeaky voice, so absorbed in his conversation he didn't even notice me come in. When he deigned to acknowledge my existence it was in the middle of a laugh he was sharing with this hyena. She held out her hand and said, I'm Kwithy. It turned out she meant Chrissy, but I didn't know that at the time. I didn't want to touch her. She looked kind of stale. And she talked like a baby, as if she thought she was awful cute or something. Ugh! I loathed her. Oh, Dowian dahling, she kept saying and giggling at everything he said. I got the impression they were both showing off for my benefit. They needn't have bothered. I wasn't the teeniest bit impressed. Whenever I said anything (which wasn't often, I can tell you), they'd look at each other like they'd seen some hidden meaning. Honestly, it was utterly disgusting.

It all went on like this for ages and I kept waiting for her to go away. Every so often I'd look at my watch but she didn't seem to take the hint. Neither did he. At last I said, Dad, I thought we were going to go to the cinema. Oh poor Matilda, was their attitude, poor little thing. Here we are chatting away and letting your precious time with your father slip by. That's actually what she said. But it didn't stop her coming to eat with us. And we never got to the cinema. Instead we went to some place that *she* suggested, where the waiters seemed to know them both. They all fussed over me. It was so fucking embarrassing. Not that I have any objections to being fussed over. But I do object to being treated like I was ten years old. I mean, Dad never treated me like that when there was just the two of us. I kept looking for some opportunity to ask him about moving, like Mum had said. But I could hardly get a word in edgeways. In the death, I just butted in and asked Dad, all kind of innocent, when we were going to move. He said, we'll talk about that another time. I mean, he actually said that! I didn't know what the sodding hell I was going to tell Mum. But as it happened she didn't ask me. So I didn't tell her anything. I just put the unspeakable Kwithy out of my mind and got on with my own life.

Such as it was. Nothing but frustration, you might think. And you might well be right. We had to rethink *Zitz*, Rodge and Ros and me. After my brave words in July, everything seemed to have gone into hibernation during the summer holidays. First Nat was carted off, and then Josh. I mean, I'd done my bit and most of the 'zine had been set up by the time we lost Nat. By September it was ready to go, only thing being we didn't have anybody who was willing to stand around and hand it out, apart from the three of us. Various people volunteered, but Rodge said we had to tell them exactly what was involved. Otherwise, it wouldn't be fair. That was when people like Slime and Emma started chickening out. I might have guessed, of course. They didn't seem to get the point that this was no wank for middle-class armchair socialists but the real thing. Then of course when they were faced with the mind-blowing reality of laying themselves and their precious career prospects on the line for their beliefs, they upped and went like we'd put a fucking rocket under their pampered bums.

Rodge said they were no loss, any of them. We'd manage somehow. And of course we did. How could we fail? Rodge and me (and Ros, of course) were a team. We were that at least. I had this totally unsettling dream about him. Not for the first time, of course. But this time it was different. Before, when I'd dreamed about him, nothing would ever really happen, if you see what I mean. I'd keep trying to talk to him, but we'd always be interrupted. Or he was just about to kiss me and I'd wake up. But this time I actually dreamed that we were making love. (When you're in love, you don't call it fucking or screwing.) The funny thing was that I was lying on top of him. I mean, it didn't seem funny in the dream, only when I thought about it afterwards. It was me making love to Rodge and he was just lying there. No, not just. He was lying with his arms all kind of flung out and his head moving from side to side. There was this expression on his face which I've never seen on anyone in real life. But it seemed to say what I was feeling. Was it rapture? Was it torture? It was both. There didn't seem to be any difference. All the time I was thinking, I don't want this to end. But as soon as I realized that, I woke up. I was sweating all over and my duvet had slipped to the floor. Everything was so quiet. So dark. I could have been the only person left on the planet.

That terrible feeling of loneliness. Rodge seemed to make it worse! But he made it better too. I kept everything he'd ever given me or sent me. I had the *Springtime* poster on the wall where I could see it when I was lying in bed. I had the letter which said, love, Rodge. I knew every word of it by heart. And I had a piece of wool from his frayed sweater, which he'd broken off and rubbed into a kind of frizz before putting it in the ashtray. I rescued it, liberated it, when he wasn't looking, and put it in my pocket. But none of it was enough. I wished I'd had a tape of his voice for every time he spoke to me on the phone. We had an answering machine but it wasn't working any more because Josh had jammed all the buttons down together in a fit of temper, the sodding self-indulgent wanker, and Mum said it would cost too much to get it mended. But even a tape wouldn't have been enough. I wished I had a film – with sound and everything – of all the time I'd ever spent with Rodge. I wished I knew what he was doing every minute of the day or night. I wished I knew what he was like when he was my age or a little boy or even a baby. I spent my whole fucking time wishing one thing or another. And nothing ever happened! Things just went on the same old way, talk, talk, talk. And Ros was always there, always talking. I couldn't understand it. She wasn't always there when Josh and Nat were around. It was almost like she didn't want me and Rodge to be alone together. Or perhaps it was Rodge who didn't want it. Perhaps he thought I was a total bore. Oh sweet Jesus, the thought terrified me, paralysed me, so that I found myself mumbling and muttering all the time. The more I thought about it, the more boring I became. Real life is so disappointing, so ordinary. It does its best to crush all the originality out of you.

All the time I wanted to *say* something to Rodge but I didn't know how to do it. I could feel this horrible *thing* growing inside me and festering like it would burst at any moment. I couldn't stand the pressure of it. I kept being afraid it would take over my whole body like some gigantic cancer feeding greedily on itself while the rest of me starved to death. I was full to bursting point and I was starving too. I was starved of Rodge. I couldn't get enough of him. And yet I didn't know how to get any more of him than I had. I kept feeling angry with him for being so stupid he could't see that I was crazy about him. Then I'd tell myself of course he couldn't see because he wasn't vain enough to suspect people of falling in love with him all over the place. At such moments I'd love him more than ever.

It wasn't that I hated Ros, exactly. I just wanted something sudden and final to happen to her so that she'd be painlessly eliminated, like a tree falling on her as she walked across Clissold Park. Mind you, I'd have settled for emigration or even a long holiday in Patagonia. I didn't wish her any harm. She'd never done me any. In fact, she was actually quite nice to me in her vague sort of way. I suppose she was an intellectual, really, and if she thought anybody wasn't quite on her level she didn't have much time for them. You felt she pitied you in an impatient sort of way for your ignorance and your inability to grasp abstractions. She never explained anything. Unlike Rodge, who always told little stories about boots or pinball machines to illustrate the principles of economics. He was so patient. And so fatherly! But I don't think Ros even knew how to explain things. She just thought naturally in complicated terms and spoke naturally in long words. I mean, there was nothing pretentious about her. She genuinely didn't live on the same plane as the rest of us. I could see why Rodge liked her. Oh, I could see it well enough. But that only made things worse. I mean, if he thought she was someone special, then she must be, mustn't she? Which is more than can be said for the Godawful Kwithy.

Then it happened – the opportunity I'd been waiting for. Ros got Asian flu. I'd had this hideous day at school when Fairfax decided to give me one of her pep talks because my last history essay had dropped a grade, and to make matters worse, I was staring out of the window in class and hadn't even heard her when she read out my name. She asked me how things were at home. Not in front of the whole class, I hasten to add, but in the corridor, which was bad enough. I said, all right. Then she asked me how Josh was. I said, all right. You're being rather evasive, Matilda, said she, is there anything wrong? So of course I said no. I mean, what else, for Chrissake? So she said there was a lot of flu about and I should look after myself and go to bed early. Meanwhile she would have a little chat with my mother. I ask you. You forget the date of one boring old Act of Parliament and it means you're suffering from some terminal disease. Love. That's what I was suffering from. And boredom. But whether either of them was terminal I wasn't prepared to say. Or even to wonder.

Rodge said, poor Ros has got flu, I'm just taking her some Lemsip, why don't you come and say hullo – from a safe distance? I said I was bound to get the flu sooner or later, so I might as well get it over and done with. Rodge said he never got flu. I said, really, why not? But he didn't know. He said he was terribly healthy and never even got colds and perhaps it was because he was a vegetarian. I said, ugh! All I could think of was the sort of food we got from Grandad. He laughed then and said vegetarian cooking wasn't all nut cutlets – in fact, he'd never had a nut cutlet in his life – and one day he'd show me how interesting it could be. We had this conversation as we were going up the stairs to Ros's room. It was the most personal conversation we'd ever had. I couldn't believe Rodge was a vegetarian. Or rather, I couldn't believe that I'd never known that about him before. Somehow the subject had never come up and I'd thought he'd had chips without fish because he was nuts about chips. Now I had this privileged information about him all to myself, to have and to hold. Well, I knew it wasn't all to myself, really. But Josh and Nat didn't know, did they?

Ros was asleep. I'd never been in her room before, but it was much as I might have expected – bare and untidy at the same time. Full of papers and files and great heavy library books. Her bed was just a divan pushed against the wall and covered in cushions like Rodge's. I hardly recognized her. For one thing, her hair was all hanging loose and kind of sticking to her scalp and face. For another, she looked truly ill, truly ghastly. And there was a horrible sickly smell in the room. I wanted to back out again, but

Rodge didn't seem to notice. He went and put the drink down on this chair littered with Ros's clothes and pulled up to the bed. Then he stood looking down at her with this expression of concern on his face. My guts turned to water. When did anybody last look at me like that? Except Mum, I mean. I couldn't even remember that they ever had. Ros opened her eyes and said, oh Rodge, as if she'd forgotten him and he'd been standing there all the time. Then she said, oh Matilda, how nice of you to come and see me. So I asked her how she was and she said, not too bad. Rodge said she was well on the way to recovery. Then they smiled at each other and my guts turned to water again.

There was nowhere to sit down, but Rodge didn't seem inclined to leave. So we just stood there like idiots while Ros drank her Lemsip. Or at least I stood there like an idiot. Rodge started telling Ros about some book he was reading, and she said the thesis sounded pretty much like Kernokov's, and he said no, there were several points of departure, and so forth. I walked over to the window which looked out over the back garden. Everything looked withered and you could see right into other people's kitchens. There were lights on everywhere but the three of us were in darkness. The book lying open on the table beneath the window was called *The Causes of Human Misery*. I shivered. I didn't want to know. I walked over to the door hoping that Rodge would come too. Ros said, thank you for coming, Matilda. Rodge said, goodbye. Goodbye! After that I'd have felt a fool if I'd said I wasn't going, wouldn't I? So I just left and walked back down the stairs ever so slowly, cursing my own stupidity.

I hadn't even reached the bottom when Rodge came out of Ros's room carrying her empty cup. He called to me and asked me if I'd like a cup of coffee before I left. I said, oh yes, why not? At least I think I did. My heart was pounding so loudly in my ears I couldn't even hear my own voice. This is *it*, I told myself, this is it. What, I didn't quite know. As it was, the first thing that happened was panic. I couldn't think of anything to say. I didn't dare say anything. I was afraid that if I opened my mouth to speak, only nonsense would come out of it. And I couldn't think what to do. Was I supposed to follow Rodge into the kitchen and help with the coffee? Or was I supposed to sit and wait? What did I usually do when Josh and Nat were around? I couldn't remember. So I hovered, if that's the word. Rodge started talking about Josh so I walked towards the kitchen so as to answer him. Then the kettle started to make a noise and Rodge started clattering mugs and spoons, so I drifted away again. And there I stood looking at all the posters and things on the walls like I'd never seen them before.

Rather belatedly I asked Rodge if he wanted any help, and he said no, why didn't I sit down? So I went and sat on the mattress where Josh and Nat usually sat, and felt suddenly lonely.

I could hardly look at Rodge as he came walking towards me. I didn't know what to do with my face, thought it would start twitching all over the place and get out of my control if it actually attempted to put on some sort of meaningful expression. So I let Rodge sit down next to me and put the mugs at our feet before I looked up from doodling with a felt pen on the knee of my jeans. Even then I just said, thanks, Rodge. But even that was an improvement. Normally I'd just have said thanks and left it at that. He asked me if I was going to do anything special over half-term. I said I never did anything special, not even at Christmas.

That's when he told me he was going to go away. At first I didn't take it in. I thought he meant he was going away for Christmas. But it turned out he was going to California. California, of all places! I mean, it's full of Californians, all made of plastic. He had some kind of job there, doing research into educational alternatives, whatever they might be. I didn't even ask. I didn't give a toss what they were. How long was he going for? That's all I wanted to know. And yet I didn't want to know. I didn't want to know anything that was going to tell me I wasn't going to see him again. Oh, not long, he said, they've only given me enough money for a year or so. A year or so! I couldn't believe it. You can't! That's what I said. You can't! Rodge looked taken aback, and said why ever not? He must have thought I meant because of *Zitz*. He said he thought I had the hang of editorial procedure by now. You can't, I said again. Because I don't want you to, I said. Because I love you, I said. Because I love you.

I thought the silence would never end. I thought maybe I'd gone deaf. And blind. I thought – well, no, I didn't think. I was kind of suspended, breath held, outside of all thought. I do remember wondering, though, if I'd died, been struck down in instant punishment for my rash declaration. Then I realized that Rodge was talking to me. He was leaning forward with his arms on his knees and his hands clasped together. He wasn't looking at me. I'm very flattered, he was saying in that gentle voice of his which made it all the more difficult to bear, and I'm very honoured, Matilda, I really mean that. I waited for the but. It didn't come. Nothing came. But, I prompted him. But you're so young, he said at last, I never dreamed, I never thought, I'm sorry. I didn't say anything, didn't move. Of course he was very fond of me, he said, of course, but I was so young. And so on. I couldn't really take it in. What did it matter what he said, anyway? I mean, what did it matter which words he used? What he was really saying was that he didn't love me and he was going away. For a year. For ever. He didn't love me. He was going away. Just like everybody else. I had been rejected.

I stood up. I tripped over my coffee cup. I ran towards the door. I didn't know what I was doing. I knew Rodge was following me, but I didn't stop. I heard him say, don't cry, oh please don't cry, Matilda. Until then I hadn't even known that I was sodding well crying. But sure enough I was. I was sobbing. I was making one hell of a row, and as I reached the door I was yelling to Rodge to leave me alone. I mean, I didn't mean it, oh, I didn't mean it. But it sounded like I did. Rodge must have believed me. He let me go. He let me rush out the front door and slam it behind me. He let me run down the street towards the park. He didn't stop me. Did I want him to? I couldn't tell. I couldn't tell anything any more. All I wanted to do was get home and shut myself in my room and never come out.

It wasn't that easy, though. The first problem was to avoid Mum. The light was on in the kitchen and when I opened the front door I heard voices, so I thought, good, now she won't notice me. Then I realized the other voice was Josh's. What the pissing hell was he doing there? He was supposed to be at school. They must have thrown him out. Well, serve him right. I didn't give a toss. Mum called to me and I called back, just a moment, and went upstairs to have a pee. I didn't want to go back down to the kitchen. Why should I? Little as I wanted to face Mum, Josh was the last person I wanted to see. Why can't he ever do what he's supposed to do? I went to my room instead and lay down on the bed. And of course the only thing I could see was that fucking *Springtime* poster. It seemed like an insult, a slap in the face. I took it down from the wall and tore it in two. That was so satisfying I did it again – and again and again until it was all in little pieces which I scattered around the room like confetti.

Mum and Josh seemed to be having an argument. Not another fucking crisis. I was sick of them. I wasn't the one who was always causing them. It was always someone else and I was just the one who had to put up with the consequences Why was life so pissing, shitting unfair? All the time? Why couldn't even *one* thing go right, just for a change? I could hear Mum saying something to Josh about education and the law of the land. And then the phone rang. While Mum was answering it, Josh came upstairs, clomp, clomp, clomp. Just the sound of his wanking footsteps made me want to scream. Mum called him. He didn't answer. Then she called me. I didn't answer either. What did any of it have to do

A.—15

with me? I turned off the light and got back into bed under the duvet, right under so as I couldn't hear Josh's record-player. Or Mum's footsteps coming up the stairs.

XXII

'Oh Claudia, how too, too predictable!' Juno's shriek of laughter, rising above the general clatter, is at the same time anomalous enough to draw the bored attention of Jeffrey and Sabina from their polite appraisal of Juno's new decor. 'If you must live in Hackney, then you must expect to get mugged.'

'You mean,' said Claudia, 'I was asking for it?'

Jeffrey puts an arm round her shoulders. 'Asking for what, darling? Some fatherly solicitude, that's what you're asking for, you poor little orphan, you.'

'Claudia's been behaving so peculiarly lately,' Juno explains. 'And now I know why. She's just told me that she was mugged on the way back from my birthday party.'

'Oh darling, how monstrous!' Sabina's huge dark eyes are avid for possible marks of the victim as she scrutinizes Claudia from limply overgrown hair to scuffed and down-at-heel boots. 'I do think it's so brave of you to live in such a dreadful place.'

'Poor little Claudia.' Jeffrey's grip tightens. 'So frail and now so tense. How could anyone do such a thing? It's like torturing a kitten.'

'Yes,' says Claudia, 'Cruelty to animals. Better call the RSPCA.'

'When we were burgled I felt just the same.' says Sabina. 'It's almost like being raped.'

'Well, they did get into your drawers, darling,' says Jeffrey, inspired to a deafening guffaw by his own wit.

Claudia takes the opportunity to slip away from him. Juno's sitting-room, its walls now resplendently intimating thoughts of blackcurrant milkshakes, is so tightly packed with guests that it is difficult to move in any direction. But Claudia tries. Her woollen dress, buttoned high at the neck and tight at the wrists, is far too hot for the occasion. Sabina, by contrast, is wearing a little black dress which leaves her arms and shoulders bare, and, to match, high-heeled sandals which consist of barely more than a strap or two. But then Sabina has come to Juno's housewarming party in her own car. Claudia has travelled by bus and tube. She notes Sabina's well-tended tan, the antique silver at her throat and wrists, and on her fingers. She notes too the network of lines around Sabina's eyes beneath the make-up and the deeper furrows on her upper lip, emphasizing the disappointed curve of her mouth. She feels a stab of compassion for Sabina, whom she dislikes but who is nevertheless female and therefore as vulnerable as herself. And yet it is not entirely the fact of Sabina's femaleness which has aroused her compassion. Something in that once pretty face reminds her of Dorian. It is its inability to forget itself or to forgive itself for changing. It is at the same time its own lover and enemy: *odi et amo*, the eternally paradoxical passion.

'What did Dorian have to say about it?' Sabina asks. 'I hope he felt thoroughly ashamed of himself.'

'Shame is not Dorian's forte,' says Claudia.

'If you were mine,' says Jeffrey, 'I wouldn't let you out alone.'

'Dorian doesn't exactly encourage it,' says Juno. 'He's done his best to keep her in a gilded cage.'

'The gilt wore off long ago,' says Claudia, 'and now the base metal stands revealed.'

Base metal is indeed what she feels her own substance to be in the presence of Juno's new and glamorous friends. How downmarket to be mugged in Hackney, like any old-age pensioner! Would rape at Highbury Corner – the true story – have any more kudos? Jeffrey would change the subject with some haste. Sabina, on the contrary, would want to know all the details, but would never admit as much, teasing them out one by one. And Juno? Claudia is afraid to put Juno to the test: Juno might fail, in which case Claudia would have lost a friend. Friends are what she needs, friends who will provide distraction and entertainment, friends who will protect her. She glimpses Greta across the room, Greta surrounded by a gaggle of young homosexuals who have typically become her admirers. Leo and Greta will give her a lift home. Claudia will insist on it. Greta is in her debt now that Clive has been restored to her possession to be shared only with Junkie June, a rival beneath consideration.

Moving through the crowd in Greta's direction, Claudia reflects that Juno seems to have gone altogether up in the world since the move to Knightsbridge. Her guests are more expensively and fashionably dressed than they used to be in Notting Hill. Indeed, they are not the same people at all. Wedged and unable to progress between two animated groups, Claudia looks round in vain for a familiar face. She can just see Greta out on the patio with one of her young men. Behind Claudia two men are discussing the relative merits of Brussels and Strasbourg as locations for business conferences. In front of her two young couples arc conducting a conversation which, to judge the number of interruptions, has a strongly competitive element. Timbo is edging his way towards her, carrying three glasses of punch above his head.

'It's the radiators I don't like,' he confides as he passes Claudia. 'That one really shouldn't be visible above the back of the sofa.'

This is beyond Claudia. 'How are you?' she asks weakly.

'In the pink,' says Timbo, 'after a few gins of that ilk. How are the children?'

'Josh's court case finally comes up tomorrow.'

'Court case?' Timbo repeats, moving on. 'You must tell me about that some time. Lovely to see you.'

Claudia cannot help feeling slightly humiliated. Of course Timbo has no knowledge of – and less interest in – Josh's case. Why did she mention it? She really must stop giving answers to rhetorical questions. In the present context direct communication, freed alike from self-enhancement and the whisper of scandal, is not the order of the day. When in Rome, Claudia. Listen to those rivalrous couples comparing their country weekends.Listen and learn.

'Oh, you've been to Knutsforth too, have you?'

'Last weekend. Duggie is such a poppet, and lavish to the point of folly – unlike the Hugget-Blandfords.'

'When we were there the other house guests were the Duvilliers d'Angevin.'

'Oh, we had Dorian Grey and – what was her name? – his girlfriend.'

'The lovely Chrissy. She's Duggie's niece, you know.'

But Claudia has heard and learned enough. She will not wait for Leo and Greta. She will leave at once. She will go home to her children. Her children – ah, how she longs to see them, to be with them, her very own, flesh of her flesh, instead of all these puppets. No longer diffident, she shoves her way through Juno's guests, spilling a drink here, stubbing an exposed toe there. Serve them right. Her coat is at the bottom of the heap on Juno's bed. It looks so thin. She shivers as she puts it on. Canadian squirrel. Poor creatures. Is their fur really so sparse against the snows? How do they survive? She will not say goodbye to Juno. Or to anyone else. She will keep her own counsel. Isn't that the better part of survival? Baby, it's cold outside. She walks briskly along the street to the tube station, her arms folded to keep her coat together, her head down as if ready to butt anyone who dares approach. At least

Juno's own parties have the advantage of beginning at six rather than nine.

The bastard. After everything he said in Cornwall. The stinking, putrid bastard. Wait, now, Claudia, wait. That was just a snatch of overheard gossip. You know that Dorian has been making an effort to see the children at weekends. Where was he last weekend? He said he had to go away. Had to. Claudia didn't ask him where, assuming that he was working. It can't be true. It can't possibly be true after everything she said about the importance of honesty. But, remember, Claudia, that's what you thought when you answered the phone on New Year's Day. Your bloke's having it off with some little tart. You thought it couldn't possibly be true, didn't you, and yet you knew that it was. It is true, Claudia, it is true. You'd better believe it. It all makes sense. It all falls into place.

Dorian has found himself another woman. He wants to live with her and not with Claudia. That is why he didn't tell her about the house. That is why he looked so pleased with himself last time she saw him. That is why he no longer talks about the future, their joint future. But why has he taken such pains to win her back again, only to reject her? He has changed his mind. It's that simple. Is it? What has made him change his mind? It is because she has been raped. He didn't like that. He doesn't want soiled goods. It is because she told him above Clive and Chaz. He didn't like that. He doesn't want soiled goods. He will not share his property. Oh no. Ownership of the means of reproduction must be exclusive. The shit. Why couldn't he have the guts to say that he had changed his mind? But surely you didn't expect him to, Claudia? Surely you can't be that naive. I am. I want to believe in reparation. I want to believe that whatever is broken can be mended. You want to, but you can't. You want to, but you shouldn't. Why don't you divorce him? He won't change. Face it. Face it now, for pity's sake, before it's too late. Forget all this striving towards honourable action. Trust your intuition instead. Remember what it has been telling you. Listen this time, just listen.

The surveyor, taking a look at the master bedroom, commended the fitted wardrobes with their mirrors and decorative chrome frames. He was even more impressed when he saw that the bed, designed to match, was fitted to the wall at the head. Must be worth a bomb, he said, have you tried it? Dorian lay full-length to one side, his hands clasped behind his head, an exaggeratedly blissful grin on his face. Claudia watched him with a distaste which was quite involuntary but couldn't be overcome. The surveyor urged her to try the bed. She shook her head, looking wildly at him and around the room, as if for escape. When he persisted and, worse, Dorian patted the space at his side, inviting her, she walked out to the landing. Her legs where shaking and, as she clutched at the banisters, she thought she was going to throw up. At once Dorian was at her side, asking what was the matter. She looked at him, unable to speak. His expression was partly amused, partly impatient, but unsuspecting, oblivious, obtuse. She couldn't say it. How could she tell him that she could never get into bed with him again?

Of course she couldn't tell him. It wasn't even true. It was probably only a temporary aversion. The body remembers. When they were all a proper family again, feelings of revulsion would be out of place and so could be vanquished. The body must learn to forget. It was only her pride, that stubborn Farquharson pride, urging her body to close its gates against a potential aggressor, a potential destroyer. The body trusts itself to preserve itself. But surely the body will listen to reason? Surely the problem is not insuperable: problems never are, if approached in a spirit of objective reality, freed from all considerations of vested interests. The body is selfish. But the body must learn to accept cultural restraints, must learn the meaning of submission to a higher authority.

Claudia catches sight of the name of the tube station. Caledonian road. She has come one stop too far. How idiotic. Now she will have to get another train back to King's Cross. When she slipped her arm through Dorian's (ah yes, it was she who touched him first) he took her hand briefly in his. Although his was the larger, its bones felt brittle in her responsive grasp, the skin dry, brushing hers like the feathers of a dead bird. That we can call these delicate creatures ours, but not their appetites. She brushed the remembered line aside as a feather duster might a couple of feathers. Let them float and fall where they will. Things are as they are, and nothing is for ever, nothing is perfect. Trudging up and sliding down the shifting slopes held loosely together by clumps of toughened grasses, Claudia and Dorian could find their new starting-point there. Their steps were those of seasoned travellers, their voices those of experience. When Aunt Hester saw their stained clothes, she tut-tutted over the foibles of young people. There was time, there was plenty of time, to begin again. There was a quarter of a century to go before Claudia attained Aunt Hester's age and thirty-five years before she reached her father's. There was a whole lifetime. The contract had been renewed, although the precise wording of the altered clauses, the nit-picking over punctuation, was yet to be worked out.

The busker in the corridor leading to the main-line station is a girl with long, blonde hair, strumming a guitar and singing 'She Loves You' in a voice hinting at a Scottish accent. She is very pretty and waif-like: a shade of the sixties. As Claudia drops 50p into the crocheted cap at the girl's feet their eyes meet briefly. What kind of creature can this Chrissy be? Doesn't she know that Dorian has a wife and two adolescent children? Doesn't she care? Oh no, there is no reason for her to care. She has no children. He has no children, if he would rather spend his time with the Chrissys of this world. What's wrong with men? That they can deceive and betray other adults is bad enough; that they can betray and desert their own children is far, far worse. Perhaps Dorian hasn't even told this one that he is a father. She must have asked him. She must know. How can the lot of women ever be bettered when there are thoughtless females like that around to sabotage the efforts of the rest of us?

There is a queue at the 73 bus stop. Nine o'clock is the slack time of the evening, and most of the buses stop here and turn round to retrace their tracks towards Hammersmith. It is beginning to drizzle and Claudia worms her way into the shelter, causing the queue to close ranks towards its head. She lights a cigarette, keeping her bag clasped firmly over her stomach to deter pickpockets. Once bitten . . . Oh, once bitten, twice and three and four times bitten. Claudia, Claudia, will you never learn? It's not as though you haven't done your homework: you know it all by heart. Why aren't you passing all your exams with First-Class Honours? Sorry, superego, sorry. Sorry, Daddy. I'll try harder in future. You'll be proud of me, honestly, you will. A 38 arrives and the queue halves. Claudia moves along the shelter to take her superior place within it. She will wait. The hand on the clock on the tower of St Pancras will complete a quarter, a half, a whole revolution, and she will wait. What else are women for?

When Dorian called round on Monday afternoon to acknowledge the first day of Josh's half-term, he looked cheerful and relaxed. Claudia's feather duster swept yet another feather out of sight: that he had spent the night with some woman. How often has it performed that same housewifely action in the name of domestic order? Never again. How often do we perceive what we prefer to perceive, what it is expedient to perceive, and discard the rest, the emperor sporting his new clothes still? No, never, never again. When Dorian telephoned this very afternoon to relay the information from Josh's solicitor, he brought good news. When he said he would see her at the court rather than collect her and Josh on his way from Ron's, she was only faintly annoyed, although taxis were hard to come by at that time of the morning. She dismissed the unworthy thought that he was being deliberately unhelpful. She had had enough of bitterness and meanness. At last Josh's case would be heard. At last everything was going to start to improve. Whatever happened, tomorrow was going to be hers, her property, in her power. She would show Sonia, for example, that a marriage didn't have to end for a life to begin.

And where was Sonia? Claudia didn't see her at Juno's party. It would seem that Juno is attempting to ostracize Sonia. Or Sonia to boycott Juno. How silly. After all, they're both adult, civilized humans – yes, they are, aren't they, Claudia? Just like you and Dorian. So Sonia was right, after all. So far Sonia has been right about everything. All men are capable of rape, she said. There is no such thing as a non-sexist male, she said. What every man feels for women in his heart of hearts, she said, is fear and hatred. But Claudia smiled disbelievingly. Poor Sonia. How limiting it must be to have such a bleakly intransigent and narrow view of human relations. As the mother of a son, she should know better. Oh poor Sonia. She is so embittered that she can't see that her own unfortunate experiences of marriage are not universal. Oh poor, poor Sonia. Hasn't she ever heard of forgiving and forgetting? What can she know of love?

With the icy calm of one who no longer possesses either a body or a soul to be hurt and has therefore become all mind, Claudia tells herself: this is a second rape. The violated woman must be reviolated by being rejected. Despoiled, despised, she is no longer a desirable, let alone valuable, property. Her conduct has nullified all promises, cancelled the contract. It was her purity, her moral integrity, which made Dorian feel a guilty and inferior being, unable to live up to her standards. But now why should he even bother to try? He hasn't been raped and in this is clearly her moral superior. He is free. Free to return to the good old double standard, such a convenience for him and his kind. He can start again with a new piece of property, undespoiled and undespised. And once again, childless and liberated from the bonds of wedlock, he can gain the undivided female attention which his mother and – alas – his wife have led him to expect. Thanks to the ministrations of a younger woman, untainted by rape, childbirth, infidelity and feminism alike, his ego can be rebuilt and his self-respect restored. Isn't he lucky?

How coolly Claudia steps onto the platform of the bus and climbs the stairs. How straight she sits in her seat, her head held high. If you look at her, she will look directly into your eyes, unwavering, expressionless. Her body has taken on the contours and the posture of Sonia's. It says, I have no more illusions. It says, I may have lost but I will not be beaten. It says, if you mess with me, I'll kill you. Things are as they are, Claudia, obstacles all of them. Kick them aside. Kick them to pieces and stick them with your stiletto heel. *Was enstanden ist, das muss vergehen.* At least you now know where you are and what you have. *Bereite dich, bereite dich, zu leben.* Now, voyager . . . Now prepare your ship of life. But I am nowhere and have nothing. Then you too are free. You have touched bottom, that is all. Now is the time to re-emerge and prepare your craft. *Was vergangen auferstehen.*

Josh and Matilda are watching television. Actors in Western costumes are galloping across the screen, intent on providing spectacle through the commission of what promises to be a bloodthirsty act. The aggressive white male will triumph, but the faithful Mexican will be sacrificed and the whore with a heart of gold give her life for the hero. Things are as they are and the nature of reality is essentially metaphorical.

'Dad rung up,' says Matilda, following Claudia into the kitchen. 'He said he'd be round at half-past nine in the morning.'

'That means ten o'clock,' says Claudia, filling the kettle. 'I wonder what made him change his mind.'

Matilda shrugs. 'He said he had to drop Ron off somewhere.'

'Are you sure it was Ron?'

'That's what he said. Why?'

'I thought it might be someone else.'

Matilda looks warily at her mother who, still wearing her coat, is unwrapping the cellophane from a pack of tea-bags with unusual precision. Her expression too, as their eyes meet, is careful. Matilda blushes. Claudia pours boiling water into the pot and gives the tea-bags a stir. Is it possible that Dorian has taken Matilda into his confidence? Surely not. Surely even he wouldn't stoop to involve his children in the deception of their mother in such a shameless and cowardly fashion. No, it isn't possible. But Matilda is looking very evasive. She has been rather evasive lately, though, rather withdrawn, and she hasn't been eating much – not since she had her row with Rodge – or whatever it was. Come to think of it, she doesn't look at all well. Claudia fetches the milk from the fridge, the mugs from their hooks, and carries them to the table. Matilda fetches the teapot and, remembering to place a mat underneath it, sets it beside the mugs. It is this unwontedly helpful gesture which prompts her mother to speak.

'Who's Chrissy?'

Matilda blushes again. 'She's in the show with Dad.'

'I see,' says Claudia.

'Oh Mum, she's awful,' Matilda says at once. 'She talks like a baby, and we call her Kwithy.'

'We?'

'Josh and me.'

'Josh knows her?'

'She went with Dad when he took Josh to school.'

Claudia can feel her scalp contract as she watches her daughter's embarrassed face. 'You mean it's been going on that long?'

But of course it has. Claudia was surprised by Dorian's offer to drive Josh to Devon. But now she understands: it was part of a weekend trip with Kwithy. Sparing Matilda any further questioning, Claudia makes a rapid reckoning. Josh went to school the day after her second visit to Dr Byng. This means that two weeks after his wife was raped, Dorian was embarking on a new love affair – if such it can be called. So soon? Can it be possible? It looks like it, Claudia. It looks as though the need for reviolation was more pressing than you have, could have, imagined. Come on, now. Why the numbness, why the shock? You knew he was dishonest. Yes, but I didn't know he was that dishonest. I thought such a degree of dishonesty would be obvious, especially to me. But it wasn't, was it? You're not quite as clever as you thought. Oh, I'm not clever at all. Mother, father, parents dear, you were wrong about me. Claudia's not the clever one, the one whose achievements you can be proud of, the one who will bring fame and honour to the name of Farquharson. What can you tell the rest of the clan now? No wonder you're disappointed. Oh mother, aren't you glad you're dead? Oh father, don't you wish you were? How can you bear the shame?

The television in the next room is silent now. Josh comes in yawning, in search of sustenance.

'I'm going to be a good boy,' he announces, 'and go to bed early so as I look all beautiful in the morning and everyone will know that I come from a good home.'

'Mum knows about Kwithy,' says Matilda.

Josh's haphazard bread-cutting comes to a brief pause before proceeding more carefully. 'Kwithy is as thick as nine short planks.'

'She's a plastic playmate,' says Matilda.

'I can't stand her smarming over me,' says Josh, 'and she stinks of some revolting perfume.'

'She can't stop talking.'

'And she keeps squeaking like a stuck pig.'

Claudia supposes that she should be gratified to learn that her easy replacement is so unworthy a successor, but she knows at the same time that her children would resent Kwithy, whatever sort of person she was. She is angry on their behalf. Dorian is telling them both by his example that the double standard still reigns supreme; that there are two sorts of women – mothers and mistresses; and that telling the truth is a matter of small importance when compared to the need for instant gratification of narcissistic impulses. Consciously or not, he is attempting to fashion his children after his own image. Learn this, Josh and Matilda: just as boys will be boys, men can do as they please and every red-blooded male will; trivialities like childcare can be left to the women; men are polygamous and women monogamous; never the twain shall meet but tell each other comforting lies; of course, it's hard on women, especially the older ones, but they were born losers, and it can't be helped. Learn this, Josh: whoring is more fun than parenting. Learn this, Matilda: anatomy is destiny. Learn again, both of you: the liars of this world shall prosper, while those that hunger and thirst after righteousness shall have their prating mouths stuffed with dust and ashes, and serve them right. Life, dear children, is a meaningless free-for-all, so grab from it what you can while you can, and don't give a toss about anyone else. Wouldn't you rather inhabit my universe than that of your pathetic little mother?

The pot is empty and Josh offers to make more tea. Claudia ascertains that Kwithy is about twenty-five, unmarried and childless, none of which comes as any surprise. By dint of further probing – she too can behave shamelessly – she discovers that Kwithy has been living with Dorian at Ron's for several weeks, weeks during which the search for a new house has proceeded, Claudia and Dorian visiting property after property and finding none on which they were prepared to agree. He has been wasting her time. And his own. Unless, of course, he has actually been looking for a new home for himself and Kwithy. What sort of game is he playing? Too cowardly himself to tell his wife that she has been superseded, he has allotted the task to his children instead. Can't he understand the enormity of what he is doing to them? It is not their business to betray their father any more than it is to deceive their mother on his behalf. And yet Dorian has managed to make all of them his accomplices.

'I'm sorry,' Claudia says eventually, 'but I may as well tell you. I shall have to divorce him. I don't see what else I can do.'

Matilda looks surprised. 'I thought you were going to, anyway.'

'We knew he wasn't coming back,' Josh says gently.

'Even before Kwithy,' Matilda adds.

'I didn't,' Claudia says faintly. 'How did you know?'

Josh and Matilda look helplessly at each other. There is, of course, no answer. Claudia sends them both to bed with a promise to wake Josh early. She sits on at the kitchen table, huddled in her coat, her chair pushed against the radiator. Even when the heating switches itself off, she remains where she is, sipping her tea, unwilling as she is to turn her attention either to the work which awaits her on her desk or to the routine of preparing her body for sleep. Simple, automatic tasks, both of them, but tasks which belong to a simpler time and a more innocent persona. The new persona sees no virtue in doing as it ought. It sees no virtue in action which is not directed towards its own resurrection. And, being unable to determine the nature of any such action, it is condemned to inactivity. When the doorbell rings she welcomes the interruption.

'Joshua Hughes?' The young policeman's voice is nevertheless peremptory.

'He's in bed,' says Claudia, adding unnecessarily. 'It's after midnight.'

'Would you fetch him, please?'

'Why?'

'His case is coming up at Highbury Magistrates' Court tomorrow.'

Claudia stares at the awkward young man with gradual comprehension. 'We knew that at two o'clock this afternoon. What do you mean by coming round here at this time of the night when you know damn well he must be in bed?'

The policeman is some twenty years her junior. He has the grace, or the lack of expertise, to blush. 'I'm sorry. We only just got the message.'

'If this is another of your techniques for harassing juveniles,' she continues, indicating the panda car parked at the kerb with a wave of her hand, 'I am not impressed. And you can tell that to your superiors with my compliments.'

He stares miserably at her. 'I'm sorry.'

'So am I.' Claudia slams the door.

But as she climbs the stairs to bed she can't help laughing. The look of guilty bafflement on the constable's face! Poor boy. It was probably his first brush ever with the Great British Public, whom he must serve and keep in check. He didn't deserve her anger. No, but how satisfying it is to be on the giving rather than the receiving side of injustice, for a change. Tonight the constable. Tomorrow, Kwithy. And Dorian. They will both get what's coming to them. Let them both sweat. Let them both agonize – if either is indeed capable of any such process. Revenge may not be sweet, but it can be fun. Claudia has it all worked out. She takes two valiums and, almost before she has smoked her cigarette down to the filter, she has fallen asleep.

At breakfast with Josh, Claudia rehearses once more the possible outcomes of his case. He will probably be fined. If so, he will have to pay the court in weekly instalments out of his pocket money. Now that he is at Abbot's Combe it is unlikely that anyone should recommend that he be taken into care, but he may nevertheless be allotted a social worker. He and Nat will, in any eventuality, have to pay for the damge to the parking-meters and vending-machine. Josh listens in silence, expressionlessly, as he eats his shredded wheat. Claudia tries to reassure him that nothing terrible is going to happen to him, and so there is no need to be nervous. Josh denies that he is nervous, says he doesn't care what is going to happen to him. His jaunty mood of the previous night has turned to one of sullen defiance. Claudia sends him upstairs to wash his face and neck while she has a second cup of coffee. This she takes into the study with her. It is almost nine-thirty. By now Dorian should have left Ron's, but at the same time he is not likely to arrive at the house for another twenty minutes or so. Claudia picks up the phone.

'Chrissy?' she enquires warmly, having ascertained that the woman at the other end of the line does indeed lisp her sixes and sevens.

'Yeth.' Kwithy's response is pleasant enough.

'My name is Claudia Farquharson.' Pause. 'Do you know who I am?'

Silence. Then, a little defiantly. 'Yeth.'

'I am Dorian's wife.' Claudia speaks slowly, spelling things out. 'I am the mother of his children. You do realise that he has two children, don't you?'

'Oh, yeth.'

'My children have suffered because of their father's behaviour. You are adding to their suffering. I am not going to stand by and allow them to suffer any longer. I will not have you meddling in matters which are beyond your comprehension. Do you understand?'

'Oh yeth. Honethtly, Claudia, I've twied to talk to Dowian about his childwen and what'th going to happen to them.'

'It's none of your business what's going to happen to them.'

'I know. I mean, I've twied to leave Dowian thevewal timeth, but he jutht won't take no for an anthwer.'

Claudia has difficulty in containing her fury. 'There was another girl earlier this year, and there were others before that. You're just one of a very long line.' Kwithy's silence seems to denote dissent. Of course. They probably all think they're different. 'People say that women are their own worst enemies. Not true. It's women like you who are the enemies of the rest of us. Women who pander to male narcissism. Childless women who are perfectly prepared to injure innocent children for the sake of getting fucked by Mr Famous.'

'I know you're cwoth with me,' Kwithy wails, 'but it'th not like that, weally it ithn't.'

'What is it like, then? Love's young dream?'

'I'm not a thilly girl, Claudia.'

'You could have fooled me,' says Claudia. 'Well, if you're not silly, you must know what you're doing. If you know what you're doing, your morals must be contemptible. I can't allow my children to have anything to do with you. And I can't allow their father to see them while he's consorting with you. He'll have to choose between his children and his whore.'

Kwithy gasps. 'How dare you talk to me like that?'

'I'll talk to you however I please,' says Claudia, nudged into calm by this gratifying response. 'Think about it.'

When she puts the phone down she finds that she is shaking all over. But she remains unashamed of her dishonest threat. Indeed, she is rather proud of herself. She has established her moral superiority over Kwithy, and that is what matters. She has made it plain that she will stand no more nonsense. And of course Kwithy is far too stupid to realize that Claudia would never dream of trying to separate her children from their father, even if such an action were at all feasible. So Kwithy will sweat. Claudia pictures her, blank-faced and open-mouthed, emitting little squeaks and waving her hands every so often. She would like to kick Kwithy's teeth in. Physical violence too could be fun. But then she supposes that the verbal sort is more dignified and thus better suited to a woman of her advanced years. It has never failed to overwhelm Dorian. And, compared to him, Kwithy is easy game.

'What are you laughing at?' Josh asks, startling Claudia by his sudden appearance at her side.

'Oh, I've just told Kwithy where to get off,' she says lightly. But Josh looks horrified. Watching his face, rejuvenated and vulnerable now that it is clean, Claudia wants to cry. Josh is so real. The fact of him, her son, hits her where it hurts. 'I'm sorry, Josh, I should have waited.'

'I think that's Dad's car,' says Josh, going to the window. 'I'll let him in.'

Claudia blows her nose. It is no good. She will never be able to make Dorian and Kwithy suffer as she and the children have suffered. It is the vulnerable who suffer, even when they are attempting to inflict suffering. Children are vulnerable. Children and those who love them. Others are unassailable. You batter them with all your might, but the blood on your clenched fist is your own. Is it worth it? But it is too late to repent. Dorian is in the room, and Josh has evidently decided not to intrude on his parents. Claudia looks at her husband as if at a stranger. His voice, when he asks her how she is, is both friendly and brisk. The very sight of him makes her feel tired, too tired to quarrel. But she can't very well pretend now that she doesn't know about Kwithy.

'Had any thoughts about Christmas?' she asks casually.

'No,' says Dorian. 'Why?'

'I just wondered if you were planning to spend another dirty weekend at Knutsforth.'

Dorian looks angry. 'I never pretended I was being celibate.'

'You pretended you were being honest.'

'I was waiting for the right opportunity to tell you,' Dorian says stiffly, 'but somehow it never came.'

'Of course not. It never does.'

'Don't start dragging the past into it.'

Claudia stares at him in amazement. 'The past is in it. This time last year you were deceiving me with some little scrubber. In July you swore you would be honest with me. But now you're doing exactly the same thing.'

'It's not exactly the same thing.'

'What is it, then? Love's young dream?'

Dorian sits down on the bed behind her and lights a cigarette. 'I don't have to tell you what I'm doing.'

'Oh, don't you?' Claudia swivels her chair round to face him. 'I was under the impression that we were married.'

'Our marriage is over.'

'When did you decide that? When I was raped?'

'No, Claudia.' Dorian's voice is patient. 'I think I knew in August.'

'When I was raped,' Claudia affirms. 'Or was it when I told you about Clive and Chaz? Ith that when Kwithy appeared?'

'Don't use that silly voice when you talk about her.'

'It's how she talks.'

'You don't know anything about her.'

'I know as much as I want to know. I've just spoken to her.'

For the first time in the conversation, and to Claudia's fleeting satisfaction, Dorian looks startled. 'What have you been saying to her?'

'I told her I couldn't allow my children to have anything to do with her.' Claudia's voice resumes the censorious tone she used towards Kwithy. 'And that I couldn't allow them to see you while you were carrying on with her. So you'll have to choose between your children and your whore.'

'You're out of your mind!'

'Probably,' Claudia says, unruffled. 'If lying, cheating and whoring and abandoning your children constitute sanity, then I'm raving mad.'

'Your choice of words would be disgusting if it wasn't laughable.'

'My choice of words is deliberate.'

'What you don't seem to understand,' Dorian says, patient with her again, 'is that none of this is a matter of morality.'

'Of course it's a matter of morality!' she yells at him. 'You behave like a prize shit and you have the gall to sit there and say it's not a matter of morality. Morality is the nub of the matter, you lying, whoring bastard.'

Dorian shakes his head ruefully with a little laugh. 'People are just people, Claudia,' he says sagely. 'Not whores and shits or saints.'

'Some people are shits,' she says, 'and you're one of them. So don't give me any of your pseudo-liberal garbage about tolerance and forebearance. You sure as hell won't get any from me.'

'I didn't expect any.' Dorian shakes his head again. 'You certainly are your father's daughter.'

'I'd rather be like my father than like you,' she says at once, though momentarily stung. 'At least he knows the meaning of integrity.'

Dorian stands up and tosses his cigarette-end into the empty fireplace. 'You really are a nasty piece of work.'

Claudia's rage is such that she can barely speak. But, remembering Josh waiting for them both, she says as steadily as she can, 'May you and your scrubber rot in hell for ever.'

Dorian smiles grimly at her. 'Shall we go? We'll talk later about Chrissy and the children.'

'There's nothing to discuss,' says Claudia. 'I've already made up my mind.'

'Mum!' Josh is calling her from out in the street. 'Come on, it's ten o'clock.'

XXIII

When Nat discovered smack it transformed all our lives. Small wonder, you may think. But if you do, you're thinking small. It was a large wonder, a glorious wonder. We'd been so fucking brainwashed about it, I can tell you. All that pious bleating you get dished up on the media about the Evils of Heroin is a load of old cobblers. One fix and you're hooked for life. That's their lying propaganda for you. Then they show you these pictures of people, not actually dressed in pin-stripe suits and over forty, shooting up, which are supposed to make everybody shudder. Or else they dig up before-and-after photographs of some wimp who's OD-ed, like it was an everyday occurrence and the natural result of depravity. Never a mention of the fact that some people (most people) know how to use the stuff properly. Never a mention of what anybody gets out of it all. Oh no, that would be giving the game away, wouldn't it? Then society in general would have to admit that what they really loathed and wouldn't stand for was the sight of anybody under the age of twenty or so actually enjoying themselves. Do you think you're going to catch the bastards doing that? You've got to be fucking joking, mate. The hypocrisy of it all is enough to make you puke. How wonderful to be young, they say. And yet they do their pissing, shitting best to make sure it's hell on earth. They smoke and drink themselves into oblivion every day of the week. They screw around with each other's wives and husbands. That's the sort of shit that keeps them going. Adult pleasures. They can keep them. We don't want them. We've got pleasures of our own.

I'd forgotten it was Josh's half-term. It wasn't the same as ours, you see, because all those jammy morons at private schools have shorter terms. His court case finally came up that week, conveniently enough. After all that, he was let off with a conditional discharge, the twice-jammy moron. Only, if he committed any more crimes in the next year he'd be charged with this one as well. So he was well pleased with himself, like he'd beaten the forces of the law single-handed.

Not so Nat. He was sentenced to continuing psychiatric care. Not that he minded. He was getting into the whole pissing thing and would keep rabbiting on about repression and Oedipal conflicts, like the best of them. This was when he started to become an expert on drugs – especially the sort manufactured by the huge Swiss companies and doled out by the State to the victims of capitalism so as to keep them quiet and able to cope with their sodding awful lives.

It was largactil that first transformed Nat's sodding awful life. He couldn't move without it. Not that he did much moving with it. Or much talking, come to that. And as for listening, well, you never knew if he was or if he wasn't. When I talked to him and Marika, all they seemed interested in was what was going on in their unit, their microcosm of madness. Who'd taken an overdose. Who'd slashed her wrists. Who'd had a fight with the staff. And then Marika refused to eat and was taken off to the main hospital where they fed her through tubes. She kept pulling them out, though. In the end they had somebody watching her twenty-four hours a day. She couldn't even blink an eye without them noticing. Not that she really minded. She wanted everybody to get their knickers in a twist over her behaviour. No doubt she thought she was some kind of heroine. Everybody else did. They all thought they were somebody really special. Jesus H. Christ, I just couldn't take it.

Not that I could take any of it any more. I couldn't be bothered with any of them – Mum, Dad, Kwithy, Josh, Nat . . . I was sick to death of them all and all their sodding problems. What about my sodding problems? Nobody seemed to think I had any. Little did they know (or care). All Dad cared about was Kwithy. And if Mum wasn't griping on about the two of them, it was about Josh who stayed in bed all day and refused to go back to school. Well, he set off twice and never arrived there. He stayed with some friends of Nat's in Dalston. The first time Mum tried to talk him into going back. The second time she pretended not to care and just left him to rot in his shit-hole of a room. It was only when he started cooking or playing the radio in the middle of the night (he never got up before four o'clock) that she started yelling at him. And of course Dad did sod all, said it was just a phase. Mum started spending more time at the library. She'd come back at about seven, have a drink and listen to 'The Archers'. By this time Josh had usually gone out somewhere or other (I didn't know where at the time) so they hardly ever saw each other. Just as well because they didn't exactly have a lot to talk about. And the same went for me. I mean, if I couldn't talk to her about Rodge, what could I talk to her about?

When she came into my room she turned the light on again and asked me what had happened. I didn't answer. Then she said it had been Rodge on the phone, asking how I was. I still didn't answer her. Serve him right if I'd committed suicide. Mum came and sat on the bed and tried to ease the duvet away from where I was holding it wrapped around my face and ears. But I hung on. Then she said in this calm little voice, not hysterical at all, I don't know what to do, I just don't know what to do about anything. I let the duvet slip and tried to sit up. Thank God for you, Matilda, she said, you're so sensible. That's when I started to cry again. I'm sick to fucking-death of being fucking sensible, I yelled. She was amazed. What had she said? And what was I doing, anyway, in bed at half-past seven with all my clothes on? And why had Rodge been so worried? She got it into her head that he'd assaulted me. I must admit it occurred to me to let her go on believing that, but in the death I just couldn't do it. I mean, it wouldn't have been fair, would it? He *had* said he was very fond of me. Not much, I know, and probably quite meaningless. But better than nothing. So I had to tell her she was wrong.

I couldn't tell her anything else, though. It was just too humiliating. I can't, I kept wailing like an idiot, I just can't tell you. She said all right, I could tell her later when I felt a bit better. I said all right too, of course, but somehow later never came. She would watch me anxiously and keep asking me questions in a roundabout sort of way. But by that time I just didn't want to talk any more. I wanted to forget it ever happened. I wanted to forget Rodge even existed. That was the only way I could carry on, the only way I could keep my self-respect. And then as soon as she found out about Kwithy, Mum didn't want to know any more.

Poor Mum. I felt sorry for her really. I suppose I thought she'd known all along. Now, I know that's stupid because of course I knew damn well she didn't know. I suppose I kind of hoped. I hoped Dad and her had talked about it, like they'd talked about Clive or Chaz. And I knew they'd talked about *them* because she'd told me herself. She said she didn't want me to get the impression that it was only men who could have affairs. I ask you. Typical Mum. As if I could have thought any such thing. I mean, they've got to have affairs *with* somebody, haven't they? It turned out she wasn't really talking about men and women but mothers and fathers. Well, of course I knew that mothers could have affairs, just like fathers. Hadn't I seen it (practically) with my own eyes? Then she went on about how infidelity was much less destructive if people were honest about it. It was one of those uncomfortable conversations of hers, with her asking me how I felt all the sodding time.

What the hell does it matter anyway? The whole concept of heterosexual monogamy was outmoded years and years ago. You can't expect it to work. I suppose Mum did expect it to, though. That was the trouble. But why? She must have seen it failing and falling to pieces all around her, long before Dad ever got it together with his bit on the side. Sometimes I think my Mum's really naive. People of her generation are, of course. I don't expect they can help it, but it gets a bit irritating when they simply refuse to believe that things have changed since their day. I mean, when she was my age, everybody wanted to get married and have children. Now you've got to be some kind of cretin like Cheryl Berners to want to grab some man who's going to keep you in slavery for the rest of your life. Even Emma wants to go to university first.

Anyway, Mum asked Josh and me all these searching questions about Kwithy. It was pathetic. I mean, Kwithy wasn't even worth talking about. If that's what Dad wanted, then let him get on with it and good luck to him, as far as I was concerned. Not so Josh. He said Dad was a sexist pig, and you could always tell what men really thought about women by the sort of woman they chose to shack up with. Coming from him, that was rich. He never had any girlfriends at all till he went to Abbot's Combe, which only goes to show he must have thought nothing of women at all until he met Lucy. And a right superior little slag she was. I only saw her once when she came over at half-term, and she said, Oh, so *this* is your sister, Josh, like I was some kind of specimen of microscopic life squirming under her probing gaze. Pretty she wasn't. Confident she was. How did she manage it? Anyway, Josh couldn't have thought that much of her, because he'd have wanted to stay on at Abbot's Combe then, wouldn't he?

As for Kwithy, we ignored her as much as possible. Jesus H. Christ, you're not supposed to *like* your Dad's girlfriends, are you? I mean, there's no law says you must. I've never known anybody who has. Nor their Mum's boyfriends neither. I mean, why should you? They don't know anything about you and care even less. Of course they always try to bribe you into liking them one way or another – flashing their money about or calling you darling and asking all sorts of idiotic questions they don't even want to know the answers to. Transparent. That's what they are. And fucking thick. Even when you let them know you can see right through them, they just keep on, smiling, insisting, watching you, showing how fabulously generous they are, and so in touch with the younger generation. Patronizing gits, the lot of them. If only they could see themselves. Not that that would make any difference. People are so fucking obtuse. Especially when they want to be.

Even Rodge. I mean, he should have known, shouldn't he? You

can't go around telling people how wonderful they are and then act all surprised when they feel the same way about you. It just isn't fair. I felt cheated, but I couldn't bring myself to hate Rodge. I knew he hadn't meant to hurt me. I knew he would never mean to hurt anybody. And in a way of course that made it all much worse. If he'd been a total shit, I could have said, good shitting riddance too. But he wasn't. I wouldn't have fallen in love with a shit, would I? I mean, you fall in love with people because they're something wonderful, don't you, not because they're shits. And then of course you're never good enough for them. No wonder they don't love you back. What else can you expect?

Rodge spoke to Mum once or twice on the phone after that, but I always refused to talk to him. And I never saw him again. And once they'd started on H (which was before me) Josh and Nat didn't either. Christ alone knows what happened to *Zitz*, including my excellent article. Don't suppose it ever saw the light of day because by Christmas Rodge had gone to California, taking Ros with him. So in a way Fairfax and Brotherton and all the forces of reaction had won. But in another way they hadn't. *Zitz* had outlived its usefulness, that was all. Its main value was shock value and to point the way forward for others to follow. If they wanted to.

What was the point of it all anyway? Why go bashing your head against a brick wall when there are better things to do with your life? What does any of it matter? Nothing's ever going to change, whatever you do. People will just go on doing exactly as they please, which is what they've always done. They're not going to change their minds about anything, just because you say they should. Why should they? And why should you think otherwise? If you think you're right about everything, then you're just as bad as they are. That's what's wrong with the world – all sorts of people yelling and screaming that they're the only ones who are right and everyone else is shit. All sorts of people killing each other to prove they're right. Who fucking cares who's right? Nobody is, not even Rodge and Ros, for all their righteous indignation. In their own way, they're just as naive as Mum. They must be if they're incapable of seeing that all political action is totally futile. The powerful will always be in power. They'll go on making bombs and destroying each other – and the rest of us too, probably. They'll make you pay for everything, and make sure you can't. They'll take away your jobs and your rights and your dignity. That's the only way they can stay in power. Let them. Why give a toss? Just ignore them.

Mum said that if Josh wasn't going to go to school he should get

A.—16

a job, which was a laugh for starters, because there weren't any sodding jobs. These days you have to have five O-levels before they graciously allow you to hump boxes around at Tesco's. Besides, could you see Josh getting up in the morning and toddling off to work every day? He couldn't even get up in time to sign on for the dole, which was Mum's next suggestion. The Social Security office shut at four, you see, so Mum kept waking Josh at about two, but he just groaned and went back to sleep again. He never even opened the shutters in his room, even when the sun was shining – least of all when the sun was shining. He never undressed, except to take off his Doc Martens every so often. And he never washed at all, to judge by the smell. Juno said Mum should pour a bucket of water over him. But she didn't. She didn't do anything except talk and yell and wail, what the hell am I supposed to do? Well, I didn't know, did I? It really got on my nerves.

It was these friends of Nat's in Dalston that Josh kept going to see in the evenings. They lived in this squat which was a whole bunch of punks from all over the place. One of them, Gordon (Gord for short) was a dealer. He'd been in the unit with Nat for a few weeks before he got too old and they chucked him out. I couldn't believe he was only just eighteen. He looked about twice that and had a beard and was very thin. I didn't like him at first. I don't quite know why. He didn't seem quite right in the head, which I suppose was hardly surprising, seeing as how he was supposed to be a nut-case like Nat and Marika. Only he wasn't like Nat and Marika. He never understood a word I said, which made me feel I was talking Venusian or something. I don't know whether he did it on purpose or not, but he'd mishear what I'd said and then repeat it. But of course he wasn't repeating it. He was saying something totally different. Then he'd laugh like it was something terribly witty, although it was just nonsense to me. I suppose he gave me the creeps. But after a while he began to seem almost normal because everybody else around him was just as freaky – at least. I still didn't like him, though. I didn't trust him.

Perhaps that's why I held out for so long when Josh and Nat were going on about the wonders of smack. At first, when I found out Josh was shooting up (not regularly, but once in a while, you understand – nobody was addicted) I thought I ought to tell Mum. I mean, I thought he was going to die or something, and she ought to know. That's how green I was, green enough to be horrified. Josh and Nat both laughed at me. I thought perhaps they were winding me up and they weren't really taking any H at all. But then they showed me. I couldn't even bear the thought of it, let alone the sight. Sticking needles into myself wasn't my idea of a good time. It seemed like just another thing boys got themselves into, like cutting themselves all over their arms and chest. And I could never see the point of that. If they wanted to mutilate themselves, then let them. I didn't want to disfigure myself. Just imagine the sort of shtick I'd have got from everybody if I'd done that. Disfigured boys are heroes. But disfigured girls are supposed to be a bit bent. Or something. I don't know what exactly. Girls aren't supposed to do anything so-called destructive to their own bodies.

Josh never persuaded me to try anything. Nor did Nat. I want to make that quite clear. I make up my own mind and I don't need any representative of the male of the species to do it for me. Oh, but you're so young, Matilda. Bullshit. It's down to me to decide how poncing young I am. I mean, if you feel like a woman, then you are a woman, aren't you? Why should you let some nurd tell you you're still a little girl? Little girls are supposed to have parents looking after them. But a fat lot of fucking use that is. Love me, love Kwithy. Who needs it? Not me. I don't need anyone to look after me. They can all go screw themselves. They can all go screw each other, and good luck to them, as long as they leave me alone. Just because they can't get themselves together, why should I have to suffer? I'm sick to sodding death of it, I can tell you. I'm going to be happy, in spite of them all. Happy, happy, happy! And in my own way. My own sweet, precious and private way.

Oh yes, I've got a mind of my own. And a body of my own too. They can't take that away from you, though Christ knows they try their damnedest. Eat this. Wear that. Stay here. Go there. Don't slouch. Don't drag your feet. You've grown. You've lost weight. What business is it of theirs, anyway? That's what I'd like to know. It's my stomach, my hair, my skin, my feet. And I can do what I pissing well like with them, any of them. If I want to stick a needle in my vein, then it's my decision. If I want to pump so-called poisons into my bloodstream, then that's my decision too, and my bloodstream, every pathetic corpuscle of it. That's the beauty of it, you see. Unless they watch you with x-ray eyes every second of the day and night (and they can't – it just feels like it) they can't control the workings of your body. Only you can do that. You don't need any money. You don't need to be clever. You don't need to have any advantages at all, because you, your body, are your own advantage and the only one you're likely to have for the rest of your miserable life, to have and to hold and to give away, if you feel like it. What else have you got, for Chrissake? Nothing that lasts. Fuck all, mate, and don't you forget it.

You can shut all the rest of them out and just live there inside of yourself in total safety. You can open your veins and your mind to another world, your own beautiful world where you are in complete control. You can walk on air, floating above the shit and the garbage of your former existence. You can he happy. I know it. And I know how to do it. I know how to take command of myself, body and mind, so that nobody can get at me, nobody can touch me. If they try, I just laugh at them. I'm stronger than the lot of them put together. Strength. Happiness. That's what I've got. Better than falling in love any day.

XXIV

Everything means something, although we may never know what, the nature of reality being essentially metaphorical and therefore, if sometimes immediately apprehensible, more often in need of unravelling, of construing. We ourselves are metaphors in the languages of the psyche, the prevailing culture and the body politic, which are three in one and one in three. Our bodies are metaphors, expressive beyond our knowledge, our understanding and even our desire. Things are what they are . . . Ah yes, but they are also what they mean. Plain, purl. And they mean what they are. Purl, plain. We are knit together by discourse upon discourse and the holes between are filled with silence. The garment is yarn and the absence of yarn. If it fits, it fits. If not, it must be remade. Grow into it. Grow out of it. Start again. You may have mislaid the pattern but you have not forgotten it. Your hands will remember, your hands will follow it and vary it, according to necessity, according to volition. Take up your handiwork, admire and put it on.

Soon it will begin to snow. The sky is gathered full and indigo but unable to contain the massed light pushing its way through. It will have to break. Standing on the pavement outside Feinstein and Delaney's Mayfair offices, Claudia looks round for a taxi. She will get home quickly and easily, in the style befitting a woman of decision. Soon the divorce papers will be served on Dorian. On young Mr Feinstein's advice, Kwithy will be named as co-respondent. Easier, he said, than having to trace the last one: neither Kwithy nor Dorian can deny that adultery has taken place when they are actually living together. Can't they? Anything is possible. Young Mr Feinstein said that Kwithy need not be cited by name, but Claudia said she wanted the record to stand clear and explicit. Why should she go out of her way to protect cheats and liars? So there it is. The case of Hughes *v* Hughes and Wrigley has been set in motion. The bonds of marriage have been loosed. Soon they will have to break.

The taxi-driver has a weary, disenchanted look. 'Nah, I'm not going north. I'm on my way home.'

'Then why did you stop?'

'Thought perhaps you was going west, didn't I?'

'OK, I'll go west.'

'Make up your mind.'

Claudia directs him to Sonia's address. Why not? Nothing of urgency awaits her at home. And, besides, she can't wait to tell Sonia that she has taken her advice and consulted Feinstein and Delaney. She leans back in her seat and unfolds her copy of the *Guardian.* The newspaper is full of the aftermath of yet another spy scandal and the illness of the deposed Shah of Iran. The world changes and the world remains the same. We ourselves change, imperceptibly, except to ourselves who see transformation in the subtlest shifts of the psyche. But Dorian hasn't changed at all. There is no paradox there. He will spend Christmas Day with Kwithy rather than with his children. Kwithy will make him feel he's a great guy, whereas his children will only make him feel guilty. Not that he evinces any signs of guilt. On the contrary, he stubbornly refuses to admit that his behaviour has been in anyway blameworthy, that he has caused any damage to others and least of all that he may be damaging himself. No. It is Claudia who is to blame. He and Kwithy are agreed on that, so they must be right. Claudia has gone to pieces when she should have been strong. She has given more importance to her own pain than to his needs. She has turned the simple matter of a marriage breakdown – such things happen all the time – into an occasion of moral censure. She has been nasty to poor little Kwithy. She is vindictive. She is a castrating bitch. What man in his senses should want to live with her? Living with Kwithy, Dorian can start again. His mother has lent him £5,000 from her savings to help set up a new home. There is no need for him to face his guilt. With any luck (and he's always been a winner, hasn't he?) he need never have to admit its existence.

Sonia's hair hangs lankly on either side of her blotched and averted face. Her quilted dressing-gown is crumpled and stained with coffee – or is it blood – at one of the lapels. Without her high heels she is smaller and plumper, reduced instantly to the vulnerability, the pathos, befitting a solitary forty-five-year-old woman. This is the woman standing next to you at the bus stop or the queue at the supermarket check-out, the mother you, in your exuberant youth, have neglected. This is the woman you will become, if you don't watch yourself. The eyes with which she looks at Claudia are little more than blank slits. Now you know, they seem to say, now you see me as I am.

'I'm sorry, Claudia.' Sonia opens the door wider to let her friend in. 'Twice a year I allow myself a day devoted to self-pity. One at Easter and one at Christmas. Christmas has come a few days early this year. That's all.'

'But something must have happened,' Claudia insists, following Sonia into the sitting-room where dust and scattered newspapers vie for domination in the peculiarly intense north light.

'Let me get dressed first.' Sonia smiles cautiously. 'I thought you were the milkman calling for his Christmas box. There's some coffee on the hob.'

The sink is full of dirty dishes, the table scattered with crumbs among the stains. By any normal standards the room is neither dirty nor particularly disordered. But by Sonia's standards, it has surely attained the status of a disaster area. Claudia searches for a clean cup. The coffee is bubbling fiercely in its glass jug and she pulls it off the hotplate. This is, and is not, Sonia. This is Sonia with a human, tear-stained face. Human, Claudia. There is no need to be so horrified. Did you think Sonia didn't suffer any more? Did you think she had it all worked out? Claudia finds a cleanish cup on the draining-board and fills it with the remains of the coffee. It is strong and bitter, as Sonia's coffee always is. It is almost comforting.

She wipes the table clean before sitting down. A blue airmail letter falls from the disarrayed pages of the day's *Times*. The name of the sender is Justin Ravel, writing from an address in Salt Lake City. Of course. No one but Justin could have reduced Sonia to such a state of devastation. Claudia tries to prop the flimsy letter against the pyramid of photographs. It will not stand up. Neither will she read it. Whatever has happened to Justin, Sonia will tell her all about it, if she wants her to know. How could Claudia ever have thought of Sonia as free? Not to love is to be free. And Sonia loves Justin.

The bathroom door slams shut and Claudia can hear the shower run. As she picks up the newspaper she can't help smiling to herself. Sonia can present herself, dishevelled and despairing, to the milkman, but is embarrassed at having to confront Claudia.

This is an aristocratic assumption: that tradesmen don't matter and it is only among equals that appearances must be kept up. Claudia's mother, on the other hand, would never have greeted any tradesman with her hair in curlers or her feet in slippers and always put on make-up in anticipation of the rent-collector's arrival. Here is the difference between self-respect and respectability. Or rather, as far as Claudia's mother was concerned, the two amounted to the same thing.

Yesterday was the sixth anniversary of her mother's death. Her father called her to remind her as much. Claudia had not forgotten, but at the same time she didn't want to be reminded. She wanted to remember her mother alone and in subjective clarity, without the intervention of her father's blurring piety. He spoke of the power of prayer, the necessity of keeping remembrance alive, and the radiant promise of reunion in the after-life. Claudia knew that he was challenging her to agree or disagree with him, a manoeuvre which she evaded. She also knew that he was asking her to remember him, now and after his death, asking her if she were capable of remembrance. As if you ever forget your parents. Obliquely she tried to reassure him, describing for him once again the last occasion on which she had seen her mother; how they had discussed her mother's dream, resembling that of Vaughan of eternity, a ring of pure and endless light. She stressed how peaceful her mother had seemed to be. She didn't mention her own turbulence, her own terror. No, she wouldn't be able to get to Cornwall over Christmas. She had problems. She and Dorian had separated. So she told him at last and waited for his shocked or disapproving response. But all he said was, oh, when is the divorce? He expressed no regret. He was going to stay with Aunt Hester for the holiday period. They wished each other the compliments of the season.

Sonia's hair is now tied back in a pony-tail, her face un-made-up. Her puffy eyes lend a childish roundness to the contours of her cheeks. She smiles almost shyly as she comes back into the kitchen.

'Only half a day of self-pity after all,' she says brightly. 'You've saved me the other half, Claudia.'

'Perhaps you can use it later – when the need arises.'

'Good idea. I must remember that I owe myself half a day.'

'It's Justin, isn't it?'

'Oh, it's Justin, all right. It's always Justin.'

'Is he all right?'

Sonia shrugs. 'Is he ever?'

'Isn't he?'

'Oh, Claudia.' Sonia sits down heavily opposite her. 'I've been and gone and sent him off to Warren.'

'I thought you never had anything to do with his father.'

'I didn't. I haven't.' Sonia is on her feet again, deftly preparing more coffee. 'But desperate remedies and all that. I'm afraid there's no milk, by the way.'

'That's hardly a desperate situation,' says Claudia. 'I'll have it black.'

'I haven't told anybody else,' Sonia says, ready to talk now that the formalities of extending hospitality have been completed. 'But I can tell you, can't I, Claudia? What happened was that Justin took an overdose. Not a little one like Nat and his friends, but a massive one. Why am I making that distinction? Not because I admire what he did. I don't. I'm just trying for the umpteenth time to face up to the fact that he really wanted to die. He even left me a note, asking me, if by any chance I returned earlier than expected, to leave him alone and not attempt to save him. How could he have asked that of me? How could he? Yes, I know he chose to come home to me to do it. And I suppose that is significant. But significant of what? He always comes home to me when the going gets rough. But he never tells me why, never tells me what's prompted the move. I've always just accepted that that's the way it is. After all, he first left home when he was sixteen. He ran off to bum around Europe with his girlfriend. I know I told you that Justin was gay, but that's not the whole story. It turns out that sometimes he's gay and sometimes he's straight. He's hopelessly confused about his sexuality. Although he says he isn't. So what makes me think he is? Is it because I can't actually accept the fact of his bisexuality? Or is it maternal intuition? Perhaps I'm the one that's hopelessly confused about his sexuality. Perhaps I'm the one that's been confusing him. How do I make any sense of it all? Does it make any sense to you?'

Claudia is too numbed to answer directly. 'You found him?' she asks instead.

'I found him.' Sonia's manner becomes less agitated: this is something she can be sure of. 'I'd been to the cinema and we were all going to eat somewhere afterwards. But I was worried about getting home and excused myself. Ever since what happened to you, I've been more than usually jumpy. It wasn't that I had any intimation of what I was going to find when I got home. And there he was, lying on the floor in the dark in front of the television. At first I thought he'd just fallen asleep, so I switched the television off and came in here to make a cup of tea. And there was the note under the kettle – well, sort of sticking out – along with two tarot cards. La Mort and Le Bateleur.'

'Le Bateleur?'

'The magician. Apparently, it signifies taking responsibility for your own life – just what Justin has never been able to do.'

'But doesn't La Mort signify rebirth?'

'Yes, it does.' Sonia sighs. 'Perhaps he did want me to find him, after all.'

'Oh, Sonia, I'm sure he did.'

'Then you're surer than I am.'

'But you did. You did find him.'

'I did. And all my fine, high principles went straight out of the window. None of that nonsense about people being allowed to take their own lives, if that's what they want to do. When it's your own son, the child you carried in your body, nursed at your breast . . . then it's different. Oh, dear God, it's different. I hauled him upright and kind of draped him round my neck. He was still conscious. He said he wanted to die. I said – trying to convince myself as much as anything else – no, you don't. And he actually laughed. Claudia, it was really macabre. So I said then that I wasn't going to let him die. I held him up while I called the ambulance. I remembered that you were supposed to walk people up and down. He fell over. He kept falling over. I thought perhaps some fresh air would be a good idea. Somehow it was easier walking him down the stairs. You know, all the time I couldn't believe it was really happening. I kept thinking, he can't die, it doesn't make sense. Just imagine, Claudia. I was expecting it all to make sense.'

'And doesn't it?'

'You tell me.'

'He wanted to be saved. He wanted you to save him. And you did.'

'Is that what mothers are for?'

'Oh, Christ, Sonia, I don't know.'

The two women look at each other in silence. Claudia lights both their cigarettes. She tries to imagine how she would feel, act, react, if she were to get home and find Josh . . . or Matilda . . . no, it doesn't bear thinking about. Her children have a highly developed sense of self preservation. But so does Justin. Justin knows that he can rely on his mother. When she makes his choices for him (as in matters of life or death) he is safe. When he makes his own (as in the matter of sexuality) he becomes confused, having made no choice at all. Perhaps Justin wandered into sexuality prematurely. Perhaps he really prefers to remain a child, his mother's child. He certainly has a definite way of making sure he still has a mother whose main emotional commitment he remains and is likely to remain. He loves her. Does he? He hates her. Can't he see how he is destroying her? He is punishing her. She was the one to bring him into the world, the one to land him with life. Such is the extent of her crime. Such are the crimes we commit in our innocence, their consequences imperceptible at first, their retribution arbitrary and undeserved.

'The ambulance took forever to arrive,' says Sonia. 'Thirty-five minutes. Can you believe it? They gave him some chewing-gum and he started laughing again. The ambulance man asked me, was I sure he'd actually taken anything, and of course I wasn't *sure*, but the question shocked me. And the way they treated him at the hospital was pretty offhand. They made it clear they thought he was wasting their time. I had to wait a couple of hours while they pumped him out. Then they told me to go home. When the psychiatrist went to see him the next morning, the ward sister said to him, what are you bothering with him for, he's a junkie. There's our wonderful, caring National Health Service for you.'

'Is he a junkie?'

'They found needle marks on his arm.'

'So he is?'

'I don't know, Claudia, I just don't know! He says he isn't, of course, but then they all say that. How can I tell?'

Claudia cannot but treat the question as a rhetorical one. How, indeed, can Sonia tell? How can Claudia herself tell? It is a brutal question, chilling in its very formulation. You can't see people's arms in December. You don't supervise your teenage children's washing and bathing. You don't tuck them up in bed. One Saturday night assorted teenagers invaded the premises, driving Claudia into her study where she sat in nervously vigilant isolation, waiting for something dreadful to happen. A strange metallic smell filled the house. But Josh swore that the polythene bag filled with a sticky, putty-like substance was not his property and hadn't been used by him. Neither he nor Matilda knew anything about the mysterious disappearance from kitchen and bathroom cupboards of bottles of turps, nail-varnish remover or shoe dye. Claudia forbade the sniffing of glue or solvents. But, Mum, it wasn't us. Claudia banned the assorted friends from the house. Josh and Matilda now spend their evenings elsewhere. Where? And with whom?

Certainly not with Rodge, who has left the country and is no longer spoken of with admiration by either Josh or Matilda. And certainly not with their father, whose sporadic invitations have been turned down on various occasions by either one or the other of his children, and sometimes by both. Emma is never mentioned. Nat and his anorexic girlfriend put in a rare appearance. Simon, though, is a frequent visitor, bringing with him others of his recently acquired kind: boys in dirty, dishevelled clothes which look as though they have been rescued from a tip and slept in regularly. These boys can hardly be called boys at all. Some of them are in their early twenties and all of them seem huge to Claudia. Sometimes, entering her kitchen, she has felt that she has strayed into a locker-room by mistake. But among these youths there is no machismo. And there is no uniform any more. They are careless of their possessions, non-materialistic and as innocent of the work ethic as are the lilies of the field. Why should they take any heed for tomorrow? There may not be any tomorrow. Is this, the generation of post-punk unemployed, the new breed?

Of course they all take drugs of one sort or another. Don't we all? They smoke a little dope, perhaps sniff a little glue or near offer. Communal activities both, undertaken in the name of fellowship and in a mutually supportive setting. Youthful exuberance. Youthful experimentation. Didn't we all? But it's nonsense to say, as do the scaremongers, that people progress as a matter of course from soft drugs to hard. It is only the wretchedly inadequate who become addicted to heroin. The wretchedly inadequate like Justin. The confused and ambivalent like Justin. But not like Josh and Matilda, who have spent their formative years in a secure and affluent home with two loving parents. Children who have such a grounding can never altogether lose their foothold on the slippery surface of self-esteem. They fall and they pick themselves up again. Claudia's children are resilient. Isn't this what everyone tells her? She worries too much. She should trust her children. She should trust herself because it is her precept and, more importantly, her example which has informed their personalities. Has she not survived? Has she not shown them that survival is what life is all about? They know, her children, what she knows. They know it unconsciously. They know that no matter what happens to us, no matter how much we are abused, still, in the unconscious, paradise persists. Of course they do.

'Was Justin so unhappy?' she asks Sonia. 'I thought he was absorbed in his music.'

'His music?' Sonia looks blank.

'I thought he was writing an organ symphony.'

'An organ symphony? Justin? You must be joking.'

'That's what Juno said.'

'Oh, poor Juno!' Sonia laughs. 'Fancy her falling for Justin's bullshit. I forgive her everything.'

'Apparently he's also a brilliant mathematician.'

'Justin? Justin doesn't even have any O-levels. He's what's known as a layabout, a kept man.'

'Unemployed?'

'Unemployable. Lazy. Fuck Justin.'

'Oh, Sonia!'

'Oh, Claudia! Don't tell me you've never felt the same. Don't tell me you've never wished you could see the back of them and get on with your own life.'

'Oh, Sonia!'

'Oh, Sonia! That's what you always say when you agree with me, but think it's not quite nice to do so.'

Claudia can neither refute nor deny this accusation. It seems to her that Sonia is speaking from the future, a future which Claudia cannot yet comprehend. Is it possible that one day she will be living like Sonia, alone in her own flat, agonizing over her absent children, having ceased to mourn her broken marriage, ceased even to think about Dorian? The possibility frightens her: she will be a different person. The certainty frightens her: she will be her own person. It takes courage. It takes courage to discard and eliminate when all your life you have been trained to preserve and maintain. It takes courage to shout when you have been taught to whisper, to antagonize when you have been taught to please. To say no. To keep on saying no. But perhaps the bravest word of all is I. Perhaps the bravest act is that of translation from bedtime story or carefully staged dialogue to continuous first-person narrative. And to do it shamelessly. Isn't this precisely what Sonia is doing with her life?

'I wish I had your courage.' Claudia sighs.

But Sonia laughs again. 'I wish I had my courage. I mean, I wish I was as brave as you think I am. You know something. I'm afraid of Justin. Afraid of my own son. Isn't that pathetic? When he came home from the hospital, all I felt for him was resentment, that I'd been conned and terrorized. All I could feel from him was hatred and resentment of me. I couldn't take it, just couldn't live with it. That's when I called Warren. That's why. Not to save Justin, but to save myself.'

Sonia always has an answer. They are never easy answers. On the contrary, they tend to seem fraught with difficulty to Claudia. The price of being Sonia in her inexhaustible selfhood is eternal vigilance, an eternal face-to-face encounter with reality in its everyday exigencies,the meaning of which is immediately apprehensible and capable of being acted upon, capable of being changed. Does she never yearn for a quiet life? Claudia does. She yearns to cease from mental fight. She yearns to lie down with the lion and the lamb in that peaceful prelapsarian oneness which – if she is fortunate enough, receptive enough – informs her dreams. Does Sonia never dream of oneness, of union, of the paradisal otherwhere? No. Her otherwhere is utopia rather than paradise, Jerusalem rather than the Garden of Eden. Sonia's otherwhere is the product of the passionate intellect rather than the unconscious. It can be fought for. Claudia's, being incapable of blueprinting, eludes definition, let alone building brick by brick, phalanstery by phalanstery, hall by shining hall. The unconscious does its own work. But the process is so slow. Life is too short. Paradise is not enough, not even as a dream.

When the doorbell rings Sonia says it must be the milkman this time. Claudia watches her fetch the appropriate envelope from the appropriate pigeon-hole in the dresser. To be Sonia and be able to say I. And yet not to be Sonia and be able to say I, because being Sonia would defeat the purpose of the word. To say I and remain Claudia, become Claudia. She shivers. It seems such a lonely exercise. Sonia comes back with a pile of Christmas cards which have arrived by a delayed second post. Claudia watches her open them and read their conventional messages with a growing sense of desolation. She will spend Christmas with Josh and Matilda. This Christmas and the next and the next . . .

Perhaps. Perhaps they will not be able to get out of bed. Josh has probably never got up before four o'clock since he made his decision not to return to Abbot's Combe. He said he no longer believed in formal education. He was an anarchist. Socialism was for idiots like Rodge and Ros who still believed in the necessity for government. All governments were the same, Labour or Conservative, Communist or Capitalist. They were all repressive. All schools were the same, large or small, comprehensive or private. They were all repressive. In vain did Claudia plead that at Abbot's Combe he had more freedom of choice than he was likely to have again for the rest of his life. In vain did she visit the school and ensure that he could devote his time there to the study of anarchy. Josh had made up his mind. Schools were institutions founded and run by adults, and adults were not to be trusted. His mother was an adult and therefore not to be trusted. This last opinion was never actually voiced by Josh, but what he implied, she inferred readily and with an increasing sense of despair. Perhaps he was right: she was not to be trusted. Mothers are supposed to protect their children, not leave them exposed to loss and grief in depriving them of their fathers. And fathers themselves? Well, how can they be trusted? They're away most of the time; they forget your existence half the time; and then, when they feel like it, they just piss off forever. Josh's professed beliefs are founded on the logic of injury. He will claim Social Security, which he will spend on dope and records, while still expecting his parents to support him. After all, that's the least they owe him, isn't it?

Now that the school term has ended Matilda too has taken to lying in bed for most of the day. When Claudia enquired after the next edition of *Zitz*, Matilda burst into tears and ran up to her room. Claudia didn't see her for the rest of the day. Nor do the children seem to communicate with each other. The institution of the family meal has had to be abolished because they are never around at the same time. Claudia buys food. It gets eaten. She buys more. She washes clothes. They get worn. She washes them again. She is catering to two strangers. They resent being questioned as to their comings and goings, but whenever she goes out, they demand to know where she is going and when she is coming back. Which is the more important element in this demand? To know when she is going to be absent so that they can act as they would and she might not wish? Or to know when they are to be granted the reassurance of her presence? Claudia cannot tell. Perhaps the two, tugging against each other, are of equal importance.

'You know,' says Sonia, 'I never send Christmas cards and yet the same people insist on sending me cards year after year. Some of them I never see from one year's end to the next. I wonder why they bother.'

'Perhaps they think you're lonely.'

'Do you think so?' Sonia seems surprised. 'Do you think I'm lonely?'

Claudia smiles, shaking her head. 'It seems irrelevant.'

Sonia is about to reply but an abrupt change – a release into whiteness – in the quality of the light alerts both women to look towards the window. The first snow of the season is falling. As it was falling on the first day of the International Year of the Child when Claudia, Josh and Matilda sat around the table playing a game of tablanette. And the phone rang, and a voice said, your bloke is having it off with some little tart. Then, counterponting intermittent conversation and the laboured conviviality of Metropolitan Radio, the sky seemed to thicken like a blanket, wrapping the matrimonial home in its own cosiness: difficult to deny, difficult to relinquish. Nothing is without significance and the nature of reality is essentially metaphorical. For in truth we cannot love those who reject and betray us, unless we also reject and betray ourselves. Now the sky seems stretched and as endless as that in Vaughan's vision, counterpointing the silence and stillness of two rapt and seated figures. We are knit and unravelled by discourse upon discourse, by silence upon silence. Until the true self, battered for so long and catching some intimation of what it is or might have been, wreaks an often terrible vengeance on that second betrayer. Or dies. Or lives.

'Come on,' says Sonia, 'Let's go out on the balcony. I want to feel it.'

'I want to taste it,' says Claudia.

Snowflakes are falling softly and sparsely from an eerie otherwhere above. They alight on Claudia's hair, settle on her eyelashes, scarcely weighing them down. They freckle her face and Sonia's as they look up at the unearthly indigo roofing them round. Claudia puts out her tongue to catch one, studies the ephemeral crystalline structure of another on the back of her hand curled round the balcony rail. Ah, but they are chill and pure and perfect. Let then continue their descent, caress by shy caress, insinuating themselves into curves and crevices, conferring beauty and the semblance of peace on even the meanest feature of the urban landscape. The upturned faces in the street below are lit with awe, with expectation, in the early dusk. Let there be a white Christmas. As St Lucy's Day is now filled with light. The world's whole sap may have sunk, dead and interred, but here is a benison trailing clouds of glory from worlds on worlds beyond.

Sonia's face is radiant. 'I love clean endings.'

'They give permission,' says Claudia, 'for clean beginnings.'

'Goodbye, seventies. I shan't miss you.'

'Hello, eighties. Be kind to us, won't you?'

'Some hopes.'

'Better than none.'

Sonia laughs. Claudia laughs too. And their laughter is tinged with wildness. The two women stand, their arms encircling each other's waists, at the giddy edge of the balcony, watching chimney, gable, tree, shrub and kerb quicken into the contours of some transcendent artifact. Claudia is alive. Sonia is alive. Josh, Matilda and Justin are alive. That should be something to be thankful for. It is, isn't it? No matter what happens to us, no matter how much we are abused, somewhere, oh somewhere still, paradise persists, only waiting to be called into conscious being. If we can't believe that, what else is there to believe? *O glaube . . . !* When you wake up, you will sing a little song. When I wake up I'll sing a whole symphony. My life began when my marriage ended. Baby, it's cold outside, cold and true as steel. Nor shall my sword sleep in my hand. *Auferstehen.*

NTOZAKE SHANGE

Sassafrass, Cypress & Indigo

'When there is a woman, there is magic . . .'

In a book of astonishing immediacy and beauty, Ntozake Shange has created a dazzling evocation of black American culture. Following on the huge success of her stage play, *for coloured girls who have considered suicide when the rainbow is enuf*, this, her first novel, reveals her magical command of the storyteller's art.

'Full of fire and humour' *Books & Bookmen*

'A telling account of being black' *Daily Telegraph*

A Daughter's Geography

In her new book of poetry, Ntozake Shange maps the expanding horizons of the black imagination today, from the indigo moods of Harlem streets to the sun-drenched colours of the Caribbean, from passionate songs of pain and outrage to the tipsy cakewalks of love's exhilaration.

Ms Shange once said that poems should 'fill you up with something/cd make you swoon, stop in yr tracks, change yr mind, or make it up, a poem shd happen to you like cold water or a kiss' – perhaps the best description of her own work. *A Daughter's Geography* will further confirm her reputation as one of the most gifted of new writers, a poet who is equally at home in the theatre, and the novel, and always in her own, exuberant, magical voice.

VALERIE MINER

Winter's Edge

Over the passing years Margaret and Chrissie's friendship, a bridge linking two very different natures, has weathered many storms in San Francisco's Geary Street. But now the shadow of a more serious and final blow falls over the street, and the two women's lives, the threat of redevelopment if Jake Carson wins the local election. As the election gathers momentum so both women are forced to re-examine their own characters and choices, and the moment for decision – and action – approaches.

Winter's Edge is a powerful and remarkable book from the author of *Blood Sisters*, *Murder in the English Department* and *Movement.*

Movement

Movement captures ten years of changes in Susan Campbell's life. Draft dodger's wife, leftist activist, journalist, committed feminist – all these are part of her passage through the seventies. Travelling from the USA to Canada, Africa and Britain, we follow her search for self-knowledge in a decade of challenge and re-examination. Valerie Miner's skills as a storyteller and insights as a reflective feminist have never been stronger.

'This is a compelling book, invigorated by Susan's idealism and enthused with her deep passion for life' *Publishers Weekly*